Praise for Mary Simses's
The
Irresistible Blueberry Bakeshop & Café

"If you liked *The Guernsey Literary and Potato Peel Pie Society,* you will devour *The Irresistible Blueberry Bakeshop & Café.* Mary Simses can write evocative detail that puts you right in the scene, with dialogue that always rings true." —James Patterson

"This charming, tender first novel emphasizes the power of simple pleasures, comfort food, and undeniable chemistry. Fans of the leads in the movies *The Proposal* and *Sweet Home Alabama* will recognize a kindred spirit in high-strung, perfectionist Ellen, and the novel's small-town setting will appeal to loyal readers of Mary Kay Andrews, Elin Hilderbrand, and Jan Karon. Simses's story of emotional discoveries, shifting priorities, and new beginnings is a delightful beach read." —Stephanie Turza, *Booklist*

"Basic ingredients, well mixed—and good to the last crumb."
—*Good Housekeeping*

"Delightful.... Simses has crafted a wholesome love story, infused with the pull-and-tug of romance and elements of mystery and enhanced by humble, low-key themes and conflicts."
—*Shelf Awareness*

The
Irresistible Blueberry Bakeshop & Café

The Irresistible Blueberry Bakeshop & Café

A Novel

Mary Simses

BACK BAY BOOKS
Little, Brown and Company
New York Boston London

Copyright © 2013 by Mary Simses
Reading group guide © 2014 by Mary Simses and Little, Brown and Company
"A Conversation with Mary Simses" reprinted with permission of Nicole Bonia, *Linus's Blanket.*

Back Bay Books / Little, Brown and Company
Hachette Book Group
1290 Avenue of the Americas, New York, NY 10104
littlebrown.com

Originally published in hardcover by Little, Brown and Company, July 2013
First Back Bay Books paperback edition, July 2014

Back Bay Books is an imprint of Little, Brown and Company. The Back Bay Books name and logo are trademarks of Hachette Book Group, Inc.

The publisher is not responsible for websites (or their content) that are not owned by the publisher.

The Hachette Speakers Bureau provides a wide range of authors for speaking events. To find out more, go to hachettespeakersbureau.com or call (866) 376-6591.

Excerpt from "Mending Wall," from the book *The Poetry of Robert Frost* edited by Edward Connery Lathem. Copyright © 1930, 1939, 1969 by Henry Holt and Company, copyright © 1958 by Robert Frost, copyright © 1967 by Lesley Frost Ballantine. Reprinted by permission of Henry Holt and Company, LLC.

Library of Congress Cataloging-in-Publication Data
Simses, Mary.
  The irresistible blueberry bakeshop & cafe : a novel / Mary Simses. — 1st ed.
    p. cm.
  ISBN 978-0-316-22585-4 (hc) / 978-0-316-24522-7 (large print) /
978-0-316-22587-8 (pb)
  1. Family secrets — Fiction. 2. Maine — Fiction. I. Title.
  PS3619.I5667I177 2013
  813'.6—dc23   2012030283

10

LSC-C

Printed in the United States of America

*To Bob and Morgan
and in memory of Ann and John*

The
Irresistible
Blueberry Bakeshop
& Café

Chapter 1

A Cold Welcome

Don't move, it's not safe!"

I heard someone yell, but it was too late. The wooden planks of the dock sagged beneath me and then gave way. Boards splintered, rotted lumber snapped, and I plunged ten feet into the frigid Maine ocean.

Maybe there was a second when I could have seen the man running onto the dock, calling out for me to stop. If I had just turned twenty degrees to my right I would have noticed him racing across the beach toward the pier, waving his arms. But I had the viewfinder of my Nikon camera pressed against my eye and I was zooming in on something across the water—a statue of a woman in a ruffled dress holding what appeared to be a bucket of grapes.

As I fought my way to the surface, my arms and legs scrambling, my heart banging in my chest, and my teeth chattering from the cold water, I knew I was moving and moving fast. A strong, swift current was spinning me around and pulling me away from the dock. I came to the surface coughing, the sea around me choppy, foamy, full of sand. And I was still moving, heading away from the dock and the beach, waves hitting me, filling my mouth and nose with salt water. My arms and legs began to go numb and I couldn't stop shaking. How could the ocean be so cold at the end of June?

I tried to swim against the current, giving the Australian crawl my best effort, kicking as hard as I could and pushing the water away until my limbs ached. I was going into deeper water, the current still moving fast.

You used to be a good swimmer when you were at Exeter, I tried to remind myself. You can swim to shore. The little voice in my head was trying to sound confident, but it wasn't working. Panic raced to the ends of my fingers and toes. Something had happened in all those intervening years. Too much time spent sitting at a desk, dealing with legal briefs and acquisitions, time not spent practicing the butterfly stroke.

Suddenly the current that had grabbed me stopped moving. I was surrounded by mounds of black water and foamy whitecaps. In front of me lay the open ocean, dark and infinite. I turned and for a moment I couldn't see anything but more hills of water. Then I bobbed up to the crest of a wave and the dock and beach appeared, far away and tiny. I began the crawl again, aiming toward shore—breathing, stroking, breathing, stroking. It was tough going and my legs felt so heavy. They didn't want to kick any longer. They were just too tired.

I stopped and began to tread water, my arms so exhausted I wanted to cry. I felt a searing pain in my chin, and when I touched my face there was blood on my finger. Something had cut me, probably during the fall.

The fall. I didn't even know how it happened. I had only wanted to see the town from the water, the way my grandmother must have seen it when she was growing up here in the 1940s. I had walked across the beach, opened a gate, and stepped onto the dock. Some of the boards were missing and a few of the handrails were gone, but everything seemed fine until I stepped on a plank that felt a little too soft. I could almost feel myself free-falling again.

A wave slapped my face and I swallowed a mouthful of water. I felt the Nikon twist and turn against me and realized it was still around my neck, like a stone dragging me down. The camera would never work again. I knew that. With my hand shaking, I lifted the camera's neck strap over my head.

A memory of my last birthday flashed through my mind— dinner at the May Fair in London, my fiancé, Hayden, handing me a box wrapped in silver paper and a card that said, "Happy Thirty-fifth, Ellen—I hope this will do justice to your amazing talent." Inside the box was the Nikon.

I opened my hand and let the strap slip through my fingers. I watched the camera drift into blackness and felt my heart break when I imagined it at the bottom of the ocean.

And then I started to think that I wasn't going to make it back. That I was just too cold and too tired. Closing my eyes, I let the blackness envelop me. I heard the swooshing sound of the ocean all around me. I thought about my mother and how terrible it would be never to see her again. How would she cope with two deaths barely a week apart—first my grandmother and then me?

I thought about Hayden and how I had assured him before leaving this morning that I would be in Beacon for only one night, two at the most. And how he had asked me to wait a week so he could go with me. I had said no, it was going to be a quick trip. No big deal. *It's Tuesday,* I had said. *I'll be back in Manhattan tomorrow.* And now, just three months before our wedding, he would find out that I wasn't coming back.

I could feel myself letting go, letting the water take me, and it felt calm, so peaceful. An image of my grandmother standing in her rose garden, holding a pair of pruning shears, fluttered through my mind. She was smiling at me.

Startled, I opened my eyes. Across the dark hills of drifting water I could see the dock and there was something—no, someone—at the end of it. I watched as a man dove off into the water. He surfaced and began to do a fast crawl, coming in my direction. I could see his arms shooting out of the waves.

He's coming for me, I thought. Thank God, he's coming for me. Someone else is out here and he's going to help me. A tiny place inside my chest began to feel warm. I forced my legs to kick a little harder and my muscles began to come alive again. I put my arm out, trying to signal so he could see me.

I watched as he came closer, my teeth chattering so hard I could barely breathe. I don't think I'd ever seen such a powerful swimmer. He treated the waves as though they were afterthoughts. Finally he was close enough for me to hear him. "Hang on," he yelled, his breathing hard, his face red, his hair dark and slicked back by the water. By the time he reached me my legs had given out and I was floating on my back.

"I'll get you in," he said. He took a couple of breaths. "Just do as I say and don't hang on to me or we'll both go down."

I knew better than to grab onto him, although I had never realized how easily a drowning person could make that mistake. I nodded to let him know I understood, and we faced one another, treading water. I looked at him and all I could see were his eyes. He had the bluest eyes—light blue, almost icy blue, like aquamarines.

And then all of a sudden, despite my exhaustion, I felt overcome with embarrassment. I'd never been good at accepting help from people, and, through some strange rule of inverse proportion, the more extreme the situation the more embarrassing it was for me to accept assistance. My mother would say it was that old Yankee stock we came from. Hayden would say it was just foolish pride.

All I knew was that at that moment I felt like an idiot. A damsel in distress crashing through a dock, getting swept away, unable to get back to shore, unable to take care of herself.

"I can...swim back," I said, my lips trembling as a wave splashed my face. "Swim beside you," I added, my legs feeling like cinder blocks.

The man shook his head. "No. Not a good idea. Rip currents."

"I was...on the swim team," I managed to say as we rose with a swell. My voice was getting raspy. "Prep school." I coughed. "Exeter. We made it...to the nationals."

He was so close his arm brushed the top of my leg. "I'll do the swimming right now." He took a few deep breaths. "You do as I say. My name is Roy."

"I'm Ellen," I gasped.

"Ellen, put your hands on my shoulders."

He had broad shoulders. The kind of shoulders that looked like they came from working, not working out. He squinted as he watched me.

No, I'm not doing this, I thought as I continued to drive my numb hands through the water. I'll go in on my own. Now that I know someone's near me I can make it. "Thanks," I said, "but I'll be okay if I just—"

"Put your hands on my shoulders," he said, raising his voice. This time it wasn't an option.

I put my hands on his shoulders.

"Now lie back. Keep your arms straight. Spread your legs and stay that way. I'll do the swimming."

I knew of this maneuver, the tired swimmer's carry, but I'd never been the tired swimmer. I leaned back, my hair fanning out around me. I felt a spot of tepid sunshine on my face. We bobbed with the waves, our bodies suspended as we floated up and over the crests.

Roy positioned himself on top of me and I hooked my legs around his hips as he instructed. He began to do a heads-up breast stroke, and we were buoyant. I started to relax as I let myself be carried. My head was pressed against his chest. I closed my eyes and felt the muscles contracting under his shirt with each stroke. His legs were long and powerful, kicking like outboard engines in between my legs. His skin smelled of salt and seaweed.

I heard each stroke that cut through the water and I felt the warmth of his body. I opened my eyes and saw that we were moving parallel to the shore. I realized what had happened. I'd been pulled out by a rip current and in my panic had failed to realize it. And because of that I failed to heed the most important rule of rip currents—don't try to swim against them; swim parallel to the shore until you've gone around them, and then swim in.

Soon we turned and began heading for the beach. I caught

a glimpse of some people standing on the shore. We're almost there, I thought, overwhelmed with relief. I couldn't wait to feel the ground under my feet, to know I had stopped drifting through darkness.

Once the water was shallow enough for Roy to stand, he picked me up and steadied me, his arms around my back. He was breathing hard. From where my head rested against his chest I could tell he had to be at least six foot two, a good eight inches taller than me.

"You'll be able to stand here," he said, drops of water falling from his hair.

I pushed away gently, taking his hands when he offered them. I put my feet down and stood in the chest-high water. It felt like heaven to touch the sand, to be anchored again to solid ground. Behind me, the ocean swirled and dipped into darkness, but just steps ahead of me the beach sparkled like a new promise under the late-day sun. I felt my muscles relax and, for a moment, I didn't feel the cold. I felt only the thrill of connection to the world around me. I'm still here, I thought. I'm safe. I'm alive.

A giddy feeling began to swell inside me and I started to laugh. Letting go of Roy's hands, I began to twirl, a dizzy ballerina in the water. I laughed and turned and waved my arms, Roy watching me with a startled expression. I wondered if he thought I had lost my mind. It didn't matter if he did. I had come from the emptiness of open water back to firm ground and there was nothing in the whole world that felt as good as that one moment.

I stepped closer to Roy and I looked into his eyes. Then I threw my arms around his neck and kissed him. A kiss for saving my life, a kiss that came from someplace I didn't know existed. And he kissed me back. His warm lips tasted like the sea, his arms, strong and sure, held me tight as if we might both be drowning. I wanted nothing more than to collapse into that embrace. And then I realized what I'd done and quickly pulled away.

"I'm sorry," I gasped, aware suddenly of all the people looking on. "I've... I've got to go." I turned and began to stride through the water as fast as I could toward the beach. I was shivering, my clothes sodden, my eyes stinging from the salt, and the embarrassment I'd felt a few moments before was nothing compared to this. I didn't know what had come over me, what had possessed me to kiss him.

"Ellen, wait a minute," Roy called as he caught up. He tried to grab my hand, but I moved out of his reach and kept pushing through the water. Pretend it never happened, I thought. It never happened.

Two men in blue jeans raced toward us from the beach. One of them wore a yellow T-shirt. The other had a Red Sox baseball cap on his head and a tool belt around his waist, with a level that flapped back and forth as he ran into the water.

"Roy, are you okay? Is she okay?" the man with the yellow T-shirt asked as he helped me toward the beach.

"I think she's okay," Roy said as he trudged from the water, his blue jeans stuck to his legs.

The Red Sox man put his arm around me and helped me onto the sand. "You all right, miss?"

I tried to nod, but I was shaking so hard I don't think my head moved at all. "Cold," I grunted, my teeth chattering.

A burly man with a beard and a buzz cut came toward me. He wore a tool belt and carried a brown leather jacket. He placed the jacket over my shoulders and zipped it up the front. It had a lining that felt thick and cozy, like a fleece blanket. I was grateful for the warmth.

The yellow T-shirt man said, "You want me to call nine-one-one? Have them take you to the hospital in Calvert or something? Won't take long for them to get here."

I had no idea where Calvert was, but the last thing I wanted was to check into a hospital, where the staff would probably want to call my mother (not good) and Hayden (worse).

"Please," I said, trembling. "I'd just like to get out of here."

Roy came over and stood beside me. "I'll take you home."

Oh, no, I thought, feeling my cheeks flush with embarrassment. Somebody else needs to take me. I can't go with him. I looked at the other two men, but neither one spoke up.

"Come on," Roy said, touching my shoulder.

I quickly began walking across the sand. He caught up and then led the way in silence. We went to the far end of the beach, where the dock was, where a house was being built. Three men were on the roof hammering shingles. I followed Roy to a dirt parking lot in front of the house and he opened the door of a blue Ford pickup.

"Sorry about the mess," he said as he moved a toolbox, a tape measure, a level, and some pencils off the front seat. "Tools of the carpenter's trade." The water squished from my clothes as I sat down and a puddle formed on the rubber floor mat below me. I looked down at my feet, covered in a fine layer of sand.

"I don't know what happened out there," I said in a half whisper. "One minute I was standing on the dock and the next..." I shivered and pulled the jacket collar up around my neck.

Roy turned the key and the engine coughed and sputtered and then started. "You're not from around here, are you?" he asked. The dials on the dashboard came to life and the radio glowed with a warm yellow light.

I shook my head and mumbled, "No."

"The rip currents can get pretty bad out there," Roy said. "And that dock isn't in good shape. It's lucky I saw you."

I closed my eyes against the memory of the current and the dock, but even more against the memory of the kiss. An image of Hayden floated through my mind—his warm smile, that lock of blond hair that always fell onto his forehead, the little wink he gave me when he liked something, his soft brown eyes, his *trusting* eyes...I could never tell him what happened.

"Yes, it's lucky," I said.

Roy looked at me and I noticed that he had a couple of tiny wrinkles on his forehead. His eyebrows were dark, but there were a few flecks of gray in them.

"Thank you," I said. "For saving me."

He glanced through the back window and put the truck in reverse. "Sure." He nodded, shifted into first, and pulled to the end of the dirt lot, by the road. We waited while some cars went by. He tapped his fingers on the steering wheel.

"You were really something out there. Where did you learn to swim like that?" I said after an awkward moment of silence.

Roy's eyebrows shot up. "That's quite a compliment coming from someone who swam in...what was it? The nationals?"

I knew he had to be teasing me, but there was barely a hint of a smile on his face.

"Oh...yeah, well, that was a while ago," I said as I watched water droplets fall from his hair onto his shirt.

His hair was thick and dark and wavy with a few wisps of gray that only made his overall appearance better. I couldn't help wondering what he would look like in a suit.

"So...were you a lifeguard?" I asked.

He pulled onto the road. "Nope."

"So you learned it..."

"Just around," he said with a shrug, as he reached out to turn on the heater. "Where are you staying?"

Just around? I wondered how someone learned to swim like that *just around.* I put my hands in front of the heating vent. He probably could have been an Olympic contender if he'd trained for it.

"So you're staying where?" he asked.

"I'm at the Victory Inn," I said, noticing a tiny scar on the side of his nose, just under his left eye.

He nodded. "Paula's place. And you're in town for...how long?"

"Not long," I said. "Not long at all."

"Well, you should get that cut looked at."

"What cut?" I flipped down the visor, but there was no mirror. He pointed to my face. "Your chin."

I touched my hand to my chin. There was blood on my fingers.

Roy stopped and put on his turn signal. "That could really use a stitch or two. I know a doctor in North Haddam I could take you to—"

I felt a rush of heat in my face and I knew my cheeks were

bright red. "No, no," I said. "That's not necessary, really." The idea of him taking me to another town to see a doctor was...well, unsettling for some reason. I wasn't going to do it.

"It's no trouble," he said. He smiled and I noticed he had dimples. "I went to school with the guy and I'm sure he'd—"

"Look," I said, my hands up in protest, my face flushed. "I really appreciate your help, but maybe it's best if I just get out here and walk back. It's not far and I've taken up way too much of your time already."

The little lines in his forehead looked deeper now. "You're not walking anywhere," he said, as we waited for a car to go by. "Didn't mean to get pushy," he added. "Just thought you should have that checked."

He touched the side of my face, tilting my chin to get a better look at the cut, and I felt a tremor go through me.

"It's fine," I said, sitting bolt upright. "I'm...um...leaving tomorrow," I sputtered, "and...uh...I'll see my doctor in Manhattan when I get back."

Roy shrugged again. "Suit yourself," he said as he made a left turn, heading for the Victory Inn.

I looked through the window, wondering if I should say something about the kiss, tell him I was sorry. After all, I didn't want him thinking that...I didn't want him thinking anything.

"I'm sorry about what happened back there," I said.

He glanced at me, surprised. "You don't have to apologize. Rip currents are dangerous. It's easy to get into trouble—"

"No, I didn't mean the rip current," I said as he pulled to the side of the road next to the inn. "I meant the other..." I couldn't say it.

He moved the gearshift to park, sat back in the seat, and ran his hand around the steering wheel. "Well, don't worry," he said with a shrug. "It was only a kiss."

If that was supposed to make me feel better, it didn't. Now I felt insulted, as though it had had no impact on him at all.

"You know," I blurted out, "people in Maine should keep their docks in better condition." I could hear the edge in my voice but I couldn't stop it. "I might have been seriously injured falling through that thing."

Roy looked at me, startled. Finally he said, "I'm glad you weren't injured—talented swimmer like you. And I'm glad I was there to rescue you." He flipped down his visor, the late afternoon sun having filled the front seat of the car with a golden hue.

I thought he had to be making fun of me again, but then I saw that his expression was serious.

"Of course," he said, smiling now, "one thing people in Maine can do is read. Now if *you'd* read the sign…"

What was he talking about? People in Maine reading? What sign?

"Of course I can read," I said, feeling even more defensive now, unable to control my strident tone. "I've had four years of college and three years of law school. I've done plenty of reading."

"Law school." Roy nodded slowly, as though he had just figured something out.

"Yes, law school," I said, staring at the side of his face. He had a five o'clock shadow I might have found attractive in some other circumstance, back in my single days. But right now he was really getting on my nerves.

He turned to me again. "So you're a lawyer."

"Yes," I said.

"And what kind of law do you...well, do?"

"I work in commercial real estate."

"Aha." He scratched his chin. "So do you know much about trespassing?"

Well, of course I knew *something* about trespassing, but it wasn't an area of the law I had many dealings with.

"Yes," I said, sitting up a little straighter. "I know all about trespassing. I'm the firm's expert in the law of trespass. I handle all the trespass cases."

A Toyota stopped across from us and Roy signaled for the driver to go. "A trespass *expert*," he said, raising his eyebrows. "Do you have to get an extra degree for that?"

An extra degree? What a ridiculous question. "No, of course you don't have to—" I stopped because the glint in his eye told me this time he was definitely teasing me.

"Okay," he said. "So with your background, all of your reading, and being a trespass expert and all, why didn't you read the NO TRESPASSING sign by the dock? Or if you did read it, why did you go out there anyway?"

What NO TRESPASSING sign was he talking about, and why was he cross-examining me? I felt a little stream of water trickling down my back as I vaguely recalled seeing a sign on the beach near the dock. Did it say NO TRESPASSING? Could it have said that? No, that couldn't be, I thought. Otherwise I was in big trouble here. He'd have every right to think I was a total idiot.

"I didn't see any NO TRESPASSING sign," I told him. "There wasn't one. I would have noticed."

Roy picked a piece of seaweed off of the leg of his jeans and tossed it out the window. "Well, maybe you didn't notice it," he said, "but there is a sign there. There's a new house being built. In fact, I'm working on it. And the dock and the house are on the same property. The sign was put up so people would stay off the property." He glanced at me. "Especially the dock."

I looked down again at my sandy feet and the puddle of water surrounding them as I attempted to put the pieces together. I tried to picture the dock again and the beach. Yes, I could see the sign. White with black lettering. What did it say? Oh, God, I think it did say NO TRESPASSING. I began to feel queasy. I must not have been paying attention at all. How could I have just walked right past the sign onto the dock? Now I was mortified. As a swimmer, I shouldn't have been caught in a riptide, and as a lawyer I shouldn't have been trespassing. I unlocked my seat belt with a loud click. I wasn't going to tell him. I could never admit what I'd done.

"You know what?" I said, conscious that my voice was wavering and that it had jumped a full octave at this point. "You should tell the owner to keep the property in better condition." I could feel my throat tighten as I thought about crashing through the dock. "They're lucky I didn't get hurt." I paused. "Or killed." I waved a finger at Roy. "Somebody could get sued over that dock. It ought to be torn down."

There, that's telling him, I thought, just as a clump of sand dislodged itself from my hair and plopped onto my lap.

Roy's expression barely changed, but there was something in his eyes again and on the edge of his mouth that told me he thought this was all very funny. I scooped the sand off my shorts and flicked it onto his floor.

He glanced at the floor, then looked back at me. "The dock *is* going to be torn down. That's why there's a gate."

"Well, the gate's not *locked*," I said, my chin starting to really burn from the cut.

"It's supposed to be."

"Yes, well, it wasn't. Otherwise how would I have gotten out there?"

He looked like he was about to say something, but I barreled on. "And another thing. Maybe you should tell the owner to put that NO TRESPASSING sign right *on* the dock and not in the middle of the sand." Great point, I thought. They ought to put it where it really makes sense.

He turned to me and this time there was no mistaking it. He was smiling—a wry little smile that made me feel I'd become the mouse to his cat. "Oh," he said. "So you *did* see the sign."

Oh, my God. I'd let myself fall right into my own trap! The man was obnoxious, detestable, insufferable. I felt the heat behind my eyes and I knew I was about to cry. I wasn't going to let him see that. I opened the car door and jumped out, leaving the seat oozing water.

"Thanks for the ride," I said, trying to sound tough so I wouldn't cry. I slammed the door and started up the front walk to the inn. Then I heard Roy calling me.

"Ellen. Hey, Ellen." He was leaning out the passenger window. His voice sounded serious and his eyes were solemn. There was no trace of that glint I saw when he was teasing me. All right, I thought. Let him say what he wants to say. I started to walk toward the car.

"Just thought you might be interested," he said. "They're having a sale at Bennett Marine Supply." Now the smile appeared and I saw his eyes light up. "Life jackets are thirty percent off."

Chapter 2

The Letter

Wet, exhausted, and humiliated, I marched up the steps to the Victory Inn. Then I cracked open the door and peeked into the lobby. Paula Victory, the owner, was sitting at her desk behind the high wooden counter, her back to me. She was humming. All I wanted to do was run up to my room, get under a steaming hot shower, and forget about the dock, the ocean, and Roy. What I didn't want to do was let Paula see me.

The woman could be a little nosy, even bordering on rude. Earlier in the day, when I checked in, I had caught her staring at my engagement ring. Then she had the nerve to ask me if it was real. Now she'd probably want to know why I wasn't wearing it. *Because an hour after coming to your town my fingers swelled up like hot dogs,* I would tell her. I could just imagine her expression then. Thank God for the room safe, I thought as I rubbed the bare spot on my finger and pictured my Van Cleef & Arpels ring safe and sound.

I took a breath and crouched down. Then I crept by the

counter, water droplets falling from my clothes, and I made it to the other side of the lobby. Thank God, I thought, pulling a piece of seaweed off my leg. I could just imagine Paula wanting to know why I was soaking wet and whose car door she heard slam outside and just what this visiting New Yorker was doing here in Beacon, anyway.

As I stepped from the reception area into the hall, I heard her voice behind me. "Forget your bathing suit, Miss Branford?"

I didn't stop and I didn't say a word. I just took the stairs two at a time to the third floor, wishing I was on my way home. I wanted to go back to New York and be with Hayden, curl up next to him on the sofa, and watch *Sleepless in Seattle*. I wanted to run my hand through his shock of thick hair and trace my fingers across his freshly shaved face. We could be drinking a bottle of Pétrus and eating takeout from San Tropez, that little bistro we like on East 60th. And instead, I was wet and cold and *here*.

Hayden was right. I should never have come. I should have put Gran's letter in the mail instead of driving all the way up here to deliver it. Or I should have waited a while longer for my head to clear before making the trip. It had only been a week since my grandmother's death. We had been so close and I was still in a state of shock. Maybe that was why I hadn't paid attention to the NO TRESPASSING sign.

From the pocket of my shorts I pulled a soggy braided ribbon with the room key attached. I unlocked the door and put the leather jacket over the chair in the corner. Then I peeled off my wet clothes and wrapped myself in a towel. I looked at my watch—six fifteen. I picked up my cell phone from the bedside table and, sitting on the edge of the bathtub, I dialed Hayden. His phone rang twice and then I heard a click.

"Ellen?"

I breathed a sigh of relief. "Hayden."

"I've been trying to get you," he said. "Everything okay?"

I squeezed my eyes shut as tight as I could so I wouldn't cry. I wanted him to hold me. I wanted to feel his arms around me. "Everything's fine," I said, but I could hear the tremble in my voice.

"Where were you this afternoon? I tried to call you a couple of times."

I thought about the splintered dock and the Nikon at the bottom of the ocean, the current tugging it along the sand. I thought about Roy and the tired swimmer's carry. I could not think about the kiss. "I went out for a walk," I said, my heart aching.

"Oh, that's good. You probably needed it after that long drive. So how's your first trip to Maine? What's Beacon like?"

What's Beacon like? I'm not sure you really want to know, I thought. You and Mom were right. It was a bad idea for me to come. Look what had happened already. Maybe it was just an unlucky place. Maybe that's why Gran left here as soon as she was old enough to go.

"Beacon?" I said. "I guess it's like a lot of other small towns." I took a deep breath. "Hayden, I was thinking...you were probably right about this whole thing. I mean, there's no harm in just putting the letter in the mail. And then I could drive back to New York tonight. If I leave by—"

"What?" He sounded shocked. "Ellen, you just got there. Why would you do that?"

"But when I left this morning you said—"

"I know what I said, honey, but I was just being...you know, *practical*. And I was worried because you were driving up by yourself. I thought you'd get lonely. It's way too late to leave now."

Way too late. I wanted to cry. I looked at the round hooked rug on the bathroom floor—bright blue, red, and gold yarns had been gathered together to create a compass. "I wish you were here."

"You know I would have come," he said, "if I didn't have that Peterson meeting tomorrow."

I knew all about the Peterson meeting. Not only were Hayden and I engaged but we were also partners in the same firm, although he worked in the litigation department. "Listen to me," he went on. "You said yourself that your grandmother wouldn't have asked you to do this unless it was really important."

I glanced at a framed print above the towel rack—a sailboat approaching a harbor at dusk. "I know, but my mother might have had a point when she said Gran probably didn't even know what she was talking about at the end. Maybe she was delirious. Maybe she thought Chet Cummings lived down the street. Who knows?"

"That's just your mother being your mother, Ellen. I know how much you loved your grandmother and I know that delivering this letter is important to you. And I'm proud of you for doing it."

Sitting on the edge of the tub in my towel, I thought about Gran on the last day of her life. Only a week ago we were together in her living room in Pine Point, the Connecticut town where she had lived for years and where my mother still lived. I could see Gran looking so elegant, sitting on the pale blue sofa, her silver hair pulled back and pinned above her neck in the chignon she always wore. She was scratching answers onto the *Wall Street Journal* crossword puzzle with a fountain pen.

"Ellen, what's a five-letter word for 'sufficient'?" she asked me.

I thought for a moment, sliding back against my chair, biting into a McIntosh apple. Through the bay window I could see the edge of the slate patio behind the house, ringed by the rose garden, and the swath of green that stretched down the hill to the iron gates at the far end of the driveway. Lawn mowers hummed in the distance like lazy bees.

"Plenty?" I said, ticking the letters off in my head. "No, that's six."

A breeze floated through the open window, trailing with it the smell of freshly cut grass and rose petals.

My grandmother muttered something and then turned the newspaper around for me to see. On the page opposite the puzzle, an ad featured a waif of a model wearing a black, boxy-looking dress made out of shiny, crinkly fabric.

"Looks like a rubbish bag," Gran said. "Whatever happened to the kind of clothes Jackie Kennedy used to wear? Now, there was an icon."

"Jackie *Onassis*," I said, correcting her.

She waved a hand at me. "She'll always be Jackie Kennedy. No one accepted that man as her husband."

"Well, I think *she* did, Gran."

"Nonsense," my grandmother said. "What could she have seen in him? Of course, he was wealthy, but he wasn't even attractive. Not like *her*."

I got up from my chair and sat down on the sofa next to my

grandmother. "Well, maybe he was attractive in his own way," I said. "She probably felt safe with him. Kind of like a father figure. After all, she'd come through a horrible experience with the assassination."

"That's not a reason to get married," she said, shaking her head and bearing down on me with her green eyes.

My grandmother began to write something on the crossword puzzle. "Aha," she said. "The word is *ample*," and she started to spell it, but when she got to the letter *p* she stopped. Her body tensed and her head dropped back against the sofa. Her eyes were closed, but there were deep wrinkles by the sides, as though she were squinting, and her mouth was rigid. I knew she was in pain.

"Gran?" I took her hand. "Are you okay? What's wrong?" My heart was pounding.

She tensed again and it looked as though everything in her body had seized up. Then her head flopped down on her chest.

"Gran!" I screamed, terrified. I clutched her hand tighter. The room seemed to be tilting, everything moving away from me. "Gran, *please*," I said. "Tell me you're okay." I felt sick to my stomach.

Then she said my name, her voice faint and breathy.

"I'm here," I said. "I'm here, Gran." Her skin was cold. I could feel the fragile bones beneath the surface. "I'm going to call an ambulance."

"Ellen," she whispered again. Her face was white, her eyes were still closed.

"Don't talk," I said. "You're going to be all right." I don't know whom I was trying to convince more—Gran or myself.

I picked up the phone and pressed the keys for 911. I had to push hard because my fingers felt like jelly. They made me spell the name of the street twice, even though it's simple. Hill Pond Lane. I must have been talking way too fast. After that I ran to the kitchen and yelled down to Lucy, my grandmother's housekeeper, asking her to find my mother at the Doverside Yacht Club and then to go to the end of the driveway and flag down the ambulance when she saw it.

I ran back to my grandmother. Her eyes were half open now but they weren't moving. She stared at me. Then, grabbing my wrist with a strength I found surprising, she pulled me close. My ear was near her cheek and I could smell her lavender perfume. "Please," she said, the word hardly more than a puff of air. "There's a letter...I've written. The bedroom." Her grip tightened again. "You...take it to him...Ellen."

"Gran, I—"

"Take him the letter. Just...promise."

"Of course," I said. "I promise. I'll do anything you—"

Her fingers fell from my arm and a wisp of air came from her mouth. Then she was still.

That night I searched for the letter, starting with the table next to my grandmother's bed. In the drawer I found three pens and a pad of paper with blank sheets, two pairs of glasses, a pack of Life Saver candies, and a copy of *One Hundred Years of Solitude* by Gabriel García Márquez.

I searched her desk—an antique cherry writing table from Paris. Wednesday's *Pine Point Review,* the local weekly paper, was on the top. Opening the one drawer in the center of the desk, I found an address book. I thumbed through the pages, feeling alternately comforted and saddened by the familiar up-and-down pen strokes of my grandmother's handwriting. There was no letter.

Her walk-in closet greeted me with the smell of lavender. Hanging rods held Chanel suits and sale-rack department store dresses side by side. Shelves displayed sweaters of every color from peach to cranberry. I brushed my hand over a pink sweater. The cashmere was soft as a cloud.

On the top of a built-in dresser stood a collection of photographs in silver frames. One showed my grandparents on the day of my grandfather's graduation from the University of Chicago medical school. He had his arm around Gran. They stood in front of a stone building with a massive Gothic arch. Her chin was tilted upward slightly as she looked at the camera, her long, swanlike neck encircled by a strand of pearls. My grandfather gazed at her, a smile spread over his whole face.

An oval frame held a photo of my grandmother and me at Alamo Square, a park across the street from my grandparents' house in San Francisco. I was ten, so Gran would have been fifty-five. Looking at the photo, I was struck by the similarity in our looks. We had the same green eyes and long auburn hair, although Gran had always worn hers up. I remembered the day the picture was taken. I had a camera slung over my shoulder and some tourists, who thought we were also tourists, offered to take our picture together. We stood in front of a huge bed of red flowers, both of us smiling, my grandmother's yellow house visible in the background.

I put the photo back and gingerly began opening her dresser

drawers, telling myself I was doing what she'd asked me to do. I sifted through a drawer where she had stashed clothing receipts, owner's manuals for long-departed appliances, paper-clipped stacks of foreign currency saved from trips abroad, years of birthday and Christmas cards she had received, and a copy of the announcement from Winston Reid when I became a partner. There was no letter.

I went back into the bedroom and sat down on the edge of her bed. Whatever she had written wasn't there. Maybe she hadn't written anything at all, I thought. Maybe she *was* delirious at the end.

My grandmother's bookshelves were laden with novels and biographies and family photographs, and I glanced across the room at them, wondering what to do next. I gazed at the paintings on the walls—seascapes and landscapes. She had even framed a couple of photographs I had taken as a young girl—driftwood on the beach and an old pair of sneakers.

I opened the bedside table drawer again and saw the book— *One Hundred Years of Solitude.* As I picked it up, a sheet of pale blue paper fluttered out from between the pages. Gran's initials were embossed in script at the top of the paper—RGR. Ruth Goddard Ray. I recognized the tall, upright letters of her handwriting as I looked at the name of the person to whom the letter was addressed: Chet Cummings. Under the name was the address, 55 Dorset Lane, Beacon, Maine. It looked like a draft; the page was full of scratch-outs and changes, but I knew I'd found the letter.

I took a deep breath and began to read.

Dear Chet,

I've thought about writing to you so many times but I've always been afraid to do it. I guess I imagined you would send my letter back, unopened, and I would find it in a stack of mail, the canceled stamp staring up at me, your handwriting scrawled on the side—"return to sender." Or perhaps you would simply ignore it, tossing it into the trash with the orange rinds and coffee grounds and the day-old newspaper, and I would never know what happened. Poetic justice either way. Still, I didn't want to face that disappointment.

Perhaps there is something about turning eighty that has created this urgency to finally write to you after sixty-two years and has given me the strength to deal with the outcome, whatever that may be. Having survived eight decades, I feel it's time to resolve matters I've neglected and, more important, to make amends.

In truth, I couldn't have written sooner because it wasn't until recently that I knew where you were. The last thing I heard was that you were in South Carolina. That was about fifteen years ago. Then one day this past March, I discovered you had moved back to Beacon. I was using the computer, looking up the address for a breeder of roses in New Hampshire. With no particular thought in mind, I typed your name into the search box and then added, "Beacon, Maine." And, suddenly, there you were! On Dorset Lane. You can't imagine my surprise. With that one little click of a key I had found you. I must have sat in front of that computer holding my breath for a full thirty seconds after I saw your name.

It took me another three months after that to decide to actually write to you. But here I am, finally putting pen to paper, and what I want to say is that I'm very sorry about what happened between us and I am writing to ask you to forgive me. I did love you, Chet. I loved you so much and I loved what we had together—our dreams for the future, our dreams of a life together in Beacon. When you came to Chicago and I told you I didn't love you anymore I was lying. I think I was trying to convince myself because it was easier that way—easier to make a clean break. At least that's what I believed at the time. And everything I did from that point on I did with that in mind—a clean break.

I know what my leaving cost you in the end and I can never forgive myself for that. If I hadn't left you the way I did, you wouldn't have left Beacon and you wouldn't have lost the thing that meant so much to you. I've always felt responsible for that loss and I'm sorry. I hope you can forgive me.

I have many wonderful memories of those days we had together. It would make me happy to know that at least a few of your memories of me are good ones. I wonder if you ever think about sitting under that oak tree, with the cicadas buzzing, and, at night, the crickets. Or how the ice used to cover the blueberry bushes in the winter, giving them that dreamy look. Or how we used to sell the pies for your mother at the roadside stand.

I still think of you whenever I see blueberries.

Fondly,
Ruth

I stood in my grandmother's bedroom, holding the letter, thinking about her writing to a man she hadn't spoken to in over sixty years. What was this love affair they had? She would have been eighteen, just a young girl. After all these years she was writing to apologize for leaving him. I sat on my grandmother's bed, holding the blue paper in my hand, wondering about Chet Cummings and what he would think when I handed that piece of paper to him. Was he really her true love? Was theirs a secret romance she never dared to speak of?

Draped in my wet towel in the bathroom of the Victory Inn, still holding the cell phone to my ear, I wondered what my grandmother's life would have been like if she had married Chet Cummings. She wouldn't have had the English Tudor house with its six bedrooms or the rose garden or the fountains or the acres of grass that were so green in the summer and smelled so heavenly when cut. She would have lived in Beacon. She would have given birth to my mother in Beacon and my mother might have stayed and married and given birth to me in Beacon. And I would have grown up a country girl, living in a small town, isolated and far from all the things I love. I couldn't imagine life without my favorite museums, the jazz clubs, coffee shops on every corner, Broadway, the Brooklyn Bridge. Life without all of that seemed so bleak.

"Are you still there?" Hayden asked.

I switched the phone to my other ear. "Yes, sorry. I was just thinking about Gran. I was wondering what it would have been like if she had stayed in Beacon."

"Well, luckily, she didn't," Hayden said. "Or I might never have met you."

A drop of water fell from my hair and landed on my lip. I could taste the salt. "Yeah," I said. "Luckily."

I glanced down at the compass rug. Maybe I needed to find out about this part of my grandmother's life for her. It was like helping her put the final letters into her crossword puzzle.

"I guess you're right, Hayden," I said. "I should stay and deliver the letter. She asked me to do this and I promised her I would." I pulled my knees up to my chest and wrapped my arms around them, cradling the cell phone to my ear. "But I miss you."

"I miss you, too."

"I'll be back tomorrow night," I said. "Thursday at the latest."

"Perfect, because the dinner is Friday night and there's only one person I want by my side."

I couldn't miss the dinner. Hayden was being honored by an organization called New York Men of Note for all of the pro bono projects he had been involved in over the years, from chairing the Literacy Coalition to spearheading the capital campaign for the Guggenheim.

"Don't worry," I said. "I'll be back long before then. I wouldn't miss it for the world." I closed my eyes and pictured Hayden being handed his award by the mayor. I was so happy he was being recognized that way. And it could only help him in his run for city council next year. Not that he needed the help, of course.

His father, H. C. Croft, was the senior senator from Pennsylvania and head of the Senate Finance Committee. His uncle Ron Croft had been governor of Maryland for two terms, and his cousin Cheryl Higgins was a congressional representative in the Rhode Island legislature. On top of that, his late great-aunt Celia had been a suffragette. Besides steel, where they had made their fortune, politics was the Croft family business, and they were naturals at it. I knew Hayden's father and uncle pretty well, and they were both charming, charismatic men who could draw a crowd while attending a charity ball or popping into a hardware store. The media were already buzzing over Hayden's decision to run.

"I'm so proud of you," I said. Then I sent him a kiss through the phone.

When I hung up I saw that I'd missed a call from my mother. My heart started flipping like a fish out of water. I couldn't talk to her. Not yet, anyway. She had a sixth sense when it came to knowing that something was wrong with me and I wasn't about to upset her by telling her I'd fallen into the ocean and almost drowned. And I certainly wasn't going to tell her that I'd kissed a perfect stranger. She'd be so worried she'd probably drive right up to Beacon. So I decided to send her a text message. All well, lovely inn, talk 2 you soon. XOX. All right, I felt guilty about it, yes. It was a bit of a stretch. A big stretch, since none of it was true. But tomorrow I'd figure out what to tell her.

I turned on the shower to let the water heat up. Tomorrow would be a much better day all around. I had a ten o'clock conference call, but that would only last about an hour, and right after that I'd swing by Mr. Cummings's house, have a nice chat, give him the letter, and then head back to Manhattan. I'd get home just in time for a vodka and tonic and dinner on the terrace if it wasn't too hot outside. Lovely.

Testing the shower with my hand, I found the water tepid. Paula had warned me about that when she showed me the room. "The hot water takes a little while to get all the way up here from the heater in the basement," she said, stretching her arms out as if to demonstrate the distance.

I waited another minute and finally the bathroom was filled with a delicious steam. Standing on the compass rug, I watched the *N, S, E,* and *W* letters disappear as the fog enveloped me.

I stepped into the shower and let the hot water cascade over my head and down my back. Running my hands through my hair, I let the water chase away the sticky salt. It was heaven. Then I emptied a tiny bottle of shampoo on my head and worked up a good lather, inhaling the clean, floral scent. Just as I was about to rinse out the shampoo, the water temperature plummeted. The water came out in an icy stream and I stood under the spray, shivering, cursing the Victory Inn, cursing Beacon, cursing the entire state of Maine. And then the tears came.

Chapter 3

Media Frenzy

When I first awoke in the semidarkness of the room, I thought I was back in our apartment in New York and for a split second I was happy. But then my eyes began to make out foreign shapes and I remembered, with a dull, lonely ache in my chest, that I was in Beacon. I remembered the dock, the ocean, the ice-cold water, the man diving in, and...

Oh, my God, the kiss. What had I been thinking? I replayed the scene in my mind. I hadn't been thinking, that was the problem. One second I was standing there looking at him and the next second I had basically lost my mind. Was I trying to jinx my own wedding? Did I not want to get married? None of that made sense. Of course I wanted to get married. I loved Hayden and I wanted to be his wife. I was sure of that.

I rolled onto my back and rubbed my eyes. I wasn't going to think about it anymore. Today was a new day, a fresh start, and it was going to be a good day because I was delivering my grandmother's letter. I tried to picture Chet Cummings. Would he have a cane? Would he live alone or have a caretaker? Would he be sweet or would he be a cranky old man? Would he remember Gran?

It was only seven fifteen, according to the clock on the bedside table—too early to go visiting an eighty-year-old man. My plan was to head over to Chet Cummings's house right after my ten o'clock conference call.

Glancing around the room, I couldn't believe I'd ended up here. My secretary, Brandy, said she had booked me into the Ocean View Suite, but whoever named this a suite needed to go back to hotel school. It was a small room, with a hardwood floor, a braided rug, and a mahogany dresser on which stood a large white pitcher in a white bowl (an *antique*, Paula had proudly pointed out). A white coverlet lay on top of the mahogany bed. There was no desk or table and only the one uncomfortable ladder-back chair in the corner. And there was no minibar. (Mini *what?* Paula asked when I inquired.)

Worst of all, there was no ocean view. The two windows looked out onto the front lawn, the street, and other houses. I got out of bed and rummaged through my briefcase until I found the confirmation Brandy had given me.

The Victory Inn
37 Prescott Lane, Beacon, Maine
Deluxe suite, with ocean view
Two nights

Deluxe suite, with ocean view. There it was.
I freshened up and put on a pair of pants and a sweater. Then

I went to look for Paula so I could tell her about the mistake and have her switch me into the right room. I checked the front desk and the lounge and the dining room and finally found her on the second-floor landing, talking to a chambermaid. I could barely take my eyes off Paula's pants—yellow with brown dachshunds all over them.

"Paula," I said. "I think there's been a little mistake. My secretary booked me into a deluxe ocean-view suite." I handed her the paper. "But the room I'm in is...well, there's no view of the ocean."

Paula's lower lip stuck out a little as she peered at the paper. "What room are you in?"

"Room ten."

"Does it say ten on the door?" she asked, taking a pencil from behind her ear and scratching her head with the eraser end.

I nodded. "Yes."

"Well, then, it's room eight."

How, I wondered, could it be room 8? Was this some strange kind of Maine hotelier counting system I didn't know about? "But the door says ten."

Paula put the pencil back behind her ear and handed me the confirmation. "It's room eight," she said cheerfully. "It's our deluxe suite, best room in the house, and there *is* an ocean view."

"But I've looked and I can't see the ocean anywhere," I said, wondering if I'd stepped into a reality show in which the producers and crew would suddenly appear, laughing about how funny all this was.

"Oh, the view isn't from the *room*," Paula said. "You have to go up to the roof."

"I don't understand."

"The roof," she repeated, in a tone that indicated the answer should be obvious. "There's a door by your closet. Go up the stairs and you'll get to the roof. We put some nice lawn chairs up there."

Lawn chairs. On the roof.

"All right, let's put the ocean view aside for a moment," I said, figuring I could find better accommodations, maybe right in town. "I have another issue. I need to use your business center to print something for a ten o'clock conference call."

Paula pursed her lips as she and the chambermaid looked at one another. Neither one spoke.

"A printer?" I said. "I have a document I'd like to have printed for…"

Paula was giving me a blank stare.

"The printer's a *little* broken," she said finally. "Sometimes the paper gets jammed." She made a twisting motion with her hands. "Probably the salt air." She pronounced it *salt eh-ah*. "But you can try it."

A little broken. I turned away and looked through the round window on the stairway landing. A man and woman were wheeling their suitcases around to the parking lot in the back. Lucky people, I thought. They were going home.

"But you have a business center," I said, turning back to Paula. "My secretary specifically asked about that. Are you sure you don't have a working printer?" I couldn't believe I was actually having this conversation. I probably could have stayed at a Ritz-Carlton, in a city, with real hot water and wireless in the rooms, but Brandy insisted this would be more convenient.

The chambermaid arched her eyebrows and shifted the stack of towels in her arms. I could see the edge of a tattoo on the side of her neck. It looked like a parrot.

Paula motioned for her to move along. "Well, we have...let's see, a printer, a fax machine, and a computer. I'll show you," she said as she led me to the first floor and into the lobby.

Maybe they didn't call it a business center, but at least they had the equipment.

"Here we go." She opened a door behind her desk. Inside a tiny closet, an old computer rested on top of a dusty fax machine. Behind them stood a monitor from the 1980s and a printer with an electrical cord that dangled lifelessly beside it, frayed wires sprouting from the end like crabgrass.

"This is the business center?" She had to be kidding. I was getting frustrated. First the room and now this. I would have to write a complaint letter to the Better Business Bureau. This place was ridiculous.

"That printer doesn't even work," I said, pointing.

Paula leaned over the printer and stared at it, as though she might will it to work. "Oh, I think I can get it fixed."

I was finally at a loss for words. I looked at Paula, who was scratching her head with her pencil, and then I walked through the lobby and out the door. I didn't know where I was going. I just knew I had to get out of there.

The morning air smelled of salt and a changing tide and I took a few deep breaths and tried to calm myself. Stopping at the sidewalk, I turned to look back at the inn, wondering why Brandy had ever booked me in there. With its three stories, white shingles, blue shutters, two chimneys, and a wraparound porch, the building sat about fifty feet back from the road, next to a gray house that was the home of the Beacon Historical Society. The place could almost be cute, I thought, if somebody would just modernize it.

After walking a couple of blocks, I turned the corner onto Paget Street, the main road through Beacon's tiny downtown. On the right was a seawall with the ocean behind it, whitecaps glinting in the sun. A young mother and two little boys sat on the edge of the wall, looking at something in a pail—shells, maybe, or hermit crabs. Or maybe it was just a bucket of sand. I wished I had my camera. It would have made a lovely photo.

I kept walking, past Tindall & Griffin, Counselors at Law; Harborside Real Estate; and the Shear Magic salon, all of them in old but well-kept houses that had been adapted for commercial use. I kept my eye out for a hotel or some other place to stay but didn't see anything. Farther along, I passed the Community Bank, its redbrick facade having faded to a pale rose, and I walked by a small white clapboard building with a sign that said Frank's Tailoring.

Which of these buildings had been around during my grand-mother's day? I wondered. Surely some of them had been. I began to feel happy imagining her on this street, seeing this view, running along this same beach. It was her town, after all, the place where she had grown up. I felt like I was walking in her footsteps.

I passed a place called the Antler, which looked like a pub, judging from the neon Michelob sign in the window. A little far-ther down I saw the Three Penny Diner, a whitewashed brick building with window boxes of red geraniums that craned their necks to catch the cool Maine sun. I suddenly felt hungry and found myself walking inside.

The diner smelled like cinnamon buns. A young waitress directed me to a booth and I ordered coffee.

"Something to eat?" she asked.

"Do you have any fresh fruit?"

She nodded. "Blueberries, melon, bananas, blueberries, blueberries." She smiled.

"I guess I'll have the blueberries."

She leaned in. "They are the local specialty," she whispered. "But personally I'd go for a cider doughnut."

"Excuse me?"

"A cider doughnut. The doughnuts are sooo good." She drew out the word as though she were stretching a piece of taffy. "We make 'em here."

I shook my head. "I think I'll just have the fruit," I said. "I don't eat doughnuts, but thanks anyway."

The table had a little jukebox on it and I flipped through the pages of songs. I found "The Way You Look Tonight," an old Jerome Kern tune I loved. I put some coins in the machine and Rod Stewart's voice came through the tinny speakers.

The waitress returned with a mug of coffee, a bowl of blueberries, and a plate with a cider doughnut on it. "It's on the house," she said, putting the doughnut in front of me. "I know you'll love it."

The coffee was rich and hot and the blueberries were bigger and sweeter than any I'd ever tasted. I peered at the doughnut, covered with fine sugar crystals. Like a siren, it seemed to beckon me. All right, I thought, one little piece won't kill me. It melted in my mouth, warm and sweet and gooey. I reached for another piece and, before I knew it, the plate was empty. Well, maybe Beacon had something going for it after all.

At nine fifty-seven, I sat on the bed, the only comfortable spot in the room, and dialed the number for the conference call. There was nothing but static on my cell phone. Looking at the signal bars, I saw they'd been reduced to nubs. No wonder, I thought. There was no signal. I picked up the room phone and found it was dead. Complete silence. Not even a click.

Grabbing my cell phone again, I darted around the room, trying to find a signal. *I need bars, give me some bars!* This was an important call and I had to get connected. How could everything be going so wrong?

Then I remembered the bathroom and my conversation with Hayden the night before. The connection had been perfectly clear. I ran in, closed the toilet seat, opened my laptop, and sat down. For the next ninety minutes I dished out legal advice on a two-hundred-million-dollar real estate deal while sitting on the toilet.

When the call was over, I reapplied my lipstick and freshened up my eye shadow in the bathroom mirror. Then I took a manila envelope with our firm's name on it—Winston Reid Jennings, Attorneys at Law—and placed my grandmother's letter inside for safekeeping. On the outside of the envelope I printed the words Mr. Cummings.

As I walked to the door to leave, I noticed the construction worker's leather jacket hanging over the back of the chair, where I'd left it to dry. Might as well drop it off, I thought as I grabbed it.

The jacket was still damp but the leather felt supple. It had a soft lining and handsome stitching. I looked at the label. Orvis. I thought they only sold dog beds and camping gear, but here was an attractive jacket. I found a plastic bag in the closet and put the jacket into it.

Paula was sitting at her desk, eating a carrot and smoothing out the fold in a newspaper when I walked into the lobby.

"Miss Branford," she said. "I think the printer will be fixed this afternoon."

"Thanks," I said, wondering who could possibly fix that old thing. "But I don't need it anymore. I got through my call without it." I started to walk on but then I stopped. "By the way, I'm pretty sure I'll be checking out today." I raised my eyebrows. "In case somebody wants that suite."

Paula glanced at me and then went back to the newspaper. "But your reservation is for two nights." She took a bite of her carrot.

The bag with the jacket was beginning to feel heavy. "Yes, I know, but I'll probably be done here today. Of course, you can keep the extra night's—"

"Whoa!" Paula's mouth was open, carrot in midair. "Somebody fell through the dock at Marlin Beach. It's here in the *Bugle*." She brought the paper closer to her face. "Yesterday afternoon, right down by the new house that's being built. And they were *trespassing*."

My stomach began to do a little somersault. "Really?" I said, the second syllable not quite making it from my throat.

Was my name in there? Could they have put my name in there? I didn't want Paula to know it was me. I didn't want anyone to know it was me. I'd always prided myself on being in control, for being able to take care of any situation. That episode with the dock was something I wanted to make disappear.

I took a step toward Paula, telling myself to calm down. No one on that beach knew my name. It couldn't possibly be in the newspaper.

"I hope they're all right," I said, trying to look concerned. "What does it say?"

"Oh, not much. Some tourist." Paula paused. "Drowning."

Drowning? They had to put that in there? I wasn't really drowning. I was just...a little tired, that's all.

Paula turned to me, head cocked, lips pursed. "A guy swam out...did the rescue. Neither one was identified."

Something twisted inside me. "A guy swam out." I tried to sound blasé. "Lucky," I said.

"Hmm?" Paula asked, still staring at the paper.

"She was lucky he was there." I edged closer to the desk, trying to sneak a look, but Paula folded the paper in half and turned it over.

"Good guess," she said, taking another bite of carrot.

"Pardon?"

She looked at me. "You knew it was a woman."

I did?

Oh, my God, I did. Think, think. Say something. I waved my hand as I headed toward the door. "Well, statistically I had a fifty percent chance of being right. It was just...a good guess." I could feel Paula's eyes on my back, as though I had a target painted there. I walked outside and down the front steps, telling myself not to worry. My name wasn't in the article, or Paula would certainly have said something.

I went around the back to the parking lot, where the sun glinted off the black paint of my BMW, reflecting the roofline of the inn. I programmed the GPS for 55 Dorset Lane, where Chet Cummings lived, and turned on the music. Diana Krall's voice filled the car with an up-tempo version of Irving Berlin's "Let's Face the Music and Dance." I could hear Gran saying, *Ellen, musically speaking, you were born in the wrong decade.* The thought made me smile.

The computer's female voice guided me toward Dorset Lane, and as I drove I pictured Chet. Puffs of snowy white hair, creases in his face, and kind eyes. He would invite me in for tea and tell me all about his love affair with Gran and how it ended. He would still be wistful. But not angry.

He would have cookies—probably Pepperidge Farm. Maybe the ones with the apricot jelly in the middle. Gran always liked those. He would take me through his house and show me an old photo album with pictures of Gran in it.

I reached Dorset Lane, a residential street lined with older, well-maintained homes, and I stopped in front of number 55. Chet Cummings's house was a white-shingled, two-story colonial with green shutters and a stone chimney. A brick path led the way to a porch that spanned the front of the house. The yard was bounded by a four-foot-high boxwood hedge.

The house looked as if it had recently been painted. The man must have some competent help, I thought, to keep the place looking this nice. I noticed a green Audi in the driveway as I picked up the envelope with my grandmother's letter and stepped from the car.

Here I am, Gran. I hope you're watching, I thought as I walked up the porch steps. I felt both nervous and excited about meeting this man who had once been so important to my grandmother. I took a deep breath and knocked on the screen door, rattling the frame. Then I stared at the wooden door behind the screen and waited for Chet Cummings to open it.

I listened for footsteps, creaking on stairs, thumping over floorboards, but there was nothing. Just a dog barking somewhere down the street. Maybe Chet lived alone and couldn't hear well. Maybe he wore a hearing aid. Gran had worn one. It used to screech when the battery was low.

Opening the screen door, I knocked on the wooden door. A white Volvo station wagon came down the street and pulled into the neighbor's driveway and a woman got out. She looked around forty. She stared at me as she carried two bags of groceries into her house, her blond hair bouncing as she walked.

I knocked again, louder this time. *He has to be in there,* I thought. *His car is here.* I wondered if he had turned off his hearing aid. I walked around to the side of the house and peered through a window. I could see a dining room with a pine table and chairs. On two of the chairs, piles of papers were stacked high, as though someone were sorting through months of mail. In the middle of the table, stretched out on its side, lay a sable-brown cat. *So he likes cats,* I thought. *I'd always been a dog person myself.*

I walked the perimeter of the house, peering through windows, tapping on the glass. When I got to the kitchen I called out. "Mr. Cummings, Mr. Cummings. Are you home?" I rapped on the window. "I need to talk to you. Please. I've come all the way from New York!" The only sound was the chatter of birds.

Disappointed, I walked across the lawn to the car. I'd been so eager to meet him, to talk to him, to find out what happened, and now I felt only frustration and emptiness. Come back later, I told myself. He's eighty, he'll be here. He can't be out forever.

I drove back to town, following Paget Street along the beach to the construction site for the new house. Relieved that Roy's truck wasn't there, I parked next to a dusty Jeep in a dirt clearing. Two men were putting tar paper on the roof and pounding nails.

The front door was open so I walked in, jacket in hand. The place looked like a maze, with studs where walls would be and cables and wires and pipes running everywhere. Circular saws whined and workmen strode around with nail guns and electric drills. Orange power cords snaked across the floor amid sawdust, chips of wood, and cigarette butts.

I walked to the back of the house and stopped in the doorway of a large room. Through the windows, the beach stretched out behind the house, black lichen-covered rocks jutting into the ocean. To the right was the dock where I'd fallen in. I noticed a new heavy black chain and padlock on the gate. Wooden barricades blocked the sides of the dock to prevent access from the beach.

"Need some help?"

Startled, I turned and saw a man on a stepladder, his big stomach hanging over the belt of his jeans. He glanced at my linen pants and silk sweater as he attached a cable to a beam with a staple gun.

"Yes," I said. "I'm looking for someone who was working here yesterday. Short hair, beard."

The man took a pencil and made a mark on one of the beams. "Oh," he said. "You mean Walter." He stepped down from the ladder and headed toward the wooden skeleton of a staircase. I followed him.

"Walter? Where'd you go?" he shouted, as he climbed the steps while I waited below.

"What's up, Hap?" came a voice from somewhere above us.

"Got a lady here needs to see you."

A moment later Walter came down, holding an electric drill. "Did you say—" He stopped and a big smile spread across his face. "Hey, how are you? You doin' okay?" He nudged Hap. "This is the girl who fell in yesterday."

Hap nodded. "Oh, yeah, I heard about that. Roy took a swim and went after you, huh?" He grinned and looked me up and down. I wondered what they had all said to one another about the incident. Had any of them seen the kiss? God, I hoped not. I could feel my neck and cheeks flush.

"Yes," I said. "He, uh, helped—"

"You doing all right today?" Walter asked, running a hand across the fuzz on his head. "You must have been pretty shook up after that."

"I'm doing fine, thanks," I said, moving out of the way as two men walked by carrying a stack of two-by-fours. "I just came by to—"

"Roy's a real good swimmer," Hap interrupted, a twinkle in his eye. "You were lucky, drowning and all." He hitched up his jeans and tucked in his shirt where it had popped out in the back.

"Well, I wasn't exactly drowning," I said, throwing back my shoulders. "I'm actually a very good swimmer. I was on the swim team in prep school and we—"

"Hey, Walter," a deep voice boomed down from upstairs. "I need a hand here."

Walter nodded in the direction of the stairs. "Sorry. We've got an inspection tomorrow. It's a little crazy right now."

"Oh, sure," I said. "I don't want to keep you. I just wanted to return your jacket." I handed him the plastic bag. "Thanks for letting me use it."

He stared at the bag. "My what?"

"I would have gotten it dry-cleaned, but I'm leaving today and I wanted to make sure you got it back."

He took the bag and looked inside. "Oh, okay," he said. "It's not my jacket—it's Roy's. But I'll see he gets it. He's at another job right now."

Roy's? That was Roy's jacket? The jacket with the cozy lining? The one that was so warm?

"Yes, okay," I said. "I'd just like to get it back to its owner, so if you could give it to, uh, Roy…" I turned and walked away before I finished my thought, suddenly feeling a little strange.

In the car I set the GPS for the Victory Inn. After a few turns, I saw a red clapboard house with a sign in front that said GROVER'S MARKET. It must be the ocean air, I thought, as I realized I was hungry again and pulled into the lot.

A cluster of people stood in the back of the store at the deli counter, waiting to order lunch. I grabbed a menu and looked at the selections. There were several tempting salads, including one with field greens, goat cheese, pecans, raisins, and fresh sliced apple. The tuna salad also looked good—albacore, diced celery, onion, capers, and mayonnaise, served on mixed greens. Capers? I'd never heard of putting capers in tuna salad. It sounded interesting.

Farther down the menu I saw the sandwiches. Rare roast beef and Brie with sliced tomato on a toasted French baguette. That sounded great, but I'd have to forgo the Brie—too much cholesterol. But then, without the Brie, what did you really have but just another roast beef sandwich? The chicken salad sandwich also looked good, with baby greens, tomato, sprouts, grapes, and crumbled Gorgonzola, but there was the issue of the cheese again. Then I saw something that really caught my eye—the Thanksgiving Special. Oven-roasted turkey breast, savory stuffing, and fresh cranberry sauce on whole wheat bread. Perfect.

Behind the counter a teenage boy and a pregnant woman were busy making the salads and sandwiches, pouring soup, wrapping cookies, and placing orders in white boxes. While I waited my turn, I studied the shelf of desserts. Lemon pound cake, carrot cake, double chunk brownies, walnut fig bars, chocolate croissant bread pudding, blueberry pie, and strawberry rhubarb pie.

Strawberry rhubarb. That was my grandmother's favorite pie, and she made it better than anyone. A memory of her San Francisco kitchen brushed by me like a tap on the shoulder. I was nine the year she taught me how to make that pie. I remember her putting on Rosemary Clooney music and demonstrating each step of the recipe as I followed along beside her, the ingredients on the counter in front of us.

We blended the flour, butter, a pinch of salt, and egg to make the dough and then formed it into balls and chilled it in the refrigerator. When it was ready, we rolled it into circles for the crusts. I always rolled my dough too thin and Gran would have to help me patch the holes. *You've got to be quick,* she would say as she showed me how to dab small pieces of dough into the gaps, her fingers moving like a magician's. *Otherwise, the heat from your fingertips will melt the butter and the dough will just stick to your hands.*

We mixed the rhubarb and the strawberries with sugar and lemon, a little cinnamon, a bit of vanilla, some tapioca and flour, and a couple of other things I don't remember, then poured the filling into the crusts. We covered the pies with the top crusts, crimping the edges with our fingers and pricking the crusts with a fork to make tiny escape holes for the steam.

While the pies baked, Gran and I danced around the kitchen to Sinatra and Shirley Horn and I peeked in the oven a million times. And, after dinner, when we finally got to taste the pie, it was sheer heaven. A little tart, a little sweet, the crust light and buttery. I still had the index card, old and yellowed now, on which Gran wrote the recipe for me in blue fountain-pen ink.

"What can I get you, miss?"

I looked up and saw a man in an apron with a pad and pen ready to take my order.

"I'll have the Thanksgiving Special, please," I told him. Then I walked to the refrigerator, looking for a Perrier but settling for a club soda. When my order was ready the apron man started to hand me a box. Then he smiled and little wrinkles appeared at the sides of his eyes, making them look like dry creek beds.

He snapped his fingers. "Knew I'd seen you somewhere. You're the gal who fell into the ocean, aren't you? The Swimmer!"

The boy behind the counter said something to the pregnant woman and she said, "Yeah, off Marlin Beach."

I heard someone behind me whisper, "A guy rescued her, she was drowning," and then a little buzz of mumbles percolated from the people in line behind me.

Oh, God, I thought, this is a nightmare. I just wanted to get my lunch and get out. I could feel everyone staring as I took my box.

The apron man leaned over the counter toward me. *"No chaaage,"* he said, waving dismissively. "You deserve it. It's on the house."

I shook my head. "No, no," I said. "That's very nice but I insist on paying. I want to pay. I'm fine."

As I raced to the cash register at the front of the store, the apron man's voice soared over the whole place. "Phil, no charge for the Thanksgiving Special. It's *the Swimmer*."

Having been directed not to charge me, Phil, who worked the register, waved me through the line and refused to take my money. "Just happy you're alive, ma'am," he said, his round face all serious, his mouth set in a determined line. "Near-death experience and all."

I was so embarrassed I didn't know what to do. I took a ten-dollar bill and threw it on the counter. He shrugged, put the money in the cash register, and motioned for the next customer to come forward. Then he winked at me. "Picture doesn't do you justice, though."

Picture?

I'd barely formed the question when I saw the answer. At the end of the checkout line, piled on crates, were two huge stacks of the *Bugle*. On the front page, taking up the top right-hand quarter of the paper, was a photo, in full color, of a man and woman standing in chest-high water. The man's face was obscured, but the woman's face was clearly visible. Their clothes were plastered to their skin, their hair tousled and sandy. Their bodies were locked together, and they were in the midst of a passionate kiss.

Chapter 4

Worth a Thousand Words

I stood by the cash register, holding my breath, staring at the photo, hoping that if I looked at it long enough the woman would turn into someone other than me. My eyes moved to the large black letters over the picture: WOMAN SAVED FROM DROWNING OFF MARLIN BEACH THANKS RESCUER. My knees began to buckle as I read the caption: "Victim is brought to shore by rescuer after being swept out by rip current."

A crowd began to form around me. "The girl who almost drowned," a man said. And then a child asked, "Why couldn't she swim, Mommy?"

I turned to the child. "I *can* swim," I said, crossing my arms defiantly.

That's it, I thought. I've got to put an end to this. What if Hayden ever saw that photo? How could I explain it to him when I couldn't even explain it to myself? Or what if the media got hold of it? I mean, the *real* media, back in New York, where they would recognize me. Maybe the chance was slim, but my heart began to rattle in my chest when I thought about what would happen to me, to Hayden. I couldn't take the risk.

The first thing I needed to do was get rid of all the newspapers in this store. I leaned over the counter toward Phil. "Excuse me," I whispered. "What would it cost to buy all of those?" I pointed toward the papers, my hand trembling.

Phil squinted at me. "You want *all* of them?"

"Yes," I said. "All of them."

His mouth twitched for a second and then he smiled. "Oh, I get it. Souvenirs."

Someone behind me whispered, "She's going to sign them and sell them."

"Please," I said, as I tried to breathe in and out slowly, the way Hayden always told me to do when I got flustered or upset. "I'm not going to sign them or sell them." *Breathe... breathe...*

"I just want to *buy* them. Please, how much?" I had my wallet out and ready.

Phil rubbed his chin. "Well, I'd have to count them. We get five hundred every day and they're fifty cents apiece—"

"Okay," I said. "Five hundred times fifty is—"

"Yes, but we've sold a bunch," Phil said, shaking his head. "So let me see..." He narrowed his eyes and looked at the ceiling.

I took out four crisp fifty-dollar bills, two twenties, and a ten. "Just take this," I said, shoving the money at him. "I'll pay for the full five hundred."

Phil looked at the money as though it were foreign currency. "Well, gee..." Then he scratched his head. "But that's too much."

"No, please," I told him, pushing the bills his way. "I insist."

It took me three trips to haul all of the newspapers to my car, as I speed-walked to and from the market, trying to avoid the stares of the customers.

I tossed one copy on the passenger seat and threw the rest in the trunk. Then I got in, slammed the car in reverse, and launched onto the road. I drove for ten minutes, with no idea where I was going, until I came to a field surrounded by a black post-and-rail fence where three horses grazed. I pulled off the road onto the dirt shoulder.

I grabbed the paper and took a good, long look at the photo. For a second I could feel his arms around me again, I could feel his lips on mine, I could taste the salt water. And it was all...

Nothing. It was all nothing. I was a happily engaged woman, getting married in three months and looking forward to it. I sat there, imagining my walk down the aisle, Uncle Whit at my side, his arm linked in mine, standing in for my late father. And Hayden would be watching me take that walk, waiting for me, looking tall and handsome, his face tan from golf or tennis or the family yacht, his hair bleached from the sun. He would give me that little nod and that wink that I loved.

I unfolded the paper and read the article.

A woman fell through the dock at 201 Paget Street off Marlin Beach yesterday afternoon and was apparently swept away by a rip current. In a daring rescue, a man dove in after her and brought her back to shore. The grateful victim gave her hero a kiss. Neither the victim nor the hero has been identified. The incident took place around four o'clock, according to Dan Snuggler, owner of Snuggler's Pet Supply on Cottage Street. Snuggler was walking his poodle, Milarky, at the time of the incident and took this photo. "It was quite a courageous rescue," Snuggler said. "It looked as though she couldn't swim." Snuggler also noted that the dock is on private property and added, "Maybe she shouldn't have been trespassing." For more photos, turn to page 7.

More photos? My hand trembled, rattling the pages as I turned them—four, five, six. Thank God, I thought as I found page 7. There were no other photos of me or Roy. Only pictures of Mr. Snuggler's poodle frolicking on the beach, which made me wonder just what kind of journalism was being practiced in this town. And what was that bit about the *daring rescue?* And the *hero? And the trespassing!*

I hurled the paper toward the backseat as the realization hit me that I had to do some damage control. I grabbed the bag from the market and took out my sandwich. Yes, damage control was definitely in order, I thought as I took a bite. The turkey and stuffing were still warm. I took another bite. The cranberries were cool and refreshing and the bread tasted homemade. I opened the bottle of club soda and took a sip.

I watched the horses graze and flick their tails at passing flies. There was no way I could have this photo circulating, even if my name wasn't mentioned and even if it was just in *The Beacon Bugle.* There was only one thing to do. I would go to every store in town that sold the *Bugle* and buy up all the copies. I would take them out of circulation. Then tonight I would find a big trash bin somewhere and dump them.

I drove around town and made six stops, ending with the Three Penny Diner, where the aroma of freshly baked cider doughnuts was overwhelming. Laying two twenties on the counter, I scooped up their copies and dropped them in my trunk. I felt a surge of relief as I slammed the lid. The incident involving the Swimmer was officially closed.

By this time it was almost two o'clock. I set the GPS for Chet Cummings's house again and headed off. When I arrived on Dorset Lane, the green Audi was in the same place. I knocked on the door several times and looked in the kitchen window again, but the house appeared to be empty.

I sat in the car and wondered what to do. I could go back to the Victory Inn, open my briefcase, and get some work done. That was one option. But the day was so clear and the sky so relentlessly blue…

I leaned back against the seat and let the breeze drift through the windows as I surveyed the neighborhood. Most of the houses were older—early 1900s, I guessed. Each one had a dark green lawn and gardens full of coneflower, lupine, black-eyed Susan, Shasta daisies, beach heather, silvery Russian sage. I could see Gran as a girl, tending one of these gardens, the same way I'd seen her so often as an adult—trowel in her hand, floppy yellow hat on her head. She would be humming to herself, pulling up weeds or deadheading old blossoms, maybe adding a little more mulch here or there.

I felt so sad to think that I would never see her in her garden again. I squeezed my eyes shut to keep the tears away. I just wanted to feel connected to her. Maybe I'd hung my hopes on finding that connection in Beacon, through Chet Cummings. And maybe that wasn't going to happen. Maybe I'd come all this way for nothing.

I gazed again at the houses on the street and began to wonder about my grandmother's childhood home. What if she had lived on this very street? What if I was looking at her house right now? And I realized that perhaps there *was* something I could do. I could find Gran's house. This was something I could easily accomplish. Real estate was my specialty. I pictured myself driving down a street of quaint New England homes, knowing that Gran's was one of them, looking for her house. I started to feel much better.

I took out my cell phone, checked the Internet, and found the number for the Beacon town clerk's office. The town clerk's office would know where the real estate records were kept. The woman who answered the phone told me the records were kept right there, at 92 Magnolia Avenue. Finally, something was going right.

The Beacon Municipal Building, at 92 Magnolia Avenue, was a one-story redbrick structure with four windows across the front, white shutters, and a white cupola above the double front doors. It looked like it had been built in the 1960s—not too modern, but not too old, either.

I stepped inside and caught a faint whiff of ammonia. A directory on the wall listed the town clerk's office as being in room 117. By the time I arrived at that door, the ammonia smell had been replaced by the smell of spaghetti sauce. A woman with short gray hair and the wrinkled face of a pug dog sat at one of two desks, eating penne and marinara from a plastic tray.

All around her were piles of paper, notepads covered with dark, scrawled handwriting, stacks of manila folders from which the edges of documents peeked out, pens, markers, and colored paper clips. The nameplate said ARLEN FLETCH.

She put down her plastic fork and looked up, waiting for me to speak.

"I'm Ellen Branford," I said, extending my hand. "From New York," I added. I beamed a big smile her way as I noticed a yellowed microwave oven in a little cabinet across the room.

Arlen looked at my hand and then shook it.

"My grandmother lived in Beacon when she was young."

Arlen nodded and stirred her pasta around in its tray. A puff of steam rose into the air.

"And she recently died…" I waited to see if there would be any reaction to that, but Arlen just looked at me again. A door closed somewhere down the hall, followed by a stream of laughter.

"I'm here taking care of some business for her," I went on, "and while I'm here I'd like to find the house where she grew up."

Arlen slipped one of the tines of the plastic fork through a piece of penne. Then she popped the food into her mouth. "So I take it you don't have the address."

"That's right," I said, relieved that she could talk. "That's what I need to find."

She looked down at her tray, eyeing it for several seconds, and I thought she was going to tell me to come back in twenty minutes so she could finish her lunch. Instead, she smiled for the briefest second and said, "Well, you've come to the right place."

She led me into an adjoining room that had no windows and smelled dry and stuffy. Except for a table with two computer monitors on it, the room was filled from floor to ceiling with books in gray metal bookcases. I knew that between the computer database and the books, the room contained a copy of every real estate document that existed for every piece of property in Beacon, from the very first sale that was recorded.

There would be deeds of title, mortgage deeds, tax liens, foreclosure notices. There would be judgment liens, bankruptcy notices, covenants and restrictions, and easements. And, somewhere, there would be a deed of title to a piece of real estate in my great-grandparents' names.

"Okay, so let me show you how this works," Arlen said, taking her pencil and waving it as though it were an orchestra leader's baton. "First, someone comes in with a document. Could be a deed of title. That's a pretty common one. Or it could be a mortgage deed or maybe a—"

"Excuse me," I said, as I started to raise my hand to stop her from wasting her time and mine, to tell her I'd spent hundreds of hours in rooms like this doing title searches as a young real estate associate. But the look on her face was so serious, so stern, that I decided I'd better keep quiet.

"Sorry," I said. "I thought I had a question, but I don't."

She nodded. "Well, then, let's say it's a deed of title. Cecil or I, he sits over there"—she pointed to the empty desk—"we put it through that machine." She nodded toward an old time-stamp machine.

"That puts the date and time on the deed so there's no question when it came in." She pointed her pencil at me. "That can be very important when people are arguing about who owns what, you know."

This was Real Estate 101, but I bit my tongue and let her continue.

"Then we photocopy it and scan it on this thing"—she pointed to a scanner— "and Alice, who comes in three mornings a week, puts it all into the computer and organizes it all in there so people can look up a deed by seller, buyer, property address, you name it."

I continued to stand there patiently while Arlen explained how to look through the annual grantor-grantee indexes for my great-grandfather's name, and how, if I found his name, there would be a notation as to what kind of document had been filed with the town clerk and the book number and page of the book where a copy of the document would be found.

As Arlen talked, I began to wonder if I would find my great-grandfather's name in this vast selection of books that contained the history of Beacon real estate. And if I did, where would the house be and what would it look like? Would it be brick or stone? Maybe it would be a clapboard house with shutters. Maybe it would have a nice porch on the front like Chet's porch. On the other hand, it might have an ugly addition pasted onto it or, worse, be run-down and falling apart. I began to worry. What if it was owned by a commune? Or a group of drug dealers? Were there drug dealers in Beacon? I wondered.

I looked up and saw Arlen staring at me. She seemed to be waiting for me.

"I'm sorry," I said.

She waved her pencil. "Federal tax lien. Ever had one filed against you?"

I shook my head. "No, I haven't." Some of my clients had, but I wasn't going to get into that.

Arlen's gray eyes seemed to light up with this topic. "You'd sure know if you had," she warned me. "Those IRS people— they're monsters."

"Really," I said in a half whisper. I dated a guy in law school who was now working in the office of the chief counsel of the IRS. I had never considered him a *monster*, although I did later find out he was secretly dating someone else at the same time he was dating me. Maybe Arlen had a point.

She put the pencil in the pocket of her pants. "You should begin here." She motioned toward a section of ancient-looking leather-bound books. These were massive things whose covers were chipped and flaking and whose yellowed pages, I knew, were filled with beautifully penned deeds and other documents that would make even Bartleby the scrivener sit up and take note. They would contain the oldest records.

"Then you can work your way up to these." She moved her hand across the room, indicating shelves of books with white plastic covers, a modern filing system to hold photocopies of doc-uments created on typewriters and, later, computers. Finally, she pointed to the table, with its two sleek black monitors. "Anything recorded in the past five and a half years is in our database and you can find it on one of those," she said.

I nodded. "Thanks. I think that will get me started."

I sat down on a metal chair and searched for "Goddard," my great-grandfather's last name. I pored over all the annual indexes for a twenty-year period, from the late 1800s through the early 1900s. Although each index had a section for every letter of the alphabet, the names in each section were not alphabetized. Grant would come before Gibson, and Gates would be after Goats. That's just the way it was with the old books. People came in with deeds and other documents to record, and the clerks entered them in their section of the book in the order they were received. On top of that, all the old entries were handwritten, which made reviewing them even slower. After two hours I'd come up with nothing, my throat was dry, and the stuffy room was giving me a headache.

Arlen was sorting through a stack of papers when I walked up to her desk. "Got a question?" she asked.

I shook my head and gave a despondent sigh. To find Gran's house would have been wonderful. It would have been so exciting to stand before it with my feet on the ground where she might have stood decades ago. I was disappointed. There was no denying that.

"No, no question," I said. "I think I'm done. Thanks again for your help."

Arlen nodded and went back to her papers.

I turned to leave and noticed a set of old postcards matted and framed, hanging by the door. I walked up to take a closer look. There were yellow-tinged street scenes of downtown Beacon showing shops and people walking on the sidewalk and cars with rounded fenders and huge steering wheels. There was a postcard of a stark white building that had once been the town hall. And there was a redbrick building sitting on a blanket of green grass. An oak tree with a gnarled trunk stood in front like a wizened sentry. At the bottom of the postcard were the words Littleton Grammar School, Beacon, Maine.

Littleton Grammar School. What was that?

I turned to Arlen. "I do have a question," I said, pointing to the postcard. "Do you know if this school was around in the forties?" If it was around then, my grandmother would have been a student there.

Arlen walked over, put on a pair of silver half-glasses, and peered at the postcard as if she had never seen it before. "That's the Littleton School," she said.

"Yes," I said. "Do you have any idea when it was built?"

"I believe it was built in the twenties." She squinted and moved to within an inch of the postcard.

"But I can tell you for sure if you just hold on a minute." Arlen went searching through a file cabinet and finally pulled something out of a drawer.

"Here it is." She waved a pamphlet at me. "One of the schools did a project last year on the history of the old buildings in Beacon. It talks about Littleton School in here."

She handed me the booklet. On its yellow cover was a child's drawing of a large green house with gables on the front. Inside were photos of a dozen local historic buildings, each accompanied by a narrative. I thumbed through and found a copy of the same postcard. Built between 1923 and 1924, the school had opened in the fall of 1924, the write-up said. Yes, my grandmother would have been a student there.

"You can have that one," Arlen said, closing the file cabinet. "We've got lots of copies."

"I have one more question," I said, "and I really appreciate your help." I clutched the pamphlet in my hand. "Is the school still around?"

She blinked her eyes wide open and stared at me. "Well, of course it's still around. It's on Nehoc Lane."

With that, she turned, went back to her desk, and picked up her phone. I noticed a tiny orange spot on her shirtsleeve when I walked by and I wondered if it was tomato sauce.

The cool late afternoon sun and fresh air were a welcome change after the stuffiness of the records room. I programmed my GPS for Nehoc Lane. It was 3.2 miles away. Maybe I hadn't found my grandmother's house, but finding her school seemed pretty good. I was beginning to feel better about Beacon. Something about this town was becoming almost appealing.

Nehoc Lane was a residential street of mostly white houses that sat back from the road, giving way to long front yards filled with gardens of lilacs and blue hydrangeas.

The school looked a lot like the postcard, but there were some major differences. One of them was the circular drive and small parking lot in the front that hadn't existed when it was built.

I pulled in and parked. Then I walked slowly around the building, studying the words LITTLETON GRAMMAR SCHOOL 1924 etched over the huge wooden front door, noticing the surprising smoothness of the brick when I ran my hand over it, peering at the mullions on the windows and the thick layers of white paint covering the trim. An addition had been grafted on to the back of the building in bright new red brick, and on one side of the school there was a large playground with a rubberized surface. A group of children played on the swings and slides while young mothers chatted at a picnic table.

I walked back to the front of the school, toward a huge oak tree with roots that rose above the ground like arthritic fingers. The giant tree canopy was full and hung over the grass like a leafy umbrella. I sat down with my back against the craggy bark and imagined my grandmother sitting there. Maybe she was six and it was her first day of school. Maybe she was eleven and she had a crush on a boy. I could feel her in the grass, in the sunlight as it snuck through the branches, in the still-warm patch of dirt underneath me.

I ran my fingers along the top of a root and felt the tears well up. They slid down my cheeks and fell onto my pants, making dark spots on the fabric. "I miss you, Gran," I whispered, my voice choking. "I miss you. And I've come here to do what you asked me to do but it's not going the way it's supposed to. First, I fell into the ocean and almost...I almost drowned, Gran. Then I tried to deliver your letter but I haven't been able to do it. And I tried to find your house but I couldn't do that, either. I wish I knew why these things were happening. I wish you could tell me." A breeze rustled the tree branches above and I put my head in my hands and closed my eyes.

Chapter 5

A Quiet Place for Dinner

I decided to try Chet Cummings's house one more time on my way back to the inn. It was five o'clock when I got there. The green Audi was in the driveway but still no one was home and I began to worry that he might have gone out of town. Maybe he was visiting a friend or there was a family emergency and he wouldn't be back for several days. I thought about leaving the letter in his mailbox but the idea seemed so disappointing. On the other hand, I couldn't stay in Beacon forever, waiting for him to return. I knew my grandmother would have understood that. All right, I thought. Tomorrow is Thursday. I've still got one more opportunity to get this done. I'll come back here early in the morning, before he has a chance to go anywhere. If he's still not here, I'll leave the letter and head home.

I returned to the inn with the idea that I would have a quiet dinner in the dining room, followed by a couple of hours of work and then sleep. When I walked up the front steps and into the lobby, it sounded like a party was going on. Three couples, all tall and tan and in their twenties, hovered around the check-in desk, laughing and talking. The men, dressed in golf shirts and khakis, were having a disagreement over a line call in a tennis match. The women, with their long, gazellelike legs, only the very tops of which were covered by their short shorts, huddled over a booklet. One of the women mentioned the Antler, the pub I'd seen downtown, and I wondered if they were looking at a travel guide.

I laughed to myself, imagining what Fodor's might say about Beacon.

The Three Penny Diner: *This is a must if you love green Formica and tabletop jukeboxes. Be sure to try the doughnuts.*

The Victory Inn: *If your fondness runs to rooftops, request the suite with the ocean view. Cell phone service available in the bathroom.*

I rounded the corner, poking my head into the lounge, and saw that someone had set out refreshments. Several bottles of wine, platters of cheese and crackers, and a bowl of dip were arranged on a table, with stacks of plastic cups and paper plates. I poured myself a glass of Pinot Noir, from a vineyard called Gallant River Winery in the Napa Valley. I'd never heard of it, but Hayden would probably know who they were. I took a couple of crackers and headed for my room.

The noise from the lobby followed me as I began to climb the stairs, and when I heard one of the women say, "Let's have dinner here tonight," I decided I'd better eat out. Maybe Paula would have a recommendation.

As I stood in front of the closet, trying to decide what to wear, my cell phone rang. I grabbed my purse, dug out the phone, and ran into the bathroom, where I closed the toilet seat and sat down.

"Hey, sweetheart. You sound out of breath." It was Hayden.

"I was just trying to get to the phone and get into the bathroom." I stretched my legs and rested my bare feet on the rim of the tub.

"Oh, well, you can call me back."

"No, no. I mean, I need to *talk* from the bathroom. It's the only place where I can get a cell signal."

There was a pause, and then Hayden said, "No cell signal?" in a way that sounded like I'd told him there was no hot and cold running water, which, come to think of it, there basically wasn't.

"It's okay," I said, not wanting to go into it any further. He would only worry. Hey," I said, "you'll never believe what I found today."

"Tell me."

"My grandmother's elementary school."

"Your grandmother's *what?*"

"Elementary school—her school. I went and saw the building. It's still here in Beacon."

"It must be pretty old."

"Yeah, it is. It was built in the 1920s. I was trying to find the house where she grew up and I didn't find that but I found the school. It was really amazing, Hayden, and I—"

"Hey, sweetie, hold on a second, will you? My other phone is ringing."

I waited for a moment, staring at a print on the wall—a lighthouse sending its beam across the water as a warning for boaters to avoid the shoals. Then I went into the bedroom and grabbed the pamphlet with the information about the Littleton School so I could read it to Hayden.

"So when are you leaving?" he asked when he got back on the line. "I was hoping you'd be on the road."

"I thought I'd be on the road, too, but I still haven't been able to find Chet Cummings. He's never home."

"Maybe he's away, Ellen. I know I said it was good that you went to Beacon, but you can't stay there forever, hoping he'll show up."

"I'm not staying here forever. I'd like to be driving home right now." I looked across the bedroom, through one of the windows, at the soft amber light ushering the day into night.

There was another pause. "Just promise me you'll come home tomorrow," Hayden said. "The dinner is Friday night and I don't want to worry about you driving home Friday, trying to get here on time. I know how you speed when you're afraid of being late. It's dangerous."

"I promise I won't speed," I said. "I won't have to, because I'm leaving tomorrow for sure. I'm going one last time, early in the morning, to see if I can find Chet Cummings."

Something began to clink and clank and sputter in the pipes behind the wall: the plumbing system was suddenly coming alive.

"What if he's still not there?" Hayden asked. "What's your plan then?"

"I'll leave the letter at his house," I said as water gushed through a pipe behind the wall. "I'll be back tomorrow, no matter what."

A crackle of static came through the phone.

"Hayden, I think I'm losing you."

There was more static.

"I can't hear you," I shouted. "I'll call you later."

I hung up and looked at my watch. It was only five thirty. Way too early for dinner. I glanced at the bed and could almost feel my eyelids start to droop. Maybe, I thought, if I lie down, just for a minute…

I lay down on top of the white coverlet and pressed a pillow under my head. The crisp cotton case smelled like powder and fresh soap and clothes hanging outside on a line.

It was nearly dark when I awoke. Someone outside, down at street level, was shouting and opening and shutting car doors. I rubbed my eyes and looked at my watch. Eight thirty. My stomach felt empty and I needed dinner.

I changed into gray Gucci pants, an ivory knit top, and a matching long-sleeved sweater. After considering my jeweled Jimmy Choo heels, I opted for a pair of flat Tory Burch sandals instead. I picked up the double strand of pearls Gran left me, slipped them over my neck, and closed the front clasp—a silver scallop shell. Then I touched up my makeup and grabbed a copy of *Forbes* from my briefcase. It was good to have reading material—dining alone was always dull.

Before I reached the second-floor landing, I could hear the din from the dining room. The gang that had checked in earlier seemed to be making most of the noise. I expected to see Paula as I walked through the lobby, but she wasn't there. I found her outside, on the front porch, smoking a cigarette, running a hand through her hair. Under the porch light, her brassy blond hair looked almost orange.

"Quite a party," I said, nodding toward the door.

She looked me up and down as she held her cigarette between the V of her two fingers and then she let a long stream of smoke trail from her mouth, like the exhaust plume of a rocket. "Uh-huh."

"Guess they're having a good time."

She nodded and looked down at her hands, inspecting her fingernails, as though she might just saunter off for a quick manicure.

I rummaged around in my purse for my car keys, finally pulling them out. "Is there somewhere in town that would be a good place for a quiet dinner?"

Paula pursed her lips and rocked her head left and right. "I'd say the Antler. They have good steaks. Fish, too. Great chowder." She pronounced it *chowda*. "And a real good meat loaf. Even the city folks seem to like it."

"Oh, yeah, the Antler," I said, wrapping my sweater a little tighter as a breeze ruffled the grass. "That looks like a pub. Do you think it will be quiet there tonight?"

Paula wrinkled her nose a little and stuck out her lower lip. "Wednesday night?" She shrugged. "Yeah, pretty quiet." She stubbed out the cigarette in a glass ashtray on the porch railing. Then she went inside.

I decided to walk to town. The evening was cool and I was feeling guilty about not having been to my health club in a week. The streetlights gave downtown Beacon a cozy orange glow. There were a dozen people out strolling. Tourists peered into windows of shops and offices closed for the night. A handful of teenagers congregated in a little group by the seawall. One of the boys took his baseball cap off and put it on one of the girls and they all laughed.

I walked to the door of the Antler, the yellow Michelob sign gleaming like a welcoming fire in the window. Meat loaf. Of all the things to eat, why would somebody want to eat meat loaf? Give me a nice piece of yellowfin tuna or a simple breast of chicken in a white wine reduction—but meat loaf? Oh, well. Maybe some people would consider my food choices equally odd.

With the *Forbes* tucked under my arm, I opened the door into a large dusky room. I could see a bar along the left side and rows of square tables on the right. Country music was playing, with the twang of a pedal steel guitar and the raspy voice of a woman singing something I couldn't decipher. There was a loud buzz of conversation, mixed with a stream of laughter and a steady clatter of utensils. Not particularly quiet, but I was already there and my stomach was rumbling. As I took a step inside I noticed a handwritten sign on an easel near the door: EVERY WEDNES-DAY NIGHT—TWO-FOR-ONE ENTRÉES. Well, I thought, that explains it. Funny that Paula didn't know.

The floor of the Antler was made of dark wood, polished to a high sheen. Wooden rafters ran across the ceiling, and light fixtures hung from the beams—copper ship's lanterns, chrome pendant lights shaped like large bells, brass chandeliers with curved arms ending in flickering, flame-tip bulbs. The bar was made of a red-hued wood that had been coated with layers of clear lacquer. The same wood had been used to make the sturdy tables and chairs that filled the room.

All the tables were occupied, as were most of the bar stools. I walked through the room, looking straight ahead but absorbing a peripheral blur of denim and khakis and T-shirts. There were a few skirts and sundresses, but this was mostly a denim crowd. I felt overdressed.

I took a seat at the far end of the bar, near the dance floor. "Your Cheatin' Heart," sung by Hank Williams, began drifting from the speakers overhead. To the right sat a middle-aged man and his wife, a buxom brunette, her hair in a high ponytail. To the left were a couple of empty bar stools, followed by two twentysomething guys in baseball caps. One of the caps had the name LOBSTER POT on it.

A stout bartender with salt-and-pepper hair came over, wiped the bar with a towel, and then placed a cardboard Coors Light coaster in front of me, its blue mountain peaks shimmering under the lights.

"What can I get you?"

I considered having a glass of wine, but then I saw a sign that said BEST MARGARITAS NORTH OF TIJUANA, and I thought, Well, what the hell.

"I'll have one of those." I pointed to the sign.

I opened my *Forbes* and flipped through a few pages, but there was so much noise it was hard to concentrate. Instead, I focused on a flat-screen TV hanging behind the bar. There was a reality show on about a truck driver taking a big rig through a remote, mountainous area at night in the middle of a blizzard. I was starting to become nervous for the driver and was about to bite my nail when the bartender placed a margarita in front of me.

I took a long sip and asked for a dinner menu. Scanning the selections, I looked for something healthy. Shrimp with rice and green beans? No, the shrimp was fried. Twin lobsters with drawn butter? Too much food, and that butter... There was a chicken breast that might work if I told them to hold the marinara sauce and cheese.

The bartender served the couple sitting next to me. The man had ordered the meat loaf, and maybe I was just really hungry, but his dinner looked kind of appetizing. There was a mound of mashed potatoes with a little gleam of butter on top, green beans that looked fresh, and a slice of meat loaf that smelled like onions and herbs. And I thought I saw mushrooms.

I wondered about the fat content and how many miles I'd have to run to burn off the calories. If Hayden were here, he'd be picking out something healthy for me. I glanced at the man's plate again. Yes, there were definitely mushrooms.

Well, Hayden wasn't here, and I suddenly felt famished for old-fashioned comfort food.

"I think I'll have the meat loaf," I told the bartender.

"Any starter?"

A starter. I thought about ordering a house salad. I looked to see what else my neighbors had ordered. The woman was having some kind of soup. I glanced at the menu again and sighed. In for a penny, in for a pound.

"Sure," I said. "I'll have the clam chowder."

I looked back at the television. The driver was crawling along the side of the mountain on a very narrow road. There was a close-up of his front wheels, chains grinding through ice. My foot began to twitch.

"Hey, Skip, can we get another round back there?"

I turned and saw someone standing in the empty space to my

left—a skinny man in a T-shirt that had a yellow swordfish on the front.

"Yeah, Billy," the bartender said. "I got you covered. Sorry, we're a little shorthanded tonight."

The man named Billy looked up and down the bar. "Where's Sassy?" Then he looked at me for a moment and I could feel him staring at me as though somebody had taped an OUT-OF-TOWNER sign to my back.

"Ah, she had to go to Portland. Sister just had an operation."

Billy shook his head. "Oh, well, hope everything's all right. Tell her I said hey when you see her." He walked toward a little seating area where there was a sofa and a couple of big armchairs, and I noticed that some men were playing darts.

I sipped my drink as Skip mixed cocktails and doled them out to customers at the bar and to the three waitresses who circled like airplanes waiting for runway assignments. Then he filled several frosted mugs with beer from a tap and said, "Bridget, take these to Billy and the guys over there, would you?" Bridget, a skinny-legged girl with bleached white hair, put the mugs on a tray and headed toward the dart players.

I looked at the television again and saw that the truck driver was off the mountain road and pulling into a big truck stop, where it appeared he was going to spend the night. Thank God.

My clam chowder arrived and I stirred it for a minute, gazing at the steam rising from the bowl. As I brought the spoon to my mouth I had the feeling I was being watched. I looked up and caught Skip peering at me.

He snapped his fingers. "It *is* you. I thought so, but then I thought, no, it's not her, but it is. You, I mean."

"Excuse me?"

He smiled a big toothy smile, showing off a space on the side where a molar was missing. "You're the Swimmer! Caught your picture in the paper. Some kiss."

I started to stammer something, but he put his big bear hand over mine and leaned closer. "Look here," he said. "This is on the house. The whole meal, in fact. We treat tourists right here, especially after a . . . er, situation like yours."

I shook my head vigorously. The last thing I wanted was any connection with swimming, near drowning, or that picture in the paper. I shuddered when I thought about Hayden ever seeing that photo. "No, no, that's fine," I said. "I really insist—"

But Skip was already in sixth gear. He stepped back and waved his hands. "Hey, everybody, it's the Swimmer!" He pointed to me. "The girl who almost drowned. The Swimmer!"

I could feel the heat in my face as I got up from the bar stool to make my escape. What was going on? I thought I had bought every newspaper out there. I wanted to run through the door and back to the inn. I wanted to leave Beacon and never return. In fact, I never wanted to see the state of Maine again.

But when I tried to leave, I didn't get farther than three steps.

A man with a ruddy complexion and DAVE stitched on his shirt came rushing toward me, followed by a group of people all talking at once.

"Hey, Swimmer, let me shake your hand," Dave said.

"Another drink for the Swimmer," a man with a shock of whitish hair shouted to Skip. "Lucky to be alive."

Oh, God, this was like a bad dream where you try to run but your legs don't work. "I wasn't drowning," I said, turning to the white-haired man, my eyes blazing with humiliation. "I was perfectly fine. That guy who helped me...I just let him do it so he wouldn't be insulted. He's...he's got a fragile ego."

"Oh, she's *funny,* too," he crowed as he slapped me on the back. "Didn't want to insult him." The crowd began to laugh.

"You know, I really need to get going," I said, trying to squeeze through the group.

A woman with a wad of gum in her mouth tapped me on the shoulder. "Did you have hypothermia? My cousin had that once and his skin started flaking off. It was really nasty."

I instinctively touched my arm. "No, I did *not* have hypothermia." I turned away.

A bald man grabbed my hand and kept shaking it. "Did you see your whole life flash before you when you fell in?" He wouldn't let go of me. "'Cause once I fell off a ladder, you know, and I swear I saw my whole life flash before me—even the night I had too much to drink and tried to put the moves on my wife's sister."

"If you don't mind," I said as I yanked my hand away. A couple of college girls from Vermont asked me if I'd ever go back in the water, and then got into an argument between themselves about whether or not I *should,* and an ex–police officer from Bangor asked me if I had been on drugs when it happened.

"Here's to the Swimmer," somebody shouted, and everybody had a glass raised...but me.

Then Skip passed a margarita to a girl and she passed it to a man who passed it to me. I drank it down in a few gulps, while people continued to pelt me with questions about whether or not I had a death wish.

The crowd was pressing in closer, and I began to feel as though people were pushing on my lungs. Pushing and pushing. I couldn't get enough air.

Then Skip said, "Hey, leave her alone, she's been through enough," and slowly the group dispersed. Skip motioned for me to come back to my seat.

"You look a little pale," he said. "I think you need to finish your soup."

I noticed that he'd placed another margarita at my spot. I gazed at the chowder. He was right; I was hungry. But I went for the margarita first, downing half of it. A sudden feeling of warmth washed over me.

Then I tried the clam chowder. It was loaded with baby clams, and the flavor of the clams was balanced nicely with diced potato and finely chopped onion and celery. Tiny sprigs of fresh dill floated on top. The combination was heavenly, and I ate every drop, doing my best not to think about what else was in there. There had to be cream—at least half-and-half—and butter for sure. And I could taste little bits of bacon. Hayden would think I'd lost my mind. But it was good. It was so good.

People kept coming into the Antler, crowding around the bar. Drinks were being passed over my head to customers standing two and three deep behind me. The music pulsed, Keith Urban's "Long Hot Summer" blasting from the speakers, and the whole place felt like it was glowing, humming.

"Skippy...hey, Skippy," I called out, but I could barely hear my own voice over the noise. For some reason, that struck me as funny, and the louder I yelled, the harder I laughed.

I held up my glass and pointed to it. "What *is* this again? What *is* this, Skippy?" I couldn't remember the name of the drink.

Skip nodded and gave me a thumbs-up, but I wasn't sure what he meant by that. I yelled his name again and held up my glass, trying to get his attention. "What is this again? What's it called?"

Before I knew it, Skip had passed another drink my way. And soon the music became even louder and livelier and people crowded onto the dance floor.

"Hey, do you want to sit with us?" A woman with a pageboy haircut and sleepy eyes was standing next to me. She reminded me of a paralegal who used to work at Winston Reid.

"I'm Bliss and this is Wendy," she said. Wendy looked like the cheerleader type, with an athletic build and blond hair.

I shook their hands and introduced myself. I was glad for the company.

"Yeah, we know who you are. You're the Swimmer," Wendy said, beaming her big smile and pulling me to a table near where the men were playing darts.

We tried to talk over the music but all I could figure out was that they were dental hygienists having a girls' night out.

Skip sent a round of drinks and menus over to us, with the message that dinner was on the house. How many drinks was this now? And hadn't I already ordered dinner? I thought so, but just to make sure, I ordered clam chowder and meat loaf again.

Bliss began talking about an argument she'd had with their office manager, and I sat back and watched the dart game. Four men were playing 301, a game I learned in college, in my junior year abroad at Oxford, where I dated Blake Abbott. Blake was British and a whiz at darts, and he taught me how to play.

One of the men threw a dart and the guy named Billy laughed and said, "Jeez, Gordon, where's your arm tonight?"

Gordon made a face. "Get real. You think you can beat me?"

A man leaning against the wall said, "Come on, get out of there, it's my turn." He stepped up and threw three darts.

"You throw like a girl, Jake," one of the other players said. I couldn't tell which one, although I thought it might have been the guy named Gordon.

What kind of a stupid comment was that? I slapped the table in front of Bliss. Maybe I hit it a little too hard, because my hand began to sting. "Did you hear that?" I asked.

Bliss looked at me, her eyes wide. "What? What?"

My finger wiggled as I pointed at her and tried to form the words. "I'll tell you what," I said. "One of those guys over there…"

"Yeah?" Bliss and Wendy looked at me, waiting.

I shook my head. "Yeah, one of those guys over there told another one of those guys over there that he *throws like a girl*." I felt a rush of indignation blast through me, sending goose bumps along my arms. "Don't you hate it when men talk like that?"

Wendy leaned toward me. "I completely hate it. There was a guy at Dr. Belden's office, the periodontist I used to work for, and he was always saying stuff like that."

I leered at the dart players, not quite sure where to cast my outrage but pretty sure that they all deserved it.

"Throw like a girl," I said. "What is *that* supposed to mean? That girls can't throw? That they can't…what? Play darts?"

I was mad. I was infuriated. I was intoxicated. And I would show them.

I pulled my wallet from my purse and rifled through the cash until I found a hundred-dollar bill. Then I pushed back my chair and climbed onto the seat. I stood there, looking across the room, feeling invincible. I would show these small-minded men a thing or two.

"Okay, I'd like to say something." I tried to project my voice over the din, but it was impossible. "Hello!" I yelled, waving my hands. "Hello. Excuse me." I tried to whistle with my two pinkies in my mouth, the way my father had taught me, but I couldn't get anything but a hiss to come out.

Finally I took a deep breath and screamed, "Quiet! The Swimmer would like to say something!"

Everything around me stopped. The conversations, laughter, arguments, clinking of glasses, clanking of forks and knives, all came to a halt. Everyone stared at me.

I held up the hundred-dollar bill and snapped it between my hands. "See this hundred-dollar bill?" I snapped it again. "I bet I can beat any of you at a game of darts. *Any of you*," I repeated, leaning over my chair like a figurehead on the prow of a ship. "Including the idiot who told what's his name...Jake over there"—I pointed a limp finger in the general direction of the group—"that he throws like a girl!"

I smiled and waited to see what kind of mountain man would come out of the woodwork and take up the challenge. There was a movement from the sofa near the dartboard. Two men were sitting with their backs to me. One of them stood up, stretched his arms, and turned around. He began walking toward me. He was tall, with dark wavy hair, a square jaw, and a slightly rugged face. He could have been anyone from an airline pilot to a logger. In another situation, he might even have been handsome. He was dressed in faded jeans, a pale blue button-down shirt, and a brown leather jacket. As he came forward and stepped into the light, I recognized the jacket, and my throat tightened. It was Roy.

"I guess I'm that idiot," he said quietly. "I'll take you on."

I stepped down from the chair, feeling a chill of sobriety pass through me. The dock, the tired swimmer's carry, *the kiss*. What had I done? The last person in the world I ever wanted to see again, and now...

"Um...hi," I said, trying to keep my voice steady. I smiled and gave him a casual wave, as though none of this was a big deal.

He put a bottle of beer and a handful of darts on the table. "I see you've recovered."

"Recovered?" I picked up one of the darts and gripped the barrel, trying to get a feel for the weight. It might as well have been an anvil.

He took off his jacket and put it over a chair. "From your swim the other day." I thought I saw a glint in his eye.

"There was nothing to recover from," I said, holding the dart to my ear and extending my arm in a practice motion.

He shrugged. "Well, good." Then he added, "Thanks for bringing back my jacket."

I nodded. "No problem." I adjusted my grip a little, hoping to give the impression that these subtle moves were part of some complex strategy. "I didn't know the jacket was yours."

He took a sip of his beer. "I hope you play darts better than you swim," he said, crossing his arms and peering at me.

I hoped so, too. Oxford was in the distant past and I hadn't exactly been keeping up my game. Add a few of those drinks Skippy kept sending me, and...

"I can play darts quite well," I said. "Quite well indeed." I flashed a big, confident-looking smile.

Roy cocked his head. "Well, name your game, then. Cricket? Three-oh-one? Shanghai?"

I began to think, trying to come up with the most straightforward game I could remember. Something that wouldn't involve complicated scoring, because math calculations were not going to be my strong suit at the moment. Finally I had an idea.

I took a deep breath. "Okay," I said. "Dead Presidents."

Roy laughed. "Dead Presidents. You want to play Dead Presidents?"

No, what I really wanted to do was get the hell out of there.

"All right, tell you what. You hit Franklin first, you get to keep your hundred and another hundred from me. I hit it first, I get the bills." Roy took out his wallet and removed five twenties. "But you've got to nail him in the face."

Nail him in the face. Nail him in the face? *Impossible.*

"That sounds fine." I shrugged and waved my hand at him as if I did this every day. Meanwhile, people had come off the dance floor, a crowd had formed around us, and someone had turned the music down low. Beads of perspiration eased their way down my back. I began to feel a little hot, a little sick.

Roy walked to the board and removed Jake's darts. All right, get it together, I told myself. *Get it together.* I rolled up my sleeves. Just get the damned things on the board. Don't throw buckshot and have them fly all over the place. He'll end up winning—that's a given—but as soon as he does, you get the hell out of here.

Roy held a fistful of darts. "Shall we warm up?" He had the edge of a smile on his face as he presented the darts to me.

I could warm up for a week, I thought, and it wouldn't help. I shrugged. "Well, *I* don't really need a warm-up, but if you insist..." I took the darts.

Okay, let's get this over with. I walked to the toe line and stepped behind it. I tried to hold the grip as I would a pencil, the way Blake had taught me, but my arm felt like it belonged to somebody else. I raised the dart until it was parallel to my ear. Then I aimed and let it float. It arced high and landed on the opposite side of the board from where I was aiming. I didn't care. I was just happy it hit the board.

I threw the second dart, aiming for the same spot. This time it went much closer. The next five were better, and as I kept throwing I realized that there was something enjoyable in this out-of-body experience I was having—holding the darts, seeing them float, watching them hit the board. I threw the last two warm-ups. They landed in the general vicinity of my targets, and that was close enough to make me feel better.

From the look of Roy's warm-up, though, I had no doubt about who would win. He was skillful and accurate and was probably already deciding what he was going to buy with my hundred dollars.

"Guess I'm first," Roy said after we threw to see who would begin and his dart landed much closer to the bull's-eye than mine. No surprise.

I took my hundred-dollar bill and folded it in thirds to reveal Benjamin Franklin's face. Then I slid the bill under the double ring, the wire closer to the outside of the board, over the four-point segment, which was roughly in the two o'clock position of the dartboard.

Please, let this be over with soon.

"Okay," I said, in a cheerful, upbeat tone. "I'm ready. One shot each, until somebody hits Franklin, right?"

Roy nodded. "Has to hit the face."

Yeah, the face. I just wanted it to hit the board. Somewhere. Anywhere.

Roy took a dart, aimed, and missed the edge of the bill by about an inch.

"Wow," somebody said, and there was murmuring among the group around us.

Beads of perspiration formed above my lip as I looked at how close his dart had come. "Not too bad a shot," I said in my most casual tone.

Now it was my turn. I held the dart, trying to relax my grip. My stomach clenched like a fist and I was so nervous my skin felt prickly. Hold it together, I told myself. Hold it together.

Roy leaned against the wall with his hands in his pockets. I looked at the tiny green face on the board. It seemed to wiggle in front of me. I looked down to clear my head. Just throw it. Just let it go. I raised my head again and lifted the dart to my ear. Then I let it fly. It made a soft arc and landed with a solid thud. For a moment there was complete silence and then a woman screamed, "She hit it!"

I stood rooted to my spot while the group around us yelled and cheered.

"She did it!"

"One shot; she got it in one shot!"

People ran up to me, clapping and laughing. I stared at the board, feeling like my knees were going to buckle under me. I walked to the board and saw that I had not only hit Franklin but I had punctured his nose. I couldn't believe it. If I tried ten thousand more times, I would never be able to do that again. I pulled out the dart and the bill and gasped at the mutilated face.

Somebody began chanting, "The Swimmer is a thrower! The Swimmer is a thrower!" Pretty soon the whole place picked up the phrase. People were clapping and saying it, slapping the tabletops and saying it. I was surrounded by the chant.

Roy came over, holding five twenties, the noise around us almost deafening. He had lost the smile but his eyes were as blue as ever. In his jeans and button-down shirt, with his jacket over his arm, he suddenly looked so handsome I couldn't turn away. He shook his head as though he, too, didn't believe what had just happened.

"Don't spend it all in one place." He smiled as he held out the money. "You've earned this. I've never seen anything like that."

I looked at the bills in his hand. Like a magic trick after you've learned the secret, they had lost their allure. I didn't really want to take his money anymore. It didn't seem right, and he seemed so...I couldn't quite put my finger on it.

The crowd continued to chant, making a circle around me and Roy. The people moved in closer. "The Swimmer is a thrower. The Swimmer is a thrower." It began to get very hot, and the noise...I wanted the noise to stop. Everybody was getting too close, and it was so hot. I needed to sit down.

I saw Roy put the money into my hand. It didn't feel like

money. It felt like dried leaves. The room began to swirl around me. I looked at Roy and tried to speak.

"I've never seen…" I wanted to tell him I had never seen anything like it, either, but my mouth stopped working and all I could do was point to myself, as though we were playing charades. Black spots began to appear around the room, removing people and objects from view as though they were being sucked into a void. My legs sagged under me. The black holes were everywhere, swallowing up the room. For one last second I saw Roy's face. And then it vanished.

Chapter 6

A City Girl Cuts Loose

Get another wet towel."

I heard a woman's voice.

"It's okay, she's coming around," a man said. His voice was close to my ear.

I opened my eyes. I was lying on my back, on something hard, looking up at a crowd of people peering down at me. Bits of conversation floated by like pods of milkweed.

"Is she all right?"

"She fainted."

"Should we call nine-one-one?"

I heard music. Maybe I was in the middle of a square dance. Fiddles and banjos swirled around in an upbeat tempo.

"All right, give her some room, please. Excitement's over." It was Roy's voice. I turned my head and saw him crouching by my side, his forehead creased with concern, his eyes soft. I could smell his aftershave, something fresh, like the outdoors, but I wasn't sure what it was. The group began to disperse.

"What happened?" I asked, glancing at a copper ship's lantern that dangled from the ceiling. Something cool was on my forehead. I touched the spot and found a wet towel.

Roy scratched his chin and gave a slight smile, prompting the dimples in his cheeks to appear again. "I'd say you fainted."

I groaned. Then I started to get up.

"Whoa, not so fast." He put his hand under my back and helped raise me to a sitting position.

I looked around and saw a crowded room with people eating at tables, clustering around a bar, and throwing darts. The Antler.

"You all right?" He gave my arm a little tap.

I took a deep breath and nodded. "I think so," I said. "I just want to get up."

He took my hand and slowly I stood up and brushed off my clothes. I ran my fingers through my hair and tried to smile. "Thank you."

"No problem," he said. "Let's get you to a chair."

We walked to a table against the wall while I tried to figure out what had taken place. Did I faint in his arms? Oh, God, please tell me that wasn't what happened. "Did you, um, catch me when I fell?"

He nodded.

I could feel my cheeks burning. First the kiss and now this. I couldn't seem to stop embarrassing myself with this man. "Well, thanks...again," I said quietly.

I sat down on a red leatherette banquette and pressed the wet towel to my forehead. Roy pulled out a chair opposite me. "No problem...again," he said.

The fiddle music was still playing and I realized it was John Denver singing "Thank God I'm a Country Boy."

"Just sit for a minute, get your bearings," Roy said.

"I'm fine, really."

He motioned toward the door. "Maybe we should go outside and get some air. Do you want to do that?"

What I really wanted was to stop making a fool of myself in this town. "No, thanks," I said. "I'm really okay. I don't know what happened."

A waitress came by and put two glasses of water on the table. "Seems like you're always coming to my rescue," I said.

"In the right place at the right time, I guess." Roy dug a hand into the front pocket of his jeans and produced a folded hundred-dollar bill with five twenties inside. "This is yours. You dropped it when you, uh…"

I looked at the folded cash, the little puncture mark on Franklin's nose. I didn't want it.

"Here," he said, putting the money in my hand.

I stared at it for a moment, and then I took out my wallet and tucked the bills into the back. "Yeah…thanks."

John Denver ended his song and the thrum of an electric guitar took over, a handful of notes followed by a woman's sultry directive: "Let's go, girls." Shania Twain's spunky voice filled the room as she sang, "Man! I Feel Like a Woman!"

We sat there for a minute while the dance floor began to fill up, and then Roy said, "Maybe what you need is to get out there. Sounds like your kind of song." He motioned toward the dance floor, crowded with gyrating bodies. "How about it?" Shania's voice echoed all around us. Some line about women having the prerogative to have a little fun.

A dance with Roy. Did I really want to do that? Oh, what the hell, I thought as I stood up. "All right." I felt my face flush.

"You know the two-step?" he asked as we found a spot on the floor.

"I know the Texas two-step."

"That'll do."

He used one of his hands to hold mine and put his other hand on the back of my shoulder, creating the proper space between us—*the frame*. I felt as though I were twelve years old and back at Trimmy Taylor's, the dance studio that used to be in Pine Point when I grew up there.

Trimmy, with her petite dancer's body and multiple face-lifts, which made her look forever awestruck, would always tell us, *Make the frame, make the frame*. I could still see her dark hair piled high in an endless bun and smell her floral perfume as she whirled about, always keeping her partner at the perfect distance.

Thank God for Trimmy, I thought as Roy began guiding me around the floor. He was so smooth I could have had glue on my shoes and it wouldn't have mattered.

"I knew you could swim, but I didn't know you could dance," I told him as we tried a couple of turns.

"Well, swimming's not my only talent," he said, twirling me.

I noticed that we were the only couple doing a two-step. Everyone else was just making random movements. We circled the floor, doing turns and moves I couldn't believe I remembered.

"They have places that teach dancing way up here in Maine?" I asked, pretending to be surprised. Roy twirled me again and then we twirled together; our hands interlocked for a moment, and the room held us in a soft embrace.

He put his hand back on my shoulder. "Maybe they do and maybe they don't."

"Ah, he's being mysterious."

Roy looked at me and smiled and I smiled, too, and then I started to laugh. It felt great to be dancing. I couldn't even remember the last time I *had* danced.

"Looks like they're all afraid of us," Roy said as my feet glided through the moves.

"What do you mean?"

He looked around and laughed. "They're all leaving."

I saw that only a few couples were still dancing. Everyone else had gone to the edge of the floor and was watching us.

Roy turned and then took my hand again. "I didn't know city girls could cut loose like this."

"I'll bet there are a lot of things you don't know about city girls."

"Well, I know one thing," he said as he guided me around effortlessly. "It's a good thing you can't swim, because—"

"Wait a minute there." I let go and stopped, pretending to be insulted, feeling a little electric spark go up and down my arms. "I object to your characterization of that incident. I clearly *can* swim, and I was doing it when you got to me. I was just a little tired from the rip current, that's all."

"Okay, okay," Roy said, waving his hands. "May I rephrase my statement, counselor? Isn't that what you lawyers say in court—*can I rephrase the question,* or something like that?"

He took my hand and we began dancing again. "Yeah, something like that," I said. "Okay, permission granted. Rephrase."

"All right, what I *meant* to say is that it's a good thing you were having *some trouble* swimming because otherwise we wouldn't be dancing right now, and you're a decent dancer."

The song ended and the people standing at the edge of the dance floor actually applauded. Roy stepped back and clapped for me and I laughed and made a little bow. Then a few lone notes on a piano signaled the beginning of something much slower. It was that awkward moment when I never knew whether to stand there and wait to see if I'd be asked again or say thanks and sit down.

"Thanks," I said as I turned to walk away. A number of couples were coming back onto the dance floor.

Roy grabbed my hand. "Wait, you can't leave yet, Swimmer. This is a good song." He smiled. The dimples were showing again.

I wondered how he could tell what the song was from only the first few notes, but then I realized I could do that, too, with songs I loved. "All right," I said.

He took my hand again, but this time he moved in close and pulled me against him. I put my other hand around his neck as Willie Nelson began singing "Always on My Mind."

Oh, God, this was starting to feel weird. Slow dancing to a love song with somebody who wasn't Hayden. Somebody who had saved my life. It was weird, all right, but it was also kind of nice. I felt small, like a ballerina, against him. His arm seemed so strong around me that I thought he could have picked me up with just that one arm. I didn't even know what my feet were doing. I was coasting along, his hand resting on my back. My face was close to his. His aftershave smelled a little bit like cedarwood, and it smelled nice.

Roy leaned his head down. "So are you always that lucky?"

"What do you mean? Lucky that I didn't hit the floor and crack my head open?"

He laughed. "Well, that, too, I guess. But I meant with the darts."

He moved his hand, just slightly, on my back, and a prickly sensation went all the way down my body. I was dancing with someone who wasn't Hayden and I was feeling…well, pretty good about it.

"Oh, you thought that was luck?" I gave a cavalier laugh. "I'll have you know I used to play darts all the time when I was in college at Oxford."

"Hmm…Oxford…and you still play?"

I laughed. "Not really, unless you count tonight."

"Well, maybe you should. Maybe this could kick off a new career."

I was about to say that playing darts wasn't the kind of thing Hayden would enjoy, but I stopped myself.

"It's hard to find the time," I said. "With work and all…" I thought about Roy's job as a carpenter and how nice it would be to work an eight-hour day and be done with it. No staying late, no bringing work home, no working on the weekends.

"You must play darts a lot," I said. "You're good."

He shrugged. Then he whispered, "Not good enough to beat you." His breath was warm against my neck.

"We're back to luck again," I whispered back. I closed my eyes and we danced in silence for the rest of the song.

"Would you like something to eat?" Roy asked when we returned to the table. "Help soak up the margaritas?"

I wondered how he knew what I'd been drinking. "Actually, I would." I realized I'd been cheated out of dinner again and wondered if I'd ever actually ever get a full meal here. "I'd love the meat loaf."

"You should try the chowder, too," he said, pronouncing it the same way Paula did—*chowda*. "It's really good here."

"Okay, sure," I said, figuring I might as well go for a third bowl. Maybe this time I'd actually be able to finish it.

He got up and spoke to the waitress, who was a few tables away, and I saw her write something on a pad. Then he came back and sat down.

"So where *did* you learn the two-step?" he asked.

There was a little white container full of sugar, Sweet'N Low, and Splenda packets near me. I spun the bowl around in the middle of the table. "Trimmy Taylor."

"Who?" Roy had a funny smile on his face, as though he thought I was making this up.

I began rearranging the packets by color. Sugars on one side, Sweet'N Lows in the middle, and Splendas on the other side.

"Trimmy Taylor. She taught all the kids in Pine Point to dance. That's in Connecticut, where I grew up."

Roy nodded, but I couldn't tell if that meant he knew of the town or not. He took one of the Splendas and moved it to where I was putting the others. His hand almost touched mine.

"Pine Point is in Fairfield County," I said. "Close to New York State. Do you know where Greenwich is? Or West—"

"I know where Fairfield County is," he said. Then he got up

and for a moment I was afraid he was going to leave—that I had insulted him or said something stupid and he wanted to get away. But he came over to my side of the table and sat down on the banquette next to me.

I felt goose bumps break out on my arms. "Well," I said, trying not to let him hear the tremble in my voice, "Trimmy had a studio and she taught ballroom dancing." I laughed. "She was a million years old. She taught everybody in town to dance."

Roy smiled. "We could have used Trimmy up here."

The waitress came back with two bowls of chowder and a basket of rolls. "Where did you learn to dance?" I asked, unable to picture anything like Trimmy Taylor's in Beacon.

He passed the basket of rolls to me. "Well, that particular dance...let's see...a girl taught me that."

"Oh," I said, taking one of the rolls. "A girlfriend?" I asked, trying to sound casual.

He nodded. "Yes." Then he added, "But that was a while ago."

I felt a little sense of relief and then I caught myself again. What was I doing, flirting with this guy when I had Hayden waiting for me back in New York?

Roy stirred his soup. "So what are you doing in Beacon?"

I tore off a small piece of the crusty roll and spread some butter on it. "I'm here because of my grandmother. She asked me to take care of some business for her."

"Here in Beacon?"

"Yes," I said. "She used to live here."

"Really? When was that?"

"Oh, a long time ago," I said, tasting the clam chowder and liking it even better this time. Something about the little sprigs of fresh dill made it just perfect. "You know, this soup is really good."

"They're known for it here," Roy said, and for a few moments we concentrated on eating.

I finished the bowl without stopping. "I guess I was hungrier than I thought," I said as I put down the spoon.

He looked at me and smiled. "Dancing will do that. And darts."

I could smell the beer on his breath, and it smelled bitter and sweet. He sat so close that his arm brushed against me twice. I wondered if he knew he was doing that.

The meat loaf came, and it was fantastic. I savored every bite, trying to figure out what they had put in there to make it taste so good. We lingered over dinner, ordering coffee at the end. Finally, Roy looked at his watch.

"It's almost eleven. I've got an early start tomorrow." He left his hand on the table. I wanted to touch it, just brush my hand over his for a second.

"Me, too," I said. "I'd better get back." I was still feeling a buzz from the drinks. "I think the walk will do me good."

"Walk? No, don't do that. I'll give you a lift." Roy slid out of the seat. "That is, if you want one."

Yes, I wanted one. I didn't want the evening to end. Not just yet. I felt too good. "Sure, that would be great."

We walked toward the door, through the aisle, where people were clustered in little groups, past the tables, where customers were drinking and telling stories, past the bar, where couples were turned toward one another on bar stools and where Skip was pulling wineglasses from an overhead rack.

Skip nodded to Roy and then did a little double take as he saw that I was walking out with him. He shot us a big, wide, missing-a-molar grin.

"Hey," he said as he gestured for me to come over. "Don't forget this." I walked to the bar and he handed me my copy of *Forbes*.

I almost laughed, recalling my thoughts when I'd put it in my purse. *So I wouldn't be bored.*

"Oh, yeah, thanks," I said, tucking it back into my handbag.

A salty breeze was blowing outside, and the street was quiet except for the waves crashing on the beach by the seawall.

"I'm just down a couple of blocks," Roy said as we walked past the storefronts, all closed for the night.

The sky was pulsing with stars. "I can't believe how clear it is." I pointed straight up. "Look, there's Orion."

"I see it," Roy said. "The three stars are the belt and those are his arms and legs." He traced the outline with his finger.

"The stars seem so much brighter and closer here," I said. They dangled over us like a net, holding us in place.

Roy looked back at me. "Maybe they are, Ellen. Maybe they are."

He opened the passenger door of the truck and I sat down on the bench seat. He got in the driver's side and tossed his jacket in the back. We drove in silence through the town, past the beach and the construction site where he worked, up the side road, and down the street to the Victory Inn, where the porch lights glowed a soft yellow. Then he pulled the truck to the side of the road.

I was holding my leather purse in my lap and Roy began to stare at my hands. I could feel him staring and all I could think about was Hayden and what he would think if he knew I was sitting in this guy's truck, having my hands stared at. And why *was* I sitting in this guy's truck, having my hands stared at? I knew I needed to get out of there, but I couldn't move.

And then Roy started tracing his fingers over mine. Over the knuckles, over the joints, up and down each finger. I felt as though I had been wired for electricity and plugged into a wall socket. A surge of heat moved through my whole body. I could barely breathe.

He turned his face to me and then he leaned in. He took his hand off mine and started to put his arm around me. Then he stopped.

"Can we move this tote bag out of the way?" he asked, nudging the purse on my lap. His dimples were showing again.

"Sure," I said in a breathy, barely-able-to-speak way. "I'll put it on the floor."

But he had already begun to pick it up. Except that he grabbed it by the side and suddenly the whole purse turned upside down, spilling out half the contents. Lipsticks and pens tumbled to the floor. My cell phone and a bucket of loose change scattered onto the seat. My wallet and iPod fell out, along with a handful of dollar bills. And, finally, the envelope from Winston Reid—the one that said MR. CUMMINGS on the outside and held my grandmother's letter—flew to the floor.

"Sorry," Roy said as he began to help me gather up the pieces. "Guess I don't know how to handle a purse."

I started to laugh. Then he picked up the envelope with my grandmother's letter in it and I saw his grin disappear and a look of alarm come over his face.

"What's this? Winston Reid Jennings, Attorneys at Law?"

"That's the law firm I'm with," I said, picking up my iPod.

"Your law firm." He sounded angry. The man who had traced Orion's belt with his fingertip was gone, and I had no idea why.

"What's wrong?"

"I know what you're doing." His eyes had gone cold. "I should have known this would happen all along."

I clutched my cell phone and a lipstick. "Should have known *what* would happen? What are you talking about?"

He waved the envelope at me. "This is what I'm talking about. Suing me over the dock—falling off."

The dock. Suing him. I couldn't get my mind around this.

"I don't understand," I said. "Why would I be suing you over the dock? I fell off, you helped me in." I was about to add that even if I *wanted* to sue someone over the dock I'd be suing the owner of the property and the construction company—the deep pockets—not someone who just worked there. But he never gave me the chance.

"You big-city lawyers," he said, shaking his head. "You're all alike. Nobody takes responsibility for themselves anymore. It's always somebody else's fault. And you lawyers have made it that way."

We were all alike? I'd made it that way? Why was he attacking me and my profession? "I still don't understand why you're angry," I said, "and I really don't appreciate you criticizing me or what I do."

He pointed to the envelope. "You're a lawyer. Lawyers sue people. You said yourself somebody could get sued because of the dock."

"The dock?" I said. "Oh, my God. All I meant was that it needed to be fixed."

He shook his head. "That's not what you meant."

I could feel the blood rush to my face. He was trying to put words in my mouth. Who did he think he was? "You're completely wrong," I said. "What's in that envelope has nothing to do with you."

Roy glared at me. "Oh, it doesn't? Then why is my name on it?"

"*Your* name?"

"Yeah, my name. Cummings."

Cummings? Was his name Roy *Cummings?* Oh, my God, he had the same last name. It was beginning to make sense. Now all I had to do was explain that he wasn't *Mr.* Cummings. Not the one I needed to see, anyway. And that I wasn't there to sue anybody. I was there to fulfill my grandmother's dying wish. That's what I should have done. But by then I was too angry. Way too angry. I grabbed my purse and got out of the truck.

"You don't know anything," I said, my voice shaking as I stood by the open door. "Not about lawyers, not about lawsuits, and especially not about me. And I'll tell you this—I'd rather be a big-city lawyer from New York than a narrow-minded guy from Maine who jumps to conclusions." I tossed back my head and looked him straight in the eye like a missile locking onto a target. "See you in court," I said, slamming the door.

I was fuming as I walked up the path to the Victory Inn. I hoped he believed I *was* going to sue him. I hoped it gave him nightmares. What a supercilious bastard. God, I was lucky I didn't let him kiss me. What the hell was I thinking?

The door creaked as I stepped inside. The lobby was empty except for the soft glow of two sconces and the blue haze of Paula's computer screen. I took a deep breath and let it out slowly, trying to calm myself.

And then I thought, Let him kiss me? Wait a minute. I would *not* have let him kiss me. That was never going to happen. I would have stopped him. I was about to stop him. I was engaged, for God's sake. My ring was upstairs in room 10—or room 8 or whatever it was. I had a fiancé whom I loved dearly and who was back in New York waiting for me. Yes, and he was brilliant—there wasn't a problem he couldn't solve, and he was refined, and he was a great dresser, and he was handsome, and he was about to be a rising star in the world of politics. I had a sudden vision of Hayden, at his desk in one of his Savile Row suits, maybe the charcoal gray with the tiny pinstripes, and a starched white shirt and Hermès tie—probably the blue one with the little *H*s all over it that were so small they didn't look like *H*s.

There never would have been a kiss.

Chapter 7

The House on Comstock Drive

A car horn wailed outside...two long blasts. Then silence. Then another long blast.

My eyelids lifted until my eyes were half open. The room was dim, with just a slice of light peeking from beneath the window shade. I turned over and tried to go back to sleep, but every muscle hurt and my head ached.

Margaritas.

I tried to swallow, but my mouth was too dry.

Margaritas.

A clump of hair was stuck to my forehead, a few strands glued to the corner of my mouth.

A chair. Someone was standing on a chair, yelling.

I pulled the hair away.

It was me on the chair. Oh, God.

People were cheering. People were raising their glasses. To me. I was standing on a chair, pointing to some guys playing darts.

Some guys playing...

Ohhh.

My stomach swerved like a planet veering off its orbital path.

There was a hundred-dollar bill and a hole in Ben Franklin's nose and a bet and I threw darts and Roy threw darts and...

Roy.

He was there. I remembered now. We threw darts and we danced a two-step and talked about Trimmy Taylor with the face-lifts and the frame and we ate meat loaf and Skip kept giving us drinks and Roy drove me home and kissed—

Hold on a minute.

My eyes burst open as I recalled my purse falling over and everything tumbling onto the floor of Roy's truck. And then he was waving an envelope at me. The envelope with my grandmother's letter in it. He thought I was going to sue him. And his name was Cummings. And he was trying to kiss me.

Outside my room, the horn went off again, and I wanted to run to the window and yell, *And they say New Yorkers are rude!* but it would have required too much effort.

I put the pillow over my head and moaned. Thank God it didn't happen. I must have been really drunk. Was I somehow seduced by his ability to use a nail gun or run PVC pipe? He'd been horrible to me. Just plain rude. Where did he come up with the idea that I was going to sue him? And all that talk about big-city lawyers. Please...

I turned to look at the alarm clock. The numbers burned with a painful brightness: ten thirty. How could it already be ten thirty? And what day was it? It took me a minute to figure out it was Thursday. And I had planned to be up at seven.

My head felt heavy as I righted myself to a sitting position, sat for a moment, and then eased my way into the bathroom. The sight in the mirror was frightening, especially under the yellow-green glow of the ceiling light. Large, dark smudges of makeup lay caked under my eyes. Had I looked that way last night?

I scrubbed the makeup off my face, swore off liquor, and then got dressed. Taking my cell phone into the bathroom, I put down the toilet seat and dialed Hayden's office. His secretary, Janice, told me he was in a long meeting. Disappointed, I hung up and listened to the two voice-mail messages my mother left while I was at the Antler. *Did you drop off the letter yet? What happened? When are you coming back?*

I started to dial the house number and then thought better of it. I couldn't handle a long, tangled conversation with her right now, and if I was worried about her sixth sense kicking in yesterday I really needed to worry today. She'd know before I said hello that something was wrong. I texted her another message: All is well. Haven't connected with Mr. C but going to try again now. Leaving today for sure. Will call soon. XOX.

I hope that will appease her, I thought as I grabbed my purse and car keys from the bureau. I'd be able to give her a full report soon. I walked down the two flights of stairs and through the lobby, where Paula was deep in conversation with a man holding a tub faucet and a wrench. She gave me a little nod as I went by.

The front seat of the car was warm. I put down the windows and was about to turn on the GPS when I realized I didn't need it. I knew the way to Chet Cummings's house. It wasn't long before I turned onto his street and pulled into the driveway behind the green Audi, which was still in the same place.

No one answered when I knocked on the door. I waited a

minute and knocked again, but there was still no response. I peeked in a couple of windows, but didn't see any signs of activity. Where did this man go every day? Did he have a job? I wondered if there was a McDonald's around somewhere. I heard they hired a lot of elderly people.

From my purse, I pulled out the envelope with my grandmother's letter in it. I ran my finger over the name—MR. CUMMINGS—as I stood on his front porch trying to decide what to do. All right, I thought, you just have to leave the letter here. You've got to leave it, check out of the inn, and get on the road. You've come as far as you can with this. Gran would understand.

A car pulled into the driveway next door—the neighbor with the white Volvo. I gave her a little wave, but she didn't wave back. She got out of her car and began walking across Mr. Cummings's lawn. She was wearing a black tank top and skinny white jeans, and I noticed that she had a nice figure. She strode right up onto the front porch and put her hands on her hips as though she owned the place.

"Are you looking for somebody?" she asked, crinkling her forehead, bearing down at me with dark brown eyes.

I was so surprised I could barely speak. "I'm looking for Mr. Cummings," I finally stammered.

She glanced at the envelope in my hand. "And what business do you have with him?"

This was too much. I couldn't believe how nosy she was. "My business with Mr. Cummings is my business," I said.

She leaned in and I caught the scent of a spicy perfume. "Well, I'm his neighbor...*and* his friend. I look out for him."

"That's very nice," I said, hearing my voice take on an edge. "But this is a personal matter and I prefer not to discuss it with anyone else."

I put the envelope back in my handbag and marched down the porch steps. Who did she think she was? *I look out for him.* There was no way I would leave the letter there now. I could just see her holding it over a teakettle, steaming it open, reading it. I'd mail it from the Beacon post office or drop it in a mailbox on my way out of town, but I would never leave it on his door.

Back at the inn, I packed all my clothes in my overnight bag. In the bathroom, I assembled my toiletries, pulled the cell phone charger and laptop cord from the outlet over the sink, and checked my makeup in the mirror.

I took a final look around the room, noticing a little hairline crack in the china pitcher on the bureau. Funny I hadn't seen that until now. I peeked into the bathroom once more to make sure I'd taken everything. The last thing I noticed was the print of the sailboat coming into harbor at dusk. I had never bothered to look at the name of the boat, but now I did. On the hull, in blue script, were the words JE REVIENS. *I return.* I closed the door to the room and walked downstairs.

The dining room was doing a brisk lunch service when I passed. Paula came through the swinging door from the kitchen.

"You leaving us?" she said, glancing at my overnight bag.

"Yes," I said, feeling bad that I hadn't fulfilled my mission. Not the way my grandmother had intended, anyway. "It's time for me to go."

I followed Paula to the desk and signed my name in the book

under a column marked DEPARTING GUESTS. Then she ran my credit card.

"Hope our little town wasn't too dull for you," she said as I slung the strap to my laptop case over my shoulder. I saw the glimmer of a smile on her face, like a spark about to ignite.

"No. It was fine."

She picked up a pen and put it behind her ear. "Well, maybe you'll be back sometime."

I shrugged and tried to smile. "I think my business here is over." I rolled my bag out the door, closing it behind me.

The air was cool, and I cracked the car windows to get a breeze. I set the GPS for home and chose the scenic route. I drove past green fields, pine trees, and yards where children played tag and, as I drove, I imagined how I would photograph each scene if I had my camera. I went by blueberry farms where roadside stands sold baskets topped high with berries and where fresh flowers were arranged in colorful bouquets on tables. I thought about Gran and her blueberry muffins and how she was able to make the tops just a little bit crunchy while the insides were perfectly moist. Just the thought of those muffins made my stomach rumble from hunger.

After fifteen minutes I came to a stone wall on the left. It seemed to go on forever, but I occasionally caught a glimpse of a field on the other side. Faded NO TRESPASSING signs appeared at seemingly random intervals, their once-red letters now pink. The field continued and the wall accompanied it, stray boulders and rocks lying by the side. "Good fences make good neighbors," I said aloud, recalling the line from the Robert Frost poem.

Then the wall ended and houses began to reappear. I passed a driveway smeared with the blues and pinks of hopscotch chalk, and then a sign that told me the highway was straight ahead.

Another hundred yards down the road I saw a small store. The sign said EDDY'S FOOD MART, although the *R* was gone from MART. You could see the outline of where it had been, though. *Mat,* I said to myself. *Eddy's Food Mat.* It sounded the way someone from Maine would say it. A single antique red-and-white gas pump stood in front of the store. I glanced at my gas gauge, saw that I was down to a quarter of a tank, and pulled in. A teenage boy with freckles and red hair ambled over to the car.

"Fill it?" he asked, shielding his eyes from the sun as he looked at me.

"Yes, thanks." I turned off the engine. "I'm going into the store for a minute, okay?"

The boy gave me a *suit yourself* shrug.

The store was cool and dark, and its four small aisles were crammed with boxes and cans, juices and cereals, vegetables and breads, milk, eggs, magazines. The floorboards creaked as I walked toward the refrigerators in the back. I didn't find any Perrier, but something else caught my eye: Higgins Root Beer. The label said BOTTLED IN MAINE FOR THAT DISTINCTLY MAINE FLAVOR, whatever that meant. I picked up two bottles, walked to the cash register, and put the bottles on the oaken counter. The wood was yellowed and scarred with pen engravings. CHARLIE AND JUNE. FITZ WAS HERE. LISA T. PETE RONIN IS A CREEP.

The girl behind the counter looked at me with a round moon face and sleepy eyes. "Is that it?"

"That's it." I took out my wallet and pulled out a wad of bills. At the bottom of the pile I found my folded hundred-dollar bill wrapped around five twenties—my winnings from Roy. I put it all back and pulled out a twenty from the top of the pile instead.

The cashier was placing the sodas in a paper bag. I was thinking of the drive home, hoping I wouldn't get stuck in any traffic jams, when I felt a tap on my shoulder.

"Excuse me."

I turned to see a woman in red pants and a blue blouse standing behind me, holding a box of frozen broccoli. It was Arlen Fletch, from the town clerk's office.

She leaned over. "I was hoping I'd run into you," she whispered, as though we were sharing a confidence. "Remember me? From the town hall?"

"Yes, of course," I said, smiling, as I reached for my bag. "We discussed the IRS."

Arlen cringed like a vampire facing a silver cross. Then her face softened. "You left this in our office."

She handed me a little scrap of paper on which I had written FRANK AND DOROTHY GODDARD, the names of my grandmother's parents—the names I had been searching for in the land records. It was something I'd meant to throw out. How odd that this woman would not only keep it but *walk around* with it. And people thought New Yorkers were weird.

"Thanks for…keeping it for me," I said, forcing a smile as I took the paper from her. "And for your help the other day." I began walking toward the door.

But Arlen followed me, past the bushels of fresh corn and tomatoes. "Oh, it's nothing," she said, dodging the stacks of canned peas piled at the end of an aisle. "I thought I might see you again. Sometimes things just work out that way."

"Yes, well, thanks again," I said, pushing open the door and walking outside.

I paid the boy with the freckles for my gas and was heading toward my car when I realized Arlen was still following me, the box of broccoli in her hand. I stopped at my car and pulled the keys from my purse. "Is there something I can do for you?"

A smile sprouted on Arlen's little pug face. "I found it."

"Yes, I know." I lifted the scrap of paper so she could see I still had it. Was she expecting a reward?

She cocked her head and squinted. "No, you're looking at the wrong side." She waved her hand. "I found the *house*. I found your grandmother's house. See? It says BRADLEY G. PORTER AND SUSAN H. PORTER. They're the current owners."

I looked at the paper and saw the names she'd written on the back. I saw the address. 14 COMSTOCK DRIVE. "You found my grandmother's house?"

Arlen gave a little shrug. "Yes-sir-ee."

"But I looked through all the indexes from nineteen hundred and—oh, I don't know, but I looked through everything and I didn't find them."

Arlen leaned in closer again. "Well, you must have missed something, because I found it." She winked at me.

I wanted to hug her. I wanted to pick her up and twirl her around. I wanted to kiss her little pug face. This would really make the trip worthwhile. I settled for just thanking her again.

"I'll put the address in my GPS and head right over there," I told her.

"Your GPS?" She shrank back. "You don't need one of those to find it. It's practically around the corner." She proceeded to recite a lengthy set of directions that included four turns, a fork, and a stream. Maybe she saw me go pale.

"You look a little confused," she said. "Hold on."

Arlen went to her car and came back with a street map, folded in thirds. Oh, God, I thought, just let me use my GPS.

The map was yellowed and smelled like a damp basement. Arlen blew off a little film of dust. Then she opened the map and laid it on the hood of someone's Toyota.

"It's right there. That's Comstock Drive." She took a pink pen and circled something.

"You go on Route Fifty-five and along here, go left there, right on Algonquin, and you turn here, on Verrick, then go across the stream here and left at the fork." She traced the route for me with her pen. "Then you'll come to Kenlyn Farm. Big stone wall. Can't miss it. You pass the farm and it's just a few streets down on the right."

My head was beginning to buzz. I picked up the map, ignoring everything except the spelling of the name Comstock so I could program the GPS.

"Kenlyn Farm?" I asked.

Arlen gave me a dismissive wave. "It's an old blueberry farm. They don't grow anything on it anymore, though. It's just a big piece of land, but you can't miss it. Stone wall on all sides."

I was pretty sure she was talking about the place I'd just driven by.

"Here, you take this," Arlen said, nudging me with the map.

I thanked her again, got into the car, and collapsed against the seat. *She found the house. She found it.* I wanted to see it and touch it and smell it. I wanted to stand at the front door, where my grandmother had stood. I wanted to trace the steps she had taken and steep myself in the wood and the nails and the plaster.

I opened one of the bottles of root beer and let the icy liquid run down my throat, and I thought again about the house and what it might look like. But this time I felt only good things. It would be small and cozy, with slanted floors and steep stairs and little rooms with ceilings that pitched downward. There would be narrow hallways and old glass doorknobs and mahogany trim stained and polished to a rich glow. And I would feel my grandmother in the rafters and in the plaster and in the layers of paint.

I threw the map on the passenger seat and programmed 14 Comstock Drive into the GPS. It showed a list of roads in the area with the name Comstock in them. There was Comstock Lane in Louderville and Comstock Circle in Tolland, but there was no Comstock Drive anywhere, including Beacon. With a sigh, I reached over for Arlen's map and tried to make sense of the route she had traced.

Then I pulled out of the parking lot and soon I was driving by the stone wall again. Kenlyn Farm, I thought. At the third street past the farm, I turned onto Comstock.

Number 14 was a New England–style home on a street of similar houses—a white clapboard two-story structure with a wraparound porch bounded by a white wooden railing. Dormers peeked out of the upper floor. A maple tree stood in the front yard, a wooden swing hanging from one of its branches. A woman in her early thirties, dressed in denim shorts and a green

Dartmouth sweatshirt, pushed a little girl, who looked about seven, on the swing.

I parked and walked toward them. "Hi," I said, waving. "I'm Ellen Branford." I extended my hand to the woman. "I'm from New York, but I'm visiting Beacon. My grandmother grew up here."

"Oh, really?" The woman shook my hand. "Susan Porter. That's my daughter, Katy."

"Sorry to bother you," I said, "but the reason why I stopped here is because…well, my grandmother didn't just grow up in Beacon, she grew up right *here*." I nodded toward the house.

"In our house?" Susan's eyes sparkled. "You're kidding."

I shook my head. "No. I got the address from the town clerk. Here's the thing…I was wondering…"

"Would you like to see it?" she asked as she took Katy's hand.

I breathed a sigh of relief. "Yes, please." I followed them across the lawn toward the house, the sun warming the back of my neck as I thought about Gran taking that same walk. Long ago, memories of my grandmother had settled within the walls of this house. I hoped the house would share some of them with me.

We walked up the front porch steps, and Susan led me to a sunlit living room, where a breeze floated through open windows. I admired a fieldstone fireplace, and she told me it was original to the house. I tried to imagine my grandmother in that room as a young girl, but I couldn't make the connection.

She showed me the family room, where toys and stuffed animals lay scattered on the floor like land mines. I followed her into the kitchen and into the dining room, which had built-in cabinets with glass doors.

"I think those are also original," Susan said, pointing to the cabinets. Touching the mahogany wood, I tried to feel Gran's presence, but couldn't do it.

A narrow flight of stairs led to the second floor. I thought I caught a faint scent of lavender when we reached the landing. Susan led the way through a pale green master bedroom, a nursery trimmed in pink gingham, and a guest room of sorts with a futon in the corner.

It was an old house and a pretty house. But that was all. Whatever I had expected to see or feel wasn't there. Whatever glimpse of my grandmother's life I thought I would divine had not materialized.

We stood in the upstairs hallway. "Thank you," I said, trying not to sound disappointed. "You have a beautiful home and I appreciate your giving me the tour." I looked down the hall. "I'm trying to imagine my grandmother here."

"How long ago was that?" Susan asked.

"Over sixty years," I said. "The Goddards lived here back when—"

Susan's eyes went wide. She put her hand on my arm. "The Goddards?"

I nodded. "Yes, my grandmother's maiden name was Ruth Goddard."

"Ruth Goddard?" she asked. "She was your grandmother?"

I took a step back, a little surprised by her exuberance. "Yes," I said tentatively. "Why? Have you heard of her?"

"Come with me," she said. "You have to see this."

Susan opened a doorway in the hall, and she and Katy led me up a set of steep, narrow steps. I could feel the trapped summer heat as we reached the attic.

"We're doing some work in here," she said, "so don't mind the mess. Brad's turning it into a home office."

I looked around at a huge square room with dormers on two sides. The windows were covered with old vertical blinds with thin metal slats. The slats were halfway open and sunlight poured in, leaving geometric patterns on the dark floor. Dust motes floated around us. A circular saw and a pile of other hand tools rested near stacks of drywall.

In one area of the room the old drywall had been stripped off the walls and the studs were visible. In an adjacent section I could see what appeared to be two layers—drywall and plaster underneath.

"Somebody put the drywall right over the plaster?" I asked. "Why would they do that?"

Susan shrugged. "I don't know. Maybe the plaster was in bad shape and they wanted to do a quick fix."

She stepped to one corner of the room, where the light was dim. "What I want you to see is this." She pointed to something on the wall.

It looked like a painting. It was about three feet high and four feet wide. I took a step closer. A young man and a young woman stood facing one another, holding hands. In the background, carefully composed, stood a lone oak tree in front of a small grove of oaks, and a weathered red barn.

The young woman wore a long green gown, the color of moss. The young man wore trousers and a shirt of earthen brown. They were surrounded by wild plants and flowers and an azure sky. There was something almost mystical about the scene, as if the man and woman had both sprung from nature themselves.

I reached out to touch the veins of a large green leaf. The paint was warm and cool at the same time, rough and smooth. The leaf seemed to come alive under my touch. I could almost feel its energy.

"What is this?" I asked.

"We found it when we ripped off the old drywall. It was painted on the plaster," Susan said.

"It's unusual," I said. "Unusual and beautiful."

She nodded. "Can you read the writing? You need to look up there." She pointed. "There are names above the people, and the artist signed the bottom right corner."

I gazed upward and saw that there were indeed names just over the heads of the two people. Above the young man, the name Chet had been printed in tiny, exacting letters, and above the young woman, the name Ruth appeared. And in the bottom right corner of the painting there was, as Susan said, a signature. I read the name, written in the up-and-down, peak-and-valley strokes that had become so familiar to me: Ruth Goddard.

Chapter 8

A Trip North

I drove away, barely conscious of anything except the pavement in front of me. If there were pine trees and yellow daisies and blue heather on the side of the road, if a spotted deer jumped into the woods and a red squirrel scrambled up an oak tree, I didn't notice. I was back in Susan Porter's attic, and because of that I missed my turn and ended up in downtown Beacon.

Feeling a little dazed, I pulled into a parking space in front of the Community Bank. Across the street, a handful of beach chairs and towels lay on the sand, and a few people were standing by the water's edge. I walked to the seawall, sat down, and took a long, slow breath as I thought about my grandmother and Chet Cummings and the painting.

The sky was full of fat white clouds, and the late June sun darted across the water. I turned my head and gazed at the row of shops—the Three Penny Diner; the Antler; Harborside Real Estate; Tindall & Griffin, Counselors at Law. Something looked different. Maybe Harborside's red brick had been touched up. Or someone had power-washed the white clapboard on Tindall & Griffin's offices. Maybe there were new geraniums in the window boxes of the Three Penny Diner. Their red blooms looked just a little brighter. I sat there inhaling the salt air, imagining Gran sitting in the same place, a paintbrush in her hand, Chet Cummings by her side. I had discovered something—a window into my grandmother's life. A life we didn't know anything about. This was a gift, unexpected and wonderful. How much more there was to learn about her I didn't know. But one thing I did know: I wasn't leaving Beacon. At least not yet.

When I pulled into the parking lot at the Victory Inn, I was surprised to see that half the spaces were already taken. Good for Paula, I thought, but then I worried that maybe she'd given away my room.

"Forget something?" she asked when I walked into the lobby. She looked me up and down. "Leave your darts behind?"

My *darts?* How did she know about that? I was beginning to understand what people meant when they talked about small-town life.

"No, I—"

"Oh, you really *are* back," she said, pointing to my overnight bag.

"Yes," I said, taking out my wallet. "Something's come up and I need to stay a couple of extra days—probably until Sunday." I placed my credit card on the counter with a little snap. "You do still have a room, I hope."

She opened the leather-bound book, turned a few pages, rubbed her chin, and said, "I can put you back in the Ocean View Suite."

"Perfect," I said, writing my name and address in the column marked ARRIVING GUESTS. I knew the drill.

Paula handed me the key with the braided ribbon and I marched up the two flights of stairs. The room looked warm and cozy when I walked in — the nautical prints, the earthenware bowl and pitcher, the bed with the white coverlet. I placed my overnight bag on the luggage rack and put away my clothes. I put my toiletries in the bathroom, on the wicker hamper.

From my briefcase I took a yellow legal pad and set it on top of the toilet tank, along with a memo pad that had a pen-and-ink drawing of the Victory Inn on it. I gathered up a bunch of pens and pencils from the bottom of my briefcase and put them in a drinking glass. I placed the glass on top of the toilet tank with the pads and nodded in satisfaction. My new office.

Then I closed the lid on the toilet seat, sat down, took a deep breath, and dialed Hayden's cell phone. He answered after two rings.

"Hayden, it's me."

"Hey, where are you?" He sounded cheerful, happy to hear my voice. "Did you pass Portland yet?"

I clenched my teeth and held the cell phone a little tighter. "Actually, I'm still in Beacon. At the Victory Inn."

"You're still in Beacon? Is everything all right? I thought you'd be on the road by now."

I could hear the concern in his voice. "Yeah, I thought so, too," I said. "But something odd happened. I was on my way to the highway and I ran into the lady from the land records office—"

"The lady from where?"

"The land records office...at the town hall." I glanced at the compass rug, with its curlicued *N, S, E,* and *W* letters.

"What did she want?"

"She found the address of the house where my grandmother grew up. So I went to the house and the owner—this woman named Susan Porter—she let me in. And guess what's in the attic?"

"The what?"

"The attic," I said. "You won't believe this. There's a painting my grandmother did…on the wall, in the attic. It's incredible, Hayden. The owners were doing some renovations and they found it…a painting of my grandmother and Chet Cummings. The two of them. She wrote their names on it and she signed it. And it's really good. I mean, really, really good."

I thought about the painting of the young girl and boy, holding hands, and I wished Hayden could be there to see it.

"I didn't know your grandmother painted."

"No, that's the amazing thing," I said, recalling the detail in the flowers and foliage, the lifelike expressions on the faces of my grandmother and Chet Cummings, the textures she used in the barn and the trees. "We didn't know, either."

"Did you take any pictures of it? Did you have your camera with you?"

I could feel the camera strap slipping through my fingers, see the Nikon silently dropping into darkness. My chest tightened as the sadness welled up inside me. "No, I didn't."

"That's too bad."

I nodded in silent agreement.

"So," he said, "you're leaving early tomorrow, then. I think you'd better take off at dawn if you want to avoid the Friday traffic. It's a long drive even without any delays, but you can't count on that so if you leave by, let's see—"

"Hayden," I interrupted, as I nervously spun the roll of toilet paper around in the holder. "I'm not coming back until Sunday." I waited through an endless moment of silence.

"Wait...I don't understand. What about the Men of Note dinner tomorrow night? You mean you're going to miss that?"

I looked at the floor, guilt pulling me down like gravity. "Hayden, I'm really, really sorry. But finding this painting is like...it's like a sign that I have to stay here and fill in these missing pieces of my grandmother's life." I pictured the painting of Gran and Chet. "And I know who can help me do that," I said. "Chet Cummings. He can tell me things about Gran that I don't know, Hayden. About her childhood, about growing up here in Beacon. About her painting. Even things my mother doesn't know. I need...a couple of days."

There was another moment of silence and then Hayden said, "I understand, Ellen." His voice was quiet, resigned. "I know you need to do this. I just didn't expect it to take this long. I really wanted you to be at that dinner with me."

"I know," I said. "And I'll make it up to you somehow." I squeezed the cell phone as if it were his hand.

I woke up early the next morning with a knot in my stomach. It was Friday and I wasn't going home. I pictured Hayden combing through his closet for the right combination of suit and shirt and tie to wear to the dinner. He would want my blessing on whatever he picked, and I wouldn't be there to give it. He would want me sitting next to him during the dinner and watching him when he received his award and giving his acceptance speech. And I wouldn't be there to do it.

The little safe in the closet opened when I entered my birthday on the keypad. I took out my engagement ring, the diamond radiant under the room light. I tried to put the ring back on my finger, but it wouldn't go on. I finally managed to get it over the knuckle with the help of some hand cream. It was still a tight fit, but at least I was wearing it again.

I sat down on the edge of the bed, turning my hand, watching the facets of the diamond catch the light. Replaying the conversation with Hayden in my mind, I began to feel worse and worse. Missing the dinner was bad enough, but recalling what he said when I told him about Gran's painting made me feel almost sick. *Did you have your camera with you?*

I closed my eyes, not wanting to think about the Nikon, but finding that's all I could think about. And then I realized I couldn't go back to New York without a camera. I'd have to find a store up here—drive to Portland, if necessary—and replace it.

Dressing quickly, I headed to the dining room. It was crowded with travelers who had arrived during the night. I looked at the selection of breakfast items on the buffet, glancing at the little handwritten sign in front of each one. The egg casserole, filled with cheese and bits of sausage, looked delicious, and I thought I detected the aroma of jalapeño peppers in it as well. I hovered over a tray of pecan-stuffed baked apples glistening with a sugary glaze, and followed the scent of cinnamon to a large bowl of homemade granola. I checked out the platters of banana nut bread and blueberry muffins, a marbled coffee cake, cereals, bagels, and a large bowl of fresh fruit salad.

All of it looked tempting, but I was eager to get on the road, so I grabbed a bagel and a banana and went in search of Paula. I found her standing outside the kitchen door, talking to the cook, and I asked if she knew of a good camera shop.

She raised her eyebrows. "Don't you have a camera? I thought I saw you with one the other day."

I wondered if there was anything this woman didn't notice. "Yes, well, that camera's *a little broken*," I said, quoting Paula to herself. This almost made me smile, but the memory of the lost Nikon was too close.

"Are you a photographer?" she asked, pulling her head back to study me more carefully.

"Not exactly," I said. "I just do it as a hobby. Kind of a serious hobby, though."

She shook her head. "Well, you won't find a camera store in Beacon. You'd have to go to Lewisboro. There used to be a place called Brewster's. They might still be around."

"How far is Lewisboro?"

"Oh, about forty-five minutes," she said. "Of course, that's in *my* car. You could do it in a half hour in yours."

I felt suddenly embarrassed about my BMW, although I wasn't sure why. In the parking lot I got the number and address for Brewster's Camera World from my cell phone. The store was still in Lewisboro and when I called, the man who answered told me they sold Nikons. This was good. I clicked off the phone with a sigh of relief and began to feel happy as I drove to Chet Cummings's house.

But by the time I turned onto his street, my mood had dampened again. I could see his driveway and the green Audi, which was still parked in the same place. There was no other car there, which meant he was out again. I drove toward the house slowly, wondering if I should knock on the door just in case. But then I saw the white Volvo in the driveway next door. No way was I getting tangled up with that neighbor again.

Frustrated, I drove past the house and, as I did, I noticed a piece of paper on the door. It was the first sign of life I'd seen, if you didn't count the cat. At the end of the street, I made a quick U-turn. When I was still several houses away, I pulled over and parked. Then I ran toward the Cummings house, hiding behind trees and bushes and fences so the neighbor wouldn't see me. When I got to Chet's house, I raced up the front porch.

The note was written with a thick black felt-tip marker on a piece of white paper, and it was stuck to the door with masking tape.

Mike—
I'll be back at 5.
CRC

CRC. Chester R. Cummings. That was Chet. So he wasn't away after all. He was going to be back here at five o'clock, and if I dropped by a little bit earlier I could catch him. This was perfect. I was so excited I could have danced a two-step right on his porch. I retraced my route, hiding behind the bushes and trees and fences again, until I got back to my car and jumped into the front seat.

Having made my plan to come back later, I set the GPS for Lewisboro, an estimated forty-minute drive. I left Beacon and headed north on the highway, surrounded by pine trees. Ahead was a horizon of more pines and a huge, billowing sky. It would have made a great photo, and I thought about how I could capture it in a viewfinder. I would keep the highway and the horizon of trees close to the bottom of the frame and let the sky open up and fill the rest of the space.

Composition.

That was something my grandmother always talked about. She had given me my first really good camera, an old Nikon F. Solidly built and completely mechanical, it was a film camera, but was state-of-the-art for its time. Gran presented it to me the summer I turned thirteen, when I was staying with my grandparents for two weeks in their Steiner Street house in San Francisco.

"I think it's time you graduated from that little Kodak you've been using," Gran said as she walked into the room where I always stayed. I called it the garden room because it had a white wooden bed, pale green carpet, and wallpaper decorated with vines and flowers.

She handed me a box covered in lavender wrapping paper. I pulled out a heavy black-and-chrome camera with a black strap.

After a moment of stunned silence, I finally managed to say thank you.

"Well, it's not new," my grandmother said. "But the man I bought it from took very good care of it. The pros use these, you know." She winked at me.

I did know. That camera was a huge step up from my old Kodak, which required nothing more than looking through the viewfinder and pressing a shutter release.

The Nikon was in another league altogether, requiring that I gain a certain degree of knowledge about single-lens reflex cameras. I had to learn how to focus the camera myself and how to set the exposure using the shutter speeds and f-stops. The only thing automatic was a simple light meter.

I walked into my grandparents' den with the instruction book, its pages dog-eared and wrinkled. Then I curled up on one of the sofas and studied the manual for two hours before my grandmother came looking for me.

"I thought you would have taken four rolls of film by now," she said, standing in the doorway. "Put that book away and come with me."

I followed her downstairs and out the door.

"But I'm still trying to figure out all this stuff about f-stops and shutter speeds," I said as I crossed the street behind her.

She led me across the street to Alamo Square, and we walked to the top of the hill, where the setting sun drenched the city's skyline in gold.

"I have to know this stuff before I can be any good," I said. "This isn't like my old camera."

"Nonsense." She flicked her hand. "I wouldn't worry about that. It all comes with time."

I let the camera hang from my neck on its long strap while she stood behind me, playfully pulling one of my braids. Then she slowly turned me around so I could see the city from all directions. Clusters of trees and park benches, apartment buildings hanging onto the steep slopes by their fingernails, the white Transamerica Pyramid, the San Francisco City Hall, and the row of bright Victorian houses called Painted Ladies, in which my grandparents' house was nestled.

"But if I don't get it right, the photos will come out too light or too dark or—"

"Aren't we technical!" She laughed. A yellow taxi stopped nearby to pick up a group of tourists who spoke with French accents. My grandmother put her arm around me.

"The most important thing of all," she said, her arm outstretched toward the skyline before us, "is composition—what your eye chooses to photograph. What stays in, what goes out." She pointed to the camera. "When you look through that viewfinder, you need to know what makes sense. You need to ask yourself if there is a better way to look at the scene in front of you—maybe a more interesting way, or a way you hadn't thought of. There are so many different ways to look at the same thing, Ellen."

She crouched down to my level and gently touched my chin. "That's something no one can teach. People either have it or they don't." She kissed the top of my head. "You don't have to worry, though. I've seen your photos. You *have* it."

I'd never really thought to question my grandmother's knowledge of photography or composition. I never wondered what qualifications she had to speak with such authority. I guess I just thought grandmothers knew everything.

Later that evening, when my parents were getting ready to go out to dinner, I told my mother what Gran had said.

"And what could your grandmother possibly think she knows about composition?" My mother laughed and raised a can of Aqua Net hair spray.

I stared at the bathroom floor, with its tiny black-and-white checkerboard tiles, as my mother sprayed a fog of chemicals around her head. I felt hurt for Gran, but I didn't know how to defend her. There was nothing concrete I could offer up as proof of her knowledge. And yet I knew that what my grandmother said was true.

Thirty-two minutes after leaving Beacon I pulled off the highway onto the Lewisboro exit and followed the signs to the shopping district. Brewster's was on the first floor of an old two-story brick building, tucked between Silver Serpent Antiques and Ross Martin Clothiers.

I stepped inside a long, narrow, dimly lit shop. The air smelled dry, like attics and old newspapers, but the store was crammed with camera equipment—bodies, lenses, tripods, filters, flash units, and other items in old oak-and-glass cabinets. Behind the counter, a man with gray-rimmed glasses was talking to a teenage boy and his father about flash units.

He nodded to me. "Somebody will be right with you," he said. Then he walked through a doorway behind the counter and I heard him say, "Pop; Pop. There's a customer—can you come out?"

A moment later an old man emerged. His forehead had deep wrinkles, like grooves, and there were grooves around his mouth, like a set of parentheses. His hair, snowdrift white, covered his head like fine fuzz.

"What can I help you with, miss?" he asked.

I told him the model of my camera and asked if he had one in stock.

He scratched the side of his face and looked at the ceiling. Then he said, "Well, miss, they've just replaced that model with another one that's a little bit different. But you're in luck," he said, his eyes twinkling. "We do have the new one in stock and I'll get it out for you. See how you like it."

He took a key and opened a case behind him. He moved a few boxes around, and then pulled out a camera and set it on the counter. "I take it you're familiar with Nikons?"

I nodded. "Yes, I've been using them for years."

He smiled. "Years, have you? Well, I'll say."

"I had an old Nikon F," I said. "I still love the feel of those mechanical cameras."

The man slapped the counter. "No kidding." He looked at me with his mouth open. "Now, that was a camera," he said. "A big deal for its time, although you wouldn't think so with all of these digital things we sell now. Everything has to have a darned computer in it." He shook his head.

"I know what you mean," I said. "Those old cameras were a lot easier. But I guess you can't stop change."

"That's for sure," he said. "Now, if you want to really know the fine points of this camera, you'll need to wait for my son, Mark, to finish with his customers over there." He wiggled a finger toward Mark.

"Oh, that's all right," I said. "I think I can figure it out."

He handed me the camera. "Okay, then, miss, give it a whirl."

I turned the camera on and put the viewfinder to my eye. "Feels a little heavier," I told him as I zoomed in on a sign behind the counter. WE PROUDLY ACCEPT VISA AND MASTERCARD. I took a picture.

Then I pointed to the front window and snapped a shot of a woman passing by outside. She had a pink fishing hat on her head.

"So you had a Nikon F," the man said, scratching his cheek again.

I looked at the photos I'd taken in the LCD panel. The woman's hat was bright and crisp. "Yes, my grandmother gave it to me one summer."

"That's a pretty nice gift," the man said.

I nodded. "Well, she was a nice grandmother." I took a picture of a cabinet full of camera bags. "In fact," I said as I looked at the display panel again to see the result, "she used to live in Maine. That's why I'm here."

The man began rearranging boxes of flash units on a shelf behind him. "She did, eh? Where'd she live? Here in Lewisboro?"

I turned on the camera's menu and started to scroll through the choices. SETUP; SHOOTING; PLAYBACK. "She grew up in Beacon," I said.

The man turned and stared at me. "In *Beacon?* I grew up in Beacon. What's your grandmother's name?"

"Her maiden name was Ruth Goddard."

His eyes burst open. "Ruthie? Ruthie Goddard? Your grandmother?" He slapped the counter again. "No kidding!" He tilted his head back and grinned. "Why, I went to school with Ruthie."

"You knew her?" I said. "You knew my grandmother?" I felt my pulse quicken, felt a tingle go up my arms.

"Sure did. Knew her from the time we were little kids. Second grade, I think. Where's she living now?"

I looked down. "Actually," I said, "she passed away a little over a week ago." When I raised my head, the man was gazing at me with soft, kindly eyes.

"Oh, I'm so sorry to hear that, Miss…Miss…what is your name?"

"Ellen Branford," I said, offering my hand.

"Wade Shelby," the man said, giving my hand a vigorous shake. "Ruthie was a sweet girl. Good artist, too. Talented."

I put the camera on the counter. "Yes. I just discovered she was a painter."

"Oh, sure," he said. "By golly, she was a painter. Got her into college. She was studying art."

Got her into college? Studying art? No, he was wrong about that. Gran went to Stanford and graduated with a degree in literature, not art. Now he was confusing her with someone else.

"Oh, sure," he said. "She went off to become an artist. A real trained one." He raised one eyebrow. "And we never got her back."

"What do you mean?"

Wade leaned in a little closer. "Well, now, she was going around with this fellow, Chet," he whispered. "Family had been in Beacon a long time. Nice kid. Pretty serious, the two of them. Everybody said they were going to get married. But then Ruthie went off to college and the next thing we heard she'd met another fellow. Some doctor or medical student." He shrugged and laid his hands on the counter. "And that was that. That city slicker took our Ruthie."

"The doctor?"

Wade nodded.

I thought about my grandmother dating Chet, going off to college, breaking up with Chet, and marrying…it was a little odd hearing my grandfather described as *that city slicker*.

"I can't believe you knew my grandmother," I said. "I've learned so much about her since I came to Maine." I took out my credit card and placed it on the counter.

"Would you like to take that camera?"

I nodded, and Wade put it in the box. Then he ran my credit card through the machine.

"What happened to Chet?" I asked.

"Chet? You know, I don't recall," he said, presenting me with the sales slip and a pen. "He was a nice kid, though." He put the box in a shopping bag. "Wish I knew more, being it was your grandmother and all." He came around the counter and handed me the bag. Then he looked at me, one eye half-closed. "You know who might know?"

"Who?"

He nodded slowly. "Lila Falk. She was a good friend of Ruth's."

I picked up the bag. "Lila Falk?"

"Sure thing," he said. "Last I heard she's still in Maine, living in a nursing home. In Kittuck, I think. Yep, she'd probably know, if anybody did."

I took the pen and scribbled the name Lila Falk on the back of the receipt. "I'm staying in Beacon," I said. "Where is Kittuck?"

"North," Wade said, waving his hand in a noncommittal way. "North of Beacon, north of here."

"How far north?" I asked.

"What kind of wheels have you got?"

"Wheels?" I said. "I have a BMW."

He smiled. "You can do it in an hour."

Chapter 9

Mr. Cummings

I sat in my car a few doors down the street from the camera store, looking for the Saint Agnes Care Center on my phone's Internet browser. It wasn't hard to find the number, as it was the only nursing home in Kittuck. Apparently it was the only one around for miles. The ad that popped up said, "Serving the communities of Kittuck, North Prouty, South Prouty, and Loudon," and then it listed a string of other towns as well.

The woman who answered the phone told me Lila Falk was indeed a resident there, but suggested that the following day would be a better one for a visit.

"Friday afternoons get a kind of hectic," she said. "We have music starting in a little while, and then some of our residents do crafts. But there's nothing going on tomorrow. Can you come then? Maybe around one or two?"

I pulled out my cell phone and checked my calendar for Saturday. The whole day was empty. "Yes," I said. "I think I can fit that in."

*   *   *

I turned into Dorset Lane at four o'clock, knowing I was very early but not wanting to take any chances at missing Chet Cummings. I could see right away that something was different—a blue Jeep was parked next to the Audi. This is it, Gran, I thought as my pulse quickened. I'm finally going to give him your letter.

I parked in front of the house, took the envelope with the letter in it, and walked to the front door, where I gave a loud knock. After knocking several more times, I still heard no response.

He has to be in there, I thought as I walked back down the steps to the lawn. I turned and stared at the house. Maybe his hearing aid was off. I walked around the house, looking in windows. When I came to the dining room, I spotted a navy blue Windbreaker hanging over the back of a chair, and I noticed that the piles of mail that I'd seen two days before were gone.

I was almost back to the front yard when I saw an aluminum ladder lying on the ground. I stopped, glanced at the window above me on the second floor, and looked back at the ladder. It might just work, I thought. Chet Cummings's hearing aid was probably off, or he was watching TV with the volume turned way up, as Gran used to do. He had to be upstairs, and there was only one way to find out.

I slipped my grandmother's letter into my pocket and then managed to prop the ladder up against the house. I climbed a couple of steps, told myself not to look down, and kept going. When I peeked into the upstairs window I saw a room with a gray rug, a wooden desk with books and papers on it, and a wall of white bookshelves. On one of the shelves was something that made my heart stop—an old mechanical camera. I knew what it wasn't—it wasn't a Nikon—but I couldn't tell what it was. A Leica, maybe? I kept staring, straining my eyes to bring the name of the manufacturer into focus.

And then I heard a voice below me. A man's voice. An angry voice.

"Just what the hell do you think you're doing?"

I froze, my knuckles white as I gripped the ladder. Then I looked down. Dressed in jeans and a dark blue T-shirt, with a faded TOWN LINE PLUMBING SUPPLY baseball cap on his head, stood Roy. *Roy.* I couldn't seem to get away from him. He was everywhere. And he was catching me in every humiliating moment. I looked around to see if anyone was taking a picture.

"I have some business here," I said, my tone cool. I was still angry with him for the way he'd acted after we'd left the Antler. And what I was doing here was none of his concern.

He put his hand to his forehead and squinted. "Oh, my God, it's...it's you!"

I descended the ladder as gracefully as I could, feeling Roy's eyes on me the whole way down. "Yes, it's me," I said, stepping off the last rung, noticing his day-old beard.

"What are you doing here? And why were you up there snooping?" he demanded.

"What am *I* doing here?" I said. "What are *you* doing here?" I brushed some dirt off my pants. "Are you following me? What's going on?"

He looked at me, startled. "*Me* following *you?* I'd say it was the other way around."

"Look, I have business here," I said. "I'm trying to find someone."

Roy glanced at the ladder and then at me. "That's how you try to find people? Looking in their windows?"

I tossed my head and stood up straight. "I don't think I need to answer your questions." He was as bad as Chet's neighbor. "Oh, and by the way," I added. "You're trespassing."

He pointed to me. "No, *you're* trespassing. This is my house."

His house? *His* house? How could that be? My mind went immediately into overdrive, trying to figure out where I'd made the mistake. I had used the address on my grandmother's letter and cross-checked it with two Internet directories and the tax collector's website. Chester R. Cummings, 55 Dorset Lane. This was the address. Still, I'd obviously made an error somewhere. Roy's name was Cummings, but he was the wrong Cummings. I couldn't believe I'd wasted four days. I was missing Hayden's event tonight, and I still didn't know where Chet Cummings lived.

"I didn't know it was your house," I said, "or I wouldn't have come. I've got the wrong address, that's all." I turned and walked to the front yard.

"You mean you're not going to leave your lawsuit papers?" Roy called out.

I spun around. "Excuse me?"

He came closer, staring at me, and then he took off his baseball cap and ran a hand through his hair. "Or maybe you found someone else to sue." He put the cap back on. "Big-city lawyers don't scare me. They still have to put their pants on one leg at a time, like everybody else. Or should I say *skirts?*"

Faded sunlight crept through the branches of a beech tree, casting patterns on the grass. "You know," I said as I felt a crease settle in my forehead, "I'm just trying to deliver a letter. I guess Cummings is a common name around here." I sighed and then gave a shrug. "I hope Chet Cummings is easier to deal with than you." I turned and marched across the front yard to my car.

"You're looking for Chet Cummings?" Roy called out.

I kept walking. I had nothing more to say. I'd go back to the inn and try to sort this out. See where I'd gone wrong. Maybe I'd figure it out; maybe I wouldn't. Either way, this was it. I'd tried my best to do what Gran wanted me to do and, as disappointed as I was to admit defeat, I'd come to the end of the road.

And then Roy called out again. "I know him."

I stopped. He knew Chet Cummings. He *knew* him. I found the wrong house and the wrong Cummings, but he knew him. In New York, the chances of that happening would be a billion to...

But I wasn't in New York. I was in Beacon, and it suddenly dawned on me that the chances of that happening in Beacon were probably pretty good. And it probably wasn't the first time people had confused two families with the same last name.

"You know him?" I said, turning to face Roy.

"I ought to," he said. "He's my uncle."

"Your *uncle?* Chet Cummings? Are you sure? I mean, it's *Chet* Cummings I'm talking about."

Roy nodded. "Yeah. I ought to know my own family."

His family. I could hardly believe it. My Norman Rockwell image of Chet and me chatting over tea and cookies in a cozy kitchen was coming back into view.

But then Roy looked at me suspiciously. "So you're the one who's been snooping around here the past couple of days," he said, waving his hand in the direction of the house.

I could feel my neck turning warm and the heat rising to my face. "I wasn't snooping."

"One of my neighbors said a woman kept coming around, knocking, looking in the windows, calling my name. Said she had a black car with New York plates." He pointed to my BMW. "That yours?"

Why did he always put me on the defensive? I planted my hands on my hips. "Yes, it's my car. And yes, I was here. I was looking for your uncle."

Something flickered in Roy's eyes. "So you weren't looking for me."

Why would I be looking for him, with his scruffy five o'clock shadow and beat-up jeans? "For *you?*" I laughed. "I just told you—no."

He stared at me. "What do you want my uncle for? Are you going to sue him, too?"

This was too much. I threw my hands in the air. "For God's sake, I'm not here to sue anybody. My grandmother asked me to do her a favor and it led me to Beacon."

Roy nodded, his mouth slightly open. "Oh, your grandmother's the one who's suing."

A gray cloud began moving in overhead. I closed my eyes and counted to ten. I needed to calm down or I would be in the *Bugle* again tomorrow, but this time I would probably be in the police blotter, having been charged with murder.

"No one is suing anybody," I finally said. "It's not about a law-suit." I began walking across the lawn to my car, thinking about my grandmother, my promise to deliver her letter, and how everything had gone so wrong. I'm sorry, Gran, I thought. I'm so sorry. Tears welled up in my eyes.

And then I felt a tug on the back of my blouse.

"Ellen, wait—"

I spun around, my hands trembling. Everything I'd been holding in since my grandmother's funeral—the anger I felt over her death, the grief, the sadness, the loneliness—burst open.

"My grandmother died last week," I shouted, tears falling down my cheeks onto my blouse. "I'm here because of her. Because she asked me right before she died to deliver something to your uncle—a letter. And I put it in an envelope from my law firm because...I don't know, I just wanted to keep it safe." I looked down. "So that's it. I don't care what you think anymore."

I turned to go, but Roy took hold of my arm. "Wait a minute, Ellen. Please." Someone's wind chimes began to jingle in the breeze. "I'm sorry about your grandmother. I'm really sorry."

A bee swayed lazily over a clover blossom and then flew away as the sky began to darken. And I realized how much I wanted to talk about my grandmother, needed to talk about her.

"We were very close," I said, my voice cracking. "She meant so much to me. And now she's gone and I'm here and everything's falling apart and I can't do what she wanted and I feel like I'm one big disappointment to her."

Roy shook his head. "I'm sure you're not a disappointment. And I owe you an apology. I'm really sorry."

I wiped my tears with my hand. "I don't understand. Why did you think I was trying to sue you?"

"Because that's what lawyers do. When I saw your envelope with my name on it—"

"It's not what all lawyers do," I said. "It's not what I do."

He nodded. "Okay."

We stood in his front yard in silence, and then he asked if I had the letter. I pulled the envelope from my pocket, and we sat down on a wooden bench. Roy took off his baseball cap.

"What does it say?" He reached for the envelope, but I held onto it.

"I'm sorry, but I can't really discuss it with you. You'll need to ask your uncle. Is this his house?"

Roy nodded.

"Sorry, but I was asked to deliver this letter to him."

Roy looked at the envelope in my hand and then at me. "Ellen, any business of my uncle's is business of mine."

"Well...I know you're his caregiver, but—"

"No, that's not what I mean." His eyes changed to a quiet, milky blue and the sides of his mouth drooped into an expression of resignation. He lowered his voice. "You're going to end up dealing with me, because my uncle died."

I felt as though all the air was escaping from my lungs, leaving them empty, lifeless. The one thing I could have done for my grandmother had now been rendered impossible. The man she had loved as a young girl was gone.

"I'm so sorry," I whispered, staring at the envelope and the name Mr. Cummings and the red salvia that ran along the edge of Roy's front lawn.

"When did he…" I let the words trail off as a drop of rain tapped my arm.

"Back in March."

Three months ago, I thought. Just three months. "I'm so sorry," I said again. I was sorry. I was sorry for Roy, I was sorry for myself for failing at this mission, and I was sorry for my grandmother.

Roy put his hand on my shoulder. "Do you think maybe you should tell me what's going on?"

The screen door opened and the sable cat I had seen lying on the dining room table two days before sauntered down the porch steps and across the lawn. He jumped onto the bench between Roy and me and sniffed at my hair. Then he rubbed his head against my cheek.

"Mr. Puddy, come here." Roy scooped the cat up in his arms.

I reached out and patted Mr. Puddy's soft head.

"I've told you everything I know," I said. "My grandmother wanted me to give your uncle the letter." I could hear the cat purring—a low, gentle sound—as he lay in Roy's arms.

"May I see it?" Roy's voice was quiet, almost a whisper.

I held the envelope, not wanting to give it up. This wasn't what was supposed to happen. I was supposed to be talking to Chet. This was all wrong.

Roy put the cat down and he scampered between the house and the hedge. "Ellen, I'd like to see the letter. Please." He held out his hand.

Finally I handed him the envelope. "All right."

He held it for a second before opening it. Then he pulled out the sheet of pale blue paper covered with my grandmother's handwriting and began to read. After a moment he looked up. "Why did she think my uncle would send this back or throw it away?"

"You just have to keep reading," I said as I felt another drop of rain.

Roy went back to the letter but soon looked up again. "She wanted to make amends." He cast a questioning glance my way. "For what?"

I shook my head. "I don't know. That's what I was hoping your uncle could tell me."

Roy read on. "South Carolina," he said a moment later. "Yeah, my uncle lived there for a long time, but he came back to Beacon about three years ago. Sounds like your grandmother was pretty surprised when she tracked him down here."

He continued to read, nodding at times. "Ah," he said after a while. "So they were lovers."

"Yes," I said. "They were lovers."

"'If I hadn't left you the way I did,'" Roy said, reading from the letter, "'you wouldn't have left Beacon and you wouldn't have lost the thing that meant so much to you. I've always felt responsible for that loss and I'm sorry.'" He looked at me. "What did she mean about the thing that meant so much to him? What was that?"

I shook my head again. "I don't know. I don't know what any of it means. She didn't tell me about the letter itself. Just that she wanted me to deliver it."

Roy smoothed the paper with his hand. Then he read the letter to himself again as a handful of raindrops spattered the wooden bench. "So we know she left him for another man."

I nodded. "Yes. My grandfather."

Roy's eyebrows went up. "Ah," he said. "Your grandfather." He shifted slightly toward me on the bench and I felt his leg brush against mine. "But we don't know why."

"Why she left him?" I looked up at the darkening sky. "Why does anybody leave anyone? I guess she fell out of love with him...or more in love with my grandfather."

"My uncle was a great guy," Roy said.

I smiled. "So was my grandfather."

He glanced at the letter again, as if some trace of his uncle might emerge from between the lines. Then he ran his finger along the tiny scar near his eye. "My uncle was there the day I got this."

I looked at the scar, a curved wisp of a line, and wondered what it would feel like to touch it. "How did you get that?"

"Learning to ride a two-wheel bike," he said. "I fell off and cut myself. Also broke my arm." He glanced at his right arm. "I was six."

"And your uncle—"

"He scooped me up and raced me to the hospital. Held my hand while they set my arm and put on the cast, while they stitched me up under my eye. I was scared to death. He told me if I made it through I'd get a medal for bravery."

I smiled. "That's sweet."

Roy's eyes sparkled. "Yeah, it was." He put his head back, as if he might divine some memory from the sky. "Believe it or not, he gave me one. A real medal. He came over that night and handed me a box. Black velvet. And inside was this medal. A Distinguished Service Cross. It was my grandfather's. He'd gotten it in World War II and given it to Uncle Chet."

"You're kidding."

"No, I'm not. And Uncle Chet insisted I take it, even though it was something I knew he really loved. I still have it on my bureau. In the box."

"That's quite a story." I was so touched by his uncle's gesture that it made me sadder than ever that I'd missed the chance to meet him.

"He was a super guy," Roy said, running his hand along the seat of the bench as if inspecting it for flaws. "He was like another father. My dad traveled a lot for his job and my uncle Chet kind of kept me out of trouble when I was a kid. He had a little marina and I used to hang around there, helping him repair the boats, patch the hulls, work on the engines, that kind of thing. He taught me to use tools—to love tools. The idea that you could fix something yourself, that you could *make* something yourself—" Roy looked at me with such intensity I could almost feel the presence of Chet Cummings there with us. "That's what made him tick."

"He must have been really talented," I said as a breeze rustled the grass. "And a great mentor."

Roy leaned back against the bench and gazed at the lawn. "If something broke," he said, "Uncle Chet could repair it. He didn't think about throwing things away and getting new ones." He paused to watch a field sparrow dart across the grass. "He was an amazing guy and I'm glad he came to live with me at the end."

I looked at the house as a few drops of rain sprinkled the bench. "So this place is yours?"

"Lock, stock, and barrel."

"But the owner's name shows up as Chester R. Cummings. That's your uncle."

"No," Roy said. "That's me, Chester Roy Cummings. But I've always gone by Roy."

"Ah," I said. "That explains a few things."

I watched the leaves of the beech tree shimmer in the breeze and thought about Chet Cummings imparting his knowledge and skills to Roy and what a great legacy that was. "You're lucky to have had a father and an uncle like Chet," I said. "I hardly had a father. He died when I was fourteen."

"That's so young."

I nodded, trying to recall my father's face, trying to strengthen the details that over time had become hazy. I knew the same thing would happen with my memory of Gran.

"It's hard to lose somebody at such a young age," Roy said. "Well…at any age." He looked down at the letter. "I wish I could help you, Ellen, but I don't know what this is about—this apology." He opened the letter and glanced at it again. "Did your grandmother ever say anything about my uncle?"

"No," I said. "She hardly ever talked about Beacon. That's why I was so anxious to meet him."

Roy sighed. "Yeah, well…" He handed the letter to me.

The air had that metallic smell of imminent rain, and I wondered when the sky would open and drench us. I noticed Roy staring at the letter in my hand. And then I realized he was staring at my engagement ring.

There was a long silence. Finally he said, "You're getting married." He kept looking at the ring.

"Yes," I said, feeling suddenly awkward, conscious of something heavy in the pit of my stomach.

He reached down, pulled a few blades of grass from the lawn, and studied them. "I didn't happen to notice that."

"I had to take it off," I said, my words steeped in guilt, as though I'd somehow misled him. "The first day I was here my fingers puffed up." I tried to laugh. "Even worse than this." I held up my hand. "Maybe the salt air..."

He nodded and turned a piece of grass over a couple of times. Then he let it blow away on the breeze.

A drop of rain landed on the letter, creating a little blue puddle of ink. I blotted it with my finger, then I folded up the paper and put it back in the envelope.

Mr. Puddy ambled by and rubbed himself against Roy's leg. "So the story of the letter," Roy said as he stood up, "is that he loved her but she loved your grandfather."

Raindrops began to hit my arm like pinpricks. I stood up and looked at the sky, now a smoky gray shroud above us.

"What was that line?" Roy asked. "'It was easier that way—easier to make a clean break. At least that's what I believed at the time.' Seems to me your grandmother might have had some regrets about leaving my uncle."

"Oh, no, she was happily married," I said, shivering as the drops flicked against my skin.

Neither one of us spoke. Finally I handed him the envelope. "You should have this."

For a second, we stood there, each of us holding one side of the envelope. Then I let go. "Well, I guess that's it, then. I'll be leaving town soon."

Roy sighed. "I guess that *is* it," he said as thunder breathed in the distance.

His eyes looked cloudy and tired. We shook hands, but when it was time to let go, he kept his hand on mine. His gaze was so intense I finally had to look away. He was still holding my hand when rain began tapping the leaves and the thunder's growl became louder.

At any moment we would be in the middle of a downpour. Mr. Puddy mewed and ran across the yard, up the steps, and onto the porch. I watched him sit down by the front door and a part of me wondered what I would say if Roy invited me onto that porch, into that house.

Instead he released my hand. "All right, then," he said, putting the baseball cap on his head. "Have a safe trip back, Swimmer."

The rain fell in a fury as I ran to the car. A clap of thunder rattled the sky as I shut the door. I turned on my windshield wipers in time to see Roy running into the house, the cat behind him. Then the porch was empty and I pulled away, the water streaming across my windshield.

Chapter 10

The Library

When I opened the shades the following morning the sky was clear. Pink clouds hung in a blue sky, full of sunlight and conviction. All signs of the previous day's rain were gone, but the memory of Roy Cummings ran through me like a streak of color in a rock—the softness in his eyes when I told him about my grandmother, the tender way he talked about his uncle, how he understood all too well the loss of a loved one.

Leaning closer to the window screen, I saw that something was going on next door, at the Beacon Historical Society. Cars were parked up and down the street, and people were making their way, like a line of ants, to the door of the gray house. I breathed in the cool, salty air and watched a boy coast down the street on a bike, the ticking from the derailleur growing softer as he faded from view. What a perfect day for a ride, I thought, wishing I had a bike and wondering if there was a place where I could rent one. I imagined myself coasting down a winding country road, camera over my shoulder, no GPS to direct my wheels. And then I remembered it was Saturday and I had an appointment to meet Lila Falk.

Saturday.

Oh, God, the Men of Note dinner was last night, and I hadn't called Hayden yet. He was going to think I didn't even care. And there I was daydreaming about bicycles and...Roy Cummings.

I grabbed my cell phone, yanking the charger cord from the wall along with it, and dashed into the bathroom. The screen said HAYDEN CROFT: MISSED CALL. I sat down on the toilet seat, my foot wiggling nervously as I played the message. *Hey, Ellen, it's about one thirty and I just got home. You really missed a great night. Everybody was asking for you. I think I did a good job with my acceptance speech. I think you would have been proud of me.*

I put my head in my hands and closed my eyes. I felt horrible. Of course I would have been proud of him. And I was sure he'd done a great job with his speech. I could picture him standing at the podium, no note cards, just saying what was in his heart. Later he would have shaken hands with the mayor, shared a humorous story.

Hayden's cell phone went straight to voice mail when I dialed his number. I left a message, a breezy, happy message, sending my congratulations and telling him I couldn't wait to see him. I ended by giving him some kisses through the phone.

I hung up, thinking how lucky I was to have Hayden in my life. Sweet, loyal, honest. The man every guy wanted as a friend. The guy every woman couldn't help but notice. Not to mention he was a Croft. And he was marrying *me*.

So what was my problem? Why had I woken up thinking about Roy Cummings? I was not interested in Roy. Not like that, anyway. I mean, he was nice enough, once you got past the lawyer paranoia. And he was kind of charming in his own way—his own small-town, boyish way. And I had to admit he was good-looking. In fact, he was quite attractive. If I didn't know him and I saw him walking down the street in the middle of Manhattan I'm sure I'd...

I clutched my cell phone in my hand. I had to stop this. I was beginning to sound like I *was* attracted to him. I was engaged, I loved Hayden, I was getting married. There had to be a logical reason why I was having these odd feelings about Roy. They couldn't have sprung out of nowhere. I gazed at the print of the lighthouse on the bathroom wall and tried to sort it out the way I would analyze a legal issue, arranging and rearranging the pieces until they made sense. Me, Hayden, our wedding. Gran, Beacon, Roy, the dock, the Antler.

And after a while it dawned on me. I was getting married in three months. That meant I would soon be out of circulation. No more flirting, no more dating. I'd be a married woman. So wasn't it logical that I might want to feel I was still attractive to men? That I still had that power? Yes, of course it was. If I felt the tiniest spark or tingle for Roy... well, that was the reason why. I was just proving I still *had it.* Didn't that make sense? I twirled my engagement ring around my finger, breathing easily again. Of course it did.

"What's going on next door?" I asked Paula as I grabbed a blueberry muffin and a glass of orange juice from the breakfast buffet.

Paula replaced an empty pot of coffee with a full one. "Annual picnic. It's a fund-raiser. They have games, contests...auction things off." A coy smile appeared on her face. "Last year Troy Blanchard had the winning bid for a year's worth of manicures and pedicures from Shear Magic. You know, the salon?"

I nodded. "Yes, I've seen it."

"Said it was for his wife," Paula went on, her eyes crinkling in delight. "But Poppy Norwich saw him in there one day, hand in the bowl of cuticle softener." She chuckled. "Oh, we gave him such a hard time. I don't think he'll do that again."

"Guess not," I said, tearing off a piece of the muffin and taking a bite. It was a little dry and didn't have nearly enough blueberries. *Why call it a blueberry muffin if you can't even find the berries?* Gran would have said. I took a long sip of my orange juice and thought about how she could teach these folks a thing or two.

Paula set a stack of napkins on the table and turned to me. "You ought to go next door if you want to learn about Beacon. They've got some nice things on display."

"Oh, really?" I said.

"Sure. You know, historical stuff. And with your grandmother being from Beacon and all..."

My grandmother being from Beacon.... Had I told her about that?

Most of the people at the picnic were already out back, milling around, talking to friends, or watching their children in the egg toss or the three-legged race.

I was happy to stay inside, where it was quiet. I strolled through the house, floorboards creaking as I walked from room to room. One room had a special exhibit of Currier and Ives lithographs. In another, vintage sepia-tone photographs of downtown Beacon were on display. I was excited when I realized that many of the buildings in the photos still existed. Another room was filled with antique furniture, including a lovely settee, desk, and cherry highboy.

In the last room, paintings by local artists were displayed. The oldest piece, of a ship at sea, dated back two hundred and fifty years. There were quiet harbor scenes and scenes of girls wading in the ocean, holding their ballooning skirts above the waves. And there were landscapes—fields and forests and farms with cows grazing lazily over mint-green hills.

But the painting that stopped me, made my heart skip a beat, was one of a small two-story shingled building, yellow with white trim around the windows. Redbrick steps led to a blue front door, over which a sign read THE IRRESISTIBLE BLUEBERRY BAKESHOP & CAFÉ. Pink roses climbed happily over a trellis to the right of the door, and through the windows customers could be seen sitting at little wooden tables.

I knew the building. The outside was white now, not yellow, and the steps were wooden rather than brick, but I could tell it was the tailor shop downtown. I also knew the artist. I would have recognized the style anywhere, but the signature confirmed it. In the bottom right corner my grandmother had signed her name.

I moved in closer to the canvas and touched the frame, tracing my finger along its ornate carving. Then I touched the painting, the blue door and the sign above it, imagining my grandmother's hand mixing the paints, creating the colors, brushing them onto the canvas. I couldn't believe I'd found another painting. Two of them now. Beacon was sharing its secrets, and I was thrilled to be the recipient. I examined each section of the canvas—the way Gran had captured the detail in the weathered shingles, the reflection of the roses in the windowpane, the burst of blue color on the door. Then I read the card on the wall. *BLUEBERRY CAFÉ BY RUTH GODDARD. THIS PAINTING WON FIRST PLACE AT THE BEACON FESTIVAL OF THE ARTS, 1950.*

The Beacon Festival of the Arts. First place. How fantastic. Gran had won the top honor. But what was the Beacon Festival of the Arts? And were there any other paintings? I'd found two. There could be more. There had to be. If Gran had painted this well, if she had won first prize in a contest, there had to be more.

I flagged down a woman who had a VOLUNTEER sticker on her sweater and asked if they had more information about the painting or the artist. "She was my grandmother," I said, pointing to the painting, astonished that the woman wasn't as excited as I was.

"Oh, you need to talk to Flynn, honey."

"Who is Flynn?"

"Flynn Sweeney," she said. "He's the director. He'll know."

She walked me to the back door and pointed to a tall man with a bit of a Humpty Dumpty build and a bulbous nose. He was hovering over a long table. The sign in front said SILENT AUCTION. Dozens of items were on the table, including a large earthenware vase, a set of home-repair instruction manuals, a crocheted blanket, fishing rods, boat cleats, a carton of previously viewed science fiction DVDs, and eight drinking glasses with Donald Duck's face on them. I wondered if Shear Magic had donated the manicures and pedicures again.

I introduced myself and told Flynn Sweeney about my grandmother's painting. "The one of the Irresistible Blueberry Café," I said.

"Oh, really?" He looked at me with deep brown eyes, the color of pecan shells, and then moved a set of steak knives from one side of the table to the other, as if he were trying to decide where they looked best. "She painted that, did she?"

"Yes, her name was Ruth Goddard and—"

"She grew up here?" he asked as he cocked his head and stepped back to view the table from a distance.

"Yes, she grew up in Beacon."

"That café was owned by the Chapman family," he said, finally leaving the steak knives on the right side, next to a bicycle seat. "For years, one Chapman or another ran the thing. A sister or a brother or an uncle or somebody...until it finally closed. I think that was around"—he paused—"oh, maybe twenty years ago."

I nodded. "Well, I was wondering if you might have any more of my grandmother's paintings. So far I know of—"

"Really too bad they closed," he said, moving a curling iron to the end of the table. "They made great blueberry muffins. Can't get a decent blueberry muffin anywhere these days."

"No, you can't," I said. He had a point there. "It's always unfortunate to lose a place that makes good food," I said. "But do you think you might have any more of her paintings? My grandmother's, I mean. Ruth Goddard. See, I'm from out of town and I came up here to—"

"Out-of-towner, are you?"

I nodded. "Yes, I'm—"

"Well, you know, that little café was a favorite of the tourists. People used to line up at the door in the morning to get the muffins when they came right out of the oven. You never had anything so good in your life, I can promise you that."

"Yes," I said. "I'm sure of it. But do you have any other work by my grandmother?"

He looked at me as though the question surprised him. "If we had other paintings by your grandmother," he said, picking up a milk-glass jug, "they would be on display."

"What about records?" I asked. "Are there any records I could check for information about her? Do you have any archives?"

He turned the jug over. "Don't know who donated this," he muttered. "Sticker fell off. Too bad."

I waited while he inspected the jug. Finally he glanced at me. "Hmm?...Oh, yes, records..." He scratched his chin. "Any information we have would be on the card by the painting."

"So that's everything?" I asked. "Just what's on the card? It said she won some kind of an art contest. The Beacon Festival of the Arts."

"Ah, yes," he said. "That was something they held every year." He squinted at me. "Did you say she *won* the contest?"

I nodded.

"Well, then, you might try the library. Look at the old issues of *The Beacon Bugle*. Maybe they published something about it."

The *Bugle*. That was a great idea. "Yes, all right," I said. "Thanks for the suggestion."

"Just check the ones published in June, July, and August," Flynn said. "They used to hold that festival in the summer."

He looked away, rubbing the jug as though it were Aladdin's lamp and he hoped a genie might appear. "Summer," he said with a sigh. "That's when the blueberries were fresh." He was almost whispering now. "Those Chapmans. They could really make a muffin. You want to see a contest? They could win a baking contest any day of the week, any week of the month, any month of..."

I didn't hear what else he said. I scooted past the makeup mirror and the Parcheesi game and the silver picture frame with the dented corner and I made a hasty exit.

The Beacon Free Library was a large white colonial house surrounded by a picket fence and located on a side street several blocks from the center of town. A plaque over the front door read 1790. I followed a sign that took me to the checkout desk, located in a sunny room where several people sat reading at tables or in armchairs.

A man with round glasses stood behind the front desk talking to an elderly woman.

"Okay, Molly. We'll let the fine go...again. Just promise me you'll try to bring these back on time, all right?" A dozen books on bird-watching lay on the counter in a tall stack. The librarian put them in a shopping bag and the woman ambled off. Then he turned to me.

"And how can I help you?" He gave me a weary smile. "Do you have an overdue book fine you want to negotiate, too?"

"No," I assured him. "I'm looking for some old issues of *The Beacon Bugle*."

"How old?"

"Summer of 1950," I said. "I'm not sure which month."

The man's black-rimmed glasses slid down his nose and he pushed them back up. "Oh, that old."

I was afraid he was going to tell me they didn't have them. "Do your archives go back that far?" I asked.

He hesitated and gave me a quick up-and-down glance. Then he said, "Yes, sure, but they're upstairs. I'll have to take you." He opened a drawer and removed a ring of keys.

"Marge," he called to a woman attempting to squeeze a manila folder into an already overstuffed drawer. "I'm going to the archives. Be back in a minute."

He signaled for me to follow him, and we walked through rooms filled with books and a reading area with comfy-looking sofas and chairs. We walked up a flight of stairs bordered by a gleaming mahogany banister. On the second floor, he unlocked the door to a small room. Sunlight poured through a mullioned window and dust motes floated in the air like tiny dancers.

"All the old periodicals are here," the librarian said, pointing to the wooden bookcases around the perimeter of the room. He ran his hand down the shelves, stopping at a series of large books bound in maroon cloth. Pulling out a volume that had the dates *June 1, 1950–June 15, 1950* embossed on its spine, he placed the book on a table in the center of the room.

"I'd start here," he said. "And if you don't find what you're looking for, you can move on to these." He indicated the five other books that housed the remainder of the summer issues. "These are all original newspapers," he said, his voice quiet now, as though just speaking of them gave him pause. "And they're very fragile."

"Don't worry," I told him. "I'll be careful."

He stared at me for a moment and then, appearing to be satisfied, left the room.

I opened the first of the two June volumes and was startled at how yellow and brittle the paper was. I ran my hand up and down the first page, amazed at the smooth feel of it. I began to turn the pages slowly, carefully, worried that I might damage or destroy them. This was Beacon's history I was staring at. I couldn't believe I was looking at an issue of *The Beacon Bugle* printed more than sixty years ago.

As I pored over the papers from that summer, I didn't expect there would be so many interesting things I'd want to read. I kept getting sidetracked. There was an article about the first kidney transplant, which took place in Chicago. The Korean War had just begun and President Truman ordered the air force and the navy into the conflict. The television show *Your Hit Parade* premiered on NBC and the movie *Annie Get Your Gun* was in theaters.

The ads and photos were amazing, too. There were pictures of women in tailored suits with cinched-waist jackets and pencil-slim skirts that fell well below the knee. Gray flannel suits seemed to be the big thing for men, and every man wore a hat. You could buy a house for eight thousand dollars and a car for seventeen hundred.

I finally found what I was looking for in the August 15, 1950, issue. The headline read, HIGH SCHOOL GIRL WINS TOWN ART CONTEST. There was a picture of Gran in a sweater, a long pleated skirt, and a pearl necklace. She stood next to an easel that held the painting. On the other side of the easel stood a man dressed in a suit and tie. He was holding a plaque. The picture looked as though it had been taken on Paget Street, right in the middle of town. I could see the seawall and ocean in the background, and part of the statue of the lady carrying the bucket of grapes.

> Ruth Goddard, 18, of Beacon, smiles as she accepts the award for first place at the annual Beacon Festival of the Arts. Miss Goddard's painting, *Blueberry Café,* won the prize for best in show. Miss Goddard, who has been awarded a full scholarship from the Art Institute of Chicago, will begin college there next month. Congratulations to our winner!

Art Institute of Chicago. I stared at the yellowed page. It was exactly what the man at Brewster's Camera World told me. That Gran had gotten a scholarship. But it didn't make sense. She talked about Stanford and she graduated from Stanford. She never said anything about the Art Institute of Chicago. Not a word. Still, there it was, right in front of me.

An uncomfortable feeling began to settle in my stomach, the feeling that there was much more to my grandmother than any of us knew. I read the article again and stared at the picture. Then I brought the book downstairs, put the page on the glass plate of the copy machine, and deposited my coins. The copier groaned and whined, and after a moment a piece of paper slid out and floated to the floor. I picked it up, gazed at the photo, and wondered, Who *was* this girl?

Chapter 11

Lila

By the time I finally left the library and headed north on the highway toward Kittuck, it was noon. I turned on some music, Sarah Vaughan singing "My Funny Valentine," but it didn't have its usual calming effect. It didn't dispel the bewildered feeling I had about the *Bugle* article.

The highway was a ribbon cutting through the Maine forest. A blur of green pine trees whizzed by my windows, and by the time I put some old Oscar Peterson music on I'd passed the exit for Lewisboro and the camera store. True to the prediction of the man at Brewster's, I made it from Lewisboro to Kittuck in an hour.

Just after two o'clock I walked into the Saint Agnes Care Center, a small, three-story brick building that would have been modern in 1990. The inside had an antiseptic, doctor's-office smell, combined with something that reminded me of old blankets and mothballs. The receptionist gave me a visitor's badge and instructed me to take the elevator to the third floor.

I stepped out in front of a nurses' station, where two women in white uniforms were working behind a counter, one studying a blinking computer monitor; the other writing on an erasable whiteboard mounted to the wall. A large clock high above ticked away the time. The woman at the monitor turned and asked if I needed help. Her plastic badge said NOREEN.

"I'm here to see Lila Falk," I said. "My name is Ellen Branford. I called yesterday."

Noreen nodded and gestured for me to follow her. "Are you a friend?"

"She knew my grandmother," I said. "When they were children."

"Your timing is good," she said, leading me down the hall. "Her daughter, Sugar, usually comes on Saturdays, but she called and said she's coming tomorrow instead."

Sounds from television shows drifted into the hall as we passed open doorways. Some of the residents sat in wheelchairs outside their rooms. A man with a few strands of white hair ambled toward us on a cane. Noreen turned to me. "Lila is almost eighty, you know."

I did know. "Yes, my grandmother was eighty when she…" I paused and took a little breath. "She was eighty."

We walked on, toward the end of the hall. "Lila also suffers from dementia," Noreen said. "It's pretty serious."

Dementia. I hoped I hadn't made the trip for nothing. After what the man in the camera store said, I had built up hope that Lila Falk would be able to tell me about Gran's childhood.

"It's up and down with her," Noreen explained as we moved to let a man in a walker pass by. "Sometimes she's fine. Other

times, not so good. Doesn't know who she is or where she is."
We stopped in front of an open doorway. "I just want you to be
prepared."

I nodded as Noreen knocked and we stepped into the room.
The walls were pale blue, and I caught the faint smell of
bleach. A tiny woman with hair like a puff of gray cotton sat in
the first of two hospital-style beds. She was watching reruns of
an old television show called *The Match Game,* in which con-
testants tried to match celebrities' answers to fill-in-the-blank
questions.

"Hi, Dorrie," Noreen said, waving to the woman. Dorrie
looked up, a smile spreading over her face like the gradual opening of a flower.

"Hello, Noreen," she half whispered, and I caught the trace of
an English accent.

We walked toward a petite woman seated in a large chair next
to the other bed. Her blue eyes seemed to have captured light
from the sky. She wore ivory pants that matched the color of her
wavy hair and a blouse adorned with a pattern of small pink rose-
buds. A pink crocheted blanket covered her lap and, on top of it,
lay an open copy of *Glamour* magazine.

"Lila, you have a visitor," Noreen said. Lila raised her head and
looked at Noreen and then at me. "This is Miss Branford. She
would like to talk to you about someone you know."

Lila picked up the magazine and turned it around for a moment to view the pages upside down.

"Well, I'll leave you two," Noreen said.

I thanked her and pulled up a chair. "Miss Falk," I said. "I
know we've never met but I believe you knew my grandmother,

Ruth Goddard." I pronounced the name slowly. "You two grew up together in Beacon."

"Beacon," she said, not looking up from the magazine. "Who is Beacon?"

"Beacon, the town." I said. "Where you grew up. Here in Maine."

Lila rearranged the blanket on her lap, moving it around carefully, as though she were following some master plan.

"Do you remember Ruth?" I asked. "You were close friends when you were young."

Lila looked back at her magazine and began turning the pages.

"You two must have gone to school together," I added. "She went to the Littleton School." I thought about the gnarled tree on the lawn. "I drove by there a few days ago, and do you know what?"

I waited for a response, but Lila just tugged at the bottom of her sleeve, which someone had folded back into a cuff. She pulled at the rosebud fabric.

"The school is still there," I said. "A redbrick building. Do you remember it?"

Lila kept tugging, as if she were trying to unfold the sleeve.

"Here, let me help you." I began to straighten out the fabric. She studied my hands as I unraveled the material. "This just needs to be undone...like that."

Lila looked at me, her blue eyes a spark in an otherwise placid face. "Ruth?"

Ruth? I smiled. "No, I'm not Ruth, Miss Falk. I'm her granddaughter Ellen."

She cocked her head. Then she reached over and touched the

clasp on the front of my grandmother's pearl necklace, running her finger over the silver shell. "It's good to see you, Ruth." She let out a sigh and gave me a little smile.

I started to correct her again, and then I stopped. Her frail hand hovered above the clasp. "It's good to see you, too," I said.

She stared at me with her piercing blue eyes. "Littleton?" The hairline cracks in her face angled away in every direction.

I pulled my chair a little closer. "Yes, Littleton Grammar School."

She looked down at the magazine, pointing to an ad for a perfume called Seven Secrets. It had a scratch-and-sniff card, which she pulled out and proceeded to scuff with her fingernail. She pushed the card in front of my nose.

"Smell that, Ruth." She waved the card.

I took a little sniff, expecting something potent, but the card smelled like gardenias, and I thought about the sunroom my grandmother had in San Francisco, with its gardenias in big clay pots, their white petals bursting like snow against deep green leaves.

"It's lovely."

Lila tilted her head and stared at me. "Your hair looks different."

"Excuse me?" I touched the ends of my hair.

She shrugged and smiled. "Pretty," she said. "But then, you were always pretty." She laid the gardenia card against her face, as if it were something she wanted to hold tenderly. "Do you remember the man in the flower shop...who used to give us flowers?"

I looked at Lila, the scented card pressed against her cheek, her eyes focused on something over my shoulder, beyond me. "Yes," I said.

She placed the card in my hand. "Daisies and carnations." She sighed. "But sometimes he gave us gardenias."

I glanced down at the fragile skin on her gnarled fingers, the faint blue of the veins running underneath. "And we'd put them in vases," I said.

"Oh, I'd put *mine* in a vase," Lila said. She looked toward the window, as though she might find a gardenia bush growing out there. Then she turned to me. "You'd paint yours."

It was as if she had opened a window into a long-darkened room. *You'd paint yours.* Of course there were more paintings. Just as I thought. I wanted to ask Lila a million questions—about the paintings, about her friendship with Gran, and about Chet Cummings. I wanted to let loose the bits of information I knew were dancing in her mind. But I sat patiently, one hand gripping the other, waiting for her to go on.

"What did you like best about the paintings?" I said.

"You could almost..." She closed her eyes and lifted her hand in the air. "You could almost touch them." She stroked the fabric of her blouse, and I wondered what she was seeing, what images of my grandmother she recalled.

Lila looked away, and I watched her fingers as they began to work the corner of the magazine cover, folding the edge down, then smoothing it back up, down and up, down and up.

Finally, with a little tremble in her voice, she said, "It was awful for him, you know...when you left."

I waited a moment, and when she didn't go on, I asked, "Awful for whom?"

"Chet," she said in a half whisper.

"Yes," I said. "Chet."

"He didn't understand, you know...how you could change your mind." She pulled the blanket to her neck and wrapped her arms around it. "And so fast. Love him and then...well, then there was Henry."

The sound of my grandfather's name startled me, and I tried to picture him as part of this love triangle so long ago. Lila's roommate stirred in the chair and mumbled in her sleep.

"Chet thought you'd come back, but I knew you wouldn't. When he got the news...when he found out..." She sighed.

"The news," I said, trying to nudge her forward.

"That you were engaged. He couldn't believe it, Ruthie. Best you didn't see him then. The poor boy was miserable. He *had* to leave." She looked down at the blanket.

He had to leave what? I wondered.

She held up her hands. "And then everything fell apart."

"You mean Chet and me?'"

"No, I mean—"

A high-pitched howl of laughter came from the woman in the other bed, and Lila and I turned to look at her. She had woken up and was watching the television again.

Lila sat up, the blanket slipping back into her lap. Her eyes, deep like glacier ice, studied me.

"You need to go see Sugar, Ruthie. She has some of your things. I just didn't have room...you understand, don't you?" She closed her eyes, as though she were glimpsing the objects. "Some photographs, I think. Some letters."

Photographs and letters. I felt a surge of excitement. "Sugar? You mean your daughter?"

Lila yawned and gave a little nod.

Of course I'd see her. If she had anything to tell me or give me of Gran's, I'd be overjoyed to see her. "Yes, I'd love to do that," I said.

Lila sighed and looked at her hands, as though they might have belonged to someone else. An announcement came over a loud-speaker: "Dr. Martin to reception. Dr. Martin to reception."

Her eyelids began to droop. "A doctor is staying here in the hotel? How convenient."

She yawned again, and her eyelids fluttered, like humming-birds' wings.

"Lila?" I nudged her arm.

Her eyes closed, her head dropped to her chest, and she was asleep.

The late afternoon sun draped the highway in a molten orange glow as I headed back to the inn. A million pine trees later, I pulled into the parking lot. It was almost six when I stepped into the foyer. The smell of sautéed onions greeted me and reminded me that I hadn't eaten since breakfast.

I didn't see Paula at the front desk. A plump young woman, with short curly hair in a shade of red not found in nature, sat behind the counter.

"Hello. May I help you?" She smiled and spoke in a slow, rolling voice.

"I'm Ellen Branford. I'm a guest here," I said. "In room eight or ten or whatever it is. The Ocean View Suite." I pointed toward the stairs, my arm feeling heavy. "Third floor, first room on the right."

The woman wore a little black pin on which the name TOTTY was printed in white letters. "Okay, dear," she said. "Nice to meet you." Totty's voice went up at the end of each phrase, as though she were forever asking questions. *Nice to meet you?*

"Is Paula off tonight?" I asked, digging around in my purse for the room key.

"Yes, she is." Totty smiled, exhibiting dimples in her cheeks that gave her face a childish quality. I thanked her and headed toward the stairs, past the lounge and dining room. Almost all the tables were occupied, and a waiter was serving soup and salad to a couple seated near the door. I waved and he came over.

"Is it possible to order something and have it delivered to my room?"

"*Sì, sì,* of course," he told me, his words coated in a heavy Italian accent. "You choose, we deliver. I get you a menu."

He returned a moment later with a menu, which I scanned.

"I think I'll try the Victory salad," I said, pointing to the first salad on the list. SPRING GREENS, CRANBERRIES, WALNUTS, AND GOAT CHEESE TOPPED WITH RASPBERRY VINAIGRETTE.

He nodded and scribbled on a pad.

"And the roast chicken," I added, pointing to the first entrée listed. HALF OF A SUCCULENT FREE-RANGE CHICKEN, ROASTED IN BUTTER AND FRESH HERBS, WITH MASHED POTATOES AND GARDEN-FRESH CARROTS. I had never eaten half a chicken in my life, but I was willing to try.

"Roast chicken," he mumbled, scribbling again.

"What's for dessert?" I said, throwing all caution to the wind and promising myself I'd make it up back in Manhattan. Maybe I'd even try to get in shape for that 10K race Winston Reid was sponsoring in the fall.

The waiter took a piece of paper from his pocket and read off the selections—cheesecake, brownie sundae, blueberry pie, and ice cream.

"The blueberry pie," I said, without even thinking. "Oh, and a glass of white wine, please. Can you tell me what you have by the glass?"

He scratched his chin. "Ah, by the glass. We have a house wine and some others. Let me find you the list and—"

I waved my hand. "Never mind, I'll just take the house wine." I'd be reviving Hayden with smelling salts if he heard me say that. *The house wine, Ellen? And you don't even know what it is?*

"*Sí sí*, we send it up." The waiter nodded several times.

I trudged upstairs and unlocked the door, letting my purse drop to the floor. Then I stretched out on the bed with my arms around the pillow. The long drive up to Kittuck and back had knocked me out. Or maybe it was Lila. Either way, I just needed five minutes to relax. To lay my head on the pillow.

I yawned and thought about the love triangle—Gran and Chet Cummings and my grandfather. I thought about Lila Falk and her daughter, Sugar, and what she might have of Gran's, and I thought about the pillow that felt so lovely under my head.

A half hour later someone was knocking at the door and I came to with a start, trying to figure out where I was.

"Miss, it's Rodolfo from downstairs." Another knock. "Miss, I have you dinner."

My dinner?

"Yes, I'm coming." I sat up, brushed some hair away from my face, and tried to smooth out the wrinkles in my clothes. Then I opened the door. Rodolfo stood in the hallway, shifting from one foot to the other. He was holding a blue tray with seashells painted on it. On the tray was a vintage wineglass of etched crystal, which had been filled with white wine, a salad of colorful greens and cranberries, a large white plate covered by a gleaming silver dome, a slice of blueberry pie, and a pink rose in a bud vase.

For a moment, I just stared. It looked so beautiful. Then I caught myself. "Come in. Please." I waved my hand.

Rodolfo looked around the room. "Where would you like?"

I thought he was joking. There was nowhere to put the tray except on the bed. "Right there, I guess." I pointed.

"*Sí sí.*" He put down the tray.

I rifled through my purse for some loose bills. "Thank you," I said, handing him a tip.

"Thank *you,*" he replied, making a little bow before he left.

I sat on the bed and tried the salad. The greens were crisp and fresh, and there were lots of big chunks of tangy goat cheese. The caramelized walnuts crunched in my mouth. Then I lifted the silver dome from the dinner plate. A puff of herb-scented steam rose into the air as I stared at the chicken. It was roasted to a golden glow and sprinkled with fresh sprigs of tarragon and some other herbs I couldn't identify. The mashed potatoes looked creamy and buttery, and the carrots were coated with a rich, dark glaze. I ate everything within minutes, right down to the pie, with its flaky crust and still-warm blueberries. I wondered if Paula would ever part with the recipes. I had underestimated her. That was certain.

Too full to move now, I pushed the tray aside and lay down again, staring at a crack in the ceiling that looked like the state of New Hampshire. Gradually, my whole body began to relax. Don't fall asleep, I told myself. You need to call Hayden and Mom and Sugar....

We are walking through a huge, overgrown field bounded on all sides by stone walls. Some of the boulders have fallen by the side and Hayden is picking them up and setting them back into the wall, finding the proper place for each one, turning them and repositioning them until he is satisfied with the way it looks. Every so often he stands back and assesses his work and some-times he takes a boulder off and tries it in another spot. I begin to pick up the smaller stones and to look for crevices in the wall where I might fit them.

"This happens after every winter," he says. "It's expansion and contraction that causes it."

"Same as potholes," I reply. "The roads do that and it makes potholes."

"You're such a city girl," he says, wrapping his arm around my neck and pulling me toward him. Then we sit on the wall and gaze across the field as a breeze ruffles the weeds.

He jumps off the wall and pushes away some brambles. "Blue-berries," he says. In the space where he has cleared the weeds, green shoots poke through the ground.

"How did you know they were there?" I ask.

"They'll always be here," he says. And then he kisses me with a passion that leaves me unable to speak.

Someone was knocking at the door. I tried to pull myself from sleep, from the field with the stone walls and weeds and blueberries.

The knocking came again, a little louder. Rodolfo. He had come to collect the tray. I could smell the vinegar from the dressing and it didn't smell that appetizing anymore. I sat up and rubbed my eyes.

Rodolfo kept knocking.

I tried to remember what was going on in the dream, but it was already vanishing, fog into sunlight. And then I remembered standing in a field with Hayden, fixing a wall. There were boulders and weeds and it was overgrown. We were lifting stones and putting them back in the wall.

The knocking continued. Rodolfo was being so insistent. Almost rude.

"Just a minute," I mumbled, moving clumsily from the bed. "I'm coming."

All right, take the stupid tray, I thought as I slid off the bed. And in that second, as my feet touched the floor, I realized the man in the dream wasn't Hayden at all. It was Roy Cummings. *Roy.* Oh, my God, Roy had kissed me. And it was an amazing kiss, even more amazing than the one on the beach. I could still feel his arms around my neck. I could feel his lips on my lips. I could taste him. He tasted like salt spray, like the end of a long summer day.

I took the tray in my hands and moved toward the door. Balancing the tray with one hand, I turned the doorknob with the other. The weeds and the blueberries and the kiss. I wanted the dream. I wanted the kiss. I wanted Roy. Something inside me began to ache.

I opened the door to hand the tray to Rodolfo, and there, in a custom-made tan raincoat of Italian gabardine, holding a briefcase in one hand and a Louis Vuitton overnight bag in the other, stood Hayden.

Chapter 12

Battle of the Roosters

Hayden!" I dropped the tray, sending plates and flatware crashing around us. A woman opened a door down the hall, peeked out, and then closed it. "What are you doing here?"

Hayden stood before me, his tousled hair golden against a gray Savile Row suit. The yellow Italian silk tie I'd given him last Christmas was knotted under the collar of a crisp white shirt. He looked very handsome.

"Are you all right?" He smiled, eyeing the scattered china.

I threw my arms around him, banishing all residual thoughts of Roy and inhaling the scent of leather and courtrooms and boardrooms with thick mahogany paneling and centuries-old Aubusson carpets. "I'm fine," I said. "Just surprised, that's all."

He pressed his lips to mine, giving me a long, soulful kiss, and for a moment I was back in New York, taking cab rides and making conference calls, riding in limousines and going to opera fund-raisers and museum galas. I could see myself in our apartment, lounging on the sofa on a Sunday morning, sipping coffee, newspapers spread out on the table, sunlight streaming in through the windows. It felt good to be there.

We picked up the scattered dishes, and Hayden followed me into the room. "Why didn't you tell me you were coming?" I asked.

"I didn't know I was coming until this afternoon."

I turned to take his coat and saw him looking around.

"This is where you've been staying?" His eyes darted from the earthenware bowl and cracked pitcher to the uncomfortable ladder-back chair to the tiny bathroom with my drinking glass of pens and pencils on top of the toilet tank.

I slipped his coat over the back of the chair. "It's not so bad."

He gave me a skeptical look. "Ellen Branford, queen of the five-star hotel circuit, telling me this isn't *so bad*. I'm impressed."

"Really," I said, taking his jacket. "I think it's kind of cute."

He raised his chin and peered at me. "You look a little...I don't know..." He paused. "Something's different." He studied my face for a moment. "Oh, you're not wearing any makeup. Maybe that's it."

"I'm not?" I touched my cheek.

"Don't look so alarmed." He laughed. "You don't need it."

I wondered how I could have forgotten to put on makeup. "I guess I was in such a rush this morning," I said. "I went to see an old friend of my grandmother's in a nursing home."

"A friend of hers up here?" Hayden asked, brushing my hair away from my face and studying my eyes.

"Yes. You wouldn't believe what I found out today." I told him about the man at the camera store and the painting at the historical society and the article at the library. "There are things about my grandmother we never knew."

He gave me a curious look. "Almost as though she had a secret life."

"Well, not a secret *life,* at least I don't think so. I mean, I hope not. But there are definitely things she never talked about."

"It's kind of like solving a mystery," he said as we sat down on the bed. "I'd love to see the paintings. You'll have to show me."

"I will. I want you to see them. But before we talk about any more of that, you have to tell me how you ended up here. I thought you were going to be in a settlement conference all day on that Dobson case."

Hayden's smile spread across his face.

"What's going on? Tell me," I said.

"We settled it this morning."

"You did? Oh, Hayden, that's great!" I threw my arms around him again. "You said you didn't think it would ever settle."

"Twenty-nine five," he said, shaking his head as though he couldn't believe it. "I didn't think it would ever settle that high."

I knew he was speaking about millions, not thousands, of dollars. Our client was getting the money, but our firm was getting a huge fee out of it. It was another feather in Hayden's cap.

"Wow, that's fantastic," I said.

He nodded. "I'm happy. Dobson's board is ecstatic. It's a good settlement for them. I'm just glad it worked out. They ended up getting a pretty fair deal. Sometimes things go the right way, and this was one of those times."

"Congratulations," I said, feeling proud of him. "You must have been extremely persuasive."

"Oh, I can be pretty persuasive when I want to be," he said, his smile turning mischievous now. "I recall using my persuasive powers on you a few times."

"Maybe," I said, feigning indifference, "but you'll never get twenty-nine five out of me."

He took my hand. "All kidding aside. You know what the best part about the settlement is?"

I shook my head.

"That I got to come up here and be with you. I was in a cab, on my way back to the apartment, and then I thought, Why don't I just go to Maine? So I grabbed a few things and got on a plane."

"Oh, Hayden." He had a way of making me feel like I could melt.

"I missed you," he said, drawing me close. "I don't like being in our apartment without you."

I put my head against his chest. "I missed you, too."

"I kept thinking about you up here by yourself," he said. "I thought this way you'd have some company and we could go back to New York together." He stood up. "And speaking of New York...I brought you something." He winked at me as he took a package from his briefcase.

"What's this?"

"Open it," he said, sitting down next to me again.

I tore off the wrapping paper and saw that it was a book. *The World of Henri Cartier-Bresson.*

"Hayden, he's my favorite."

"I know. And it's a first edition."

"It's beautiful." I began flipping through the pages of black-and-white photographs. "The father of modern photojournalism."

"Yes, he definitely was."

I paused at a photo of a man riding a bicycle through a narrow street in France. The picture was taken from a stairway. "I love this one. Look at the curve of the steps and the iron railing, how beautiful the shapes are. And the man whizzing by on the bike, almost a blur. He had a half second to take that picture. Incredible. 'F-eleven and be there.'"

"Hmm?"

"It's that old saying photographers use," I said. "You know— it means the technical aspects aren't as important as being in the right place at the right time." I pulled Hayden toward me and kissed him. "What an amazing gift. I can't wait to go through every single photo."

"I'm glad you like it," he said.

I closed the book and held it against my chest. "I love it."

He smiled. "So tell me what's been going on. Did you finally get to meet the famous Mr. Cummings?"

I looked down and shook my head. "No. I'm not going to meet him."

"Why not? What happened?"

I pulled at a loose thread in the coverlet. "Chet Cummings is...well, he died."

Hayden took my hand. "Oh, honey, I'm so sorry."

I nodded. "Yeah. Me, too."

"When did it happen?"

"Three months ago."

"Oh, no. What bad timing. You came all the way up here and...well, I'm sorry."

A cool breeze blew through the window. Feeling a chill, I closed the sash, walked to the thermostat, and turned on the heat. Something groaned and clanked, and then a fan whirred. A metallic smell rose from the radiator vent on the floor, and a gust of lukewarm air shot out.

Hayden put the pillows against the headboard, kicked off his shoes, and lay down on the bed. He loosened his tie and motioned for me to join him. I settled into the crook of his arm.

"So tell me what happened," he said. "You couldn't deliver the letter and—"

"No, I did deliver it," I said. "I gave it to his nephew."

Hayden looked at me. "His nephew? Who's his nephew?"

"A guy named Roy Cummings. Chet was living in his house."

"Oh." He paused and then said, "What's he going to do with it?"

"I don't know, but I thought he should have it. Don't you think?"

Hayden gave me a quizzical look. "I don't know, Ellen. I'm surprised you did that. The letter wasn't addressed to him. I would have given it to the executor of the guy's estate or the court-appointed administrator if he...is this guy the executor?"

I tried to remember what Roy said to me in the front yard. *Any business of my uncle's is business of mine.* Something like that. He hadn't actually said he was his uncle's executor, but that was the feeling I'd gotten. That he was taking care of his affairs. I hoped I hadn't jumped to conclusions. What if I did the wrong thing? Was I losing my edge?

I nodded. "Yes, I think so."

"You *think* so?"

"No, I mean he is. He's the executor."

"Well, then, I don't see a problem with that."

Hayden stretched and let out a loud sigh. I helped him take off his gold cufflinks, the ones with the family crest on them, and he placed them on the bedside table. Then he began to kiss my neck. I closed my eyes and felt his breath, warm and familiar, his hair soft against my skin. His hair smelled like citrus, like the shampoo in our apartment.

He unbuttoned my blouse, his fingers moving gently along the fabric. I pulled off his tie and undid the buttons of his shirt. Then he leaned in and kissed me. The crack on the ceiling that looked like New Hampshire became soft and fuzzy and, as crickets hummed outside the window, we undressed and made love.

Hayden was already up when I awoke on Sunday morning. Sitting next to me in bed, in his boxers and a blue T-shirt, he clicked away at his laptop.

"Good morning," I said, yawning and rubbing my eyes. "What time is it?"

He looked at his watch. "A little after nine."

I could see a strip of light beneath the window shade. "Does it look like it's a nice day?"

He continued to type away. "I don't know. I haven't checked yet."

"You haven't looked?"

He shook his head. "I've been working." He gave me a kiss on the cheek.

"Listen, Hayden," I said. "I really want you to see Gran's paintings. I doubt the historical society is open today, but maybe we can go over to the Porters' and see the one in their attic."

"Sounds good," he said. "I'd love to see it."

"I'll call Susan in a little while." My stomach rumbled and I realized I was famished. Something was happening to my appetite. I felt hungry all the time now, and the food I wanted to eat wasn't the superhealthy variety I was used to. It was comfort food. Meat loaf and mashed potatoes, chicken and dumplings, macaroni and cheese, pot roast. I turned to Hayden. "Do you want to get some breakfast?"

"Yeah, just give me a minute," he said. "I need to finish one thing." He grabbed my arm as I walked toward the bureau, his hand sliding down my bicep. "Mmm, still got great muscle tone." He smiled. "You've been working out up here."

"Not really." I wondered if there even was a place to work out. I took a pair of shorts and a top from the drawer. "Oh, wait," I said. "I forgot—I did some swimming."

"Swimming?" He gave me a quick glance. "Oh, yeah, you used to be on a team. Exeter, wasn't it?" He took the cap off of a pen and began scribbling on a pad.

"Yep, Exeter," I said as I zipped up the shorts and pulled the top over my head. I raised one of the window shades and the sun exploded into the room. Leaning on the sill, I looked out and breathed the cool, grassy air.

After a minute Hayden looked up. "It's so quiet here."

I couldn't tell if he meant quiet *good* or quiet *bad*. "Yeah, it's quiet."

I stepped into the bathroom, ready to pick up my toothbrush, and then I froze. Tucked into the corner of the mirror above the sink was an ivory card. The black lettering was raised, and I recognized the typeface: French Script. I stepped closer and read the words.

Mrs. Cynthia Parker Branford
requests the honour of your presence
at the marriage of her daughter
Eleanor Newhouse
to
Mr. Hayden Stewart Croft
on Saturday, the seventh of October
at half after six
Saint Thomas Church
New York, New York

I began to feel a little twinge in my chest. I took the invitation from the mirror and held it in my hand as I sat on the edge of the tub. Saturday, October 7. The letters were dark, definitive, engraved into the paper.

"So what's the verdict?" Hayden called from the bedroom.

"The verdict?" I was trying to remember how many invitations we had ordered. Two hundred? Two hundred and fifty? All I could recall was the number on the bottom of the guest list—three hundred and thirty-seven people. They were all being invited to watch us get married. Family, friends, business associates...

"The invitation," Hayden said, sounding impatient. "What do you think? Isn't it great?"

I pictured the church—candles lit, flowers arranged, pews being filled, the string quintet playing the pieces we'd selected. I felt something prickly in my stomach. "Yes, it's beautiful."

"Didn't I tell you Smythson was the best?" Hayden said, appearing in the doorway. "They're not engravers to the queen for nothing."

I nodded. "No, I'm sure they're not," I said.

"You can't get that kind of quality here in the States."

I ran my finger over the letters and wondered why I was suddenly feeling just the tiniest bit nervous. Maybe it was the thought of all those invitations making their way across the country to dozens and dozens of people, beckoning them to come to this event, to witness Hayden and me taking our vows.

Maybe every bride got a little nervous at the first sight of her wedding invitation. Why not? It was probably a normal reaction. After all, there was something so...well, concrete about it. *No room for error now,* it might as well be announcing.

Error? Well, that wasn't the right word. That wasn't what I meant at all. I just meant...what did I mean?

I must be going crazy, I thought as I stood in front of the mirror. I'm engaged to the most fabulous man in the world, and we've got a beautiful wedding coming up.

Suddenly, Hayden was next to me, his head over my shoulder. He took the card from my hand, gazed at it, gave a satisfied smile, and tucked it back into the corner of the mirror.

"Engravers to the queen," he said with a little nod.

"Yes." I put my arms around him and held him as tightly as I could.

Totty, the night shift woman, was not at the front desk when Hayden and I walked by on our way to breakfast. Paula was back, and she did a little double take when she saw Hayden.

I smiled cheerfully. "This is my fiancé, Hayden Croft. Just in from New York." I turned to Hayden. "Paula Victory, the owner of the inn."

Paula blinked. "Your *fiancé*." She drew out the word, as though it had six syllables. Then she looked at Hayden. "*What's* that name?"

"Croft," he said. "C-R-O-F-T."

"Never heard it before."

"It's English. My ancestors—"

"Oh, no, I meant your first name. Did you say Haven?"

Hayden adjusted the collar of his polo shirt. "No, Hayden, with a *y*."

"Aha," Paula said, glancing at me. "Your *fiancé*." One side of her mouth turned up in a half grin. "Well, isn't that nice?"

She looked Hayden up and down. Then she gave a little approving nod.

"I should thank you for taking care of Ellen," Hayden said, putting his arm around me.

Paula laughed. "No need to thank *me*," she said. "Ellen seems to be taking care of herself."

I pulled Hayden toward the door before Paula could say anything else. "Yes, well, we're off to breakfast. See you later."

"Shall we take the car?" he asked, stopping at the bottom of the front steps. "I'll drive."

"Drive? It's a five-minute walk."

He looked surprised. "You can walk to town from here?"

"Of course," I said.

We strolled down Prescott Lane, passing houses with clusters of white beach roses bursting from picket fences. I pulled off a blossom and held it to my nose. It smelled like dew and early morning sunshine. At the end of the block we turned right onto Putnam and headed toward the water.

At Paget Street we turned again, and the ocean opened up before us, a mosaic of blues and whites under a flashing sun.

"This is the whole town?" Hayden gazed down the street, adjusting his sunglasses.

I took his hand. "Yes. This is Beacon."

I led him into the Three Penny Diner. Almost all the tables were occupied, and only one booth was empty. The young waitress I spoke to my first day there approached us with menus. Her red hair tumbling in crescents, she flashed a smile and showed us to the booth. We sat down opposite one another, ordered coffee, and studied the menus.

"I already know what I want," I told Hayden. "Apple cider doughnuts. You have to try them. They're incredible."

"Doughnuts?" He looked up at me with a puzzled expression. "You're eating doughnuts?"

"What do you mean?"

"I don't know. Carbs? Calories? You never eat doughnuts. I'm just surprised."

He glanced back at the menu, and I thought about the doughnuts, hot out of the fryer, the outside covered with sugar, the way they crunched when you bit into them, the soft inside part that tasted of apple and melted in your mouth. They couldn't possibly be good for you. He was right.

The waitress returned and set two mugs of coffee in front of us. "Have you folks decided?"

I knew I should have ordered oatmeal or asked if there were any whole-grain cereals hiding in the back, but the memory of the cider doughnut was too vivid. I ordered one, handing over my menu with a slight feeling of resignation.

Hayden looked at me for a second, but didn't say anything. Then he flashed a big smile at the waitress. "I'd love an egg-white-and-chive omelet with some sliced tomatoes on the side and a piece of twelve-grain toast—no butter, please."

An egg-white omelet with chives? It wasn't even on the menu. I wanted to remind him this wasn't New York, but I kept quiet.

The waitress clicked her pen a couple of times. "Sir, I'm sorry but we don't have that item. We don't even have chives here or that kind of bread."

"Okay," he said, raising his hand in a conciliatory gesture. "An egg-white omelet with sliced tomatoes and... what kind of bread *do* you have?"

She clicked her pen again. "White, whole wheat, rye."

He thought for a moment and then said, "I'll take whole wheat."

The waitress gave a quick smile and was gone.

I took a sip of coffee. It tasted like hazelnuts and evenings by a warm fire.

"I'd love to find a *Wall Street Journal,*" Hayden said. "Do you think there's any chance of that?"

"There's a little store down the street that might have it," I told him.

He stood up and looked around. "I saw some newspapers when we came in... oh, there they are." He walked toward the cashier's counter and returned with a *Boston Globe* and a *Beacon Bugle.*

"This should be interesting," he said, looking at the headline on the front page of the *Bugle:* STONES ON ROUTE 9 STOP TRAFFIC. Underneath was a photo of a traffic jam and a pile of rocks that had fallen from a truck onto a road.

Thank God it's not my picture he's looking at, I thought. "I guess it was a slow news day," I said.

Hayden tossed the *Bugle* onto the table and picked up the *Globe*. "It's amazing that such a small town can keep a daily paper afloat. How many of those could they possibly sell—four, five hundred copies a day?"

"More like three thou—"

He looked up. "Hmm?"

I waved my hand. "Nothing."

The waitress returned with our breakfast, and I tried to get Hayden to taste my doughnut. "Come on, you're in Maine now." I nudged him. "Chad will never know."

"Ha!" he said. "Chad's been my trainer for seven years. He'll know." But then he picked up the doughnut and took a small, cautious bite, chewing it slowly, savoring the flavor the way I'd seen him taste wine a hundred times.

"Wow," he said. "I didn't know a doughnut could be this good."

"Welcome to Maine."

Something inside me bubbled with joy. It was a beautiful day and we were going to share it. This mini vacation in Beacon would turn out to be a nice break for the two of us.

I leafed through the *Bugle,* scanning an article about a police officer who had received a special commendation, an announcement about a rummage sale at Saint Mary's church, and a letter to the editor complaining about a property tax increase. I turned the page and saw an ad for a country fair sponsored by the Maine Organic Farmers and Gardeners Association. I wondered what it would be like. Butter-churning contests with girls in white aprons? Milk tastings? Could be fun.

"Hayden, I think we should go to this." I pushed the paper toward him.

"A country fair?" he said. "With horses and cows? That kind of thing?"

"I guess. Why don't we check it out?"

He took a bite of his omelet, and then he said, "I'm not really into horses and cows, but for you, Ellen, I'll do it."

We lingered over breakfast, had seconds on the coffee, and then I folded up the *Bugle* and we walked outside. I called the Porters' house, but the phone rang and rang. Their voice mail finally picked up and I left a message, asking if I could bring Hayden to see the painting.

On the way back to the inn, we passed the Beacon Dry Goods store, its front window filled with denim clothes and work boots and camping gear.

"Let's stop in here for a second," I said, tugging Hayden's arm. "I want to buy a pair of jeans."

"Have I ever seen you in jeans?" he asked as we stepped inside.

I laughed. "I can't remember the last time I wore a pair. But then, I can't remember the last time I went to a country fair."

I tried on a pair of straight-legged, low-rise faded jeans with a lot of stitching on the pockets and seams. Hayden whistled when I came out of the dressing room.

"I'll take these," I told the salesman. "And I'm going to wear them." I turned to Hayden. "How about you?"

He looked down at his khakis and Top-Siders. "I think I'll stick with this."

We walked back to the inn and unlocked the car. "If we go to this country fair," Hayden said, "am I going to have to look at chickens or anything like that?"

I got into the passenger seat, holding up my hand as though I were taking an oath. "No chickens, I promise. Maybe just a couple of pigs."

He shook his head. "Pigs. Ugh." Then his eyes lit up. "I'll tell you what. I'll go to the fair if you find a place around here where I can play a little golf."

I shook my head. "Sorry, honey. There isn't any place around here to golf."

"Maybe just a driving range?"

He started the engine while I looked at the *Bugle*. There was a map showing the location of the fairgrounds. It wasn't far from Kenlyn Farm.

We drove for fifteen minutes and passed the farm and then the Porters' house. "That's Gran's old house," I said, pointing as we went by the empty driveway.

Shortly after that, we turned into the fairgrounds, and a man directed us to a dirt parking lot, where people were emerging from cars with children and strollers. Teenagers leaned against the sides of pickup trucks.

At the edge of the lot, wildflowers had taken over, forming a thick border. I stopped to pick a bouquet of gold buttercups and yellow-and-white oxeye daisies. I plucked a sprig of Queen Anne's lace and watched a black swallowtail butterfly land on a branch of goldenrod. Then I stretched and took a deep breath. The air was mellow and sweet. "All right, I'm ready," I said, admiring my flowers as we followed the crowd to the entrance.

A sign noted the fair's activities, which included a donkey-and-mule show, a draft-horse obstacle course, an antique tractor pull, sheepdog demonstrations, an apple pie contest, and presentations with titles like Sharpening the European Scythe Blade and Introduction to Worm Composting.

The fair took up several acres, with tents, booths, vendors, and food and demonstration areas. There were lines for the rides, which included a Ferris wheel and something that spun its riders around in pods. Fathers balanced toddlers on their shoulders and elderly people sat on folding chairs. The aroma of wood-fired pizza and apple crisp hung in the air.

We walked toward booths where people were selling flowers and herbs. I picked up a pot of thyme and held it to my face. It smelled like chicken roasting in my mother's kitchen. I saw a pot of lemon verbena, and I took a leaf and rubbed it between my fingers. Now I was on the patio at Gran's house, sipping iced tea.

We ambled around, checking out the local goods—maple syrup, dog biscuits, hand-dyed yarn, pottery, and paintings. We bought a box of blueberries and ate them as we wandered. We watched women spin fleece into yarn and saw German shepherds demonstrate sheepherding.

"Let's go over there," I said, pointing to a large tent. People were milling around the entrance. A rooster crowed as we got closer.

Hayden smirked. "I thought we agreed, no chickens."

"Come on," I said, taking his hand. "Let's just see what's in there."

The smell of grain and animals hit me as soon as we entered. The first thing I saw was two dozen wooden-and-wire cages. Inside each one a chicken clucked and pecked and scratched around as viewers walked by and admired them.

"Oh, Hayden, look how pretty they are." I pointed to a black Jersey Giant and a blue Andalusian with a plumy tail. The Andalusian cocked his head and scratched at the floor of the cage.

"I guess they've got a certain kind of, um, charm," Hayden said with a cringe. "I think I'll see what else they have in here besides chickens." He strolled on ahead.

I moved to the next cage, where a Barred Plymouth Rock clucked away. Its black-and-white zigzag feathers made it look like an abstract painting. I bent down to get a closer look.

"Aren't you a pretty bird?" I got down to eye level. The chicken bobbed its head at me.

"Yes, you're so pretty."

"Ellen?"

I turned around. A man stood behind me, dressed in jeans and a faded red New England Patriots T-shirt. A Red Sox baseball cap was on his head, and a day's growth of beard was on his face. It was Roy.

For a second I thought all the blood was rushing to my feet. I managed to say hello.

The Plymouth Rock rooster chose that moment to crow, sending an earsplitting greeting through the tent.

Roy tipped back the brim of his cap. "Hello yourself. I thought you were leaving."

His eyes were too blue. Nothing could be that blue. "I was supposed to leave today," I said. "But I had to see someone yesterday and now there's been a little change in plans."

"In that case, I see you're using your time wisely." He smiled.

"Looking at roosters and picking..." Roy took my hand and opened it. I had forgotten I was still holding the flowers.

"Hmm," he said. "Buttercup, Queen Anne's lace." When he let go, my hand felt empty. I could barely speak.

A little girl, maybe four, approached one of the rooster's cages with her father.

"Don't get too close," he said. "It might be dangerous."

Roy looked at me, cocked his head, and scratched his chin. "You're wearing jeans. I knew there was something different."

I couldn't tell whether he approved or not. "It's my weekend look."

"Suits you," he said. "You can really fit in at the Antler now." He smiled.

The Andalusian hen, with her fancy tail, preened her feathers and bobbed her head toward the adjoining cage, as though she were trying to get the attention of the rooster next to her.

"What's that one doing, Daddy?" the little girl asked, pointing to the hen. "Why is it dancing?"

The dad wrinkled his brow. "I don't know, honey. Maybe they're trying to have a conversation."

The girl giggled and they strolled away.

"All right, I've seen every damned chicken —"

It was Hayden walking toward us. He stopped when he saw Roy.

I let the flowers fall from my hand. "Hayden," I said, adding an extra bright note to my voice. "This is Roy Cummings. Remember, I told you about him — Chet Cummings's nephew?" I turned to Roy. "This is my fiancé, Hayden Croft." My throat felt dry as I watched them shake hands. I thought I saw something change in Roy's face. Maybe his jaw tightened, just a little.

"Hayden surprised me last night," I said. "He showed up at the Victory Inn, where I'm staying."

The Plymouth Rock rooster began strutting around, looking a bit agitated, ruffling its black-and-white feathers and clucking.

Roy put his hands in the pockets of his jeans. "That's great. You came from where? Manhattan?"

Hayden nodded. "Yes, I settled a case yesterday and I thought, Why don't I just fly up and celebrate? So I did." He paused and then added, "Ellen tells me you're from Beacon."

"That's right," Roy said, nodding. "I grew up here."

"Seems like a nice place," Hayden said. "Pretty quiet, though. What do people do for R-and-R? Any golf courses around?"

Roy studied Hayden, from his Top-Siders to his cantaloupe-colored polo shirt. "Oh, you're a golfer?"

Hayden nodded. "Yeah, but not often enough. Are you?"

"No. Never really got interested in it," Roy said. "There are plenty of other things to do here, though. In the winter you can cross-country ski or snowshoe or go ice skating. Drive a skimobile." He paused, and we stepped back from the chickens as a group of teenagers passed through.

"In the summer," he went on, "people fish. A lot of folks have motorboats, or they go sailing. Some people like to swim." He glanced at me.

"Yes, Ellen told me she's been doing some swimming," Hayden said.

I shot Roy a warning glance. "Hayden was glad I was able to get some exercise."

"I didn't think you'd ever go in such cold water," Hayden said.

Roy tipped his cap back. "But if you were on the Exeter swim team and you made it to the nationals, I would think..."

"That was a long time ago," I said, glaring at Roy. I saw him stifle a smile.

He leaned against a display table. "So how long are you staying?"

"Just a few days," Hayden said, putting his arm around me and pulling me closer. "I thought I'd better come up here, since I can't seem to get Ellen to leave."

I forced a smile.

Roy cocked his head and stared at me. "Is Beacon growing on you, Ellen? That happens to people, you know. Sometimes they come and they never leave."

"I just need to stay a couple of extra days," I said. "Tie up some loose ends in connection with my grandmother."

Hayden squeezed my shoulder. "I'm not too worried about Ellen overstaying her welcome here. She's a city girl if I ever saw one. I don't think she'd survive in a town this small. She's used to moving way too fast... she doesn't have the patience."

I wasn't sure how I felt about Hayden's remark. Yes, I'd lived in the city for years and no, I didn't have any desire to live somewhere else. But did that mean I *couldn't* do it if I really wanted to? He made it sound as though I were incapable of change.

Roy shrugged. "Sometimes people don't realize they can slow down until they do it." He looked from Hayden to me. "I think Ellen could probably live and be successful anywhere, including Beacon."

"Well, thanks for that vote of confidence," I said, trying to laugh and make light of Roy's comment. There was a strange undercurrent in the conversation, like voltage barely registering on a gauge, and it was making me feel uncomfortable.

Hayden's hand stiffened against my shoulder. "I didn't mean she couldn't do it," he said. "I just don't think she'd be as happy living outside of an urban area." He turned to me. "Right, honey?"

What was going on here? I felt like I was in the middle of a tug-of-war. "I don't know," I said, Hayden's arm suddenly feeling heavy on my shoulder. "I live there now and I'm happy, but I think I could be flexible."

"Well, there you go," Roy said, smiling. His dimples were showing again.

"We're leaving in a few days," Hayden said in a tone that indicated he was through discussing this topic.

I slid out from under his arm. "Well, I think we ought to get going, Hayden, don't you?" I took his hand so I could guide him away. "Maybe the Porters will be home and we can stop by." I turned to Roy. "I found the house where my grandmother grew up and I want to show Hayden. So I think we'll—"

"Oh, that's great that you found her house," Roy said. "Where is it?"

"On Comstock Drive."

Roy nodded. "Near Kenlyn Farm."

"Yes, right by there," I said. "We passed that on the way here. Somebody told me it used to be a blueberry farm."

"Yeah, it was," Roy said. "A long time ago."

"Looks like it's just gone to ruin now," Hayden said. "Too bad. It's a huge piece of undeveloped property. I'm surprised somebody hasn't come in and built something there. Houses or condos." He grinned at me. "Maybe a golf course?"

"Hayden's got golf on the brain," I said, smiling, as a crowd of children entered the tent, escorted by two young women who were instructing them to stay with the group.

"Why does it need to be developed?" Roy asked, a little edge to his voice. "Why does everything have to be turned into houses or condos or...a golf course? Why can't some things just be left alone?"

The black Jersey Giant rooster, with its bright red comb, began pecking anxiously at the floor of his cage.

"Well, I was only kidding about the golf course," Hayden said, glancing at me. "Ellen can tell you I'm always—"

"I can't count the number of stories I know about nice towns that got ruined by overdevelopment," Roy said, shaking his head. "People come up north from the city, developers wanting to make money...you know. They find a place like Beacon and they think it's nice because it's pretty and it's quiet. So they build a bunch of houses or condos." He looked toward the black rooster but I could tell he was seeing something else.

"Yeah, then they put in a golf course and a country club," Roy went on. "A big marina and a bunch of restaurants. And pretty soon they've got the Gap and Victoria's Secret and Bed, Bath and Beyond right there on their doorstep. And then they wonder why it's not pretty anymore and it's not quiet." He looked at me. "And then they move on to some other place while the people who have lived there all along are stuck with a town they don't even know anymore."

The black Jersey Giant rooster shook its wings and let out the loudest screech I'd ever heard. I jumped. "That thing's got quite a voice," I said with a nervous laugh.

"Yeah, he does," Roy said, his mouth a thin, straight line, like a dash between his ears.

I rubbed my arms to get rid of the goose bumps that had appeared. "Let's hope Beacon never ends up with a mall and chain stores. That would be horrible."

Roy glanced around the tent. "Yeah, well…we'll see." When he turned back to us, the blue of his eyes had vanished into slate. "It may already be happening." His voice was flat, cold, like something buried deep underground. "Kenlyn Farm is being subdivided into a million pieces and they're all being sold. So your idea about developing it"—he looked at Hayden—"it's already happening. Maybe the golf course will be next."

Neither Hayden nor I said a word. And before I could think of an appropriate response, Roy tipped the brim of his baseball cap, muttered, "See you," turned, and was gone.

Hayden and I looked at one another.

"What was that all about?" he said.

I grimaced. "Not sure. He didn't seem too happy about the idea of that farm becoming a golf course."

Hayden shook his head, confused. "What did I say? I wasn't trying to insult the man."

"I know, Hayden. Let's just forget it."

"And what was that lecture about developers?" Hayden began walking toward the entrance to the tent. "Let's just get out of here."

I followed him through the fairgrounds, his pace steadily quickening as we wove around blueberry vendors and rides, passed the HOMEGROWN FROM MAINE displays, and veered through the arts and crafts area toward the exit.

"Wait up," I called when he got too far ahead.

"Come on," he yelled back. "Let's get out of this hayseed place." Then he turned to look at me and tripped over a stack of lobster pots artfully arranged as a display. He went sprawling to the ground, landing on his stomach, arms and legs splayed.

"Hayden!" I ran and crouched down beside him.

His eyes were closed in a grimace. A few people stopped and stared, and an old man sprang out of a nearby booth to see what happened.

"My ankle," Hayden moaned.

"What's wrong?"

"I don't know, but it hurts like hell. Why'd they leave those stupid cages in the middle of the street, anyway?" He tried to raise himself to a sitting position.

"Do you want some help?" I offered my hand.

He waved me off. "No, I can do it," he said brusquely. Gradually he sat up. Then he clutched his ankle and took several deep breaths.

"Maybe I should get some help," I said.

"No, let's just go." Leaning on me, he slowly stood up and dusted himself off.

"Are you going to be okay?" I asked as he limped toward the parking lot, using my shoulder as a crutch.

"No, I'm not going to be okay. I think I sprained the damned thing. I told you I didn't want to see any chickens."

They were mostly roosters, I thought. But I wasn't about to correct him.

Chapter 13

Never Make an Enemy
of the Media

Hayden didn't say another word until we got back to the car. "You'd better drive," he said, hoisting himself into the passenger seat and pulling his injured leg in after him as though it were a package he was bringing along for the ride. He shoved his seat belt into the holder with a loud snap.

I backed out of the parking space and headed down a row of cars toward the exit. "Sorry the fair turned out...um...you know. Sorry about your ankle."

Hayden moaned as he wiggled off his shoe. His ankle had swollen to the size of a grapefruit. "Oh, God, look at that." He winced.

"You're going to need some ice," I said, turning out of the parking lot and onto the road. "I'll stop at the first place I see."

He flipped down the visor to block the sun. "I can't believe I tripped over those damned cages."

I bit my lip so I wouldn't laugh, but I couldn't entirely suppress the smile.

"What? What?"

"They were lobster traps."

He waved me off. "Yeah, I know. That's what I meant."

I turned by a sign that read SCENIC ROUTE, realizing too late that I might not have gone this way before. I followed a road that meandered through a little shingled town and a harbor where people were packing coolers into motorboats and hoisting sails on sloops. We drove by an inlet where weathered houses stood watch on a hillside and small children in swimsuits carried silvery galvanized pails full of things I could only imagine. Minnows flickering in ocean water. Sand. Shells.

Hayden craned his neck and looked around. "Do you know where you're going? This isn't the way we came. Maybe you should turn on the GPS."

I had no idea where we were. "Of course I know where I'm going," I said, looking for something familiar. We needed ice and a quick route back to the inn, and I didn't need Hayden any more stirred up than he already was. At the edge of the water I spotted a restaurant with an outdoor patio and umbrellas over the tables. "I'll run in there and get some ice."

"I could use some food," Hayden said. "I'll come with you."

He hobbled along beside me to the patio, where a dozen tables were covered with plastic red-and-white checkered cloths. A woman in a T-shirt directed us to a vacant table. We ordered drinks and I asked for a bag of ice, while Hayden put his leg up on an empty chair.

The menus included a number of lobster-related items that looked appealing, but when I thought about the cause of Hayden's injury I dropped the idea.

"I'm having the fried clams," I told him, closing the menu. "And a house salad."

Hayden squinted at me. "Fried clams? *Fried?*"

"Just this once. They taste good and I don't eat them every day, so it's not going to kill me." I took his hand and squeezed it. "Come on, we'll get some ice for your ankle, you'll be fine."

"I guess," he said with a resigned shake of his head. The waitress returned with two iced teas and a bag of ice, which Hayden immediately draped across his ankle. Then he ordered my clams and, for himself, a grouper sandwich. "But could you please make sure they broil it?" he asked.

After the waitress left, we sat and watched boaters walking up and down the pier with fishing poles and tackle boxes. I sank farther into my seat, closing my eyes, feeling the sun on my shoulders.

"I wanted to wait for the right time to tell you this," Hayden said.

I opened my eyes. "Tell me what?" I couldn't predict if this was going to be good news or bad news. He wasn't smiling, but he didn't look alarmed, either.

He adjusted his position in the chair. "At the Men of Note dinner, one of the people I met was the editor of the *New York Times* Styles section."

"Really?" This didn't sound like bad news. I took a sip of iced tea and reached for a pack of sugar.

"Yes, Tom Frasier. He wants to do a story about our wedding."

"Oh," I said as I began to stir in the sugar. "One of those 'how they met' pieces?" I could handle that. They would probably just do a quick phone interview with us and publish something light-hearted.

Hayden adjusted the bag of ice. "Well, actually, it's a little more complicated than that. They want to do a feature article about us and the wedding. With photos...you know, the whole thing."

Feature article...photos. This was sounding like a bigger deal. I felt a twinge in my chest. "What do you mean, a feature article? What do they want to write about? Did he say?"

"All kinds of things. Who made your dress? Where are you getting your hair done? What color nail polish are you wearing? I don't know."

"Nail polish? I don't even know myself," I said.

"Well, they probably won't ask you that, Ellen. I'm just saying ..."

His voice faded into the background as I put down my spoon. This new information was descending upon me like something cold and dank. Sure, I'd been in the newspaper before. An Internet search would reveal dozens of things about me, like the articles in the *Times* itself on the Sullivan project and the *Wall Street Journal* pieces about the Cleary Building and the Battery Park deal, not to mention a few radio interviews and magazine mentions. But that was different. That was work-related. This was personal. I didn't want my personal life invaded by the media.

I watched a group of tan college-age boys get into a Boston Whaler with a cooler and fishing gear, part of me longing to take off with them and never come back.

Hayden put his hand over mine. "It will be fine, honey," he said. "And the more you do this kind of thing, the more you get used to it."

Somehow, that didn't make me feel any better.

"How does this work?" I said. "Do they meet with us in person? Together? Separately?" I hoped they weren't going to ask me any tricky questions, try to make me say something foolish or something that would embarrass Hayden or his family. "They'll meet with us together, right?"

"Don't look so worried. I'm sure we can do it together."

I took a big gulp of iced tea. "And what about the photos? Where do they take those?"

"Well, they'll definitely be taking photos in the church," he said. "And they'll be at the Metropolitan Club for the reception."

The wedding and the reception. They were covering both. I reached for another sugar packet.

"And...well, there's something else," Hayden said.

I emptied the packet into my glass. "Yes?"

"They're interested in our family backgrounds. Mine because...well, the political connections. And yours because your father was such a financial guru and all..."

My skin was starting to feel prickly.

"Anyway, Tom Frasier called me early this morning, when you were asleep, and when I told him where we were and what you were doing up here, he got kind of excited about it. He said he might want to include it as an angle for a sidebar. You know, girl with small-town roots marries into big political family."

A sidebar? My family was becoming a sidebar?

"Hayden, I don't want to be a sidebar. I don't want any of this."

Hayden gazed into my eyes and ran his hand along my cheek. "Look, sweetie, I knew you might be a little concerned, and I want you to know that I thought this through very carefully. I analyzed it from every possible angle, I promise you. And no matter which way I looked at it, I came out with the same result—we should do it."

"But—" I raised my hand.

"Just hear me out. Please." He leaned in a little closer, his eyes focused, his tone of voice the one I'd heard him use in court, steady and convincing. "First of all," he said, raising an index finger as though he were ticking off numbers. "My father's always telling me you should never make an enemy of the media. And he's right. We don't want to get them mad. They never forget." He raised another finger. "Second of all, we can use this to our advantage. It won't hurt either of our professional lives to have a little extra media coverage and let people get to know us better, will it?"

He didn't wait for me to respond. "We'll just make sure we get in the points *we* want to make," he said, "no matter what they ask." I imagined that might be harder than it sounded, but I knew it was useless to interrupt him. "And third," he went on, raising a final finger, "it could also help my run for city council next year. Just one more way to get my name and face out there." He looked at me, waiting for me to concur.

My foot twitched under the table. "Hayden, I'm really not comfortable with this. You've come up with all these rationales for why we should do it, but they don't make me feel any better. This is our *wedding*."

He looked away, his eyes fixed on something across the patio. "I can't tell them no, Ellen. The *Times* is already calling our wedding the social event of the season. There are places to draw the line in the sand, but this isn't one of them. And anyway, we're inviting over three hundred people. A couple of photographers will barely be noticed."

The social event of the season? I began to bite my nails. "I feel like our wedding is turning into *Entertainment Tonight.*"

He shook his head. "No, it's not, honey. I'd never let that happen."

The waitress returned and placed two straw baskets on the table with our meals in them. I glanced at the fried clams, but I didn't feel hungry anymore.

Hayden removed the bun on the top of his grouper sandwich and inspected the fish.

I pushed the clams to the side and stared at the harbor. A lobster boat chugged toward the dock.

Hayden touched my chin, turned my face toward him, and kissed me. I couldn't feel anything but panic. I knew I wasn't going to be able to dissuade him and I would be stuck with this plan he'd agreed to. I kept thinking, What have I gotten myself into? What am I doing? And then all of a sudden I stopped. What I'd gotten myself into was exactly what I should have expected all along, and I knew it. I was marrying Hayden Croft, and that came with certain responsibilities. I'd told myself in the beginning of our relationship that I would have to deal with this kind of thing when the time came. Well, the time had come.

"Hayden," I said, forcing a smile, "I'll do this. I can deal with it and I'll be fine." I clasped my hands and hoped I sounded convincing. "And you're right—the more I deal with these things, the more I'll get used to it. I'm a little out of my element up here, but I know once we get back to New York and I put my business head on again I'll click right in and in a couple of weeks I'll be ready for anything. You can throw the whole New York press corps at me and I'll be fine."

Hayden looked down at his grouper sandwich and then back at me, his forehead scrunched up. "Well, here's the thing…"

Uh-oh; this time it *did* look like bad news.

"They're coming here in two days."

I felt the burn of a headache igniting right behind my eyes. I slid to the edge of my chair. "Who's coming? And what do you mean, *here?*"

"The *Times*. They're sending a reporter and a photographer to Beacon."

"Oh, my God!" I stood up, knocking a spoon off the table. It hit the cement patio with a clang. "Why here? Why two days?" I clutched the tablecloth. "I'm not ready for this." I touched my hair. It felt dry and brittle. I looked at my fingernails, the pink polish chipped, the nails bitten and broken.

Hayden grabbed my hand and pulled me back toward him. "You know," he said, "besides keeping the press happy, there might be another benefit from the media exposure."

I looked at him.

"This down-home, small-town thing might be good for us. It could show another side of two hard-boiled Manhattan attorneys." He took a fried clam and ate it. "Peace offering?"

I tried to smile. I could hear the lobster boat as it chugged closer. My head throbbed. I picked up the spoon that had dropped, and when I looked at my reflection in its curved surface I noticed that my face was upside down.

*   *   *

"You should never have let me eat that clam," Hayden groaned as he limped through the door of the inn, clutching his stomach.

"Let's just get upstairs," I said.

Paula stared at Hayden. "What happened to you?"

He frowned. "Lobster traps."

"Oh, my word. You got your leg caught in a lobster trap? Were you trying to poach them? That's illegal, you know."

Hayden's face went red. "I'm a law-abiding citizen," he said. "And besides, I wouldn't even know how to poach a lobster."

Paula half closed one eye, as though she were considering this. Then she nodded at me. "You had a telephone call." She held out a white slip of paper. "A gentleman." She glanced at Hayden.

The paper had a pen-and-ink drawing of the Victory Inn at the top. Hayden shuffled toward me, reading the message over my shoulder.

2:15
Ellen Branford —
Roy called. Says he's sorry.

"Okay, thanks," I said, trying to sound uninterested as I looked at Roy's name written in Paula's small, cramped handwriting.

"Let me see that." Hayden pulled the paper from my hand. "At least he had the sense to apologize — to you, anyway." He looked at me with a little smirk.

We ascended the stairs like mountain climbers, one slow and

deliberate step at a time, Hayden making full use of the banister and my shoulder. I unlocked the door and he shuffled straight to the bed, propping his ankle up with a pillow.

"Do you think it looks worse?" he asked. "I do."

I couldn't really tell. "I think it looks a little better," I said. Hayden was a bit of a hypochondriac. It was best to err on the positive side.

"Well, it feels worse," he said. "I could really use some more ice."

"I'll find some," I told him as I dumped the watery remains from the plastic bag into the bathroom sink.

"It really hurts, you know," he told me as I put my hand on the doorknob. "And my stomach is killing me. Really bad pains. From that clam. I know it."

"Do you want me to get you a doctor?"

He shook his head. "No, no. I'll be all right."

I walked downstairs, trying to figure out why men were so confusing. It really hurts, but don't get me a doctor. I've got terrible pains, but I don't need any help. It was more fun to complain, I figured.

One of the maids filled the plastic bag with ice. When I returned, Hayden had both pillows under his leg. I placed the bag of ice around his ankle.

"Oh, that's great," he said with a sigh. "Thanks, honey." I was about to sit down next to him when he added, "I was just wondering..."

"Yes?"

"If maybe an Ace bandage would help, and a bottle of Pepto-Bismol for my stomach."

An Ace bandage. Pepto-Bismol. I glanced around the room, as though they might pop up out of nowhere. "Okay, I'll go to the pharmacy downtown."

"Ellen, you're the best." He patted my hand. As I got up again he added, "Could you please pick up some Alka-Seltzer, too? I might need that."

I gazed at him, lying there. He looked so pathetic, so uncomfortable, the bag of ice melting around his puffed-up ankle. "It's all right," I said. "I just want you to get better."

Chapter 14

Kenlyn Farm

I plodded down the three flights of stairs, my mind heavy with worries about the invasion of the press in two days. I got into the car and sat for a minute, staring at the fine coating of salt on the windows. Then I drove toward town and found an empty parking space in front of a shop called the Wine Cellar. The sign was pretty—a burgundy wine bottle under an arch of purple grapes. Opening the door to the shop, I stepped inside a cozy room filled with old mahogany wine racks. Hundreds of bottles sparkled under tiny lights set in the ceiling. I spotted a sign for French wines and walked toward it with no expectations. To my surprise, I found several good Bordeaux selections, including a Château Beychevelle 2000 Saint-Julien. I picked up the bottle, the familiar single-masted ship on the label like an old friend.

On the far wall of the store was a long oaken counter with a varnish job that would have put a bowling alley to shame. Behind the counter, a man with a round, sunburned face was reading a boating magazine.

I walked over and placed the bottle on the counter. "I'll also need a corkscrew, please."

"That's a nice Saint-Julien," the man said, looking at the label. "Have you tried it?"

I told him I had.

"Yes...very nice." He grabbed a plastic corkscrew and a paper bag. "I love that nose of licorice and black currant."

I pulled a fistful of twenties from the bottom of my purse and set them on the counter. "Yes," I said. "So do I."

"I don't sell too much of that," he said, putting the bottle and corkscrew in the bag. "We do get the occasional tourist who buys it, and there's a fellow in town who orders a couple of cases every now and then." He passed the bag to me.

Must be a good customer, I thought, knowing the wine was pricey. I thanked him and walked toward the door.

"Miss? Uh, miss?" The man called to me and I turned. He waved something in the air. "Is this yours?"

I walked back and saw that he was holding the phone message Paula had given me. The one from Roy.

"It was stuck to your money," he said.

I looked at Paula's scrunched-up writing:

2:15
Ellen Branford—
Roy called. Says he's sorry.

I thanked him and left.

Outside in the sunlight I looked at the note again and wondered what Roy was apologizing about. Leaving so abruptly? The lecture on developers and their supposed effects on small towns? I did think he was being overly sensitive about any changes happening in Beacon. Why Roy got his nose out of joint in the first place was beyond me. Hayden was only joking about that golf course idea. I had tried to tell him that.

I got into the car and headed away from town, ignoring the turn onto Prescott Lane, which would have taken me back to the inn. I headed toward Dorset Lane and Roy's house, telling myself I was just going there to let him know I'd gotten his message and that I wasn't upset with him.

Halfway down the street I saw the Audi sitting in the middle of Roy's driveway like a green light at an intersection. I pulled my car in behind it, walked up to the front porch, and rang the doorbell three times. Nothing.

I drove back to town, past the shops and along the beach, to the place where the new house was being built. There, parked in the dirt area in front, sat Roy's blue pickup, the late afternoon sunlight glinting off its hood.

Walking around to the back of the house, I expected to see the door open, to hear the whir of a saw or the ping of a hammer, to see Roy with a tool belt slung around his hips. But the house was quiet, and then I remembered it was Sunday.

As I looked toward the ocean, I saw someone standing on the rocks, throwing stones into the surf. Although his back was to me, I could see it was Roy. I called his name, but he didn't hear. I walked toward him, the surf crashing, salt spray hanging in the air, and called to him again.

He wheeled around, a couple of stones falling from his hand. "Ellen. What are you doing here?" His hair looked wiry and windblown, his face sunburned, like he had spent an afternoon on a boat. His eyes looked tired or maybe mad. I couldn't tell.

Oh, no, I thought. This is a bad idea. I stuffed my hands in my pockets. "I got your message." A wave broke over the rocks, and I stepped back to avoid the spray.

He held a gray stone in his hand and rubbed it between his fingers. "Yeah, okay. I'm glad you got it," he said, hurling the rock into the ocean.

A valley of silence slid between us. "I didn't have your number," I told him. "And I wanted to let you know I'd gotten it. The message, I mean. Thanks for the apology." I picked up a blue mussel shell from a pile at my feet. It was dark and smooth. As the waves whirled toward the rocks, I thought about the feel of Roy's arms around me and the determined look in his eyes the day I fell through the dock.

"Yeah, well, okay," he said, tossing another stone. It flew far out, made a graceful arc, glistened for a moment in the sun, and then disappeared.

"I drove by the house," I went on, "but you weren't there." I shivered as the wind blew through my shirt.

"I called," Roy said, "because I wanted to tell you I was sorry. I know I walked off in a huff."

"Yeah, we couldn't figure out what happened."

"I just got a little upset…about what your fiancé was saying."

I shivered again and rubbed my arms. "He didn't mean anything."

"Is he a developer? Is he some kind of wheeler-dealer?"

"Hayden?" I started to laugh. "Wheeler-dealer?" I thought about his work as a litigator, his charity involvement, the run he would soon make for city council, the *New York Times* reporter and photographer who would be here in a couple of days. He was a wheeler-dealer, all right. "He's an attorney."

"Same thing, isn't it?"

I sighed.

A seagull veered overhead, banked, circled, and flew off. Roy turned to me. "I want to show you something. Do you have a couple of minutes?"

I looked at my watch. It was five fifteen. Hayden would be waiting for me, waiting for the ankle bandage and the Pepto-Bismol and the Alka-Seltzer. I needed to get back.

Roy's keys dangled in his hand, sunlight flickering off the metal.

"Yeah," I said. "I do have a couple of minutes."

We drove down roads now familiar to me, Roy shifting the truck and fooling with the radio, trying to tune in a station. We came to the stone wall I'd driven past three days before and drove on, the road running parallel to it. The sun was a yellow haze on the horizon, beginning its late afternoon descent. Finally the wall opened up, just enough to allow the intrusion of a dirt path, and we turned in.

"This is Kenlyn Farm," Roy said, the truck rattling over a patch of bumpy ground.

"Yes, I've passed this several times," I told him.

"My grandparents used to own this land."

"They owned this?" I said, taking my first glimpse of what the wall had hidden from view.

Acres of wildflowers and tall grasses grew unimpeded. I hung my head out the window, gazing at the black-eyed Susans, butter-cups, Queen Anne's lace, purple lupine, and goldenrod running riot up and down the hills. I suddenly understood a lot more about Roy and why he'd been so sensitive about this place.

"It's been out of the family for a long time," he said.

"It's beautiful," I whispered, afraid I might break the spell. "Is it all right that we're in here?"

He shrugged, ignoring the question. "I'll show you the best view. It's at the top of that slope there."

He pointed to an incline ahead of us, and we drove toward it, stems and branches crunching and crackling under the truck's wheels, rustling beneath the metal frame. He stopped a few yards from the wall and stepped out of the truck.

Then he came around and opened my door. "Be careful." He took my hand and helped me down. The wildflowers were dense and high, almost to my knees, and from them came the steady hum of grasshoppers, crickets, and bees.

"Is it true that this all used to be blueberries?" I asked, turning around to take in the view from every direction.

"Yeah, it was once all blueberries," Roy said.

We walked to the stone wall, which stood about three feet high at its tallest point. Much of the wall was lower, due to the ef-fects of time and weather and obvious indifference on the part of its owners. Rocks and boulders had scattered to the ground as though they had jumped overboard to freedom.

Roy found a foothold and climbed up. Then he offered me his hand again, and I scrambled up and sat down on a large flat rock, swinging my legs over the wall next to his.

I gazed over the field, down the slope to a grove of pine trees at the bottom. "You're right about the view." I would have loved to photograph it in the late afternoon light.

Roy moved a few loose rocks from a pile on the top of the wall and placed them in some of the gaps around us.

"There's a poem about fixing a wall," I said.

He nodded. "Robert Frost. 'Mending Wall.'"

I picked up a loose rock. "'Something there is that doesn't love a wall.'"

Roy looked down the length of the wall, with its lichen-covered boulders and tufts of green weeds sprouting in gaps between the stones. "'That sends the frozen-ground-swell under it,'" he said. "'And spills the upper boulders in the sun, and makes gaps even two can pass abreast.'"

I sat there with my mouth open. "Do you know the whole thing?"

He smiled sheepishly. "Used to. Memorized it once for school. Could probably dredge it all up if I had to."

"Impressive," I said. A bee buzzed lazily at my feet.

Roy stared across the field. "I thought maybe if you saw this you'd understand why I got upset this afternoon."

"Oh...you mean your lecture on developers?"

He nodded.

"I think I do understand. I know development can be a double-edged sword."

"Don't get me wrong," he said. "I'm not one of those crazy activists, those people who are against every new idea. I don't think all development is bad. But I've seen some bad things done in the name of progress and improvement."

He moved a little closer to me on the wall. I held my breath.

"And I come from a long line of stubborn Maine Cummings folks who felt the same way," he said.

"Really? How far back does your family go in Maine?"

"Five generations." He pointed to the sun, which had become a soft ball of putty on the horizon. "Pretty, isn't it?"

"Very."

"My people were all from Augusta," he said as he fit another stray rock into a small crevice between us. "That's the state capital," he added with a wink.

"Yes, I know that."

He stared at me again. "You've got nice eyes. A little green, a little blue. I can't really figure them out." He continued to look at me, leaning in closer.

"They're green-blue," I said, pulling back.

"I think I just said that." He smiled, letting his gaze rest on me a little too long.

I was beginning to feel uncomfortable. I couldn't let him make a pass at me. No, that would be horrible. But then why did I come here? Just to tell him I'd gotten his message? Or was I feeding my ego with his attention? "So your ancestors were from Augusta?" I asked, turning the subject back to his family.

Roy picked up a small stone from the top of the wall and pointed to a shiny pink streak down the middle. "Yeah, until my grandfather broke the mold and moved to Beacon."

"Why did he do that?"

"He met a woman from Beacon," Roy said, "and he fell in love."

The breeze ruffled the wildflowers below us. I could feel him staring at me again.

"The woman was my grandmother," Roy said, running his hand lightly along my arm.

I jumped down from the wall, ignoring the tingling feeling that was spreading inside me. "Well, he ended up in a beautiful place," I said, looking around. "Look at all these flowers." I tried to pick a tiny blue flower, but the stem was tough and wouldn't break.

Roy walked up beside me. "You can't do it like that." I could feel the warmth of his body next to mine. We were almost touching. "You've got to do it like this." He snapped the stem in his hand, his arm brushing against my side. Then he picked several more and handed the flowers to me, our fingers briefly touching.

The sun continued to drift toward the horizon as we walked along the wall, the insect sounds becoming softer.

"What happened then?" I asked. "To your grandparents."

"Oh…well, they bought this property. My grandfather wanted to start a blueberry farm."

I watched a grasshopper jump from a thicket of brush in front of us. "That sounds nice."

Roy nodded. "Yeah, this was a big area for blueberries way back when. You saw the statue in town?"

"The statue?"

"The woman with the pail of blueberries."

It sounded like the statue I was trying to photograph when I fell through the dock. "Yes, I think I know the one."

"Different, isn't it?" he said. "Most towns would have a statue of the founder, somebody like that. We have the blueberry lady."

"I thought she was holding a bucket of grapes."

Roy's eyebrows shot up. "Grapes? Don't ever admit that to

221

anybody else from Beacon. They'll ride you out of town on a rail."

I laughed.

He reached out and touched a spot above my right eye.

I flinched.

"You've got something on your face," he said, trying to brush it off.

"It's a freckle. It won't move."

He leaned in. "Oh, yes, I can see that now."

I started walking again. "So then what happened?"

"What happened? Oh, with the farm? Well, my grandfather learned everything there was to know about blueberries. Then he figured out what kinds of blueberry plants would be best for this piece of land."

"I didn't know there was more than one type."

Roy looked surprised. "Of course there's more than one."

"Interesting," I said. I wondered how they grew. Somehow I pictured them on vines, in thick clusters, growing over trellises. "They grow on vines, right?"

He scowled and brushed an insect off his shirt. "Vines? Blueberries? They grow on bushes."

"Oh, yeah, bushes. Of course."

He picked a black-eyed Susan and handed it to me. "This is nice, Ellen," he said. "I like it."

"Yes, it's pretty." I twirled the stem between my fingers.

"I wasn't talking about the flower."

I gave a nervous laugh and felt the heat rise in my face. I had to get him back to the story. "So then what happened?"

Roy smiled. "I think my grandfather could have grown anything from alfalfa to artichokes. That's what Uncle Chet always said. He knew what worked and what didn't. What made stronger plants, bigger berries, that kind of thing."

"Sounds like he found his calling," I said.

"Yeah, I guess it was his calling." He brushed a piece of hair off my forehead. "There," he said. "That was in your eyes, and your eyes are too pretty not to be seen."

I looked down at my bouquet so he wouldn't see me blush. "So they had the farm."

"Yeah, they had a good business. They sold to grocery stores, restaurants, hotels, that kind of thing. And my grandmother had a blueberry stand."

I thought about all the blueberry stands I'd seen so far in Maine. "And they did well?"

"Yes, they did all right. Then my grandmother had Uncle Chet. From the time he could walk he was out here running around in the bushes, pulling off the berries, and eating them. He used to tell me he always had purple stains on his clothes. He had all of my grandfather's talent. Maybe even more. He loved this place."

Roy stopped at a spot where several boulders had fallen from the wall into the field. He picked them up and hauled them back in place. "There," he said, wiping the dirt off his hands.

I pictured a boy in overalls running through the rows of blueberry bushes under a warm summer sun. "It sounds lovely."

"I'm sure it was." Roy paused. "But nothing lasts forever." He looked away, toward a robin that landed on the wall and was fluffing its wings. "My grandparents eventually sold it. They just got too old to keep it up."

We came to a corner of the farm where a group of oak trees clustered together and one huge oak stood off by itself, like someone at a cocktail party who didn't want to join the group.

"Didn't they have your uncle to help them? If he loved it so much..."

Roy walked toward the lone oak and leaned against its trunk. "No, he left Beacon when he was twenty and he didn't come back for years." He looked up at the canopy of branches and leaves suspended above us like a sculpture. "Something happened—he never wanted to talk about it, but the farm only made him sad."

I let my gaze drift from the stone wall at the top of the field, across the meadow, and down toward the pine trees at the very bottom. "I can't believe he didn't miss it, though."

A spot of sunlight flickered through the trees and landed on Roy's shoulder. "Oh, I think he did," Roy said. "In fact, I never heard it from him, but other people told me it was really hard for him to come back and see the farm in somebody else's hands. Live in this town and have to drive by it all the time."

"So why did he come back?" I said.

The patch of sunlight slid across Roy's face. "I guess because it was still his home."

I thought about that. I wondered if you could ever really get your true home out of your system. Probably not.

"Who owns the land now?" I asked him.

"Some guy from Boston bought it a few years ago, but he died and his kids inherited it. They don't live around here. They want to sell it, but they want to subdivide it first. You know, slice and dice."

Slice and dice. Yes, I did know. I had done that very thing

for more than one client, and I'd never given it any thought other than what price per acre it would ultimately yield. I never thought about what the land had been or what it might have meant to the people who lived there.

"Could you buy it?" I asked.

Roy laughed. "Not really. Besides, what would I do with a hundred acres? I'm not a farmer."

"I don't know. I guess it was just wishful thinking. I was hoping you could get it back into your family. That way maybe you could do something with it one day when you got married. Or you could give it to your children." I plucked a stem of Queen Anne's lace and added it to my bouquet.

"Yeah, well, I doubt I'll be getting married any time soon."

"No? A nice, good-looking, gainfully employed man like yourself? I would think you'd be in demand."

Roy stopped and gazed down the hill. "The right girl's not in my life." He shook his head. "Gotta have the right girl to get married."

I wondered if he'd ever been married. He stopped and I watched in awe as he gently removed a ladybug from his sleeve and deposited it on a stem of purple lupine.

"Came close to being married once," he said, as though he were reading my mind. "But I waited too long. She ended up with another guy. They have a couple of kids, last I heard."

"How long ago was that?"

He thought for a moment. "Oh, about six years."

"And nobody since?"

"Nobody serious," he said as he picked up a fallen rock and placed it back in the wall. "If I ever get lucky enough to find the right girl, I'm not going to mess it up again. I'm not going to let her go."

I smiled. "What are you going to do? Put her in handcuffs?"

"I don't know," he said. "Probably not handcuffs." He scratched the back of his neck and half closed his eyes. Then he smiled. "Maybe I'll build her something. Maybe I'll build her a palace."

"A palace...now, there's a thought. Like the emperor who built the Taj Mahal for his wife. How romantic is that?"

"But didn't she die in childbirth?" he asked. "Isn't that why he built it?"

He was right. That probably wasn't the best example. "I think she did die in childbirth," I said. "But putting that aside, what woman wouldn't want a palace?"

"I guess I'll find out someday."

We stood in silence for a moment and then Roy said, "I'd better get you back."

We walked to the truck, and I turned around to take one last look at the view. "Well," I said, "if you can't buy it, you're not going to be able to stop them from subdividing it."

Roy turned to me, his blue eyes quiet, resigned. "I can't stop them from subdividing it, Ellen."

We stood there for a moment as a hawk flew overhead, its wings barely moving, its body suspended like a whisper above us. Then Roy opened the passenger door.

"Hold on a second," I said as I noticed something near the truck's front wheel. Next to the tire track, where stalks of wildflowers lay crushed and matted, a cluster of purplish-blue caught my eye. I pushed back the flowers and pulled on a gnarled branch. It snapped, and I held a piece in my hand. On the branch were three tiny blueberries.

Everything around me seemed to stop—the insect hum, the breeze, the slow descent of the sun. I held up the branch, my hand trembling. "Look," I said. "They're still here."

He touched the tip of the branch. "Blueberries can be pretty hardy. They can survive for a long time in the right conditions." He smiled at me. "Kind of nice to know, isn't it? Some things keep going no matter what happens around them."

I thought about the woody stalk with its three bright berries living on after Chet, after Gran. I held onto it as I climbed into the truck. The sun cast threads of golden-red over the field. The insects had quieted, as if they, too, knew the end of the day was near. Roy started the engine, and we drove out of the farm and onto the main road, the cool evening air streaming through the open windows.

"You never really explained why you're still here in Beacon," he said.

We drove alongside the farm and then turned left at the intersection, heading back toward town. "Do you remember," I said, "how I told you I found the house where my grandmother grew up?"

Roy slowed down to let a squirrel dart across the road. "Yeah. You said it's on Comstock Drive."

"There's a painting in the attic of that house, done on plaster. The people who own the house found it when they were renovating, when they pulled off the drywall. My grandmother was the artist. It's really an amazing piece of work, and the painting is of her and your uncle."

Roy turned abruptly and stared at me. "My uncle? And your grandmother? She painted the two of them?"

I nodded. "Yes. They were teenagers, standing under an oak tree. It's kind of...almost mystical, I guess. And beautiful. Really lovely."

"I'd like to see it."

I wanted him to see it, although I wasn't sure how I'd be able to work that out. I told him about the painting at the Beacon Historical Society and the *Bugle* article in the library, and the camera shop, and my meeting with Lila Falk.

"Wow," Roy said as the road meandered up a hill and around a bend. "You've been busy. And all the stuff you found out—you didn't know about any of it?" His voice was so animated. It made me feel even more excited.

"No, we didn't know any of it," I said. "And I keep finding out more and more. That's why I've stayed. We never knew Gran was an artist or that she went to art school. And her paintings are so good." I looked out the window and watched the woods, thick with pine trees, slide past. "I just wish she hadn't kept it a secret."

Roy downshifted and turned a corner. "Maybe she sent you up here to uncover the secret. Maybe that was part of her plan."

Could that have been part of the plan? Could she have wanted me, expected me, to uncover all of this? I wanted to believe it, but it didn't seem likely. "How could she have known I'd find her painting in the Porters' attic?" I said. "It was buried under plaster until recently. Or that I'd end up at the camera shop and then meet Lila Falk?"

Roy slowed the truck as we headed toward a stop sign. "Well, maybe she didn't know exactly *how* you'd find out, but she might have figured if you came up here you'd find something." Roy looked over and smiled. "And you did. You found a legacy that might have been lost forever if you hadn't come."

Maybe he was right. Maybe, along with delivering the letter, she was hoping I'd uncover her past.

"I guess you could be right," I said.

We drove on without a word, the only sound the hum of Roy's tires against the road. Then he turned onto Paget Street, and the ocean and the buildings of downtown Beacon came into view. When we got to the construction site, he pulled up next to my car, walked around, and opened his door for me.

"Thanks for showing me the farm," I said, stepping down from the truck.

He stood by the hood. "Thanks for finding the blueberries." He put his hands in his pockets, and I could see the slight suggestion of a smile on his face, accompanied by the tiniest of wrinkles near his eyes.

"What?" I asked. The way he was looking at me made me nervous. "What is it?" I clutched the bouquet of flowers and the blueberry branch.

He took a step closer. "Why did you come here today, Ellen?"

The question was a lot more difficult than it sounded. Why had I come? I still wasn't sure myself. Was it just to let him know I'd received the phone message? Or was there something more? Was I falling in love with him? Is that what was happening? I wanted to look away, but I felt trapped.

"What do you mean?" I said. I could hear the nervous tremble in my voice.

"I just mean what made you come here?" He moved in even closer. I could almost feel him without touching him.

"I told you. I felt bad about what happened this morning and..." I began to gesture, my fingers twitching like marionette hands. "I knew you were upset and when you called I figured it would be good if...I mean, I thought maybe I should...that..." I looked away. Oh, God, what was I *saying?* I wasn't making sense.

Roy cocked his head, the smile still on his lips. He stared at me, almost as though he knew that if he looked at me long enough he might get me to do something crazy, like throw my arms around him again or admit that I couldn't stop thinking about him. Another second or two and I would be totally under his spell. His eyes were so bright and so blue, like the waters of the Caribbean, clear and deep and full of bright yellow fish and purple ferns and red coral, and they were pulling me in, those eyes, and I was going under, ready to hold my breath and take the dive....

And then I heard his voice. "Yeah, okay," he said. "You wanted to make sure we were back to having a clean slate." He smiled and, with a little shrug, he added, "Okay, done."

Was that it? Was he letting me off the hook? But I didn't want to leave anymore. I wanted to stay there and float away in his eyes.

Roy opened my car door, and I slid into the driver's seat in a fog. I watched him get into his truck. I watched him shut the door. I watched while he started the engine and I heard the sputter of the motor. He put up his hand, a motionless wave. I put up my hand, and I could almost feel us touching.

*   *   *

I took the key with the braided ribbon from my handbag and unlocked the door to the room. I was shocked to see Paula and a
man wearing a white doctor's coat in the room. What was going
on? How long had I been gone?

Hayden was still lying on the bed, but the man in the white
coat, who reminded me of my twelfth-grade physics teacher, was
wrapping Hayden's ankle with a bandage.

"What's going on?" I rushed to Hayden's side.

"It's all under control," Paula said, giving me a confident wave.
"Doc's taking care of him."

I looked at the man unrolling the bandage. Then I turned to
Hayden. "What happened?"

"It just got worse," he said, wincing. "Puffed up like a basket-
ball." He looked so pale and, suddenly, so small. "I called down
for more ice, and when Paula came to deliver it, she took one
look at me and rang for Dr. Herbert."

"Thank God," I said, taking Hayden's hand, wondering how
I could have been so callously wandering around Kenlyn Farm
with Roy Cummings when I should have been here with Hayden.

"It's hard to find someone on a Sunday," Paula said. "Especially for a house call." She smiled at the doctor. "But Doc here
is married to my cousin, Laurie, so I knew he'd come."

"Thank you, Doctor," I said. "I'm Ellen, his fiancée."

"Glad to help," Dr. Herbert said as he secured the bandage
with clips. "I'm going to give you a couple of prescriptions," he
told me. "One for the pain and one for the swelling." He took
a pad out of his pocket and scribbled something. "He's probably

torn the ligament, but he should be better in a day or two." He handed me the prescriptions. "Just keep him off of it for a couple of days."

"I will, Doctor. Thank you very much. You're so kind to do this. Let me give you my card and you can send me the bill."

He picked up his black doctor's bag and I handed him my card. Then he followed Paula out the door.

I sat on the bed next to Hayden, weighed down by my guilty conscience. "Sweetheart," I said, leaning over to give him a hug. "I'm really, really sorry I didn't get back sooner. I had no idea you were feeling this bad." I kissed his forehead.

"It's all right. I knew you needed some time on your own to decompress."

"I never even went to the pharmacy," I admitted sheepishly. "Thank God Paula got that doctor over here."

Hayden adjusted his bandaged leg on the pillows. "I guess you'll have to go to the pharmacy now, though. What did he prescribe, anyway?"

"Let's see." I looked at the first prescription. "Tylenol with codeine." Then I saw something odd. Little paw prints across the top of the prescription sheet.

Paw prints?

Underneath the paw prints I saw the name: PETER HERBERT, DVM, HERBERT ANIMAL HOSPITAL. The guy was a vet.

Chapter 15

Sugar

The next morning it poured. I took one look at the rain pelting the windows and wished I could stay in bed all day. But it was Monday, and I had an important appointment to keep.

Hayden was already awake beside me, reading *The Art of Negotiation: How to Argue Like a Five-Year-Old,* a book that had been on the bestseller list for twenty-six weeks.

"Are you feeling any better?" I asked.

He nodded. "A lot better. I think it's fine."

I looked at his ankle. It still looked puffy to me. "Well, you need to be careful. You know what the...uh...doctor said." I would take the knowledge that Dr. Peter Herbert's patients typically had four legs with me to my grave.

Hayden took my hand and pulled me toward him. Then he wrapped his arms around me and kissed me, his hands drifting through my hair. "I love you, Mrs. Hayden Croft."

Mrs. Hayden Croft.

"Ah," I murmured. "I love you, too, Mr. Hayden Croft."

"Maybe someday," he said, kissing my neck, his breath warm against my skin, "we'll be Senator and Mrs. Hayden Croft."

"Maybe we will," I whispered. Closing my eyes, I imagined us at a fund-raiser, in black tie, at the Museum of Natural History in Washington, D.C. We're navigating our way through a packed room full of dinosaur skeletons. People are grabbing us, shaking our hands. *Senator, Mrs. Croft, over here.* I'm wearing Oscar de la Renta and giving air kisses.

"Sounds pretty good, doesn't it?"

I opened my eyes to find Hayden smiling at me. He kissed me again and then began to pull my T-shirt over my head. Yes, he was feeling much better.

"You are *not* coming with me," I told Hayden as I pushed him back down on the bed. He had put on khakis and a button-down shirt and was now trying to get a sock over his ankle bandage. Sometimes he could be so stubborn.

"Sugar lives all the way up in Pequot," I said. "That's a two-hour drive at least. You're staying here."

Lila Falk's daughter, Sugar, had not seemed too anxious to meet with me when I called her. In fact, it was only after I suggested I might be willing to pay her a nominal "storage fee" for taking care of my grandmother's things that she perked up and became a little more accommodating.

"I can't very well send you to see this woman by yourself," Hayden said, still working on the sock.

"What are you talking about? You make it sound like she's crazy or something. Trust me, she's not. Besides, I've been all over this state by myself already."

He pulled the sock up the rest of the way. "That may be so, but now that I'm here I'm going with you."

"But you're not supposed to be on that leg. Doctor's orders." I bit my lip.

Hayden flung an exasperated hand at me. "I'll put the seat back and lie down. What's the difference whether I'm lying down here or in the car?"

I thought about that. He wasn't a litigator for nothing. "All right, but when we get there you'll stay in the car, off the leg, right?"

He smiled and did this little squinty thing with his eyes that meant he was agreeing but he wasn't necessarily committing.

We borrowed a couple of umbrellas from the inn, and Hayden put the passenger seat in the car all the way back as I set the GPS. We drove to the highway, heading toward Pequot, a town northwest of Beacon.

Three hours later, I slowed down in front of a small gray ranch house. A tattered American flag fluttered in the rain above the front door, and a decaying off-road vehicle, some sort of camper, sat on blocks, in puddles, by the side of the house.

"This is it?" Hayden said, scanning the yard. "Are you sure? Looks like a dump."

"Look at the number on the mailbox," I said, biting my nail. "It says two-seven-seven. That's what she told me." I pulled into the driveway.

Hayden glanced at the mailbox and then stared at the camper, with its rusted fenders and patches of primer and assorted paint colors. "I'm not letting you go in there by yourself."

I took another look at the house and didn't argue. Under

sheets of rain we crossed the yard, Hayden limping beside me as we dodged the puddles. We took shelter by the front door, beneath a small overhang of partially rotted wood. I searched for a doorbell and, seeing none, gave a hard rap on the door.

A moment later it opened and a fiftyish-looking stick-thin woman with dirty hair stood in the doorway. With a cigarette dangling from her mouth like an unanswered question, she looked us up and down and then motioned for us to come inside.

"I was only expecting one of you," she said as we stepped into a tiny living room that smelled of smoke and cabbage. A brown Naugahyde sofa, covered with spiderweb cracks, stood against a wall, accompanied by a coffee table made from a wagon wheel and a circular piece of dusty glass.

Sugar looked us up and down again, tucking her head in like a turtle. She studied my silk pants and sweater, and I began to wish I'd worn my jeans and a T-shirt instead.

"You must be Sugar," I said. "I'm Ellen and this is my fiancé, Hayden Croft." I offered my hand and thought she was going to shake it, but instead she reached across me and tapped her cigarette ash into the pot of a large, wilted plant. Then she blew out a thin, wavering stream of purple smoke.

She eyed Hayden. "What kind of a name is Croft, anyway?"

Hayden brightened up. "It's British, actually. My ancestors came over on the *Mayflower*."

Sugar raised her eyebrows and pursed her lips. "And I went on a Carnival cruise once, so I guess that makes us even." She put her head back and made a coughing sound that I realized, after a few seconds, was a laugh. A look of quiet alarm came over Hayden's face.

"You wanna sit down?" Sugar asked. With the burning end of her cigarette she motioned to the sofa.

I moved toward it cautiously, examining the sticky-looking patches and fissures from which tufts of gray stuffing erupted. Glancing down at my silk pants, I slowly lowered myself to the edge of the cushion. Hayden perched beside me, the two of us like birds ready for flight. Sugar sat across from us and hung her cigarette over the side of a sagging armchair.

"So you've been to see Ma." She made a crooked half smile and pushed her chin-length hair away from her face with the heel of her hand. Her hair displayed the results of multiple experiments with dye—clumps of gray, brassy gold, and auburn amicably shared space with a patch of green, the color of penicillin growing on stale bread.

"Yes, I went to see your mother," I said. "We had a nice chat. She's very sweet."

Sugar winced. "Hmm. I guess everyone's entitled to their opinion." She put her head back and laughed again, hacking away and waving her cigarette around like a gymnast waving a ribbon.

I could feel Hayden's knee pressing against mine. "Yes... well," I went on. "As I told you on the phone, your mother mentioned that you had some things of my grandmother's. She said I should come by and get them."

"Some things?" Sugar sat up and glared at me, her head in a nest of smoke. "Oh, yeah, I got *everybody's* things." She folded her arms across her chest. "Ma's, Ronny's, Doug's. I got forty-year-old comic books, beer bottles from around the world, football jerseys from who knows where. And let me ask you, does this place look *big*? I mean, does it?"

"I'm not sure I..." I glanced at Hayden, who started to speak, but Sugar cut in.

"No, no, Mr. Mayflower. I'll tell you the answer. It's not big. It's *small.*" She blew a plume of smoke toward us.

I could see the muscles in Hayden's neck tense. "Mrs. Hawley, we're just here to collect Mrs. Ray's possessions," he said. "The things that your mother—"

"The name's *Sugar.* And that's my point, Mayflower." She smiled, exhibiting a gray front tooth on the upper right side of her mouth. "I got everybody's junk here and it's costing me a bundle to keep it all."

Hayden's face went red. "Look, my name's not Mayflower. It's Hayden. Hayden Croft, and—"

Sugar waved him off. "Aw, come on." She shrugged. "I was just having a little fun."

Hayden took a breath and let it out slowly, composing himself. He glanced around the room, noting the stacks of vinyl record albums and cardboard cartons overflowing with ancient-looking leather-bound books.

"Maybe you should consider selling some of this," he said. "If it's valuable."

Sugar exploded into another hacking fit of laughter. "Well, aren't you the bright bulb in the pack? That's exactly what I'm doing!" She shook her head. "It's slow going, though, writing up them ads and having to take the pictures. And my camera's not too good. Could use a better one." She winked at me.

"A better camera?" I said. I leaned closer to Hayden and whispered, "I did tell her I might be able to pay her a little something for storage."

"She gives me the creeps," he whispered back. "Don't go overboard."

I opened my purse in search of my checkbook. "I'm sorry you've had to store Gran's possessions," I said. "We really need to get going, but if you'd bring me her things I'd be happy to pay you something for your inconvenience."

Hayden's arm launched out and grabbed mine. "I think we should see what Mrs.—uh, what *Sugar* has first, Ellen."

Sugar stood up. "I'll go get it. One less box." She peered at a purple frog ashtray on the coffee table, moved it about two inches, nodded, and left the room.

I glanced at Hayden.

"Really weird," he mouthed to me.

I nodded. "Let's get the stuff and get out of here."

Sugar returned, holding a cardboard box not much larger than a man's shoe box. Well, this couldn't have taken up much space, I thought as she handed it to me.

I opened the box and, one by one, I took out the items that were inside and placed them on my lap. There was a little sketch pad with a pink paper cover, a packet of handwritten notes in what looked like my grandmother's writing, a silk scarf of water lilies on a blue background, a black fountain pen with an ornate silver band around it, a book of poems by American poets with a number of pages dog-eared (I made a mental note to see if "Mending Wall" was in there), a magnifying glass with a carved wooden handle, a book called *Native Flowers of New England* with a ragged cloth binding, another clothbound book called *The Berry Farmer's Companion,* and a stack of twenty faded black-and-white photographs. A few of the photos were of my grandmother; the rest were of people I didn't recognize. I was hoping there might be a school yearbook or a diary, but I wasn't disappointed. I clutched the box, anxious to get back to the inn, where I could spread everything out on the bed and study the items one by one.

"So this is it," I said, brushing my hand over the top of the box. "Thank you."

Sugar stared at my engagement ring. "Some rock. He get that for you?" She tilted her head toward Hayden. "Mr. Mayflower?"

Hayden stood up, his jaw rigid. "Let's go, Ellen. I think we've taken up enough of Mrs. Hawley's time. There's nothing here anyway but a lot of junk." He glared at Sugar. "Forget eBay. You couldn't *give* this stuff away."

Sugar's eyes smoldered. "Well, aren't you two all high-and-mighty? Just like your grandmother." She pointed to me. "Oh, I know all about her. Ma used to tell me stories. Ruth this and Ruth that. How they were such great friends. Personally, I think your grandmother was nothing but a big snob from the sound of it. Thought she was too good for Beacon."

"What are you talking about?" I said, my voice rising in indignation. "You didn't even know my grandmother. You have no right to say that."

"I know enough to have my own opinion. Sugar's opinion." She pointed to herself. "I know the type. Your grandmother couldn't wait to get out of here. She wasn't going to end up spending her life picking blueberries, so she ran off with some big-shot doctor from *Chicago*."

How dare she, I thought as I stood up and turned to Hayden. "I'm ready. Let's get out of here."

Sugar tugged at my sleeve. "Oh, hold on. Wait a minute

there." Her voice turned quiet, almost saccharinely sweet. "You think old Sugar's just got junk? Well, you might be interested in seeing what else I got—you're so fascinated by all this family stuff." She raised one eyebrow. "Follow me."

Hayden and I looked at one another. I could see he didn't want to go any farther. "What if she has something else of Gran's?" I whispered.

We followed Sugar down a narrow hallway, stepping into a dark bedroom that smelled like cough medicine. By the light of two small windows I saw boxes piled high, bookshelves crammed, and shopping bags and storage bins overflowing with Sugar's collections. I inched my way farther inside as she switched on a lamp.

"Now, your grandmother's stuff is over there." She pointed across the room.

"My grandmother's stuff?" I glanced at Hayden. "So there is something else."

Sugar led us around the bed to a corner where five piles of rectangular boards, some as large as three feet by five feet, leaned against a wall.

"What is this?" Hayden said, moving closer.

As I stepped forward, I could see that some of the boards had wooden strips running around the edges and wires strung from one end to the other.

"These are paintings," I said, moving in quickly. "We're looking at the backs."

I grabbed one and turned it around. The piece measured about two feet by three feet and depicted, in lively brushstrokes and smears of dancing color, a sailboat regatta. Three small sailboats, bursting with wind, took up the foreground. A smattering of smaller boats skimmed the water in the distance behind them. The waves swirled in bits of blue, and white froth leaped above the hulls. It was Maine. I could smell the salt. I looked at the bottom right corner and saw the name in the loopy up-and-down handwriting I knew so well. Ruth Goddard.

Hayden took the painting and set it down. We stepped back to view it, and my mouth went dry. "Wow," I said.

"Wow is right," Hayden said. "Your grandmother did this?"

I nodded. "I guess so." I took a step closer and touched the paint she had swirled together to create the water. I felt the surface of the sails. I could almost hear the boats cutting through the waves. And I could picture my grandmother creating this. I didn't know when or where she did it, but I had an image of her, before an easel, dabbing paint on top of paint.

I grabbed the next painting, a slightly smaller one, and turned it around. There was a young man in a field of blueberries with a red barn in the distance. He stood between two rows of bushes, picking the berries with one hand and holding a red pail in the other. Sun glinted off the pail and the plants and the young man's sandy brown hair. His nose was freckled. It looked like a younger version of the Chet Cummings in Susan Porter's attic.

"Look at this," I whispered, tracing my finger over the painting, feeling the edges of paint, the grooves of the brush. "I think this is Chet Cummings." I ran my hand down to the right corner and brushed my finger over the name. Ruth Goddard.

"Beautiful," Hayden said, setting that one next to the first. "Let's try this group," he said as he pulled a painting from one of the other stacks. A gray-haired woman wearing a white apron stood proudly in front of a little hut in which baskets of fruit were displayed for sale. In another painting, two boys played with yellow wooden boats in a tide pool. The name on both paintings was Ruth Goddard.

I turned to Sugar. "They're all my grandmother's, aren't they?" She puffed a trail of smoke at me. "Sure are."

I sat down on a small empty space on the edge of the bed and stared at the sailboat regatta. Something about the reflection of the boat in the water, the red hull shimmering in a million colors in the blue-black sea—triggered a memory.

I was on a dock with my grandmother, at a harbor. We were looking at the reflections in the water, at the hulls of the boats, and she asked, "What colors do you see there, Ellen?"

I pointed to a boat with a yellow hull. "Yellow," I told her.

"Ah, and what else?" she asked. "What other colors do you see? There are lots of colors in that reflection." And then I looked more closely and I saw the other colors—orange and green, purple and a little gray, gold and even pink. I named the colors and she said, "That's right, and if you keep looking you'll keep seeing more and more. That's what it means to be an observer, Ellen. There's always more there than you think."

Hayden was inspecting the sailboat regatta in small sections, staring at the brushstrokes. I got up from the bed and stood next to him.

He leaned closer. "This is good-quality work," he whispered. "Very nicely done." He turned to the canvas of the boys in the tidal pool and leaned in again. "Quite stunning," he said. "These remind me of the American impressionist Childe Hassam."

"I've heard of him," I whispered back, "but I don't recall his work."

"Some say he was the greatest American impressionist ever," Hayden said. "His use of sunlight was superb. He painted scenes of everyday life, like these."

I nodded and then gazed at the stacks of paintings, amazed that Gran had done all this work. "My God, there must be twenty paintings here," I said.

"Twenty-five," Sugar corrected me.

They are beautiful, I thought, my hands trembling as I turned over a canvas showing six horses in a thick green field and another depicting three children fishing on the bank of a quiet river. We looked through the rest of the paintings.

"I can hardly believe this," I said, turning to Hayden. "All these paintings in one place. Now we just have to figure out the best way to get them out of here." I began a mental calculation, trying to determine what kind of a vehicle I would need to rent to take the paintings to my mother's house. "I guess I'm going to have to rent a van or something."

Sugar, who had been standing off to the side, moved closer. "Get what out of here? What do you need a van for?" She smacked a spider crawling up the wall.

"To take these paintings."

Sugar's eyes dissolved to pebbles. "You're not taking these paintings anywhere."

I froze. "What do you mean?"

"You're not taking them. That's what I mean."

"Why not? They belong to my family, to my mother." I looked at Hayden.

The lights flickered and dimmed for a moment, and a roll of thunder spread over the house. "Because I've sold them," Sugar said.

I felt the ground shift under me. "You *what?*"

She repeated the words slowly, one at a time. "I. Sold. Them."

"How could you do that? They belong to my family."

"Hah." Sugar threw back her head. "Where's your family been for the past sixty years, then? How come they never came for these?"

Hayden stepped forward. "What are you talking about? Her family didn't even know these paintings were here."

Sugar pointed at me. "Her grandmother gave them to my mother."

I took a step closer to Sugar. "Look," I said. "I'm sure my grandmother didn't *give* them to your mother. There's obviously some mistake."

"Oh, there's no mistake," Sugar said. "Your grandmother didn't want them. She wanted to get rid of them."

"That's a lie," I said. "I don't believe that for a second."

Sugar smiled, her gray tooth glowing. "Sugar doesn't lie. And yep, I've sold them. I'm getting ten thousand bucks for the whole heap." She swept her arm over the stacks of paintings. Then she put her hands on her hips and raised a finger. "Unless, um..."

"Ten thou—" I couldn't even finish the word. How could she let these go for only ten thousand dollars? It was insulting. It was crazy. "For God's sake, you said there are twenty-five paintings here, and—"

Hayden put a hand on my arm, his signal for me to watch my temper. "Excuse me, Ellen," he said. Then he turned to Sugar. "Unless *what?*"

"Well...Mayflower..." She pointed at Hayden and almost touched him, causing him to take a step back. "I was just thinking you two might want to make me a better offer, in which case—"

"How much? What do you want?" I began to dig for my checkbook again.

Hayden stopped me. "Wait a minute here." He turned to Sugar. "We're not just going to write you a blank check."

I glared at Hayden. "What he means is that the amount needs to be...somewhat...reasonable. That's all. What were you thinking?"

Hayden waved his hands. "Hold on, hold on. You said you've already sold these?"

"Well, yeah," Sugar said. "He took one painting already and paid me for it."

"Who took one?" I asked.

Sugar shrugged. "An art dealer from Boston."

"Well, did you sign anything?" Hayden asked. "Put anything in writing?"

I held my breath.

"Sure. I signed some paper he gave me."

"Some paper," Hayden echoed. "Do you have it? Could we see it?"

Sugar left the room and came back with a sheet of paper folded in thirds.

Hayden read it and then looked at me. "She's sold them to some place called the Millbank Gallery in Boston."

He turned to Sugar. "Mrs. Hawley," he said. "As lawyers we can assure you that these paintings were not yours to sell. They were being *stored* here by your mother, and she wants Miss Branford to have them. We intend to stop any further so-called *sale* of these paintings to this Millbank Gallery."

Sugar crossed her arms and pursed her lips. "Well, we'll just see about that, won't we?"

Sugar's cat crept into the room, hovering around a collection of empty jelly jars piled in a three-foot-high pyramid in a corner. The cat looked as though it wanted to leap to the top.

"Let's get out of here," Hayden whispered. "We can't get the paintings out today, but I'll get them for you. Don't worry."

He hobbled down the hall, one hand on the wall for support. Just before we got to the door, he addressed Sugar one last time. "Mrs. Hawley, I suggest you make sure these paintings stay right where they are, unless you want to be involved in a very expensive legal battle."

Sugar stood in her spot, her mouth slightly open. "You don't scare me, Mayflower. Nobody talks to Sugar that way."

"You'll be hearing from us," Hayden replied as I opened the door.

It was still pouring outside, cold sheets of rain that pelted the cracked gray driveway and sent streams of mud from Sugar's yard out to the street. We stood under the overhang and then dashed to the car as fast as we could, Hayden listing with his bad leg like a wind sock in a hurricane. The last thing I heard, as we stepped away from the porch, was a loud crash from inside the house, as though a hundred Welch's jelly jars had gone smashing to the floor.

Chapter 16

It's Just Like Cici Baker

Hayden was right, I thought as I sat on the bed in our room the next morning. Sugar Hawley was crazy. And because of that, despite his confident assurances that he would get those paintings for me I knew it wasn't going to be that easy. I glanced around the room, stopping at the crack in the ceiling, as I listened to him talking on his cell in the bathroom.

"I think we've got a good shot at winning the motion," he was telling another attorney from our office. "And that's what I told Elizabeth. She understands, but they've got a new regime over there now and everything's up for grabs."

I poked my head into the bathroom and pointed to my watch. It was eleven fifteen. We were supposed to be at the Porters' house at eleven thirty so I could show Hayden the painting and take some photos of it.

He put his hand over the phone and whispered, "You'd better go without me. Ashton Pharmaceuticals. Another mess."

"Are you sure?" I whispered back, disappointed.

He nodded. "Take lots of pictures. The people from the *Times* might want to see them, too."

The people from the *Times*. Oh, God, they were arriving tonight and had scheduled Hayden and me for an interview and photo session tomorrow morning. I picked up my camera and walked downstairs, trying to think of other things.

I sat in the car for a minute, staring at the dashboard. Then I began browsing through my music selections, looking for something to distract me. Finally, I chose Ella Fitzgerald singing "Skylark" and let her honey-layered notes drift out the window as I headed toward the Porters' house. Gran loved Ella; I loved Ella. Her voice and the comforting sounds of the Nelson Riddle Orchestra were perfect medicine for my nerves.

I spent about a half hour at the Porters', talking to Susan and her husband and then photographing Gran's painting. It was just as I remembered—vibrant and almost magical, lovingly depicting Gran and Chet, the oaks and the barn. By the time I left I was in a much happier mood.

On my way back to the inn, I drove past Kenlyn Farm and, seeing the opening in the wall and the dirt road leading inside, found myself turning in. The sun flickered off my car as I kept my wheels in the flattened-brush path that Roy's tires had made the day before. Parking near the wall, I began to walk up the slope where Roy had driven, my feet in the trail of the truck tires.

At the top, I put the camera's viewfinder to my eye and slowly turned, the way my grandmother had taught me. From every vantage point something remarkable filled the screen—clusters of wild red columbine, fallen boulders forming geometric designs against the wall, crusty green lichen gnawing on rocks, a Baltimore oriole popping from a thicket of brush, and, at my feet, a grasshopper clinging to a stem of purple aster. I could spend a day here and barely scratch the surface.

The sun felt warm on my shoulders as I bent down to capture the blossoms of yellow star grass, the feathery purple petals of spotted knapweed, and the lacy wings of two yellow jackets as they alighted on tiny white blooms of Labrador tea. By the time I finished taking photos of a monarch butterfly resting on milkweed, I realized an hour had passed.

I began to walk back down the slope to the car, enjoying the conversation of birds, the aroma of lanky grass and wildflowers, the earthy scent of the ground under my feet. To my right I saw the grove of trees and the lone oak against whose trunk Roy had stood two days before.

That would make a nice photo, I thought—the single tree with its craggy bark and umbrellalike branches and the other trees clustered behind it, like children lagging behind a parent. I walked closer, placing the viewfinder to my eye, moving my head to the left, to the right, adjusting the aperture and zooming the lens in and out to compose the shots I liked the best.

You have to look at a thing from all angles before you can really see it, Gran said. I moved around, taking photos of the tree and the grove from different vantage points, until I saw something that made me stop.

In my viewfinder I had placed the lone oak tree on the left, with most of the grove behind it on the right. And in the far right corner I noticed something I hadn't seen, couldn't have seen, two days ago. Half buried in the wildflowers, I saw what looked like the remains of an old stone foundation. The position of the tree, the grove, and the foundation were lined up in exactly the same way the tree, the grove, and the barn were lined up in the painting in Susan Porter's attic. I knew that was where the barn had once been, right there in front of me, where part of the foundation was still visible. The only things missing from the scene were Gran and Chet.

The tingle going up my spine worked its way into my arms as I edged closer. Sections of three crumbled walls emerged here and there from the carpet of wildflowers. The boulders peeking through the growth were gilded with large yellow and green patches of lichen, as though someone had splashed paint over them in a moment of creative frenzy.

I stood there, the field humming around me, and I thought about Gran and Chet Cummings. I could feel her spirit in the soil under my feet, in the sun-baked boulders that had once formed the base of the barn, in the stalks of wildflowers that brushed against my legs like memories calling out to me.

I stepped into the foyer of the Victory Inn, camera in hand, excited to tell Hayden about my discovery at Kenlyn Farm. A woman in ivory pants stood across the counter from Paula, her ash blond hair neatly styled in loose waves, a pair of jeweled sunglasses perched on top of her head. She had a small ostrich suitcase by her side.

I blinked in surprise. "Mom?"

My mother turned. "Darling!" She headed toward me, arms outstretched, gold bracelets jingling as she kissed me on both cheeks.

"Mom, what are you doing here?" I looked her up and down, not quite believing she was there.

She took a step back, scrutinizing me. "You've changed your hair. It's so... different."

I ran a hand through my hair. "Really?" I laughed. "I probably just forgot to brush it." All of a sudden I was eleven again. My fingers scurried through my scalp, trying to create a part. "So why are you here? What—"

My mother stared at me as though I told her I'd kidnapped her yoga trainer. "Sweetie, you're getting married in three months. This isn't the time to stop caring about your appearance."

Paula cleared her throat and Mom and I turned. "So do you want to put this on a card?"

"Oh, yes, of course," my mother said, opening her wallet.

Paula took the card, a virtually clear piece of plastic, and held it to the light. She narrowed her eyes. "Never seen one of these before."

I turned to Paula. "They're not very common," I said, feeling the need to explain. "You don't apply for it. Actually, you can't," I said. "The company chooses *you*."

Paula drew her head back in surprise.

I pulled Mom aside. "Would you please tell me what you're doing here?" I whispered. "What's going on?"

"I'll need a driver's license, too," Paula added.

My mother placed her license on the counter. Then she turned to me and crossed her arms. "Why am I here? Ellen, that ought to be obvious. You haven't returned my calls for days."

I tried to avoid her gaze. "I sent you some text messages."

"I *called* you," my mother said. "More than once. And I expected a call in return. You know, that old-fashioned custom where you actually hear the other person speak."

"I'm sorry," I said. "Things just got a little busy." I tried to smile as she stared at me, doing her sixth-sense reconnaissance, attempting to figure out what wasn't adding up.

"So where is my mother's room?" I asked breezily as Paula took one last look at the transparent credit card before handing it back to Mom.

"I put your mother in room twelve," Paula said. "Right across from you."

"Lovely," Mom said, eyeing me. "We have so much to catch up on." She wasn't smiling.

Paula's eyebrows rose like a pair of trained dogs. "I guess so," she muttered.

My mother took out a gold compact. "I'm going to my room to freshen up," she said, looking in the mirror and fluffing the back of her hair. "Then you can take me out for a latte, which I desperately need, and you can tell me all about what's really going on here."

What's really going on, I thought. That would take a lot more than a latte. "I'm going up, too," I said. "I need to talk to Hayden. I'll tell him you're here."

"Hayden?" My mother's gaze turned from the mirror to me. "What a surprise. I didn't know he was here."

"He settled a case," I said. "It's a long story."

"Wonderful," my mother said. "Let's go say hello."

Paula handed my mother the receipt. "Actually, Mr. Craft's not up there. He went out a little while ago with two other guests. A man and a woman. A looker, too," she said, glancing at me.

"It's *Croft*," I said, correcting her.

A man and a woman. She had to be talking about the *Times* people. "Are they from New York?"

"Sure are," Paula said, glancing at her guest register.

"Those are business associates," I said. "From the *New York Times*." A looker, indeed. I wondered what Paula's imagination was churning up. She had too much free time on her hands.

Mom closed her compact and then leaned in and whispered, "Why is Hayden talking to someone from the *Times*?"

"That's a long story, too."

"Great. I'd love to hear it." She pointed to her overnight bag. "Can someone please take that up to my room?" She glanced back at me. "And I wouldn't mind a scone or a croissant or something like that. I'm famished."

"I'll take you to the Three Penny Diner."

"A diner?"

"They have great apple cider doughnuts."

She cocked her head. "Since when do you eat doughnuts?"

The diner was practically empty when we walked in. I led the way to a table by the window. "Isn't this pretty? You can see the ocean."

Mom pulled out one of the worn wooden chairs and sat down. She eyed the mini jukebox and green Formica table. "Interesting," she said, taking in the vinyl phonograph albums on the walls and the black-and-white photos of Buddy Holly, Jerry Lee Lewis, the Platters, and other 1950s bands. "I feel like I've gone back in time. Do you suppose that's the intent?"

I shook my head. "I don't know, Mom. I guess the owner just likes it this way."

A waitress with thick gray hair, almost like animal fur, handed us menus and disappeared.

"No latte?" my mother asked as she scanned the choices. "And no croissants, either."

As she studied the menu, I watched a cluster of children on the beach, playing with shovels and pails, and a group of teenagers congregating by the wall. I thought about Gran and wondered if she had run along that beach under the Maine sun as a child or sat under the moon on the seawall with Chet.

The waitress returned and Mom closed the menu. "I'll have a cup of coffee and one of your blueberry muffins." She sighed and looked at me. "Your grandmother was such a good cook. Her blueberry muffins were extraordinary."

"Yes, they were," I said, and I was back on Steiner Street again, Gran and I taking muffins from her tins and placing them on a wire rack to cool, the smell of baked sugar hanging in the oven-warmed air, the muffin tops covered with rivers of blue where the berries had melted from the heat.

I turned to the waitress. "I think I'll have a muffin, too," I said.

Mom clasped her hands and placed them on the table. "Ellen, since we're talking about your grandmother, there's something I wanted to tell you."

I looked up.

"It has to do with the trust."

The trust. Gran told me a long time ago that she'd set up a trust for me, but I didn't know the details or whether it even still existed. "There is a trust?" I said.

"Yes, of course," Mom said. "In fact, I met with Everett a couple of days ago." Everett was Gran's estate lawyer. My mother leaned across the table. "There's a fair amount of money in that trust, Ellen."

The waitress set down our coffee mugs. I caught the faint scent of pecans.

"It'll be just a minute on those muffins," she said. "They're coming out of the oven now."

I poured some milk into my coffee and began stirring it. "What do you mean?" I asked my mother.

Mom lowered her voice to a whisper. "Six million dollars. In the trust."

I stopped stirring and stared. "What?"

She didn't blink. "I've seen the investment statements."

"You've got to be kidding."

"No, I'm not, Ellen."

I couldn't speak. Gran had left me six million dollars. Six million dollars. I didn't know what to say. I made a good living, and so did Hayden. But a six-million-dollar trust...well, that was like a security blanket. A big security blanket.

I shook my head. "I don't know what to say." I pictured my grandmother in Everett's office, sitting tall in one of his mahogany chairs, the sheaf of trust documents on the table in front of her. I could see her holding a fountain pen, her hand scurrying across the pages, leaving a trail of signatures in bright blue ink. "I wish she were here," I said, a heavy feeling in my chest. "So I could thank her. She did so many things for me and she's still doing them. I miss her."

My mother reached across the table and took my hand. "I miss her, too."

"I didn't get to thank her for this."

"Yes, you did," my mother said. "You thanked her by how much you loved her."

We sat in silence as the waitress placed our muffins in front of us. After a while, my mother began to cut her muffin into small pieces. Then she took a bite. "Mmm," she said. "You know, this is actually quite good...although it's not as good as your gran's."

"Here's to Gran," I said, raising my coffee cup. Mom raised hers and we tapped our mugs together. "Here's to Gran," she said.

"I've been meaning to ask," my mother said as we finished eating. "How did you end up in that strange little...what is it, a bed-and-breakfast? The room doesn't even have a mini fridge."

Next she'd be asking why there wasn't a spa.

She inspected the nails of her right hand. "I wanted to get a manicure. And maybe grab a massage. I pulled a muscle in my leg playing tennis last weekend and it's very painful." She began rubbing her calf.

Oh, my God, she *did* want a spa. "I hate to tell you, but the spa is closed for renovations," I said. "They're going to reopen it when they reopen the fitness center...and the golf course." I started to smile.

My mother smirked. "Okay, I get it. No spa." She looked around the diner and then out the window. "This really *is* a small town, isn't it?"

"It's small," I said, "but there are some nice things here. They have a—"

"I'm sure it's all very sweet," my mother said, leaning toward me, "but I'm dying to get you back home. We have so much to do before the wedding and so little time. I can't imagine what's kept you here."

She opened her purse and removed a checklist. "Let's see." She ran her finger down the page. "We need to schedule the final fitting for your gown...and for the bridesmaids." She paused. "And review the floral arrangements one more time." She turned over the paper. "And, of course, get those invitations addressed." She circled something with a pen and then put the list on the table. "Oh, I almost forgot to tell you. Beezy and Gary Bridges are definitely coming. They're postponing their safari so they can be at the wedding."

I struggled to remember who Beezy and Gary Bridges were as images of the wedding took shape in my mind. Saint Thomas Church, ten bridesmaids, ten groomsmen, three hundred guests, to have and to hold, in sickness and in health. I could feel my throat tighten. It was all so...*final.*

"That's nice of them," I said, trying to sound excited. And then, recalling who they were, I added, "I thought they were going to get a divorce."

Mom twirled one of her bracelets around her wrist. "Yes," she said cheerfully. "They were. But they decided to get a new house instead."

I nodded, trying to understand that logic, as Mom placed her coffee cup on the saucer with a little clink.

"So tell me," she said. "Why are you still here, and why didn't you call me back? How could it take so long to deliver one letter? And why is Hayden here? What's going on, Ellen?"

I wondered what to tell her and where to start. The painting in the attic? Lila Falk? Sugar? I wasn't about to mention the dock. That would send her into a tailspin.

I told her about delivering the letter to Roy and discovering that Chet Cummings had passed away. Then I told her about all of the paintings and the places where I had found them, ending with the visit to Sugar Hawley.

"Did you know Gran was a painter?" I asked.

My mother drank her coffee. "I find that hard to believe, Ellen. I think someone else must have painted them. Your grandmother wasn't artistic."

I leaned across the table. "Mom, I've seen the paintings. Sailboat races, portraits, a blueberry farm that used to be owned by Chet Cummings's family. She painted all of them. And if you don't think she was artistic," I said a little defiantly, "then you should have been there when she taught me about photography."

My mother listened with halfhearted interest. "I think if she was that talented, I would have known."

"I'll take you to the Porters' and to the historical society, and you can see the paintings for yourself," I told her. "Then you'll know."

The waitress appeared with a pot of coffee. "Refill, ladies?"

"No, thank you," Mom said.

"I'm fine," I added.

The waitress glanced at me and then did a double take. She kept staring. Finally, she walked away, but a moment later she came back with something rolled up under her arm.

"Yep, I thought so," she said, looking at me with her head cocked. "I thought it was you." She nodded. "I was hoping you'd come in here so I could get your autograph."

"My auto..." I tried to speak but my voice caught in my throat.

"Yeah, I saved this copy just in case." She unrolled an issue of *The Beacon Bugle* and placed it on the table. There, on the front page, was the photo of Roy and me, ocean water up to my waist, white T-shirt plastered to my skin, my arms tight around Roy's neck, my lips firmly planted on his.

I shrank back.

The waitress placed a pen in front of me. "You know, there's not one copy of this issue around anywhere. It just sold right out. Isn't that amazing?"

I nodded, unable to speak.

"Would you sign it for me?" she asked. "Could you put 'To Dolores, with love from the Swimmer'?"

"What is this?" Mom asked, turning the newspaper toward her and putting on her reading glasses. She covered the side of her mouth and whispered, "And why does she want your autograph?"

"Maybe I'd better explain something," I said. My mouth had gone dry. I could feel the bottom dropping out of my stomach.

"*The Beacon Bugle*?" My mother smoothed out the crease. Her eyes darted up and down over the page.

I held up my hand. "Mom, I really need to talk to you about this. Could we please go back to the—"

"Right there," the waitress pointed to my picture. "Could you sign it right there, by the photo?"

My mother saw where the waitress was pointing. She began to read the caption. I wanted to grab the paper and run, but my feet wouldn't move. Nothing would move. All I could do was sit there and feel the cold sweat breaking out on my back.

Mom pushed her reading glasses farther up the bridge of her nose as she looked at the photograph. There was a frightening second of silence and then a shriek. "Oh, my God!"

She brought the paper close to her eyes and then back to arm's length, as if the proper distance might change what was printed or, better yet, make it disappear. "It's you! Ellen, what are you doing in this newspaper? And who in God's name is this man you're kissing?"

"I told you I needed to explain."

My mother's eyes were wide with alarm and her face had lost all its color. I grabbed the pen and scrawled "To Dolores, with love from the Swimmer" next to the photo. "Take this out of here, please," I said, handing the paper to the waitress. She scurried away, thanking me several times.

"I think I need another coffee," I said.

"I think I need a Scotch."

"You don't drink Scotch, Mom."

"This might be a good time to start." She looked at me, steely gray lie-detector eyes sizing me up. "What's going on? You were *drowning?* Who was that man?" With each question, her voice went up about four notes.

I raised a finger. "Just to clarify something—I don't think I was really drowning. They got that wrong. I was just a little—"

"Is this why you didn't call me? Because you're having an affair with this man? Oh, my God." She looked up toward the ceiling, rubbing her forehead.

"No, Mom. Listen. I'm not having an affair. I can explain. I fell through this dock and—"

"A *dock?*" She sat up straight.

261

Oh, God, why did I mention that? "Yes, but I was fine, really. It's just that there was a rip current and it took me—"

"You got into a rip current? Ellen!"

Somehow the truth was coming out, whether I wanted it to or not. "Mom, I told you I was fine. The guy in the photo... he swam out and brought me in."

"When did all this happen?"

"My first day here."

She leaned across the table, lowered her voice, and demanded, "Why didn't you tell me about this?"

"I didn't want you to worry."

"Well, now I *am* worried."

"I'm all right."

"It doesn't matter. You still should have told me." My mother gave me an uncomfortably long look. "And what about *the man?* This *hero,* as they call him in the paper? What's going on with him?"

"Nothing's going on, Mom." I waved her off.

"That photo didn't look like nothing to me."

"That just happened," I said. "I think I was so glad to be back on the ground that... I don't know." I glanced out the window, to the place where the blue drift of the ocean met the sky, and I thought about Roy setting me down in that water, my feet against the grainy sand, and how I put my arms around his neck, my mouth on his, and how he tasted like salt and late afternoon sun. "It just happened... and then it was over."

My mother raised her chin and peered at me through half-shut eyes. "You're not giving me the whole story. There's something more going on."

"No, no. There isn't. We're just…we're just friends." I looked down and ran my finger around the rim of my coffee mug. "Well, I think he'd like to be more than friends, but he knows I'm engaged. Now he knows, anyway."

My mother lifted an eyebrow. "*Now* he knows?"

"He didn't know the night at the Antler. When I fainted and he caught me…" I stopped, realizing again I'd said too much.

My mother gasped. "You *fainted?* Ellen!"

I raised my hands. "I was fine, Mom. He caught me. It was lucky he was there. And then we…kind of danced, and, well, he's a nice guy. He really is. There's something charming about him." I thought about the Antler and the two-step and how easily I floated across the floor in Roy's arms.

"And that's all?" my mother said. "That's everything?"

I glanced toward the beach and saw a boy unfurling a kite. The blue plastic shape fluttered and flapped in the wind as he gradually let out the string. I could feel my mother's gaze boring into me. "Okay," I said. "Maybe I do find him kind of attractive." I clasped my hands under the table. "But I think it's just because I'm getting married in three months, and it's nice to know I can still get attention from men."

My mother didn't move a muscle. I wasn't sure she believed me.

I looked away, toward the beach again. The boy's kite rose into the air as he held the end of the string. My mother didn't say a word. A wall of silence slipped in between us.

"Maybe that's not quite true," I finally said. "Maybe something else is going on. But I don't know what it is. I'm not in love with him or anything…I love Hayden. But there's something about Roy…and I can't…"

My mother's face had gone white. "Oh, dear God. Ellen, who is this man? Where is he from? Who are his *family?*"

"He's from Beacon, Mom."

"He's from *Beacon?*"

"He's Chet Cummings's nephew." I told her how I'd gone to Chet's house several times, finally running into Roy and finding out that Chet had died and that Roy was his nephew.

"And what does this man do?" my mother asked.

"He's a carpenter. He builds houses."

She blinked. "A carpenter. With a tool belt and a pickup truck? That kind of thing?"

"That pretty much covers it."

She looked away, as though she were staring at something far down the shoreline. Maybe it was the yellow dog racing into the water or the woman and the little girl at the ocean's edge. Or maybe she wasn't looking at anything.

Finally she got up from her chair and moved to the empty seat beside me. A patch of sunlight flickered against the Formica table. My mother put her hand on mine. Her eyes were soft, like blue sea glass. "Do you love Hayden?" she asked.

I nodded. "Of course I do."

"And do you still want to marry him?"

"Yes, yes."

My mother nodded. "Okay, sweetheart, I see what's going on here, and it makes total sense." She had that all-knowing-mother look, which made me feel like I was six years old again. "I can tell you that you're having a perfectly normal reaction." She pushed a lock of my hair over my shoulder and smiled. "Thank God, because now we can both breathe a sigh of relief."

"What are you talking about? Normal reaction to what?"

She sat back in her chair. "Didn't I ever tell you the story about Cici Baker?"

"Who?"

"Cici Baker. My old tennis partner. Don't you remember her?"

"Oh, yes, I think so."

"Well, about five years ago she found out she had cancer." My mother squinted at me. "I'm sure I told you this.... Okay, anyway, she went to a doctor...oncologist in Manhattan... Sloan-Kettering. He absolutely saved her life, and after that she developed a mad crush on him."

"On her oncologist?"

"Yes, of course. And he wasn't at all attractive—short, stocky, and I think he had one of those hair weaves." My mother grimaced. "But Cici didn't see any of that. He saved her life. She worshipped him."

"So what happened?" I asked. "Did they end up getting married?"

"Married? No! Turns out the man was gay."

I crossed my arms. "Well, what's your point?"

Mom put her hand on my shoulder. "Two months later she'd forgotten all about him. My point is that it's normal to become infatuated—maybe even think you've fallen in love—with someone who saves your life. It doesn't really mean anything."

I watched the color return to my mother's face as I reflected on the sequence of events from my fall through the dock to hitting the water to the moment Roy appeared to finally feeling the sand beneath my feet when he pulled me onto the beach and I gave him that...*kiss*. Was my attraction to Roy just based on what he'd done to help me that day? If Cici Baker thought she had fallen in love with her oncologist...I mean, the man had a hair weave.

My mother stared at me. "Ellen, you are not in love or interested or anything else with a carpenter from Beacon, Maine. Believe me, you're not." She smiled. "You've worked far too hard to get where you are. This is a momentary infatuation with a person who helped you out of harm's way. Don't give it any more stature than that." She put her hand under my chin. "Everything is going to be fine. Trust me."

Chapter 17

Chet

I followed my mother up the walk to the Victory Inn, thinking about how clever she was. Whatever attraction I felt for Roy was surely the result of his helping me the day I'd fallen through the dock, just as Mom said. It had to be. Someone saves your life and you're in awe of him. I could see how that could certainly lead to...well, infatuation, even with a man as wonderful as Hayden in my life.

"Now," my mother said, stopping at the front steps. "Why don't you pick the nicest restaurant in town...or anywhere up here," she added with a flick of her wrist, "and I'll take you and Hayden to dinner tonight."

The nicest restaurant. I wondered what that would be and if my mother were really up to the task. She was used to a certain level of...well, a certain level. I wasn't even sure I wanted to go out to dinner. Not that I didn't appreciate the invitation and the fact that she'd come all the way to Beacon. But I needed to be alone with Hayden, to get things back on track, and I thought we could start with a romantic dinner in the dining room at the inn. Candlelight, a corner table, a nice bottle of wine—well, anyway, a bottle of wine...

"Mom, we'll at least have drinks together, and tomorrow night we'll take you to dinner, okay? Tonight I think I need to spend a little time alone with Hayden."

"Good idea," she said, her eyes dancing.

My cell phone began to ring just as my mother opened the door to the lobby. The area code looked familiar, but I didn't recognize the number.

"I've got to take this out here," I said. "No bars in there." I nodded toward the building.

She gave me a little wave and walked inside.

I put the phone to my ear. "Hello?" There was a second of silence.

"Ellen?" It was a man's voice. "Hey. Roy Cummings."

Roy Cummings? I felt something skip around inside me. It was strange hearing his voice over the phone. Strange and almost intimate. "Oh...hello," I said, ready to bite my nail. Why did he make me so nervous?

"I got your number from Paula," he said.

So Paula had given him my number. Hmm.

"I hope you don't mind my calling, but there's something kind of important I need to talk to you about." He paused for a second. "And show you. Do you think you could stop by?"

"You mean come to your house?"

"Yes."

Now I had a right to be nervous. Roy Cummings's house? Probably not a good idea. "When?"

"Well, now would be great if you could do it."

"Right now? What is it you want to show me?"

"I really think you should come over," he said. There was urgency in his voice. "It has to do with your grandmother and my uncle."

I looked at my watch. Three fifteen. Maybe Hayden was still out with the *Times* people. Maybe I could just run over to Roy's for ten minutes.

"Okay," I said. "I'll be right there."

Roy answered the door within seconds of my knock. I stepped into a small entry and followed him to the living room. The floor was chestnut-colored wood, and a white sofa and two chairs flanked a dark coffee table. The effect was simple but lovely. Built-in bookcases ran along one wall, filled with photos and objects that looked like antique tools—a wooden level, a set of planes with beautifully varnished handles, a wooden ruler with hinges that allowed it to fold. I wondered if they had been Chet's. And then there were the books. Hundreds of them—small, large, hardbound, paperback. I wondered if the older books with the faded cloth covers had belonged to Chet as well.

Roy gestured for me to sit down. "Can I get you a drink or something? Water, soda, juice? Wine? I've got a nice Beychevelle you might like."

A *Beychevelle?* Was *he* the one who was buying it from the Wine Cellar? Part of me was tempted to accept his offer, but I knew that was probably not a good idea. "No, thanks," I said, deciding I'd better see what he had to show me and leave.

"I'll be right back," Roy said as I walked to the bookshelves.

There was a brass object I thought might be a plumb bob, but I wasn't exactly sure what a plumb bob looked like. Next to it was a framed photo of Roy, looking like he was in his early twenties, and two older men who could almost be twins. The family resemblance among the three was obvious.

"That's my dad," Roy said, coming up behind me and pointing to the man on the left. "And that's Uncle Chet."

"Those Cummings eyes," I said, turning to Roy. "You all have them. They're so blue."

We sat down, Roy at one end of the sofa and I in a chair opposite him. He held a wooden box in his hand, a little smaller than a shoe box. The outside was varnished to a satin gloss. It looked like cedar.

"When my uncle died," he said, "he left a lot of things— clothes, personal effects, you know." He leaned back against the sofa. "I really didn't want to look at that stuff then. I was too upset. And besides, I figured there wasn't any hurry to go through it." He glanced at the box in his hand. "But the other day, after you came over here and I found you on the ladder..."

I looked down, embarrassed.

"And I was telling you about the marina...well, I knew my uncle had some old photos of the two of us taken there. And I thought maybe it was time to look at his stuff. I kept thinking about you and all these things you're finding out about your grandmother and I thought, If Ellen can do it...so I figured I'd look for the photos. And I found them." He hesitated for a moment. "But I also found something else."

He handed me the box. "Go on, open it."

I lifted the brass hinge on the front and opened the lid, letting the scent of cedar into the room. Inside the box lay a stack of envelopes, in slightly varying shapes and sizes, tied up with a brittle-looking piece of twine.

The edges of the envelopes were wrinkled and worn, the paper having faded to shades of cream and tan and even orange. Some of the postage stamps were visible. Like tiny works of art, they were printed in muted blues and reds and greens, with designs that appeared soft, almost out of focus. Large round cancellation marks showed that the envelopes had been mailed not once but twice.

The envelope on the top of the pile bore a three-cent stamp printed in a violet-brown, with a picture of Casey Jones in the middle and train locomotives on either side. In the middle of the envelope the name Ruth Goddard appeared along with a Chicago address. The fountain-pen ink, which I guessed had once been blue or black, had faded to an earthy brown, but the handwriting still looked neat, compact, and bold.

I ran my finger gently over the address. "From your uncle to my grandmother."

Roy leaned in closer. "I didn't want to read them without you." He reached over and carefully untied the string. It broke apart in his hands.

I picked up the envelope on top of the pile. The paper felt thin and dry. On the back flap, the name Chet Cummings appeared above a Beacon address. I looked at all the other envelopes. They were all addressed to my grandmother in Chicago and they were all from Chet Cummings. Not one had been opened. On every envelope, Gran had crossed out her name and address and, in her neat cursive writing, had written "Return to Sender."

I looked at Roy, sadness welling up inside me. "He wrote her all these."

Roy nodded.

"From December second, 1950," I said, looking at the cancellation marks, "to July ninth, 1951. All these letters and she never opened one."

"That's what it looks like."

Roy had said he wanted to read the letters, but I wasn't so sure I could do it. These had to be love letters. I began to get a queasy feeling in my stomach.

"You really think we should read these?" I set the box on the coffee table. "These are all your uncle's private thoughts, written to my grandmother."

"Yes, I do," Roy said with such total conviction it almost startled me. "I think we should read them."

He walked to a window, stared at something, and ran his hand through his hair. "I'm not saying I'm completely comfortable with it. Yeah, it's kind of like invading somebody's privacy, I guess…but look, Ellen, your grandmother brought you into this, and now I guess my uncle has brought me into it. And we need to deal with it, for their sake and for ours, and move on. Whatever happened with them, we all need to let it go."

I thought about his choice of words. We *all* need to let it go. All of us, including our ancestors, who, as Roy said, had brought us into this. What he said made a lot of sense. I wondered if maybe, without realizing it, I had begun carrying some of my grandmother's burden on my shoulders ever since I found out I couldn't deliver the letter to Chet. *We need to deal with it and move on.* He was right.

"Okay," I said. "In that case, I guess you should start."

Roy picked up the envelope on top, the one with the oldest cancellation dates, and ran his finger under the flap. The single sheet of paper he removed, once white or cream, had faded to a warm tan. He opened the paper, smoothing out the deep creases, and as I sat on the edge of my chair, he slowly began to read.

December 2, 1950

Dear Ruth,

I'm still in shock since returning from seeing you in Chicago. It's one thing to read something in a letter and another to hear it in person. I can't believe you're really in love with him. I can see how you might be flattered by his attention. He's a medical student. He'll be a doctor someday. He's different from anyone you've ever met. And you're away from home for the first time in your life. But please examine your heart and be sure this is real.

Can you so easily turn your back on what we've had together? Can you really forget the past three years? We are so alike, you and I. We come from the same place; we want the same things. I know what you're thinking before you know it. Can you say that about Henry? How can he possibly know you the way I do? Or love you the way I love you?

What you believe is a romance could be simply an infatuation that will wear thin in a few months. You and I have memories. We have a past—the farm and the summer blueberries, listening to the radio on your parents' back porch, your easel and paints under the oak tree by the barn. I know we have a past and I thought we had a future. Please don't jeopardize

that. Take your time and think it over. Don't do something you
may regret. That's all I ask. Remember, there is no one who
loves you more than me.

Chet

I let out a long sigh. It felt strange hearing Roy read a letter
from his uncle to my grandmother. It made me feel as though I
needed to put myself in my grandmother's place and apologize
for her refusal to look at it, to acknowledge Chet's feelings. But I
wasn't my grandmother and Roy wasn't his uncle, so what good
would it do?

"My uncle wasn't the kind of a guy to give up easily," Roy said,
putting the letter back in its envelope and handing the next letter
to me.

The second one was dated less than a week after the first. Chet
asked my grandmother again to take her time and told her how
much he loved her. Then he described his life that Maine winter.

I saw George Cleary and Ruby Swan walking up Hubbard
Hill with a toboggan yesterday and I thought of you. I thought
about last winter, you and I hiking up that same hill together,
fresh snow crunching under our feet, our breath making clouds
in the air. It's cold here without you. The blueberry bushes are
bathed in ice and all night the wind howls like a hungry ani-
mal. I miss you. I love you.

"That's beautiful," I said, my eyes misting.
Why, I wondered, couldn't she have read these? Why couldn't

she have written him back? I felt terrible for Chet. I wished I could conjure up their spirits in a séance and let them speak to one another and say all the things they should have said when they were alive.

"I never knew my uncle was such a poet," Roy said, glancing at me. "He certainly was in love with your grandmother."

I nodded, not knowing what to say. I handed him the next letter, written in January of 1951.

I looked for you everywhere in town over Christmas week. I was hoping you would be home and that I'd catch a glimpse of you driving your father's Studebaker or see you at the skating pond. Then I heard you'd gone to California to stay with Henry's family for the holidays. My heart broke all over again. The winter is so long without you.

Two weeks later he wrote:

The Chapmans hung your painting on the wall of the café. It looks good in there. People point to it and talk about you winning the art contest. I'm glad you did the painting in the summer. It helps me remember what this place is like without all the snow.

In February, Chet told my grandmother he heard of her engagement to my grandfather. "I wonder how I can go on," he wrote, "knowing you will be his wife, knowing he's in the place where I long to be."

In May, he wrote a letter from Vermont.

I moved here because I had to leave Beacon. My cousin Ben got me a job in a lumber mill. Although the spring is finally here, I couldn't bear to be around the farm. Without you, its beauty is gone, and what I once felt for the land has left me. There are only painful memories. My father doesn't understand. He still persists in wanting me to run the place. He says he's getting old and it's time for me to take over. But that was never the plan. You and I were supposed to do that together. Isn't it odd how something you feel is so important becomes meaningless in the end?

I heard that you're leaving Chicago and that next fall you'll be in college in California. It makes me sad to know you will be even farther away. I also heard that you stopped painting. If that's true, it's a terrible mistake. You're so talented, Ruth. Don't ever stop painting.

By the time Roy finished reading, my heart was breaking for Chet. Gran had ignored every one of his letters and, in the end, he'd left his farm and his hometown all because of her.

I took the letter from Roy and read it silently. As I did, I began to realize what my grandmother's apology was really about, what she felt so bad about.

"I know what Gran meant in her letter," I said. "When she wrote that part about your uncle giving up the thing he loved the most." I looked at Roy. "It was the farm."

He nodded. "Yeah." His voice was quiet. "I think you're right."

We sat there for a moment, both of us staring at the cedar box, and then Roy picked up the last envelope and opened it.

July 9, 1951

Dear Ruth,

I saw you last week in Beacon. Isn't it strange that we were both back in town at the same time? I came to help my mother clean out the house. I don't know if you heard, but they sold the farm.

I saw you with Henry, sitting on the seawall. You were holding his hand. At first, I only saw you from the back, but I knew right away it was you. I know every wave of your hair, the silhouette of your face, the tilt of your head. I watched you for a while. You turned to look at him and you laughed. You put your head on his shoulder. He pointed to something. I think it might have been a flying fish. I watched you for a while, and then I said good-bye to the girl I used to know.

For months I thought if I ever saw Henry or saw you with him, it would be the death of me. But it wasn't. Maybe it's because you looked so happy. I was glad for that. I want you to be happy. And maybe it's because now I understand that what happened when you left Beacon was your destiny.

Chet

I began to cry, tears rolling down my cheeks. "I hate that she never read these. I wish I could apologize for her."

Roy put down the letter. "Ellen, you don't need to apologize. Your grandmother already did that. She wrote a letter. She sent you up here to deliver it. She wanted to make things right." He leaned in a little closer. "If you want to know the truth, I feel sad for *her*."

I wiped a tear away with my hand. "You do?"

"Yes," he said. "She was still thinking about my uncle when she died. Doesn't that tell you something? That she felt terrible about it to the very end. She carried all that inside of her for years. That's awful."

I hadn't thought about it that way. How much of my grandmother's life, I wondered, was wrapped up in the events that took place more than sixty years ago? "Maybe you're right," I said, picking up one of the envelopes and smoothing out the wrinkles. "But why did it have to be so complicated?"

Roy shook his head and gave a little shrug. "I don't know. Because love is complicated, I guess." He put the letters back in the box. "Here's what's really sad. Think about it—what did she do that was so wrong?"

He stared at me so intently, his blue eyes like pulsing stars, I thought he could see into my soul. I looked down.

"She fell in love with someone else, Ellen. That happens to people. I'm not saying it was no big deal that my uncle got hurt, but it's part of life. He went on. Eventually he married my aunt. Things work out, you know."

Roy put his hand on my arm. "Let's let it go. They've made their peace with one another."

"You're right," I said, committing to memory the feel of his hand. "They've made their peace."

I turned the key and put the car in drive, but I didn't press the gas pedal. I moved the gearshift back into park and sat there for a minute, in front of Roy's house. What was it he'd said? *She fell in love with someone else... that happens to people.* Was he talking only about my grandmother, or was he also talking about me?

I glanced back at the house. Did Roy think I was in love with him? Did he really think that? I clasped the gearshift with my hand.

Well, I wasn't...was I?

Chapter 18

Return to the Antler

I sat on the bed at the Victory Inn, a towel around me, my wet hair dripping from the shower. I was still thinking about my grandmother and Chet and the letters. Roy was right. It was time to let it go. They'd made their peace. The clock on the bedside table said five fifty. Hayden had been gone for hours with the *New York Times* people, but he'd finally left a message when I was in the shower and said he was on his way back.

I picked up a bottle of Caution to the Wind nail polish, gave it a shake, and began to brush the red liquid over the nails of my left foot while I went over the plan for the evening. Hayden and I would have cocktails with my mother in the lounge downstairs. Then he and I would have dinner at a cozy table I'd reserved in the dining room, and afterward we would come back upstairs for Champagne. I'd managed to get Paula to part with a few candles, and I had a bottle of Dom Pérignon chilling in an ice bucket. I would have preferred a 1996 vintage, but I settled for the '98 because that was all they had at the Wine Cellar. I was all set. We'd enjoy our dinner, pop open the Champagne, get a little drunk, get a little romantic. It sounded pretty good. It sounded...

"Oh, great, I'm glad you're getting ready."

I looked up and saw Hayden breeze into the room.

"We're meeting Jim and Tally for dinner," he said, checking his watch. "At seven."

"Who?" I put the cap back on the bottle.

He dropped the car keys on the bureau. "The *Times* reporter and photographer. I told them we'd have dinner with them."

"Tonight?" He couldn't mean tonight. Not the one night I wanted us to be alone, *needed* us to be alone.

Hayden opened the closet door. "I'm sorry, honey. I know it's last-minute, but they really want to meet you and they didn't have any plans, so...oh, by the way, Paula told me your mother's here. That's a surprise."

"Yes, Mom's here. She got into one of her worried modes because I didn't call her back. You know how she—"

"We'll take her with us," he said, placing a pair of trousers and a shirt on the bed.

I turned to him. "Oh, Hayden, I was thinking maybe we could eat here tonight. You know, just a nice quiet little dinner in the dining room...by ourselves. We're spending the whole morning with them tomorrow on the photo shoot and the interview. And I got a bottle of Dom."

He sat down next to me on the bed and draped his arm around my shoulder. "Sweetheart, this is the kind of thing we have to do. I promised them we'd go out. They really want to see the town." He brushed his hand across my cheek. "We'll have the Champagne when we get back.

"And besides," he added as he began to change clothes, "guess where Tally, the photographer, grew up?"

"I don't know, Hayden."

And I really don't care, I thought as I shook the bottle of nail polish again and began to apply a second coat. Why were these people dictating our whole evening?

Hayden buckled his belt. "Right down the street from my uncle Greer in Locust Valley. She knows my cousin Debbie."

He walked into the bathroom before I could say anything. I could see him combing his hair in front of the mirror.

"Oh, you'll love Jim and Tally," he called out as he buttoned his shirt. "And it's just one night. They've picked out some place called the Anchor." He began to run the water in the sink.

The Anchor. "I hope it's not far," I said. "I'm really not up for a long drive." Maybe, if we got finished early enough, we could wedge in half of a romantic evening together.

"I think they said it's in Beacon."

I thought for a moment, the nail polish brush in my hand. "The Anchor? Never heard of it." That meant it could be twenty miles away. I wasn't happy.

Hayden appeared in the doorway, drying his hands. "Oh, maybe it wasn't the Anchor. But something like that." He paused. "The Antler? Yeah, I think that's it."

The brush fell from my hand, depositing a bright red glob of nail polish on my ankle. "The Antler?"

I wasn't going back to the Antler! I couldn't go back to the Antler. What if the bartender recognized me? "I've heard their food's not that good," I said, trying to rub out the spot with my finger. "Why don't we try some other place?"

"Tally really wants to go there," Hayden said as he glanced in the bathroom mirror and fussed with his part one last time.

Tally again. Why was she calling the shots?

He turned to me. "She said she wants to pick up some of the local flavor, and the Antler looked like a good place to do it."

Local flavor. Who did she think she was, Margaret Mead?

I could see I was fighting a losing battle. "Yeah, all right," I muttered, trying to convince myself I had nothing to worry about. After all, they had to have more than one bartender. Maybe it would be Skip's night off.

A poster board outside the Antler announced LIVE MUSIC BY THE RIPCHORDS & KARAOKE NIGHT! Mom followed Hayden inside, and I followed Mom. She had shed her country club attire for a pair of cotton pants and an Indian print tunic I'd never seen before, and her gold bracelets were gone, replaced by a simple beaded cuff.

Even before my eyes adjusted to the muted light and orange glow I knew the place was packed. People were laughing and shouting, and a steady buzz of conversation hummed around us.

Hayden glanced at me. "Looks packed for a Tuesday night."

I bit my lip and nodded.

"Do you see the people we're meeting?" my mother asked.

Hayden looked around. "No, but let's keep walking toward the back. We'll find them."

We passed crowded tables loaded with food and pitchers of beer. About halfway across the room, I thought I heard someone say the word *swimmer*. Don't get paranoid, I told myself as we squeezed through a cluster of people.

Someone called Hayden's name, and a tall man in his early forties waved to us from a table in the corner.

"Come on," Hayden said. "That's Jim."

I walked toward the table, staring at the woman sitting next to Jim and suddenly feeling underdressed in my white cotton pants and tan sweater. Tall and lean and wearing a powder-blue dress that intensified the color of her eyes, she reminded me of a sleek sports car. Her chin-length hair, very smooth and naturally blond, looked like it had been cut and then pressed into place one strand at a time, it fell so perfectly around her face.

On the other hand, Jim seemed the complete opposite—laid-back in his khakis and polo shirt, his hair a little disheveled, his tortoiseshell glasses slightly askew on his face. Hayden made the introductions, and when Jim shook my hand and smiled I noticed he had a crooked upper front tooth that gave him an endearing look.

Mom sat down next to Jim, and Hayden and I took seats on the opposite side of the table.

"I don't think I've ever heard the name Tally before," I said, turning to the photographer. "Is that a family name?"

Tally smiled and blinked her long eyelashes. "Not in the usual sense," she said. The pitch of her voice was low, and she spoke slowly, as if she were choosing every thought from a long-established repertoire. She emphasized the *u* in "usual," drawing out the sound to take up more than its initial place in the word. "My real name is Sally, but my younger sister always called me Tally and it just stuck. You know how those things go."

Never having had siblings, I wasn't sure I did, but I nodded. "Hayden tells me you grew up in Locust Valley, near his uncle."

"Until boarding school," she said. "I knew his cousin Deborah." She smiled at Hayden. "Good tennis player."

"Yes, she still is," Hayden said.

"I beat her in the club finals, though," Tally added with a beaming smile and a flick of her hair.

"Well, then..." Hayden said, giving a little laugh. He turned to Jim. "Have you been here before?"

"Do you mean Maine or Beacon?" Tally said, ignoring the fact that Hayden had directed the question to Jim. "Or," she whispered, a faint smile on her lips, "the Antler?"

"Maine or Beacon," I said, looking at Tally and then at Jim and then at my mother, who wore a polite smile but who, I knew, was taking all of this in.

Tally placed her long manicured fingers around the stem of her wineglass. "My family has a little place in Kennebunkport so I know a few things about Maine, but I've never been to Beacon."

Jim laughed. "A *little* place in Kennebunkport?" He let out a low whistle.

Tally elbowed him. "Don't you start in on me now."

Jim took an olive from his martini glass and popped it into his mouth. "Well, it's not little. I think you have to agree with that."

Tally waved him off and then adjusted her gold necklace so that the pendant, a sailboat, lay flat against her skin.

"This must be a very popular place," my mother said, glancing at the crowd standing two deep at the bar.

Jim raised his martini glass. "Good thing I made a reservation."

Hayden looked around, eyeing the hanging lanterns, the sepia-tone photos of Beacon in its early years, the heavily varnished bar with its orange hue. "Yes, good thing," he said, a look of bewilderment on his face as he glanced at the moose and deer heads on the walls.

A waitress descended upon us with a stack of menus and an order pad. She had a pen behind her ear. "Skip, the *baa-tendah*, told me to get you a round of drinks on the house." She shot me a grin. "After all, you're famous here."

I turned toward the bar and caught Skip looking straight at me. He waved and smiled, dimples forming in his round cheeks. "Hey, Swimma, welcome back!"

Hayden looked from Skip to me. "What did he call you and why is he giving us a round of drinks?"

I saw Mom's face go slightly ashen.

Tally raised an eyebrow. "You're famous at the Antler?" She let out a little laugh and then leaned toward me. "And just what does one have to do to become famous here?" she said, half whispering. Then she smiled in a conspiratorial way, as though we were old friends sharing a secret.

I shook my head and tried to give a casual shrug. "I guess I look like someone else."

Hayden glanced at Skip again and turned back to me. He was about to say something when the waitress interrupted.

"So what'll it be?"

For a split second I saw a look in Hayden's eye, the kind of look people get when they suspect they're not in on the joke, but then it vanished and he turned to my mother. "Why don't you start, Cynthia?"

"All right, then," my mother said. "I'll have a Bacardi daiquiri."

"I thought you quit drinking rum," I murmured to her, a

frightening visual of my mother dancing at her neighbor's anniversary party coming to mind.

"Oh, it's fine," she muttered back, waving me off.

"Sure thing," the waitress said, scribbling on her pad. Then she turned to me. I was about to order a glass of wine when she added, "Hey, I'm real sorry I missed the big night last week." She gave me an apologetic look. "The dart game and the Dead Presidents. Way to go!"

The dart game and the Dead Presidents. I could feel my throat start to tighten up.

"Dead Presidents?" Hayden asked. "Who are they? A band?"

The waitress laughed. "That's funny, pal. You got a sense of humor." She clapped Hayden on the back. He coughed and then turned to me, startled.

The waitress placed coasters in front of us. "You know you got a ringer here?" she said to Hayden. "She's good. Wow."

Hayden, Mom, Jim, and Tally all stared at me. "A ringer?" Jim said, smiling. "What's this all about?"

I glared at the waitress. "I think you've got me confused with someone else."

She glanced toward the bar. "But Skip said you were—"

I held up my hand. "Yes, I know, but I think Skip needs glasses."

"He wears contacts."

"Well, new contacts, then."

"He has new contacts."

"Well, *something*," I said, now totally flustered. The last thing I needed was for Hayden to find out what happened, and she was about to blow my cover.

"Look, could we just finish up the drink order here?" I said. "I'd like a diet cola, please." No way was I going to have anything with alcohol in it. I needed to keep my wits about me. That was certain.

"Yeah, all right." The waitress shook her head, mumbled something, took the other orders, and walked away.

Hayden leaned toward me. "Did she just say you should have kept drowning? What in the world was she talking about?"

"Hayden, I think your hearing's going. And you're not even forty." I forced a smile.

Jim laughed, but Hayden kept staring at me, as though he knew something wasn't right. All of a sudden it felt like the temperature in the room had risen twenty degrees. I could feel my face flush, and now everybody at the table was looking at me, waiting for me to say something more, but my mouth wouldn't move.

Then a miracle happened. The back door opened and the band members came trooping in, carrying guitars, drums, an electric piano, and some other instruments, and the whole restaurant erupted with applause and hoots.

"They must be popular," Hayden said, looking surprised.

"Let's hope they're decent," Tally said, tipping her chin up slightly, as though she were resting something on it. "We're a little far from civilization here."

The band started tuning up, and after a few minutes the waitress returned with our drinks and then went around the table, taking the dinner orders.

I hadn't even looked at the menu, but there were two things I remembered from my first night here, meat loaf and lobster. I didn't want the meat loaf again, so I blurted out, "Twin lobsters with drawn butter. Oh, and fries." I snapped the menu shut and put my hands in my lap.

Hayden's eyes almost popped out of his head. "Drawn butter? Fries? Have you lost your mind? I thought you were always so worried about your cholesterol, Ellen. You'll need a prescription for Lipitor before you leave this place." He shook his head, stared at me a moment longer, and then turned to Tally. I heard him ask her something about Kennebunkport.

Here goes, I thought. I took a drink of my diet cola and tried to hear what Tally was saying, but it was impossible because at that moment the band broke into a rendition of the Johnny Cash song "Ring of Fire." Several couples got up to dance, including a husband and wife with matching "I ♥ Maine" T-shirts. I watched the husband lead his wife around the floor, occasionally stepping on her feet. The band finished "Ring of Fire" and then went into Van Morrison's "Wild Night."

Jim leaned across the table and asked me how long we were planning to stay in Beacon. I tried to have a conversation with him, but it was hard shouting back and forth, and after a little while I gestured that I couldn't hear anything.

I looked at the dance floor, which had turned into a mass of gyrating limbs under the dim light. Then I glanced toward the door and, as I did, I saw Roy Cummings walk in. He was wearing a blue Windbreaker, and he moved slowly through the crowd, occasionally tipping his Red Sox baseball cap or pointing to someone and smiling.

Oh, no, I thought, feeling a breath of air lodge in my lungs like a trapped bubble. Roy and Hayden in the same place again. This couldn't be good.

Roy saw me and waved. Then he walked to the table. "Well, this is a surprise, Ellen." He tipped his hat. "Guess you're a real fan of the Antler."

I could feel Hayden staring at me. I said hello and made some clumsy introductions to Mom and Jim and Tally, ending with, "You remember Hayden."

"Yeah... golf courses," Roy said, shaking Hayden's hand.

I laughed nervously, glancing from Roy to Hayden, my mother peering at me.

"Would you like to join us?" Jim asked. "We can pull up another chair."

Hayden's face stiffened.

"No," Roy said, "but thanks. I'm just stopping in for a minute."

"Jim and Tally are from the *New York Times*," I said, trying to think of something to say.

"The *Times*?" Roy said, turning to Jim. "You should meet Scotty Bluff. He's over there." Roy pointed across the room. "He's the publisher of the *Bugle*. That's our local paper." He glanced at me. "I think Ellen is familiar with it."

I could feel a red glare slide across my face.

Roy put his hand on the back of my chair. "Hey, Ellen, could I talk to you for a minute?"

I looked up at him. He didn't have the razor stubble. His face was smooth. He had a glint in his eyes. "I don't know. I've got guests here, and—"

"I just need a minute."

"Hayden, do you mind?" I whispered. "This is probably about my grandmother and his uncle."

"Do what you've got to do," he said, putting his hand on mine.

"I'll be right back," I told him.

I followed Roy as we elbowed our way through the crowd to the door. Outside, he led the way down the street, past a half dozen stores, and then stopped in front of Frank's Tailoring. I could see racks of clothes inside, hanging in gossamer plastic sheets—skirts and dresses in summer colors and men's suit pants and jackets. In the front window a vintage wedding gown was on display. I imagined for a second the bakeshop that had been there for so many years, cookies and cupcakes in baskets on a counter, and the promise of something warm and delicious when you opened the door.

"Thanks for stepping out a minute," Roy said.

"Yeah, well, fancy meeting you at the Antler." The little tremble in my voice was back again.

Roy took off his Red Sox cap and ran a hand through his hair. "It wasn't a coincidence. I went to the inn looking for you."

I didn't think I'd heard him right. "Pardon?"

He put the cap back on his head, giving the brim a little tug. "I went looking for you at the Victory Inn."

He went looking for me. I felt like I was going to melt.

Inside the shop, a ceiling light flickered, sending out a soft glow, like heat lightning. "Paula said you'd be at the Antler."

He had asked Paula where I was. He had gone there to find me. He must have found something else of his uncle's, something more about Chet and Gran.

"Why were you looking for me? Did you find something else?" I stared at the *B* on his baseball cap until the letter dissolved into a blur.

He shook his head. "No, it's not that." He paused. "I'm leaving in the morning. I have to be away for a couple of weeks… some work stuff."

The light inside the tailor shop flickered again, and my heart began sinking at the thought of him being away. He was leaving in the morning. And I was leaving in the afternoon, once the interviews and photo shoot were done. That meant I'd never see him again. I felt like I was plummeting into a hole.

Roy leaned against the window. "I really wanted to talk to you before I left," he said, and then he stared at the pavement for a full half a minute, rubbing the back of his neck.

Finally he took a small bag from the pocket of his Windbreaker and handed it to me.

Whatever was inside wasn't very heavy.

"Open it," he said.

I put my hand in and pulled out something square, tiny. Holding it up to the window light, I saw what it was, and my heart stopped. It was a miniature wooden house, exquisitely crafted. Painted white with sky-blue trim, the house was no more than five inches in width or depth or height. It had a wraparound porch, three chimneys, two dormers, wooden shutters, and windows made of real glass. I had never seen anything so small and yet so beautifully detailed.

"Where did you get this?" I asked, my voice dissolving to a whisper.

Roy smiled. "Do you like it?"

"It's beautiful." Mesmerized, I turned it over, studying it from all angles.

"I made it," Roy said.

I couldn't believe it. This was the kind of thing that could only be made with tweezers and toothpicks and the kind of patience I couldn't fathom.

"It's amazing," I said, marveling at the tiny porch railing and the red-painted chimney bricks.

"Ellen," Roy said as I held up the house and peered through the miniature windows. "I told you if I ever found the right girl again I'd build her a palace. It's not the Taj Mahal, but it's the kind of palace I could build for us."

He had built me a palace. He was saying I was the right girl. I gazed at him, with his dimples and his smile, and he looked so handsome and so confident and so accomplished.

He brushed his hand across my cheek. "I'm in love with you, Ellen. That's the bottom line. I'm in love with you and I want us to be together. I know I can give you a good life. I know I can make you happy. That's a promise."

I looked down at the tiny house nestled in my hand. How could I tell him that I felt something? That of course I felt something. That I couldn't stop thinking about our dance that night at the Antler. That when he took my hand in the wildflowers at Kenlyn Farm, a vibration went through me like the vibrato of a note played on a violin string. And that even though I tried to convince myself that my feelings for him were just an infatuation, because he'd boosted my ego or saved my life, I knew, standing there, that it was something more primal.

But I had made a commitment to Hayden. And we were too

far down that path. I couldn't back out now. It was crazy to even think about it.

I took a deep breath. "You're a nice guy," I said. "A really wonderful man, in fact. You have a certain way about you...a certain charm that's different from anyone I've ever known." Oh, God, this was sounding so stupid. "And I appreciate all the things you said. It's all lovely, really lovely." I stopped to collect my thoughts. "And this little house"—I held it up—"it *is* a palace. It's magnificent and it's amazing and it deserves to go to someone who will love you and share your dreams."

I looked down. "But that person isn't me. I can't be with you." I held up my engagement ring and let the diamonds dance under the streetlight. "I'm engaged to Hayden. And I'm getting married in a few months. It's all planned, and Mom's halfway through her checklist."

I thought about my mother and how I'd be letting her down, too. She loved Hayden. And she loved the idea of Hayden and me together. "Mom has it all figured out," I said, "and when we get back we'll be sending out the invitations. They're printed. I've got one in the room, in fact." I pointed in the direction of the inn.

"The invitations," Roy murmured, looking past me.

"Yes," I said, imagining the ivory card tucked into the mirror—the date, the time, the place. "It's all arranged," I said. "All final."

Roy's eyes caught mine and he held me in his gaze.

"And Hayden's a good person," I rushed on. "He's wonderful, really. We're cut from the same cloth. I know I'll be happy with him." I nodded emphatically. "And let's face it, I live in New

York City. That's hundreds of miles away. And I have a good career going. I'm pretty well respected for what I do."

"I'm not asking you to leave your job," Roy said. "I'm just telling you that I know I could make you happy, Ellen."

Two teenagers on bicycles, a boy and girl, pedaled lazily past us down the darkened street. I watched them until they turned a corner.

"Look," I added. "Putting all that aside for the sake of argument, you don't even know me. And if you did, I'm sure you wouldn't like me. I'm stubborn and I act like I know everything and I'm high-maintenance and I grind my teeth at night."

Roy leaned against the wall of the tailor shop. "I already know all that," he said. "Except for the teeth-grinding part. And I probably know a lot more about you than you think. I even looked you up on the Winston Reid website. Picture's pretty good, by the way."

He had looked me up on the website. He liked my picture. Oh, God, why did he have to keep saying these things? "That picture's awful."

"No, it's good," he insisted. "And everything about you on the Internet—I read it all. And then I found every article that mentioned you. And I found your photographs."

"My photographs?"

"Yeah, the ones you have on that blog. The pictures you took in Italy...I liked those the best. The way you see things, Ellen..." He paused. "You have a way of looking at the world that's really special. It's beautiful. It's a gift."

I felt my heart do a double beat. I wanted to collapse into his arms. I wanted him to hold me forever and tell me these things again and again.

But I couldn't do that. I was getting married.

"Roy," I said. "You did your research. You know a little bit about me, but—"

"No, wait a minute." He stepped closer. "I know a *lot* about you, Ellen." He had hooked me in his gaze again, and I couldn't look away.

"I know you're smart and you're funny. And I know you love your family very much. That's obvious by the way you talk about your grandmother and by the fact that you came up here for her. I also know you're loyal and dependable, that you never want to let anyone down once you've given your word. And you're an artist, just like your grandmother. Even if photography is only a hobby right now, you need to keep doing it, because you're great at it."

He tilted back his head and peered at me. "And yeah, you're right. You do go around thinking you know everything. I figured that out right away in the ocean. You were in the middle of whitecaps trying to convince me you didn't need any help because you were on the swim team at Exeter." He smiled, and I couldn't help smiling myself.

"But I know that's just the way you are on the outside," he said. "And you know what?" He lifted my chin and gazed at me. "I love that about you. I love that about you because... well, because I love you."

I looked away so he wouldn't see the tears brimming in my eyes. The wedding gown in the window swirled with beading and lace. I gazed at the tiny pearls stitched into the bodice, the yards of fabric carefully sewn together for some magical day long ago. I thought about everything Roy had told me. And then I told him what I really wanted to believe.

"Look, I'm sorry," I said. "I'm really, really sorry, but I'm just not in love with you, Roy. Infatuated, maybe. Interested, maybe. But not in love. I'm in love with Hayden." I paused and forced a smile. "And I'm going to marry him."

Roy stared at the moon, a silver crescent in the sky. I stood there, not sure whether I wanted him to believe me or not. Finally, he turned back to me. "Well, that's another story," he said. Then he shoved his hands into his pockets. "I can't change the way you feel, Ellen. I thought I was pretty good at figuring people out—I really thought you felt something like I did or I would never have come here tonight. But I see now I was wrong."

He glanced down at the pavement and then back at me. "Well, I guess that's that." His voice sounded lost; his eyes looked tired. He reached into the pocket of his Windbreaker and took out a folded sheet of blue paper. My grandmother's letter.

"I've been carrying this around with me, but now I think you should have it back," he said.

"But I wanted you to keep—"

"No, Ellen. You should have this. It might be the last thing your grandmother ever wrote."

I looked at the letter and then reached out for it. Roy took my hand, held it for a moment, and then let my fingers slip through his. "Well, Swimmer, good-bye, then." He gave me a little nod, turned, and walked down the street.

I heard his footsteps on the sidewalk. I watched him get into his truck and heard the purr of the engine. I saw the lights come on and I watched him drive away, the red taillights fading into darkness.

Chapter 19

Confession

I walked back to the Antler, the salt air heavy in my lungs. I had done the right thing, the only possible thing to do. I felt certain. I opened the door and pushed my way through the crowd. The band was playing "Don't It Make My Brown Eyes Blue," an old Crystal Gayle tune. The tall brunette girl who was singing was doing too good a job with the song, her voice drenched in sadness, and it made me feel like I could cry any second.

Edging my way through the crowd, I made it back to the table. Hayden was talking to Jim and Tally. A man with a handlebar mustache was standing at the other end of the table, chatting with my mother. I sat down next to Hayden.

"So what was all that about?" Hayden asked.

"Nothing much," I said, trying to sound upbeat. "Just some things about his uncle. About the farm."

"The farm?" Hayden peered at me. "He came here to tell you something about that farm?"

298

"He's going away for a couple of weeks."

Hayden took a sip of wine. I could tell he was mulling this over. I could feel him looking at me, wondering if there wasn't something more to the story. In a deposition, this is when he would begin his methodical interrogation of the witness.

I noticed the waitress out of the corner of my eye and flagged her down. "I'd like a drink, please. Right away."

"Another soda?"

"What kind of Scotch do you have?"

"Uh, let's see." She began ticking off the names on her fingers. "We've got Dewar's, J and B, Johnnie Walker…" She rattled off a couple of others.

Hayden blinked. "Scotch, Ellen? Since when do you drink Scotch?"

From the corner of my eye, I could see Jim stabbing the olive in his drink with a fork. "Since now," I said. "I'll have a Johnnie Walker Black." And then I added, as if I knew what I was doing, "On the rocks."

"Got it," the waitress said as she picked up a couple of empty glasses and hustled off.

Hayden leaned in. "What's going on with you tonight? You're like a different person. People here think you're someone else, you're drinking Scotch, eating lobster and fries. Maybe you *are* someone else."

"Maybe I wish I was," I mumbled.

He looked at me, surprised. "What do you mean?"

"Nothing," I said, waving him off.

The man with the mustache left and Mom moved to a seat across from me. "I just met the publisher of the local paper," she said. "Do you know he moved here from New Jersey? Fascinating man. He wants me to play darts later."

"Darts?" Hayden and I asked.

"Yes, darts. With a board and a target." She smiled like a little girl and rubbed her hands together. "What fun."

This was too much. Roy Cummings's declaration of love; my mother throwing darts with the publisher of the *Bugle*. When my Scotch came, I took an enormous gulp, letting it blast its way down my throat. I began to cough, feeling as though my lungs were constricting.

"Kind of like drinking jet fuel," I gasped.

"You're supposed to sip it," Jim said, eyeing me with a wry smile.

"So I've heard." I took another long drink. It burned the whole way down.

The band began to play "Proud Mary," an old Creedence Clearwater Revival tune.

"I always liked this song," Hayden said.

"Me, too," Tally said. "Maybe Ellen would let you dance with me." She gave me a wink, as though she and I were plotting this together.

The nerve, I thought, but then I placated myself with the knowledge that I'd have the last laugh. Hayden would never get up and dance in a place like this.

"Don't take it personally, Tally," I said, "but Hayden isn't one for..." I stopped because he was already getting up from his chair to escort her to the dance floor. Upset and angry, I watched them walk away.

The *Bugle* publisher with the mustache returned, and the next thing I knew my mother got up as well. She winked at me and made a little motion as though she were throwing a dart. I felt like everyone was deserting me.

Jim moved to the seat across from me, cracking an ice cube between his teeth. "Want to dance?"

"Not really," I said, lifting my glass to take another drink, but getting only ice cubes.

He nodded and stirred his drink with his finger. "You know," he said after a moment, "you've got an interesting way of drinking Scotch, hammering it down like you do."

"I usually drink wine," I said. "And I sip it."

He seemed to be considering this. Then he leaned across the table. "My editor, Tom, is really excited about doing this series on you and Hayden. Looks like it's going to be quite a wedding."

I reached for my glass and rattled the ice. "I didn't realize we'd become nuptial standard-bearers," I said, taking a couple of sips of ice water.

Jim raised his eyebrows. "Oh, no? I'm under the impression that anything you do, you do quite well, Miss Branford." He grinned and cracked another ice cube. I liked his smile and his crooked tooth.

"And how would you know that, when we've just met?" I glanced at the dance floor, looking for Hayden, but all I could see was one solid mass of moving bodies.

"Ah, I do my research. And one of the things I read was that piece about you in *New York* magazine."

"Oh, God, the Lark-Hawkins thing?" I grumbled. "I don't know why that was in the headlines so much. Zoning issues usually put people to sleep."

"It was a big development," Jim said. "There was a lot at stake."

"That article was hardly about me," I said. "And anyway, it's ancient history."

Jim sank back in his chair and peered at me. "It was three years ago and the writer was very complimentary." He raised his empty glass at our waitress, who bustled by without stopping.

"Complimentary? He hated me. Said I was a skirt-wearing shark, as I recall."

Jim shrugged. "Maybe. But he said your plan was brilliant. I remember that."

"All right then, I'm brilliant."

"Agreed." He craned his neck for a waitress, then pointed to my glass. "You want another one? I'm heading to the bar."

I nodded.

When he returned he was clutching an armload of drinks.

"That's enough for the whole table," I said.

"Affirmative, Captain. Skip, the bartender, insisted. Said they were on the house."

Well, I thought, if you can't beat them, join them. I picked up a glass of Scotch, tilted it, and let the amber liquid glide down my throat. It was starting to taste pretty good—warm, almost smooth.

The waitress came over with a tray laden with plates of food.

I stared at the lobsters on the platter she put in front of me, feeling suddenly ravenous. "Do you think we should wait for the others?"

Jim put his napkin in his lap and picked up a fork. "No, I don't."

I ate some french fries and gaped at the lobster before me. It looked daunting.

"So," Jim said. "How does it feel now that you're just a few months away?"

"A few months away from what?" I asked, eyeing the metal lobster cracker and wondering if there were tiny instructions printed on it somewhere. I picked it up, but didn't see anything. I'd never been too adept at using them.

"A few months away from your wedding."

"Oh, is the interview starting now?" The room had become warm and fuzzy all of a sudden, the lights radiating a red glow.

"Just background."

"Okay," I said, drawing out the last syllable while I tried to remember what the question was. Oh, right—something about how I was feeling now that the wedding was so close.

"Well, I'm happy about it," I said. "Of course. I mean, how else would I feel?"

"Oh, I don't know," Jim said. "Sometimes people get a little nervous when they get closer to the actual date. You know, they worry about whether everything will go well, all be perfect, that kind of thing."

I shrugged. "Not me. It's all under control. Mom's helping me and she's very—" I was about to say she was very organized, but before I knew what was happening, something else came out. "Actually, she's a professional wedding planner. Yeah, and a very good one, so I don't have to worry about a thing."

What was I saying and why was I saying it? It was obviously the Scotch talking, but I couldn't help myself.

Jim looked surprised. "A wedding planner. Wow, that's

lucky." He raised his glass to take a drink, as ice cubes floated around like tiny glaciers.

"No kidding," I said, feeling as though I was having an out-of-body experience. "Good thing she was able to squeeze us in."

Jim looked shocked. "You mean she's that busy? She might not have been able to handle *your* wedding?"

"Oh, she's busy all right," I said. The words were tumbling out now, faster than my brain could keep up with them. "Well, not just with the wedding stuff. She also travels a lot." I paused. "Dart tournaments." I stirred my drink with my finger, as Jim had.

He eyed me skeptically, one side of his mouth turning up. "Darts?"

"Yeah," I said, pointing toward the end of the restaurant where the dartboard was located. It was impossible to see what was going on, though, because so many people were in the way. "She's over there now, probably giving tips to the other players."

"That's...amazing," Jim said.

I could tell he didn't know what to think. "Do you know," I said, leaning in closer, "that she paid for our summer house on Nantucket with her winnings one year?" This was becoming fun.

He let out a low whistle. "Impressive." He cocked his head. "I doubt there are many people who can do what she does. Wedding planner and tournament-level dart player." I could see a faint smile on his lips. "My mom's just a plain old CPA."

I took another drink. It tasted good, and I was finally feeling good, light and floaty. I started tapping my foot to the beat of the music. The band was playing Faith Hill's "The Lucky One."

"So," Jim said after a moment. "I was wondering—did you two meet at Winston Reid?"

I sat back in my chair. "Yes, we met in the cafeteria. There was only one bok-choy-and-noodle salad left, and Hayden let me have it."

"The mark of a true gentleman."

"Yes, it was," I said. "Then, on our first date, he took me to a fund-raiser for the governor. We just"—I clasped my hands together—"hit it off."

"I hear Hayden's interested in politics himself. That he's going to make a run for city council."

I stared at the lobster again, with its hard, shiny shell. Then I looked for the waitress to see if someone in the kitchen would crack the shell for me, but the waitress wasn't in sight.

"City council?" I said, dragging some french fries through a mound of ketchup and popping them in my mouth. "Yeah, he is." I washed it all down with more Scotch. The room was radiating, throbbing, moving, a little off-kilter. "He wants to do that."

Jim nodded and sliced through a steaming baked potato. "And what about you? Are you interested in politics?"

"Who, me?" I laughed. "Nope. I don't want to run for anything. I want to do something different." I stabbed another fry.

Jim leaned back in his chair and gazed at me. "Different. Like what?"

Like what. I tried to think of something clever. And then a vision of Gran and her blueberry muffins slipped into my head.

"Like...well, open a bakery," I said.

Jim looked surprised.

"Of course, my specialty would be blueberries." I gave him the most earnest look I could muster. The Scotch was really ramping up now, and I was enjoying this.

"Blueberries?" he asked, shaking his head, as if he hadn't heard right.

I nodded. "Sure. It's an untapped market, you know. I could make blueberry muffins. My grandmother was great at those." I closed my eyes and pictured her stirring the batter. *Don't overmix it, Ellen, or they'll be like rubber.* "Yeah, this place needs a better-quality blueberry muffin." I raised a pointed finger. "And I could provide it."

"You sound pretty sure of yourself," Jim said, placing a pat of butter on his baked potato.

"And there are always blueberry pies," I said, pausing to think of other possibilities. "Turnovers, cakes, croissants..." I popped the fry into my mouth. "I don't think anybody's done blueberry croissants."

"No," Jim said slowly. "I don't think they have."

"Of course, I'd sell some other things, too. Can't all be blue-berries," I mused as I began to envision the bakery—a tray of lemon pound cake, peach cobbler in a fluted casserole, a basket of pomegranate-and-ginger muffins. I could see myself pulling a baking sheet of cookies from the oven, the smell of melted choco-late in the air. There would be white wooden tables and chairs in the front room, and people could order coffee and sandwiches. Maybe even tea sandwiches, like the ones Gran used to make. Cucumber and arugula. Bacon and egg. Curried chicken. And people could sit and read the newspaper, and...

Someone tapped my arm. I looked up and saw Jim staring at me.

"Where'd you go?"

"Sorry," I said. "I was just thinking about the bakery."

"I gather you like food."

I nodded, trying to envision what color accents would look nice in a room with white tables and chairs. Blue? White and blue was always a great combination. Fresh. Beachy.

"But what about politics?" Jim asked.

Yes, white and blue. Did he say politics? I looked across the table at Jim. "Excuse me?" I grabbed another french fry with my fingers.

"I was just wondering, given Hayden's family...and Hayden wanting to run for office. Do you like the world of politics?"

Did I like the world of politics? The question caught me a little off guard. I looked down at my lobster...the spiny legs, the claws. Sure, I was interested in politics. Who wasn't? But did I really like it? I'd always thought most politicians were liars and crooks, Hayden's family excepted, of course. I was afraid my answer might be *No, I don't really like the world of politics.*

"Of course I like it," I said. "What's not to like?" The french fry slipped from my hand, landing on my pants. I picked it up, noticing the grease and ketchup stain it left behind.

Jim nodded and watched me as I tried to remove the stain with a water-soaked napkin. A two-inch wet circle appeared around a red center, like a target.

He took a bite of his potato, and I looked for the waitress again. There had to be somebody in that kitchen who could deal with this lobster shell. Finally, giving up, I placed the cracker around the tail and, *whoosh,* the cracker slid right off the surface, hitting a little dish of drawn butter that shimmered like a reflecting pool. I grabbed the tail again and pushed the cracker with all my strength. This time the shell exploded, sending shards of lobster meat all over the table, onto my blouse, and onto Jim's clothes.

"Oh, my God, I'm sorry," I said, grabbing a clean napkin from Hayden's place and handing it to him. And then, even though I knew I shouldn't, I started to laugh.

Jim began to wipe the specks off the front of his shirt and his sleeves, and as he looked at the mess he began to laugh, too. We continued to wipe off our clothes, but every time we looked at one another, covered with lobster debris, we started up again. We couldn't stop laughing. By the time we did, we were both out of breath, our eyes tearing.

I had finally gotten myself back under control when a cheer went up from the crowd of people near the dartboard, and one of the men yelled for a round of beer. I looked over and was able to catch a glimpse of my mother, holding a dart up high, as though she were just about to throw it. Then she let it go, but I couldn't see where it landed.

"That's my mom," I said. "I told you she was a champion."

I went to pick up the lobster tail again, but he grabbed it from me. "I'd better help you with this." He took the crackers and snapped down on the shell, which opened in one clean break.

I sat there in awe, admiring his skill.

"You'd never survive life in Maine if that's how you crack a lobster," Jim said.

Life in Maine.

He grinned, and I knew he meant it as a joke, but all I could think about was Roy Cummings and the little house he made for me and the beautiful things he said as we stood outside.

I looked down, my eyes welling up with tears. *I'm in love with you. I know I can make you happy.* I put my head in my hands and closed my eyes. But there was no getting away from it. I could still see his face, the quiet, defeated look when he said good-bye.

"Are you all right?"

I opened my eyes. Jim was looking at me, an expression of concern on his face.

"I don't know."

"Can I help?"

I shook my head. I wanted Hayden to come back and take me to the inn. Where was he? "I'm fine." I kept looking down.

Jim pushed his dinner plate to the side. "All right, Ellen, I'll make you a deal."

When he didn't say anything else for a moment I finally glanced up at him.

"Look," he said. "Tonight you just consider me a friend, okay? I'm taking my reporter hat off." He pretended to lift something from his head and toss it behind him. "It's gone, okay?"

I stared at him. He had lovely brown eyes, trusting eyes, like a dog.

I nodded. "Yeah, okay."

He leaned forward and whispered, "So tell me what's going on."

I put my elbows on the table, too. Then I leaned in closer. "You know the guy who was here earlier? Tall, dark hair."

"Red Sox cap?"

"Yeah," I said. "That's Roy."

Jim looked confused. "I'm not sure I—"

"His name is Roy. Roy Cummings."

I gazed at the watered-down Scotch in my glass. My head felt very heavy. Something was happening inside me from all the alcohol.

"Here's the thing," I said, my words starting to sound a little like slushy. "I'm three months away from my wedding…" I held up three fingers. "And everything's all set to go, all ready.…And then I meet him. Roy. Roy Cummings. Just walks into my life out of nowhere."

I waved my hand. "No, wait, that's not true. Not out of nowhere. Out of Beacon, Maine." I pointed to the floor. "Right here. And he tells me he's in love with me. Oh, God." I tossed my head way back, which was a bad idea, because suddenly everything in the room was spinning.

"Whoa," I said, righting myself.

Jim moved to my side of the table and took the seat next to me. "Are you all right there, Ellen? You think maybe I should take you back to the inn?"

"This is what's confusing me," I said, feeling the need to finally get all this out. "How can he be in love with me? I only met him a week ago. A *week*. I mean, really. That's only seven days." I put what I thought were seven fingers in the air, but I must not have gotten it right, because Jim put down one of them.

I looked at my plate of lobster, with the splintered shell and the exploded shards. "Of course," I said, "I told him there was no way. *No way*. I'm getting married in three months, see?" I held up my left hand. "Van Cleef." I took a breath and let it out. "And Arpels."

Jim nodded. "Beautiful," he said. "Lovely."

"Of course it is. Hayden does nothing but the best." Tears began slipping down my cheeks. "I told him, I'm not in love with you. We can't be together."

Jim looked startled. "You told Hayden that?"

"No, I told Roy that."

Jim was eyeing me with a curious expression. I think he was about to say something when one of the band members, a man in a red-and-white checkered shirt, stepped up to the microphone.

"We're going on break for a while, folks, but the entertainment isn't. Marty Eldon is here, so get ready for karaoke and sing your hearts out!"

"It sounds like you've got some serious issues going on, Ellen. Maybe you ought to figure out how you feel. I mean really feel. That might be a little harder than you think."

I didn't want to figure it out. He was right. It was too hard and way too painful, and I wished I'd never brought it up and I wished he'd stop talking about it. I twirled my engagement ring around my finger. I wasn't going to think about it anymore.

"That's the only way you're going to resolve this," he said.

Okay, just leave it alone. Let's change the subject now.

"You just have to do some real soul-searching," he said, "and the only—"

"Hey, you know what?" I blurted out. "I'm *really* good at karaoke. I think I'd like to sing." I moved my chair back.

Jim looked shocked. His forehead was full of lines. "You sure you think you can do that?"

"Of course I can," I said. "Two years ago I was at the annual New York State Women Lawyers Association retreat. I led the whole group in a rendition of 'Respect.' You know, the Aretha Franklin song?"

Jim nodded. "Sure, I know it."

"Yeah, well, we sang it to celebrate the fact that a senior

partner in another firm, this guy named Steve Ajello, finally got nailed on sexual harassment charges." I paused, savoring the memory. "Everyone said I had a great voice."

I stood up. "So here goes."

The legs under me didn't feel like my own. I grabbed the back of the chair for support. A huge ketchup stain was on my pants, and I wondered how it had gotten there. I picked up a lobster bib that lay folded next to my plate and opened it up. Printed in white, on a red background, were the words GET SOME TAIL AT THE ANTLER! I wrapped the bib over the stain, knotting the ties in the back. That was better.

I began making my way through the crowd, heading toward the stage. After a few steps I could feel that I was dragging something with my foot. When I looked, I saw that a hollowed-out lobster claw had locked onto the strap of my sandal. I tried to reach for the claw but couldn't grasp it. It was too long a way down.

I got to the stage, finally spotting Hayden, who was standing in the crowd, waving frantically, trying to get through. Every drop of color had left his face, and I could see he was yelling, trying to tell me something. But the noise was too loud. I couldn't hear him.

Don't worry, Hayden, I thought. You don't know this, but I'm a great karaokist. You'll see. Was *karaokist* even a word? I wasn't sure.

"It's okay, Hayden," I put my hands around my mouth and tried to shout over the din. "You're in for a surprise!"

I took a step onto the stage and glanced around at the blur of faces under the warm orange lights. They were smiling, expectant. Even Skip, standing behind the bar, raised an empty glass to me in a salute.

The DJ looked at the red plastic bib around my leg, and then his eyes wandered to my feet. He smiled and shook my hand. "You must be the Swimmer. Real pleased to meet you."

He passed me a notebook of song titles, indicating that I should pick something. I began turning the pages, going through the different sections of music—pop, rap, rock, Top 40, country. There were dozens of songs on each page, and the titles began to float and bend in front of me.

"Do you have any jazz?" I asked. "Old jazz classics, that kind of thing?"

He thumbed through the book and then handed it back to me, open at a page entitled "American Standards."

Great, I thought. Closing my eyes, I brought my finger down on one of the titles, "Our Love Is Here to Stay." It was one of my favorite Gershwin songs. Maybe that was a good sign.

"Okay, this one," I said, pointing.

He handed me the microphone, and in a moment the music began. The arrangement was lush, with lots of strings and a long introduction, in the style of those old songs. The crowd quieted down, and I glanced across the room toward my table and saw Mom staring at me nervously, holding a trophy in one hand. *A trophy?*

Next to Mom sat Jim and Tally and, on the very end, Hayden, gaping at me with the horrible curiosity of a car-crash observer. No one was talking.

The introduction ended, and the words to the song appeared on the monitor. I began to sing, lines about love outlasting everything else, outlasting radios and telephones and even mountains. As I sang I gazed around the room, and the faces that had been blurry came into focus.

Arlen Fletch from the town hall was sitting at a corner table with two other ladies. At a table against the wall I noticed Phil, the cashier from Grover's Market, where I'd first seen my picture in the paper. He was with a woman I guessed was his wife. When I looked at him, he waved. Susan Porter, her husband, and two other couples were seated at a round table in the middle of the room, and the young waitress from the Three Penny Diner was right up front, holding hands with a cute blond boy.

I caught myself looking for Roy, searching for his Red Sox cap and his easy smile. I wanted him to be there. I scanned the crowd, but after a moment I was no longer seeing them. Instead, I was imagining Roy, the tiny wrinkles by his eyes when he smiled, his wavy hair, his dimples.

I saw us floating in the ocean, his legs hooked around mine in the tired swimmer's carry. I felt the sun on my face and my arms around him, and the water didn't feel cold at all. Then we were standing outside the tailor shop, and he was telling me he loved me. He was holding my hand. *I know I can make you happy. That's a promise.* I could feel his fingers on mine, just before he let go and said good-bye.

The music ended, and there was a moment of dead silence, a white hush that fell over the room. Oh, God, I thought, I was terrible. They hated it. Why did I even think I could sing? Why did I drink so much? Why did I—

But I never got the rest of the thought out, because the whole place suddenly exploded with applause and cheers and hoots and howls. Some people even stood up. I couldn't believe it. I kept looking to see if they were clapping for someone else, but there was nobody up there except me.

My hand shook as I held the microphone. "Thanks," I said. I could hear my voice shaking. "That's really nice of you."

Somebody shouted, "Go, Swimmer!" and everyone laughed.

I stood there, clutching the microphone, and something began bubbling up inside me—advice Gran used to give me—and it seemed very important at that moment.

The DJ reached out for the mike, but I didn't let go. I glanced around the room again, at the amber liquids lined up in bottles behind the bar, the ship's lanterns dangling from the ceiling, the chalkboard with scores from the last dart game.

"You know," I began, my tongue suddenly thick and heavy. "I like to take pictures." I could feel I was slurring my words. It sounded as though I'd said *pishers*. "I take lots of pishers." A couple of people whispered.

"And sometimes," I went on, waving my hand, "when I think I'm taking a pisher of one thing...it ends up being a pisher of another thing." I glanced at the DJ. He looked worried. Maybe I wasn't making myself clear.

"You know," I said, "like a pisher of a flower. I go to take the flower and I'm looking through the...the thing...the viewfinder." I closed my right eye, as if I were holding my camera.

"And I could take the pisher. I mean, it would be fine and it would probably come out nice." I glanced at Arlen Fletch and gave her a little wave. She waved back. "But if I *really* take a good look I'll start to see...you know, other stuff. Stuff I really didn't see before. Like maybe...a leaf that's pretty because the sun is shining behind it, making it glow." I heard a few more people whisper, but I kept going.

"And then I want to get the leaf in the pisher, too. Or maybe, there's...um...a shadow that looks interesting. Maybe the flower makes a shadow I hadn't noticed before. And maybe," I added, "the shadow is even more interesting than the flower....That can happen, you know." I nodded a few times.

Then I looked directly at Hayden. He was sitting on the edge of his seat, not a trace of color in his face. "Here's the thing," I said, my mouth so dry I could barely speak. "I wouldn't have figured it out, Hayden, if I didn't stop...and really look. Look at everything...so...you know, so carefully. Because in the end that's what you gotta do."

A tear rolled down my cheek and I took a deep breath. "Hayden, I'm really, really sorry," I said. "But I can't marry you."

Chapter 20

Welcome Home, Swimmer

I tried to open my eyes but the lids were stuck. I rubbed them and blinked and rubbed and blinked again. My mouth was dry, and my hair smelled of fish. My head lay on a white pillowcase, and in front of me were a small table and lamp I didn't recognize. My watch was on the table, along with a glass of water. I turned my head and saw that I was in a room similar to mine—room 10 or 8 or whatever Paula called it—except that there were twin beds, a few different pieces of furniture, and on the bureau was a trophy with the figure of a person holding...what? A dart? I rubbed my eyes again.

My mother stood across the room, folding a pink cashmere sweater. Her suitcase lay open on her bed. What was I doing here? I struggled to put the events of the night in order. There was the Antler and people were dancing. Hayden and...Tally? Yes, Hayden and Tally. And Mom was...I had this fleeting image of my mother holding a dart. I tried to shake it off.

Then Roy came in. Oh, God, *Roy*. He told me he loved me.

He gave me a palace. I looked on the bedside table for the little house, but it wasn't there. And then I remembered I'd given it back to him. And he'd given me back Gran's letter. An image of the two of us standing in front of the tailor shop, with the lights flickering, flashed through my mind.

Then there was Jim. *Jim.* What had I told him? I was drinking all that Scotch. Scotch, for God's sake. I never drank Scotch. And then…karaoke? Did I really get up and sing? Sing and…oh, no, what the hell was I ranting about? Something about taking pictures.

And then… *Hayden.*

Clutching a piece of the bedsheet with my hand, I squeezed my eyes shut against the memory. Had I really broken off my engagement? I opened my eyes and stared at my hand. My ring was gone. Yes, I'd given it back to Hayden last night.

"Mom?" I called, my voice raspy.

She placed a pair of silk pajamas in her suitcase and looked up. "Good morning." She sounded a little cool, a little businesslike.

"Morning," I said, slowly bringing myself to a sitting position. I took a long drink of water. "I guess…a lot must have happened last night."

She began packing her cosmetics into a pink case. "Yes, you could say that."

I pulled the covers up to my neck. "So where is everybody?" I asked timidly, glancing at the bedside table, where I'd left my watch. It was almost ten. "I know they must have canceled the interview and photo shoot, but I was—"

"They've all checked out," my mother said as she put the lid on a jar of moisturizer. "Those people from the *Times* were leaving this morning when I went down to get coffee."

"And Hayden?" I asked, in a half whisper.

"Hayden's gone, too."

Mom walked to my bed and handed me an envelope. It had the pen-and-ink drawing of the Victory Inn on the front flap and my name written on the back. The handwriting was Hayden's.

"He left it under the door," she said, and then she went to the bureau, removed a pale blue shawl, and packed it in her suitcase.

I opened the envelope, afraid of what I would find. Inside was a letter written in black ink on a sheet of white stationery.

Dear Ellen,

There are so many things going through my mind right now. I'm trying to sort them out and make sense of everything. At first, I sat down and wrote a long list of questions I wanted to ask you about you and Roy. I thought they were things I needed to understand and that once I had the answers, I could tell you where you were wrong and why you were wrong. And I could convince you that this whole idea of being with him is crazy and that if you proceed down that path, you'll never be happy. But then I realized this isn't the time for a deposition or a cross-examination. This isn't a legal matter I'm dealing with here. It's your heart.

I don't know what's in your heart, Ellen. I thought I was there. And I hope I still am, in some way. I'm going to assume that whatever you think you feel for Roy is just a crazy idea that won't last. Maybe you're nervous about getting married. Maybe taking that final step is harder for you than you thought it would be. That's the only way any of this makes sense to me. I'm counting on the idea that once you return to Manhattan you'll transform back into the Ellen I knew, the one who loved me.

The only advice I'd like to give you is to take some time to figure out what you really want. Stay up here for a while. Think about it carefully. And then, if you believe with your whole heart that Roy Cummings is the only man who can make you happy, you'll have my blessing.

Hayden

I pulled the covers over my head. How could I have done this horrible thing to Hayden? He loved me, and...well, I still loved him. It's not that I felt anything less for Hayden, it's just that I felt something more for Roy. And how could that be? How could I have loved Hayden enough to want to marry him and then suddenly fallen for someone else? What did that say about me? That I was erratic? Untrustworthy? That I didn't know my own mind?

I must be crazy, I thought. I must be out of my mind. I'll never trust my judgment about men again. Now I think I'm in love with Roy, but what if I'm really not? What if Hayden's right and all this is just infatuation? Then I'll end up doing the same thing to Roy that I've done to Hayden. Was I going to ruin both of their lives? They didn't deserve that.

No, I can't do it, I thought. I've done enough damage already. The best thing I can do now is to walk away from both of them, steer clear of romance altogether. If my judgment is this bad, there's only one way things can go now. It's over with Hayden and it's never going to get started with Roy. I'll just be alone. That's what I have to do.

"What did Hayden say?" my mother asked.

I slowly pushed back the covers. She was standing at the foot of the bed. "He thinks it won't last," I said, my throat tightening at the thought of how I'd hurt him. "He thinks it's just an infatuation."

My mother nodded.

"He said he hoped when I come back to Manhattan I'll turn back into my old self. The one who loves him."

Mom nodded again, sighed, and went back to her suitcase

"Thing is," I said as I watched her tuck a jewelry roll into the corner, "I do love him. Just not..."

She turned and raised her eyebrows expectantly.

"Just not enough."

She looked at me and made that face she was so good at—one-third concern and two-thirds frustration.

"Why are you making that face?" I asked.

"Breaking off your engagement with Hayden," she said, placing a bottle of cologne in her suitcase. "You come up here for a week and you turn everything in your life upside down. You almost drown, so you think you're in love with some, some...carpenter who saves you. Then you break off your engagement. I suppose now you're going to quit your job, move up here, and bake bread or something."

"Mom, you're being ridiculous."

"Darling," she said, walking over to me. "Do you know how many women would take Hayden Croft in a heartbeat? The man is smart, handsome, and accomplished." She sat down next to me. "And he comes from a wonderful family."

"Then maybe you should marry him," I said as I got out of bed and began picking up the clothes I'd left strewn around the night before. "This whole wedding has been more about you than me anyway."

"Nonsense!" Mom said, her face turning red.

"No, it's true. You just don't see it. You're the one who turned the whole thing into the social event of the season. You and Hayden."

"I thought you wanted it that way," she said, looking shocked. "Don't try to tell me you didn't."

"You're right, I did. But I wanted it because *you* wanted it," I said. "It's always been about what you wanted. Everything looking a certain way; everybody acting a certain way. That's all you, and it's what you've taught me."

"I don't know what you mean." She stood up, went to the bureau, and began fussing with her hair in front of the mirror.

I walked over to her. I wasn't going to let her get away with this. "I'm talking about appearances, Mom. How things look. That's your stock-in-trade."

Something inside me was starting to give way. I could feel it unraveling like a rope, strand by strand. I looked in the mirror at the reflection of Mom and me, two generations of Branford women, bound together by so many things. But there was still room for me to be different.

"Appearances used to be my stock-in-trade, too," I said. "But that's not what I want anymore."

Mom turned away. "Yes, I know. That was obvious last night when you announced your breakup in the middle of a drunken karaoke performance."

"Look who's talking! You were up there playing darts, and if memory serves me you had a few daiquiris under your belt."

"The difference, Ellen, is that *I* was holding my liquor. And anyway, so I threw a couple of darts. So what?"

"Threw *a couple?* Mom, you walked away with a trophy, for God's sake."

"Well, no one will ever know, except for a few people from Beacon. At least I didn't make a public announcement about it."

She went back to her suitcase, packing a pair of white pants on top of the other clothes. "And anyway, I couldn't help it. Those people at that pub were so insistent that I play. When I told them I was your mother they just…" She waved her hand. "I think they had some notion about darts and genetics."

"About what?"

She shrugged and picked up a silk scarf. "I could hold my own in college, that's all."

"What do you mean? Hold your own *what?*"

She placed the scarf on top of the pants. "Darts, dear, darts." She turned to me. "I was on the team at Princeton." She zipped up her suitcase. "We made it to the nationals."

"You *what?*" I took a step closer. "What in the world are you talking about?"

She took the trophy from the bureau and held it up, an impish smile on her face. "You didn't think that was just luck, did you? I was a pretty good tournament player in my day."

"You're kidding me," I said. "You've got to be kidding." I sat down on the bed and stared at my mother with the trophy in her hand. And then I began to laugh. I laughed until I shook, until the bed shook, until my mother started to laugh with me. And then she sat down next to me, the trophy between us, and we both laughed until tears rolled down our faces.

I was still trying to catch my breath when the room phone began to ring. Mom looked at me. "You get it," she said, giggling.

"No, you get it," I said, giggling back.

The phone kept ringing.

"All right, all right." My mother dabbed her eyes with a tissue and then picked up the phone. "Yes? Hello?"

There was a moment of silence. Then she said, "Okay, I'll tell her. Thank you." She turned to me. "That was Paula. There's a package for you downstairs."

"A package? I didn't order anything."

Mom handed me a tissue. "Well, she said something's down there for you."

I got up. "All right, I'll go get it."

I splashed some water on my face and quickly brushed my teeth. Then I threw on some clothes and walked downstairs.

Paula was in the lobby talking to a young couple who were checking in.

"And I'll need to use your business office," the wife said, a briefcase slung over her shoulder.

I looked at Paula and a smile began to form on my lips.

"I'll see what we can arrange," Paula said. Then she slid her pen behind her ear and glanced at me. I could swear she winked.

The couple walked toward the stairs, and Paula pointed to a cardboard box against the wall. "Delivery service just dropped that off for you."

"Delivery service. You're sure it's for me?"

"Got your name on it," she said.

The box was large, probably three feet by five feet, but only about six inches deep. An envelope taped to the front said CROWN COURIER DELIVERY SERVICE at the top. In the middle, someone had written my name.

"Hey," Paula said. "Before you go..."

She slid something across the counter toward me. "Today's *Beacon Bugle*," she said. Then she pointed to a large full-color photo on the front page. "I could swear that lady looks just like—"

"Mom!" I shrieked.

There she was, glassy-eyed, a rubber smile on her face, hair askew, holding her two-foot-tall trophy at a forty-five-degree angle. Oh, my God, and they'd printed her name in the caption. "Cynthia Branford from Connecticut wins first place at the Antler's annual summer darts tournament."

I started laughing. I couldn't help it. The whole thing was just so perfect. Paula drew her head back a little and stared at me. For once, she was at a loss for words. I slid the newspaper back toward her and pointed to the photo of my mother. "You know," I said. "I think if you ask her, she might autograph it for you." I was still giggling when I got to the third floor.

"What's that?" Mom asked, eyeing me as I walked into the room. I leaned the box against one of the beds.

"I don't know," I said. "But there's a packing slip or an invoice or something here." I opened the envelope and pulled out a handwritten note on a small sheet of white paper. Yesterday's date was at the top.

E,

I've arranged to have your grandmother's paintings sent to your mother's home in Connecticut—all except for this one, which I wanted to surprise you with. I can't wait to see your reaction.

Love,
H

He'd written this before the debacle at the Antler. That was just like Hayden—quietly and capably resolving the whole issue of the paintings and arranging for this to be delivered. I bit my lip so I wouldn't cry.

My mother walked toward me. "What is it? What's going on now?"

I handed her the note without a word, praying she wouldn't say *I told you so.*

"Oh, dear," she said, putting her arm around me after she read it.

I pulled the packing tape off one end of the carton. Then I removed something wrapped in thick padded paper. I placed it on the bed and studied the scene. In the middle of the canvas was a white farmhouse and, next to it, a red barn. Near the barn stood a single oak tree, a cluster of smaller oaks behind it, and, in the far background, acres of blueberry bushes. In the foreground, a grassy lawn ran down to a small dirt road, and on the edge of the lawn was a roadside stand with a hand-painted sign: BLUEBERRIES.

"That's Kenlyn Farm," I said, my breath caught in my throat. "That's where Chet Cummings grew up."

Mom stood beside me in quiet amazement as she studied the work. "My mother really was an excellent painter, wasn't she?" I could hear the pride in her voice. "I had absolutely no idea."

She stepped closer. "This is beautiful. Look at the detail in the grass." She pointed to brushstrokes of greens and yellows and tans. "You can see every blade. And the blueberries. See the reflection of the sun right there? And look at the roof of the barn. The way she's blended those colors." She had a dreamy look on her face, as if she had just run into an old friend whose name was on the tip of her tongue and she was still trying to remember it.

"There's something written on the bottom...right there." She pointed to a little spot in the grass. "I can't read it, Ellen. What does it say?"

I looked where she was pointing. The words were in my grandmother's handwriting. "It says OUR FARM."

"Our farm," my mother repeated, turning to me.

"It was supposed to be theirs." I said. "Chet's and Gran's. I guess when they got married." I leaned the painting against a wall and stepped back. "They were going to own it, run it together. That was their big dream. But then Gran went to college and met Poppy—"

"Well, I know what happened after that," Mom said.

"You don't know all of it," I told her as I stared at a patch of dappled sunlight on the oak tree and wondered how Gran had painted it. "After Chet heard they were engaged, he left Beacon. He didn't want to be around all the...well, you know, the things that reminded him of Gran. He was still in love with her."

"Where did he go?" my mother asked.

"He went to Vermont and I don't know where else, but he was

away for a long time. Because he left Beacon, his parents ended up selling the farm."

"This farm? The one in this painting?"

"Yes," I said. "Kenlyn Farm." I touched the thick red paint my grandmother had applied to the barn. "And I think that's what bothered Gran the most. She knew how much the farm meant to Chet. She thought it was her fault that it fell out of the family's hands."

Mom cocked her head and looked at me. "And how do you know all this?"

I gazed at the white farmhouse and the little hut, where baskets of blueberries were piled high. "Because Chet wrote to Gran after she broke off their relationship. He wrote to her for months, but she sent all the letters back unopened." I sat down on the bed. "Roy found them and we read them yesterday."

Mom sat down next to me, and she didn't say anything for a little while. She just looked at the painting. "Well," she said finally, "the fact that she was still thinking about this after all those years...it's kind of incredible." She looked at me, her eyes soft. "And sad." She let out a little sigh. "She was looking back on her life and she was thinking about..." Her voice trailed off.

I gazed at the floor, the wide boards with their cracks and crevices. "Yes," I said. "I guess that's the lesson in all of this—not to be eighty years old, looking back on your life, wondering if you made the right choice or how your life might have been different if you'd done one thing and not another."

Sunlight flickered through the windows and landed in mottled patches on the bed. I thought about Gran just before she died, asking me to deliver the letter. And I thought about her as a young girl, standing under the oak tree at the farm with Chet. I wondered what her life would have been like had she stayed in Beacon. But now, when I considered that possibility, the prospect of her life here didn't seem as grim and lacking in luster as I'd pictured it a week ago. The prospect seemed happy and beautiful and full of potential.

My mother brushed a strand of hair from my forehead. "Sometimes I forget that you're an intelligent, grown woman and that I need to respect the decisions you make, even if they wouldn't be my decisions." She put her arm around me. "I'm just stubborn and set in my ways, Ellen...and I'm sorry for that." She pulled me close.

"I love you," she whispered.

I rested my head on her shoulder. "I love you, too."

We held each other as a breeze blew through the windows, fluttering the curtains and sending the faint scent of salt water into the room. Above us, in a tree somewhere, a woodpecker tapped out a song.

I pushed the pedal to the floor as I pulled into Dorset Lane, a squeal coming from my tires. As soon as I saw Roy's house, my hands went cold and an empty feeling seeped through me. The truck was in the driveway and the Audi was gone. He must have left. I banged my hand on the steering wheel in frustration, accidentally sounding the horn.

Maybe he's still here, I thought, even if the Audi isn't. I pulled into the driveway, left the car idling, and raced up the porch steps. Yanking open the screen door, I gave several loud knocks.

"Roy, Roy, it's me, Ellen. Are you in there?"

There was no answer. Only a meadowlark singing in the field behind the house.

"Roy, open up please," I said. "It's Ellen."

"He's gone out of town."

I turned, startled to see Roy's neighbor at the foot of the porch steps. Dressed in a pink jogging suit, she was holding hand weights.

"I'm doing my power walk." She sounded out of breath. "I usually do two miles a day."

I stepped to the edge of the porch. "What was that? Did you say he left?"

"Yeah, about a half hour ago. Gone for a couple of weeks." She bent down to tie the lace of her pink sneaker. "I'm taking care of Mr. Puddy, his cat." She stood up. "He gets really upset and tears up the place when he's left alone too long, but he's fine with me. Roy says I've got the magic touch." She picked up her weights and darted across the lawn toward the street. "See ya."

"Yeah, see ya," I said. A cloud hovered overhead, blocking the sun, and a breeze rustled the grass. I walked to the car.

The neighbor, now a couple of houses away, turned her head and called out, "Looks like you sure broke his heart." Then she marched on.

There was nothing I could say. I got into the car, my eyes burning. I glanced at Roy's house one last time—at the windows where I first called out "Mr. Cummings," looking for Chet; at the ladder by the side of the house; at the bench where Roy and I sat reading Gran's letter. And then I set the GPS for Manhattan.

*　　*　　*

I'd already driven down Bidwell Road and onto Route 20A, heading toward the highway, when I realized there was one more thing I needed to do for my grandmother. Or maybe it was for me. I needed to give her a proper send-off. And to do that I needed to drop her letter in the ocean. Roy said we all had to put this behind us and move on, and he was right. Maybe that was the way to do it. I turned the car around and headed back toward town.

In ten minutes I rounded the bend at the edge of town, and the ocean appeared. The salt air filled my car, and I was struck by the rich cobalt blue of the water, the meringue of white chop, and the sky full of seagulls. I thought about the different ways I could frame the picture in my camera lens.

I drove between the beach and the shops, passing the Three Penny Diner, Tindall & Griffin, and the Beacon Dry Goods store, passing the Wine Cellar and Frank's Tailoring, once the home of the Irresistible Blueberry Bakeshop & Café in Gran's painting. I drove through the town and all the way to the end of Paget Street, where the new house was being built.

I was startled to see how different it looked from the day I'd arrived in Beacon. The roof was finished and shingled now, and the pipes and wires and chips of lumber and other debris that had once lay scattered across the dirt yard were gone.

A white van and a tan Jeep were parked in the area in front, and between them sat Roy's green Audi. He was here. He hadn't left yet.

I bolted from the car and ran toward the back of the house,

colliding with one of the workers as I rounded the corner. He dropped a coffee can and hundreds of nails went flying everywhere.

"Sorry," I said, out of breath, as I crouched down and tried to scoop up some of the nails. I threw them back into the can. "Is Roy Cummings around?"

The man peered at me, his quiet brown eyes coming alive for a second. "Hey, aren't you the Swimmer?"

"Yes," I said, nodding. "Yes, I'm the Swimmer. That's me. But *please*, I need to see Roy Cummings."

"I think he's inside," the man said with a shrug, and I ran off.

There were easily twenty workers in the house, installing kitchen cabinets, laying bathroom tile, putting up light fixtures. I went from room to room looking for Roy, but he wasn't anywhere. Finally I ran downstairs and out the back door. And then I saw it.

The old dock was gone, and a brand-new structure stood in its place. The broken planks, missing handrails, and rotted boards had all been replaced with new, pressure-treated lumber. And a shiny black gate with fancy scrollwork had been installed. I looked toward the end of the dock and saw a man standing there. It was Roy.

Running across the sand, I jumped onto the platform and flung open the gate. Roy watched as I raced down the length of the dock, my shoes pounding against the wood. I got to the end and stopped.

"Hey," I gasped.

He looked me up and down. "Hey yourself. What are you doing here?"

"I've been looking all over for you," I said. "I thought you'd left."

"Not yet," he said. "I'm going in a little while. I have a meeting upstate, about a job."

Oh, no, I thought. He's going to get a job with another company and he's going to leave Beacon. "You're moving away?" I asked. I could hear the panic in my voice.

Roy tilted his head and squinted at me. "What?"

"Are you getting a job with another construction company?"

"Another construction company..." He shook his head. "No, I'm... Ellen, what are you doing here?"

I looked down at the brand-new boards under my feet. They felt strong, solid. I gazed across the water toward the beach, where a boy was throwing a ball for a golden retriever. Then I looked into Roy's eyes. "I'm not going to marry Hayden."

He squinted at me, a confused expression on his face. "You're not?"

I shook my head. "No." I held up my left hand and wiggled my fingers. "No ring. See?"

He took my hand and turned it from front to back. Then he let it go. "What happened?"

I thought about the Antler and the karaoke and my drunken speech. "You know, I've never had trouble holding my liquor in New York, but up here...that's another story. I got a little tipsy at the Antler again last night."

Roy grinned. "You didn't."

"Oh, I'm afraid I did."

"Dead Presidents again, Counselor? Or was it Steeplechase this time?"

"Neither one. I wasn't playing darts," I said. Then I remembered my mother's trophy. "Oh, but Mom was, and she won the annual summer tournament! I had no idea she could throw."

Roy's eyebrows shot up. "Your mother? Wow. I think I'd like to get to know her."

"I'd like that, too," I said, and I smiled. He held my gaze and we stood there for a moment.

Finally he said, "So what happened?"

I told him about the karaoke and my rendition of "Our Love Is Here to Stay." "I think the Gershwins must have been rolling in their graves, but the crowd loved it. Maybe they were just rooting for the underdog."

"They were rooting for the Swimmer," he said.

"I guess. I don't know. The thing is, the whole time I was singing I kept thinking about you and wishing you were there. And then I started saying all this crazy stuff about taking pictures, and...I don't know. But at the end, in front of everybody at the Antler, I told Hayden the wedding was off." I could hear the water lapping against the dock pilings as Roy stood there, taking this in.

"Why did you do that?" Roy asked after a moment.

I took a deep breath. "Because I can't go back to the way things used to be. I came here expecting one thing and getting something completely different. Everything's changed. I've changed. And I can't marry Hayden if I'm in love with you."

He tilted his head. "What did you say?"

"I said everything's changed now, and I can't go back to—"

"No, I mean the last part."

I took his hand. I took a deep breath. "I said *I'm in love with you.*"

He closed his fingers around mine. "But what about all that

stuff you told me last night?" He looked down. "You said you weren't in love with me."

I shook my head. "I was afraid of the truth. The truth can be pretty messy sometimes. I've hurt Hayden a lot. I know that, and it's something I have to deal with. But I can't help being in love with you."

"What about New York and your career? What about grinding your teeth when you sleep?"

I laughed. "You know, I don't think I've been grinding my teeth since I came to Beacon." I thought about my grandmother and the money she left me, and I thought about Kenlyn Farm and the fragment of the blueberry plant I found there.

"And I've suddenly got this crazy urge to own a blueberry farm. Maybe start a bakery. I could sell great blueberry muffins and blueberry pies and..." I looked across the beach toward town and the statue of the blueberry lady. "Have you ever wondered why you don't see blueberry croissants? Maybe I could make those, too. You know, I hear there's an old blueberry farm for sale."

A flying fish leaped out of the ocean, its body a jolt of silver against the blue water. Roy looked at me and smiled. "I think you're crazy, Ellen Branford. But I love you." He started to pull me toward him.

"Wait," I said. "There's something I have to do."

I took my grandmother's letter from my pocket. I unfolded the paper, smoothed out the crease, and gazed at my grandmother's writing one last time. Then I walked to the edge of the dock and let the paper go. It fluttered in the breeze and settled on the water.

Roy came and stood beside me. "Maybe she's finally found some peace."

"I hope so."

"I think she'd be very proud of you," he said.

"You do?"

"Of course. I'm proud of you."

"Thanks," I said. We leaned against the railing for a moment, watching the breeze ruffle the water.

"The last thing I ever expected was to see you on this dock again," Roy said.

I smiled. "Well, here I am. And I much prefer this dock to the old one."

He laughed. "You like it?"

"It's beautiful," I said.

"I think the owner was afraid he'd get sued. You know, by that woman who fell in."

"Oh, right," I said. "That lawyer. You think she'd sue?"

He shrugged. "I don't know. Maybe. Maybe not. It could be...a conflict. Conflict of interest?"

I shook my head. "I don't think so. Why would it be a conflict of interest?"

"Well, she just told the owner she's in love with him."

"No I didn't. I...wait a minute. *What?*"

Roy was grinning.

"You're the owner?" I said. "You?"

"C. R. Cummings Construction, LLC." He put out his hand for me to shake.

I know I must have looked confused. He was trying not to laugh. "So you're telling me you own the dock?" I said.

"The dock and the house. They go together, remember? I own them until I sell them, anyway. I know you thought I was a carpenter. And I am, but I'm also a general contractor. I own the company."

I looked down the length of the dock to the new house, knowing now that it was there because of Roy, admiring it as if for the first time. "You're pretty impressive, Roy Cummings."

He grinned sheepishly. "Well, that's what my meeting's about later. I'm seeing somebody about a project. A huge piece of property with a lake, and they want to...oh, hey, we don't have to talk business right now. I can think of better things to do."

He looked into my eyes, took my hand, and pulled me close. Something inside me fluttered, like the heart of a caged bird suddenly freed and about to take flight.

"You know," he said, "this might sound crazy, but I think I've been in love with you since the first day I saw you out here, when you were drowning."

I pulled away. "When I was *what?*"

"When you were drowning," he said matter-of-factly.

I put my hands on my hips. "I wasn't drowning, Roy Cummings. I was never drowning."

"I see." He tried to suppress a smile. "Then why were you thrashing around in the water, looking panicky? Was that just to attract my attention?"

"I've never looked panicky in my life." I threw back my shoulders. "Especially when it comes to swimming. When I was at Exeter—"

Roy pulled me toward him again. "Yeah, yeah, I know. You made it to the nationals."

And before I had a chance to utter another word, his arms were around me, his face against mine. He kissed my forehead. I could feel the stubble of his beard and smell his aftershave as he brushed his face against my cheek. He smelled like the field of wildflowers where a farmhouse once stood, where blueberries grew and would grow again.

He kissed the tip of my nose and then he moved his lips to mine and everything around me—the boards under my feet, the sigh of the ocean against the dock pilings, the blue granite sky—every single atom of existence outside of Roy and me quietly slipped away.

Epilogue

One Year Later

Grabbing the pot holders, I pulled the blueberry muffins from the oven. The aroma of cinnamon filled the air as I placed the two baking tins on a cooling rack. I think Gran would have liked my twist on her recipe—sprinkling the tops with cinnamon and sugar to make them even more crunchy.

Standing in the café kitchen, oven mitt in my hand and Cole Porter's "Night and Day" playing in the background, it seemed hard to believe that it had been a year since my grandmother's death and my journey to Beacon. I think she would be proud of what I'd done, and I know she would have loved the café, especially as I'd named it after the Irresistible Blueberry Bakeshop & Café of her youth.

There were touches of Gran everywhere. I could almost see the two of us dancing in this kitchen, the way we did in hers, while muffins baked and Ella Fitzgerald sang "Bewitched, Bothered, and Bewildered."

As I walked into the front room, her painting of Kenlyn Farm welcomed me. I smiled at the images of the red barn and the little roadside stand and thought about how happy Gran would be to know that Roy and I had bought the farm and that some of the money she'd left me had found its way there. It would be a few years before the blueberry bushes we planted would bear fruit, but that was okay. We would wait.

Next to Gran's painting hung the blackboard where I posted the specials. I took a stick of bright yellow chalk and wrote "Chilled Carrot Ginger Soup," "Apple Pecan Chicken Salad Sandwich," and "French Baguette with Smoked Ham and Brie." Roy would want the smoked ham and Brie when he stopped by. We topped it with field greens and finished it with a Dijon mustard sauce that he loved. He would probably come in wearing faded jeans and his Red Sox T-shirt, poke his head in the kitchen or find me in the closet I called my office, and kiss me with his scratchy Saturday morning beard, all of which I would love.

Roy and I were getting married in the fall—just a simple wedding with family members and a few close friends. It would be perfect. We had booked the Victory Inn for the reception and the out-of-town guests, and Paula even threatened to buy new chairs for the roof.

An elderly couple rose from their table, leaving behind a copy of the *New York Times*. I picked up the paper, noticing a headline that read, CROFT POISED TO WIN COUNCIL SEAT BY LARGE MARGIN. I felt a little thrill of excitement for Hayden. The election wasn't until November, but he seemed to have a lock on the seat for his district, which was no surprise to me.

I thought about the e-mail Hayden sent me a couple of months back. He told me he'd run into Tally at the New York

City Ballet spring gala and that they'd begun dating. I wrote back, wishing him well and letting him know I had seen Jim, who had become a food critic for the *Times*. Jim had come up here in April and given the café two stars in a review he wrote for a series the paper ran on New England comfort-food restaurants.

Sometimes I think about New York and I wonder what my life would have been like if I had put my grandmother's letter in the mail and never come to Beacon. Now I can't imagine living anywhere else or being with anyone but Roy. It's strange how my grandmother's death, while so tragic, led me to something so wonderful. Maybe Roy was right when he said Gran sent me here to uncover her secrets. Maybe she sent me here to uncover my own as well.

I set down the yellow chalk and pulled my grandmother's tin recipe box from a shelf behind the counter. Hand-painted blue-and-white flowers, worn and scratched but still visible, adorned the front. I ran my finger over the surface and opened the lid. My grandmother's handwriting filled the yellowed index cards, her letters tall and elegant, directing the creation of breads and cakes, pies and pastries, cookies, and, of course, muffins. Even in the faded peacock-blue ink, her words lived on.

Acknowledgments

Many people assisted me in connection with this book and I am most grateful for their help.

My husband, Bob, supported me in every way while I wrote and rewrote and rewrote the manuscript. ("Are you still working on that book?" he would often ask, especially at one thirty in the morning.) In addition, as one of my first readers, he provided me with a huge sense of relief when he laughed in all the right places.

Several family members and friends also read the manuscript and gave me terrific suggestions, all of which I appreciated and most of which I incorporated: Michael Simses, Kate Simses, Christine Lacerenza, Suzanne Ainslie, Ann Depuy, Rebecca Holliman, and Angela Rossetti.

The team at my publishing house, Little, Brown, has done incredible things to turn my tale into a book. Michael Pietsch, my publisher, has been wonderful (thank you for giving me this chance!). Judy Clain, my editor, came up with such brilliant ideas and insights — they made the story and the writing far better than I could have imagined. And everyone else at Little, Brown — all those who worked so hard to get the story from manuscript to print to bookstore shelves—has been a joy to know and to work with.

Special thanks go to Sue and Jim Patterson for their ideas and suggestions, which were critical to strengthening the story and enhancing the drama in key places (providing the "icing on the cake"). I am especially grateful for Jim's graciousness in bringing the manuscript to the attention of Little, Brown.

Finally, I want to express my gratitude to Jamie Cat Callan, friend and author, for being my mentor during the writing of this book and for providing me with guidance and encouragement throughout the process. It was Jamie's rallying cry that eventually convinced me to put away the short stories I'd been working on and go for something bigger. She kept telling me, "You have to write a novel!" And finally I did.

About the Author

Mary Simses grew up in Darien, Connecticut, and spent most of her life in New England, where she worked in the magazine publishing industry and, later, as a corporate attorney. She wrote fiction "on the side" for many years, and several of her short stories have appeared in literary magazines. Mary now lives with her husband—who also happens to be her law partner—and their daughter in South Florida. She enjoys photography and listening to jazz standards. She also makes a fine blueberry muffin. This is her first novel.

Reading Group Guide

The

Irresistible Blueberry Bakeshop & Café

A Novel by

Mary Simses

A Conversation with Mary Simses

Would you give us a bit of introduction and let readers know who you are, how you got started writing, and what kind of books you like to write?

I grew up in Connecticut, where my mother's family has some fairly deep roots (several generations). I'm an only child and we lived in Darien, a suburban town on the Connecticut coast. When I was young, I was always writing short stories and poems, and my teachers encouraged me to write—especially my ninth-grade English teacher, with whom I'm still in touch.

By the time I started college, I decided I'd better take up a "practical" career, as I didn't think I could ever make a living writing fiction or poetry. I decided to major in journalism because at least that way I'd still be writing, although doing a very different kind of writing. I spent a couple of years after college working for a small trade magazine in Connecticut (fortunately, an interesting one that covered the field of magazine publishing) and then ended up going back to school to get a law degree. I worked for a law firm and then spent fifteen years working in the legal department of a large corporation in Westchester County, New York.

It was during that time that I realized I had to start writing fiction again. I kept imagining scenes and thinking of dialogue, and I figured I'd either have to write or I would drive myself crazy. I enrolled in an evening fiction-writing class at Fairfield University in Connecticut. And that was it. I was totally hooked again—but now, as an adult. I wrote "on the side," whenever I could—late at night, on weekends, traveling, any time I could squeeze it in.

Over the next few years, several of my stories were published in journals and literary magazines. Then my husband, also an attorney, was transferred to South Florida, so we moved there. After that, I had our daughter, Morgan, and I put the writing away for several years, during which time we opened our own law firm. But, once again, I came back to writing fiction and began to work on more short stories. A close friend and author kept telling me I needed to write a novel, and, finally, I took the big leap and wrote what became *The Irresistible Blueberry Bakeshop & Café*.

My stories, and my novel, are all relationship-driven. The characters define the stories. Locations are important to me as well, however. I tend to set my stories in small towns and my favorite small towns are those on the New England coast. I like to use fictional towns so I can create them from the ground up, exactly the way I want them to be. In *Blueberry Café*, the location is Beacon, Maine, a small coastal town where Ellen, the protagonist, goes to deliver a letter for her recently deceased grandmother, who wanted to set something right before she died. I guess small coastal New England towns and characters dealing with "unfinished business" in their lives are my themes. Those two elements are also in the new book I'm writing.

Can you share with us any routines, food or recipes, or favorite books or rituals that help you through the writing process?

This is hard. My only real routine is probably the lack of one! Actually, that's not quite true. One thing I find is that I like to write in the same place, at least when I'm home. There is a little "nook" in our bedroom, with a banquette against two of the three walls and windows, making it a nice, bright spot. I usually sit on the banquette with my laptop on a small table, and that's where I write. We do have a home office, but I use that to pay bills, sort mail, work on photographs (I love photography and have been taking pictures since I was a child), and that sort of thing. I don't write there.

I also find that my best schedule (when I can stick to it) is to write in the morning, before I get distracted and the day gets away from me. To do that, I really have to "x" out time on my calendar for myself. Otherwise, it will get filled in with appointments and things I could, at least for the most part, just as easily do in the afternoon. If I'm getting really distracted by being in the house, I just pick up my laptop and go somewhere else to write—preferably somewhere outside, if it's not too hot.

That said, I don't always write in the morning and there are periods when I don't write at all. Then I'll have several days where I knock out a ton of pages. It's also not unusual for me to write until the wee hours of the morning when I really get going.

I usually have something to drink next to me, such as my one cup of coffee in the morning or a cup of tea. Cinnamon, one of our two cats, is typically hanging around, looking to be petted or threatening to walk on my laptop keys, which he loves to do. (Sometimes he sleeps on the keyboard!) He's not the best writer, though, so I try to discourage him from coming too close.

What are some of your favorite books and authors? Has writing your own book changed the way that you read?

Some of my favorite books are: *To Kill a Mockingbird* by Harper Lee, *The Great Gatsby* by F. Scott Fitzgerald, *The Catcher in the Rye* by J. D. Salinger, *A Prayer for Owen Meany* by John Irving, *The Secret Life of Bees* by Sue Monk Kidd, *Angle of Repose* by Wallace Stegner, *The Liars' Club* by Mary Karr, *Major Pettigrew's Last Stand* by Helen Simonson, *The Last Time They Met* by Anita Shreve, the novels in the Deptford and Salterton trilogies by Robertson Davies, *Pride and Prejudice* by Jane Austen, *David Copperfield* by Charles Dickens, *A Room with a View* by E. M. Forster, and *Brideshead Revisited* by Evelyn Waugh.

For humor, I love David Sedaris and Bill Bryson.

If writing has changed the way that I read, I think it's given me an even deeper appreciation of great literature because now I know how hard it is to craft a book and do it well.

Did you know what you wanted the title of the book to be? How involved were you in choosing it?

For the three years while I was writing the book, I was using the working title *The Letter*. Not terribly exciting, but I thought it got the point across, as the main character's journey comes about because of a letter. The author James Patterson, who lives in our town and who read and liked my manuscript, asked me if I had a title. When I replied, *"The Letter,"* he just looked at me and said, "You need a really good title," which told me all I needed to know! Being the mastermind that he is, Jim put his head back and thought for a moment. Then he said, "I think *The Irresistible Blueberry Bakeshop & Café* would be a good title," and that was it. I had the biggest-selling author in the world handing me a title. You can't do much better than that!

Do you ever look back on your early work? How do you feel your writing style or approach to writing has evolved since you first began?

I don't look back very often. It's funny because even when I first started, most of my work (short stories) dealt with small-town life. And a couple of them were set in Maine. One of my earliest stories, which I just reread in order to answer this question, was about a young woman who traveled from Seattle, Washington, to Camden, Maine, to visit her mother, who has dementia. Even though the story was serious, the mother said some things that really made me laugh, confirming my suspicion that it's always been hard for me not to throw in a few humorous lines, no matter what I'm writing.

In terms of style, I think I'm probably a more fluid writer now. I guess that just comes from writing a zillion sentences. And, of course, age and stage of life have a lot to do with it. Twenty years ago I couldn't have written what I write now or the way I write now. Nevertheless, when I read a story that I wrote a long time ago, I'm usually still fairly happy with it, at least in terms of what it represents for its time. I'm often struck by certain phrases or sentences or descriptions that I like. It's an odd feeling, because although it's my own work, in a way it also feels as though it belongs to someone else.

What were your experiences with reading when you were growing up? Was there a pivotal moment in discovering literature when you knew that you wanted to be a writer?

The strange thing is that although I read as a child, I was never an avid reader the way I am now. I don't know exactly when all of that changed, but I think it was during college. I remember one summer when I decided I wanted to read a lot of plays. I'm not sure why, but I just did. So I went to the library and took out huge volumes of work by several American playwrights—Tennessee Williams, Lillian Hellman, Eugene O'Neill, and a few others—and I just read them from cover to cover. I think that might have been the beginning of my deep love of literature because I haven't stopped reading since.

As far as having a pivotal moment when I knew I wanted to be a writer, that's a tough question because I started writing stories when I was about eight years old. I can't say that I remember a particular moment at that age; I just remember always writing, at least as a child. But there was a pivotal moment when I started writing fiction as an adult and I realized I would always be writing, at least as a side venture. That happened in the evening fiction-writing class. One week, I read a story I had written for the assignment. Afterward, there was a lot of discussion about the story and the characters, and a lot of positive comments, all of which I found very encouraging. But the most amazing thing was what took place after class. A young man, probably in his early twenties, came up to me and told me how much the story had moved him and how, at one point when I was reading it, he thought he was going to cry. I drove home that night feeling as though I was floating on a cloud. I'd written something that had really touched people and I was ecstatic. I knew then that I would always keep writing.

As a published author, what's been the biggest surprise about life after the publication of your first book?

The biggest surprise—and pleasure—has been the number of wonderful responses I've been getting, through my website, Facebook, and Goodreads. People have written me such kind notes, telling me how much they've enjoyed *Blueberry Café,* and I really feel honored that they think so highly of the book. There are so many great books out there—thousands of choices—and readers are giving up time, and usually money, to read them. It makes me feel great when I know that someone is happy with the investment he or she has made in my book.

Another big surprise is how much I've enjoyed giving book talks. I love meeting and talking with people, so the book signing part was never an issue. But I was worried about giving the talks—What would I say? What stories about the book would I include? Would people be bored? Would I be nervous? Fortunately, everything has worked out very well. I *haven't* felt nervous, and people in the audiences have told me how much they enjoy hearing my story. I've also discovered that a number of people who come to my talks are writers who are working on stories or books themselves or are people who are interested in writing but haven't done it. If I can help or inspire them in any way, that's an extra bonus for me.

This interview with the author first appeared on the blog *Linus's Blanket*. Reprinted with permission of Nicole Bonia.

Questions and topics for discussion

1. How does the setting of *The Irresistible Blueberry Bakeshop & Café* enhance the story? What imagery does Maine or New England create in your mind?

2. The author tells us a great deal about the narrator of the book in the very first pages. What qualities do you see in Ellen that make you like or dislike her? Does she surprise you?

3. Why doesn't Ellen tell Hayden right away about her mishap at the dock?

4. Both Ellen and Roy "jump to conclusions" about each other during the first forty-eight hours of their meeting. What are these assumptions? Do Ellen and Roy deliberately mislead each other or are they simply projecting stereotypes onto each other?

5. Ellen's relationship with her grandmother is a true and genuine bond. "There are so many different ways to look at the same thing, Ellen" (page 130), her grandmother tells her when she is a girl. What are some of the many legacies that Ruth leaves to Ellen, besides money?

6. In what ways is Ellen like her grandmother? In what ways is she different? How do those similarities and differences affect the decision Ellen makes in the end?

7. How does Ellen change over the course of the book? Are there specific turning points for her?

8. Do you believe in love at first sight?

9. Ellen's father died when she was fourteen. How might that affect her choice of a suitor, or what she thinks she wants?

10. Both grandmother and granddaughter ultimately make a decision between two men, although Ellen's decision differs from her grandmother's. Do you think Ellen's grandmother set Ellen on this path deliberately?

11. Ultimately Ellen brings her grandmother's journey full circle. Does her relationship with her mother help to explain that?

Mary Simses's Irresistible Blueberry Muffins

2 cups all-purpose flour
½ cup sugar
2 teaspoons baking powder
8 tablespoons (1 stick) unsalted butter, melted and cooled
¾ cup whole milk
1 egg, slightly beaten
1 teaspoon vanilla
1½ cups fresh blueberries
1 heaping tablespoon sugar (optional, for tops)

Preheat the oven to 350 degrees F. Grease a 12-cup muffin pan. In a large bowl, combine the flour, sugar, and baking powder. Reserve one tablespoon of the mixture and use it to coat the blueberries. In a smaller bowl, combine melted butter, milk, egg, and vanilla and mix well. Add the milk mixture to the flour mixture and stir with a spatula or whisk until just blended (the batter can be lumpy). Do not overmix or your muffins will be too dense. Toss the blueberries with the reserved flour mixture and gently fold the blueberries into the batter.

Fill muffin cups ⅔ full. Sprinkle tops with additional sugar, if desired. Bake for 20 to 25 minutes. Cool the muffins for 15 minutes before removing them from the pan.